Praise for *The Angel of Montague Street*

"Norman Green's Silvano Iurata is an intriguing character. . . . Green is a gifted writer with a style as understated as Iurata, a man of substance who's slow to reveal himself. *The Angel of Montague Street* . . . establishes Green as an author worth looking for—and recommending."

—*Albany Times Union*

"*The Angel of Montague Street* shows the Brooklyn of a generation ago when the borough retained its separate identity. Green acts as a guide through the leafy neighborhoods, the mean slums and such places as Rockaway and Jamaica Estates. . . . Green is a skilled storyteller, slowly building tension, adding ingenious distractions leading to a raucous finale."

—*St. Louis Post-Dispatch*

"As in his dark debut . . . Green presents a cast of folks who talk like Elmore Leonard but live in a reeking urban hell right out of George P. Pelecanos—along with their sense of grim fatalism in the face of impossible odds."

—*Kirkus Reviews*

Praise for *Shooting Dr. Jack*

"In his first novel, Norman Green sketches such indelible portraits. . . . The reader is drawn in."

—*New York Times Book Review*

"A self-assured debut. . . . Will invite comparisons to Elmore Leonard."

—*Publishers Weekly*

"A heart-catching novel of perception and intelligence. The language is fresh and poignant. With its moody underpinnings and subtle redemptions, Green's book is a powerful and emotional story."

—Perri O'Shaughnessy, *New York Times* bestselling author

"A powerful debut from a gifted new writer. It's got the narrative drive of a thriller, the unflinching reality of a literary novel and characters that come alive and stay with you after the story is finished. You get the feeling that Norman Green could go anywhere from here."

—T. Jefferson Parker, *New York Times* bestselling author

"Norman Green has an original voice that takes us into the edgy shadows of human nature. The blood of New York is so strong in this book that you can feel it pulsing in your veins. *Shooting Dr. Jack* should not be missed."

—Robert Crais, *New York Times* bestselling author

"A gritty, dark and totally original debut, *Shooting Dr. Jack* packs a helluva wallop. I can't wait to see what Green comes up with next."

—Harlan Coben, *New York Times* bestselling author

"Can this guy write! Fast-paced with complex, interesting characters, this is one terrific debut novel."

—Ridley Pearson, *New York Times* bestselling author

"With his debut novel, *Shooting Dr. Jack,* Norman Green eloquently puts into words the struggle we all face: getting through the day, getting one step closer to love and happiness and possibly making a few bucks along the way."

—*Sun Herald* (Biloxi, Mississippi)

"Even considering the sharp New York scene-setting and fast-paced plotting, the best thing about *Shooting Dr. Jack* is the characters."

—*Tampa Tribune*

"This gritty urban tale is a strong debut."

—*Seattle Times*

"This novel mixes elements of *The Sopranos* and *Traffic* and comes up with the best qualities of both."

—Associated Press

"Green tells an emotionally provocative story while keeping readers on edge with suspense."

—*South Bend Tribune*

"Fast, stylish and morally centered, *Shooting Dr. Jack* is an auspicious debut from a gifted writer who wears his rough edges proudly."

—*Florida News-Press*

"Green's greatest triumph is the development of three realistic characters readers can relate to and care about."

—*Register Star* (Rockford, Illinois)

Carina Salvi

Norman Green is the author of *Shooting Dr. Jack, The Angel of Montague Street,* and *Way Past Legal.* He lives in New Jersey with his wife.

www.normangreenbooks.com

ALSO BY NORMAN GREEN

Shooting Dr. Jack
Way Past Legal

The Angel of Montague Street

A NOVEL

Norman Green

An Imprint of HarperCollins*Publishers*

This book is a work of fiction. The characters, incidents, and dialogue are drawn from the author's imagination and are not to be construed as real. Any resemblance to actual events or persons, living or dead, is entirely coincidental.

A hardcover edition of this book was published in 2003 by HarperCollins Publishers.

HarperCollins books may be purchased for educational, business, or sales promotional use. For information, please write: Special Markets Department, HarperCollins Publishers Inc., 10 East 53rd Street, New York, NY 10022.

First Dark Alley edition published 2004.

Designed by Joseph Rutt

The Library of Congress has cataloged the hardcover edition as follows:

Green, Norman.
The angel of Montague Street/by Norman Green.—1st ed.
p. cm.
ISBN 0-06-018819-7 (alk. paper)
1. Vietnamese Conflict, 1961–1975—Veterans—Fiction.
2. Brooklyn (New York, N.Y.)—Fiction. 3. Italian American
families—Fiction. 4. Organized crime—Fiction. I. Title.

PS3607.R44 A84 2003
813'.6—dc21 2002032885

ISBN 0-06-093411-5 (pbk.)

04 05 06 07 08 ❖/RRD 10 9 8 7 6 5 4 3 2 1

For Christine

The author wishes to thank Richard Boes, Silvana Rivituso, Patrick Henderson, Charlie Boiselle, Brian DeFiore, and Marjorie Braman.

The Angel *of* Montague Street

■

THE MONTAGUE WAS AN OLD WHORE OF A HOTEL; she stood on the corner of Henry and Montague Streets in Brooklyn, New York. She was a couple of decades past her prime when Silvano Iurata landed there in the fall of '73, but if you squinted your eyes hard enough to filter out the grime you could still see something of what she used to be when she was young and glorious, green marble columns in the lobby thirty feet high, floor-to-ceiling windows, ornate wainscoting, carved mahogany front desk, plaster lions molded into the ceiling, so far up you could barely make them out, up there snarling down at you in sooty malevolence. She was maybe eighteen stories high, the lower floors more desirable than the upper ones because only one of the three elevators worked. One of the other two was generally shut down for repairs and the third was broken and sealed off for good. In one corner of the lobby was a bar, a dimly lit room behind swinging doors that had the image of a piano frosted into the thick green glass.

Silvano flopped on an ancient couch and waited for the night manager to locate his paperwork. He glanced in the bar's direction but he had no real desire to go in; bars were not his thing, particularly when they were small, dank, and heavy with the smell of beer, urine, and unwashed bodies. He wasn't that thirsty, couldn't imagine being that thirsty. An old guy with a cracked leather face and a red potato nose watched him from the bar doorway, and after a while, his beverage in his hand, he made his way carefully over to where Silvano sat.

"Excuse me," he said, in that whispery voice guys get when their upper teeth are gone. "I know you from someplace. Someplace overseas."

Oh, I hope not, Silvano thought, keeping his expression blank. He looked at the old boy's face, trying to picture what he might have looked like before time and bad habits had worked him over. "I don't think so," he said. "You don't look familiar."

"You sure? I was a news service photographer during the fifties and sixties. I worked the Middle East and North Africa. I swear I ran into you over there someplace."

Silvano shook his head, relieved. "Not me," he said, "late sixties, I was in Southeast Asia."

"Damn. I was so sure. Damn. Guy must've been your twin, then." He chuckled and drained off what was left in his glass. "Maybe you'll meet the guy some day. What did you do, in Southeast Asia."

"Worked for a messenger service."

"Ah," he said, looking down into his glass. "One of those guys. You with the Company?"

Silvano shook his head. "No. I was just an observer for the Defense Department."

"You don't look like an observer. You look more like a participant." He had a wry smile on his face. "Well, anyway," he said, rattling his ice cubes, "I need a refill. Come on in and join me sometime. I'll buy you a drink, we can talk about the bad old days."

"Yeah, sure."

Silvano shook his head as he watched the old boy make his way unsteadily back over where he'd come from. Funny, he thought, when you're young and you're spending it, you never think you're gonna get old and have to struggle to make the payments. You see some old bugger just hanging on, just trying not to die today, he looks like some kind of an alien creature, but he's you, brother, just as sure as that little shit who went to high school was you, and you'll get there all too soon. He tried again to place the old man's face, going back in his mind, remembering, until he caught himself at it and pulled back. Bad neighborhood, he told himself, you can't afford to hang out there. You got to stay in the now.

Easier said than done, though. He kept waiting for things to be different, but he kept winding up in the Hotel Montague or someplace like her, back in the arms of some old blowser who would give him shelter for a while. Someone had once said, he couldn't remember who, that home is where you can go, and they have to let you in. Maybe that's what kept him where he was, or maybe he was supposed to learn something, maybe he was supposed to have some sort of an incremental awakening before he could go on to the next level. But whatever the reason, he always felt more comfortable in the low-rent joints, where you didn't need to worry if your shirt or your haircut or your politics were right, if you had the price of a round they'd be glad to see you no matter how you looked or how badly you'd treated them the last time out, and they'd say, welcome back, sonny, have a seat, tell us where you been this long time.

There was still a lot of old fleabags like the Hotel Montague in that part of Brooklyn, from the Brooklyn Bridge stretching south and west along the waterfront past the Port Authority docks. The Hotel Montague was about the best of the bunch, at the time. Some of the others were pretty bad, like the Lady Margaret or the Stanford. With those two, it was only a question of whether they burned down before they fell down, or vice versa. The Castle Arms was another one, big square brick building with a parapet on each corner. It was not a bad place, relatively clean, still had some normal people in it. It had a big empty room on the first floor that had once been a restaurant, and a huge ballroom one floor down. No one had danced in the ballroom for a generation, it was dark and piled eight feet deep with chairs and old hotel furnishings that were covered with a thick coat of dust. There was a narrow pathway through it all to the back door. Upstairs, though, it looked nearly normal, like a regular hotel almost, all the elevators worked, all the doors had locks, all the toilets flushed, the whole bit.

And then there was the St. Felix. The St. Felix took up an entire city block, from Clark to Pineapple and from Henry to Hicks. It hadn't started out that way, originally it had just been a large white tower on one half of the block, but it sucked in all the other buildings like a tumor eating up healthy cells until the whole block was one big amorphous funky-smelling conglomeration with a few stores stuck to the outside, a deli and a liquor store and whatnot, and an arcade where you could catch the big elevator that went from street level through the basements and subbasements, all the way down to the subway.

The original part of the hotel, the white tower, was mostly empty in those days, except for cats, pigeons, rats, and winos, but one of the elevators still worked, some of the rooms had electricity, and some had running water. The rest of the hotel was inhabited by crazy people; it was party central—neurosis, psychosis, self-medication, and the occasional homicide or suicide.

What happened, sometime in '72 someone decided that there were too many people in the puzzle factory who weren't crazy enough, and it would be cheaper to put them on the street. Mainstreaming, they called it, and suddenly big welfare hotels and outpatient clinics became growth industries. A lot of the people who got mainstreamed had a bad time of it. Take a person with a tenuous grip on reality, lived most of his or her life on the inside, it's a scary thing to be put out on your own. Got no family, no friends, everybody looks at you, well, like you're crazy. A lot of them died from loneliness. They find you in the river, say that you drowned, but it was being alone killed you.

THE NIGHT MANAGER found Silvano's paperwork, finally, and gave him a room on the fifth floor. That meant four flights of stairs up and four down every time he went out, that or wait for the elevator. Silvano did not like waiting. Even if the thing was sitting there with the door open you had to go in, push the button, and stand there while the D.C. circuitry in the elevator's primitive brain decided to close the doors and slowly hoist you to your destination.

Silvano banged through the stairwell door on the fifth floor into a long dark corridor. He could hear her before he saw her.

"Claaark," she said, in a mournful voice, "Claark, let me in." She was sitting on the floor in front of a door, looking like a refugee from the Haight-Ashbury of half a dozen years ago, she had long straight blond hair, a velvet choker around her neck, a big yellow Indian-print shirt, bell-bottom jeans. Take one look at her face, though, and you could see how it had all gone to hell, she wore a troubled, confused expression and her blue eyes were clouded and unfocused. She was probably under thirty, but some of those years had to have been hard ones. She had a shopping bag on the floor next to her. Silvano looked at the number on the door where she was sitting, and then the number on his key.

"Terrific," he said.

She ignored him. "Claaark," she said again. "Please let me in, Clark."

Some of us, Silvano thought, paid a higher price for the sixties than others. "This is my room, sweetheart."

"No," she said in that lost and confused voice, "this is Clark's room. He's inside, he's waiting for me but sometimes he doesn't hear."

Silvano checked the number again, shook his head. "If Clark's in there, he'll be right out. C'mon, move your ass." He pushed her bag out of the way with his foot and she pivoted with it, crablike, still sitting down. He stuck his key in the lock and opened the door.

It was a small room, twelve feet by twelve feet, walls and ceiling painted pale green. Asbestos tile floor, one double bed, one small metal desk, one metal chair, one lamp, one metal bureau, four drawers. One window, bathroom off to one side, out of sight.

"See? No Clark. He musta split."

She peered over his shoulder into the empty room. "Clark?"

Clark, Silvano thought, you must've been really fucked up. "He moved out. They gave me his room. Go on downstairs, maybe they'll tell you where he went."

"But he was, he was . . ." She looked around uncertainly, and her voice got higher and more frantic. "But he was waiting for me!"

"Yeah, well, he ain't here now. Go on, get lost." She inched reluctantly down the corridor a few feet. He closed the door, but he could still hear her voice.

"Claark?"

Oh, Jesus, he thought. Wonderful.

He liked the room, liked the emptiness; he was comforted by the almost claustrophobic embrace of the place. You could see everything from anywhere in it, so there could be no surprises. Nothing hidden, no dark corners. He sat in the metal chair with his back to the wall next to the window and stared at the bathroom door. Nobody's in there, you already checked, he told himself, but he could feel the worms chewing at his guts and he knew it would get worse and worse until he went over and looked. Was it the war, he asked himself, or are you just fucking crazy? He could feel his anxiety building. The hell with this, he thought, and he got up and went to look. No place to hide in there, either, there wasn't even a window to climb through, nothing but the sink, the rusting metal shower stall, and the john. He turned and looked back into the room. Go on, he told himself, you're going to give in to this shit, you might as well go all the way. He dropped to one knee and looked under the bed. Monsters in the closet, he told himself, except there's no closet, so they hide up in your head. Jesus.

It didn't take him long to move in. He unzipped his bag and left it open on the floor, and that was about it. Not much in it anyway, just some clothes, toothbrush, and like that. The stuff he didn't want stolen he'd already stashed in a locker in a bathhouse over in the St. Felix.

Out of his window you could see the brick side of the next building, maybe six feet away, and a narrow slice of Montague Street, all lit up. The bed was starting to look good, but Silvano wanted to have a look around.

She was not in the corridor, but when he got down to the lobby she was on the far side of the room. She spotted him coming out of the stairwell door and made a beeline for the elevator. Silvano stopped at the front desk.

"What's with Mrs. Clark?"

"Who?"

"Mrs. Claaark."

"Huh? Oh, her." He chuckled. "Don't worry about her, she's harmless. You just caught her on a bad day."

Silvano stared at him.

"No, really, man, most of the time she's almost lucid. She gets to be a pain, let me know, we'll move you."

"Is there a real Clark?"

"Never seen one."

THINK OF A LONG row of bookshelves leaning drunkenly against a wall. The top shelf is the Promenade, a pedestrian walkway of octagonal paving stones, park benches, wrought-iron fences, small private gardens in the backyards of pricey brownstones. One shelf down and slightly out from the wall run the northbound lanes of the Brooklyn-Queens Expressway, another shelf down the southbound lanes of the same expressway. The bottom shelf is Furman Street, lined with trucks waiting to pick up or deliver to the freighters that were still coming to the Brooklyn waterfront, docking at the busy Port Authority piers. And the floor itself, stretching away from the wall, the floor is the East River, which is not a river at all, but which is, like the city that surrounds her, deep, fast-moving, dark, beautiful, also treacherous and unforgiving. On the far side the buildings of Lower Manhattan are stacked thick and close, so close you can see nothing of the land they stand on, nothing of the island itself, just the buildings, with another highway perched on stilts, running around the outside, just above the water. A row of piers stick their thick fingers out into the river, giving shelter to some wooden sailing ships from another century, ferries running to and from Staten Island and Governors Island, tennis courts under inflated cocoons, and a dock for seaplanes and helicopters. Behind the piers is the narrow slice of the South Street Seaport, a working fishmarket. No boats unload there anymore, the fish is all delivered in trucks, and men in dark suits set prices that hold firm as far north as New Bedford and Gloucester, as far south as Baltimore.

Silvano walked the few blocks from his hotel straight down Montague Street to the end, where he stepped onto one end of the Promenade and turned right. Streetlights from the New York City Parks Department kept the night at bay, and people walked their dogs, pushed their baby carriages, and young gay men walked slowly, eyeing one another speculatively. For the most part they ignored Silvano because he was not young or pretty, did not look prosperous. Even the guys into rough trade gave him a wide berth, knowing somehow that he wasn't one of them, that his troubles were uncomfortably real. He was medium height and he looked lupine, underfed for those fat years. He still walked with an athletic grace but his dark hair was beginning to show streaks of gray, and he had two days' growth of beard on a lined face that looked older than it was. He could have passed for a street cop in plain clothes, or a hockey player, or maybe an aging middleweight who had stayed in the game a little too long. He had that kind of build, he had the scars, he had hooded, hollow eyes that told you the only real sin was not to see it coming.

He leaned against the rail. The awareness of that vast open space behind him itched at him, but he ignored it and watched the crowd. There may be people behind you, he thought, but it's not a stretch to trust that none of them are looking through a scope right now, lining you up. Didn't make it easy, though. He stayed there with the people flowing slowly past him until he felt a little better. You're just a voyeur, he told himself, you don't understand them, so you stand and you watch, wondering what the hell they're doing. You think you've gotta see every dog in the bushes, he told himself derisively. What a fucking wreck.

He pushed himself away from the railing and walked north on the Promenade. He stopped a little farther on, where an apartment building that had no rear garden butted up against the fence. He sat on a park bench with his back to the wall of the building and he watched again. It was an idiotic habit, he knew that, it only slowed him down, there were just the normal dangers on this nighttime walkway, nothing extraordinary, there were no trip wires on the Promenade, but something deep in his subconscious would not accept that. Some days he would fight against the paranoia, other days he found it easier just to go along, pick his spots to stop and scan the faces, look into the dark corners before he passed them by. A VA shrink once told him it was neurosis, but Silvano preferred to think it was just that he no longer believed in normalcy.

He became conscious of the cacophony of automobile horns, louder and angrier than seemed reasonable even for Brooklyn, so he walked to the railing and looked down. Below him the southbound lanes of the expressway were empty, and the north-bound lanes were stopped dead. A few people had gotten out of their vehicles to crane their necks and peer ahead, looking for the cause of the tie-up. He continued north, and soon the massive stone towers of the Brooklyn Bridge came into view, all lit up in the darkness.

The helicopter that was hovering near the Manhattan tower

was a police chopper, built by some company in France, that was why it hadn't registered. It made a different noise than the Army choppers he was used to, whose whop whop whop sound had imbedded itself deep into the nether regions of his mind. It was shining a spotlight on the guy wires that ran from the big bridge cables down to the roadway. The roadway was ablaze with flashing lights from a crowd of police vehicles and ambulances, and there was a police boat in the river, bow pointed into the current, wake streaming out behind as it remained more or less stationary beneath the bridge. Below Silvano, the car horns crescendoed and died away, only to start up again farther on.

In the space of maybe four city blocks he got to the other end of the walkway. There were about a dozen people there, leaning against the railing, watching. Silvano looked again, made out a human shape clinging to a guy wire about thirty feet above the roadway of the bridge. Ten feet below was another figure, one arm held up in supplication, had to be a cop saying, don't do it, buddy, let us help you, come down, goddammit. Silvano stopped at the outer edge of the small group that stood watching. For one tiny fraction of a second his control slipped and he was out there on the bridge with the guy, whoever he was, holding on but leaning out, closing his eyes, and it wasn't that you wanted to go but that you couldn't stay because you didn't have it anymore, couldn't suck it up one more time, couldn't go into battle again and couldn't run away, just couldn't get it up for one more fucking sunrise. The man next to him turned to make eye contact. "It's just like the ones that jump in front of subway trains," he hissed. "They always wait for rush hour. Gotta have an audience." He rolled his eyes, turned away, and stalked off into the night. The next guy over, a young light-skinned black man with a cane, was laughing.

"There's compassion for you. Reminds me of the New York version of mouth to mouth. You heard of it?"

"No." He gritted his teeth, angry with himself, and the door that had cracked open slammed shut again. He worked hard to keep the clamps on his emotions in the hope that his demons would stay buried. It didn't always work, but it was all that he had. The other guy, oblivious, finished his joke.

"That's where you kick the guy in the ribs and yell, 'Breathe, damn you!'"

"Very good." Silvano looked at the man's olive drab fatigue jacket, irked that the jacket could be so popular when the institution was so disliked. "You Airborne?"

The man looked down at the insignia sewn onto the jacket. "Me? Hell, no. Jacket was Airborne, I was in the brown water Navy."

"River rat, huh?"

"Yes, suh." He regarded Silvano with heightened interest. "Yourself?"

Silvano twisted the truth, as was his wont. "I flew medevac."

"Oh, my," he said. "Always glad to see one of you guys, even if you do be walking."

"You think this guy's jumping?"

"Yeah. He's had enough. He been out there too long. He was gonna come down, he'd a given up by now. Got traffic fucked up from here to Kansas, got half the cops in New York waiting on his ass, he already got his money's worth, he was gonna back out. No, this guy's gonna jump."

"They'll have to pull him outa the river."

"No way, baby. Too far to fall, and the current is a mother. Odds are, he'll wash up on Staten Island in a few days, or over on the Jersey side."

"Sounds like you seen this before."

"Every so often. Brooklyn Bridge is a pretty popular spot for it."

Silvano watched and he wondered if this might not have been the way his brother Nunzio had gone, into the river, never seen again. It would explain why no one had heard from him in a year. The thought made his eyes water just a bit, and some part of his mind called out unbidden, Noonie, where are you, Noonie, for the umpteenth time.

"Aw, shit, there he goes." Silvano could hear real sorrow in the man's voice as they both watched the figure cartwheel down through the night air into the river. Police divers went off the back of the boat as the helicopter swooped down to shine its spotlight on the surface of the water. "Son of a bitch."

Several of the other watchers turned and departed, and over the next few minutes the rest left one by one, leaving Silvano and the young black man standing alone at the railing.

"He must have figured it was his time."

"You can't think that way, man." He glanced over at Silvano. "Especially guys like us, guys from Nam. I seen too many of us go like this. Too many suicides. It ain't right, you can't think that way."

"Why not?" Silvano was looking out at the black water. "You gotta go sooner or later anyhow. What the hell's the difference."

"Well, that might be true, but I was raised Pentecostal, so I got a few attitudes left over from that, and one of 'em is, you can't go early. You gotta wait until the man upstairs says it's time for you to go. Otherwise, you show up ahead of schedule, you might piss the old boy off, wind up worse than if you'd just hung in there to begin with."

Silvano looked at him. "I guess we were better off than you guys, because we had Purgatory."

That got a laugh, which was choked off by a deep, hacking

cough. "Aaa," he said, finally, clearing his throat. "Why would Purgatory be a good thing?"

Silvano shrugged. "I always knew I wasn't gonna be a first-ballot Hall of Famer, you know what I mean? But with Purgatory, at least you got a shot, you know, because there's a back door."

"You know, I never thought of it that way. So you figure the veteran's committee is gonna vote you in?"

"That would be assuming a lot. You from around here?"

"Nope. Where I'm from, my old man was the first black dentist in the State of Maine. He had gone to dental school back in the forties, on the GI Bill, and after he graduated he moved from Philadelphia to Portland, Maine, and he went to work for a French Canadian dentist up there, wound up marrying the boss's niece, and then I came along."

"That where you grew up? You ain't got the accent."

"Been gone a long time. Yeah, I grew up in South Portland, there was a few brothers there at the time, but not many. Few more now. But I'll tell you what, I didn't hear too much shit about black and white, I got it worse for having a French Canadian mother than I did for a black father, because sometimes French Canadians talk funny, they would say something like, 'Hey, t'row me down the stairs my hat.' My mom said it didn't matter, she said up in Quebec they'd tell Newfie jokes, you know, ranking on people from Newfoundland because they talk funny. I don't know what kind of jokes they tell in Newfoundland."

"Probably tell the one about the white guy from New York City, jumped in the river."

"Poor bastard. How you know he was white?"

Silvano looked out at the lights reflecting off the water. The guy's probably sucking in a lungful of black water right now, he thought. Dying in the deep embrace of the East River while we stand watching. "In the joke, it don't matter."

"I suppose not."

"Listen, you live around here? You know a good place to eat?"

"I live up to the St. Felix. Yeah, plenty of places, we got anything you want. My personal favorite, nice Greek place up on Montague, cheap, BYOB, they got sidewalk tables, you can sit and watch the world go by."

"St. Felix, no kidding. You know a guy named Nunzio, about so high, thin, not all there? People usually called him Noonie."

"Name don't ring a bell. He owe you money?"

"No, he was my brother. Went missing a while back."

"Ain't that the way it goes? Go off for a one-year tour, when you get back, the whole world's changed."

It didn't feel like a year, it felt like half a lifetime. He pushed himself away from the railing. "I'm gonna go try out your restaurant. You hungry?"

"No. I appreciate the invite, but I came down here to cop, not to watch some poor bastard take a header into the East River. I got business to transact, and the thing is, guy like you, down here at night, ain't queer and ain't walkin' your dog, gotta be the po-lice. You too mean-looking to be Joe Citizen."

"Prejudice is such a mother, see, people think they know something about you . . ."

That got another laugh. "Hey, listen, you staying here?"

"Yeah, I'm at the Montague."

"Maybe I'll see you around."

SILVANO WALKED AWAY from the northern end of the Promenade, out onto the local streets. The first building he passed was the Lady Margaret, a tall, narrow wood-frame hotel with a dirty white exterior and a smell to match. A stocky woman with white hair and a face like Tip O'Neill stood in front of the steps to the hotel and eyed him belligerently.

"Thirty years of niggerism!" she bellowed at him hoarsely. "Thirty years of niggerism and a cellar full of garbage!"

"Oh, nice," Silvano told her. "And how are you tonight?"

"Fine," she said mildly.

He passed the Castle Arms a block later and then he stopped at the liquor store in the St. Felix and bought a bottle of Chianti. The clerk slid the bottle into a paper bag and handed it smoothly to Silvano along with his change without ever once looking at him. Back out on the street, Silvano continued on with the bottle tucked under his arm. He paused on the sidewalk outside the arcade, the big opening in the hotel that gave pedestrians access to the elevator to the subway. To get into the arcade you had to go through two sets of swinging doors, an inner and an outer set, three pairs of them were set side by side in the grayish brick facade. As Silvano watched, an old woman with a cane came through the center set of doors, and in the vestibule space between the inner and outer doors she suddenly began swinging her cane wildly, wielding it like Errol Flynn in some old movie, and then exiting the outer set of doors she stopped to recover her breath and her composure. Then she set off down the sidewalk as if nothing in the world were more normal. Fear, Silvano thought, maybe she got mugged there once, and her fear makes her irrational and antisocial. Just like the rest of us.

It was a ten-minute walk from the St. Felix to the Greek restaurant on Montague. The neighborhood was called Brooklyn Heights, and she was still undiscovered, a little nicked up and past her prime, but beautiful, with a sort of silver-haired grace. The brownstones and brick buildings spoke of time and endurance, the old slate sidewalks and the trees arching over the streets gave the place an air of solidity and permanence that Manhattan's steel and glass towers could never duplicate. Silvano took his time, stopping here and there to look around.

Finally he found the restaurant, sat down at a tiny table under an awning out on the sidewalk. A waiter came, pulled the cork from his bottle, took his order. He sat there alone, watching the people go streaming past, people on their way home, couples out for a stroll, a crowd of young men with unfashionably short hair, all of them seeming to shout at the others, trying to be heard, laughing uproariously. Silvano sat by himself, off to one side, like always. No crime in being alone, he told himself, but he'd had the inner debate about his solitary existence so often he was tired of it and he choked it off.

When he was done eating he left money on the table, and catching the waiter's eye, he jiggled the Chianti bottle to let him know there was still something in it. The waiter pinched the inside of his pantleg between a thumb and forefinger and shook it, giving Silvano his opinion of the wine. Silvano shrugged, left it there anyway. Communication without speech, he thought. That's where I'm headed. He walked off down the sidewalk, but when he looked back, the waiter was pouring the rest of the Chianti into a water glass.

Couldn't have been that bad, Silvano thought. Bet he's had worse.

THERE WAS A BANK of pay phones on the sidewalk in front of the hotel, next to a large green box that opened out into a newspaper kiosk. Silvano had noticed the phones there before, on his way out. He'd expected the kiosk to be closed this late at night, but it was not. The dark-skinned man sitting inside on a stool was passed out, breathing noisily, cheek pressed against worn plywood. A row of skin magazines with unfamiliar names pinned to the top of the kiosk over his head fluttered in the breeze. As Silvano walked past, two neighborhood kids raced by him, grabbed handfuls of change from the counter of the kiosk, and took off again. The dark-skinned man woke with a start and looked around wildly. Indian, Silvano thought, or Pakistani. He could see the imprint of the wood grain in the side of the man's face as he began to close up hastily. Silvano paused in front of the payphones, considering. Been six months, he thought. You really should call her.

He walked over and stood in front of a phone, steeling himself. Why is this so difficult, he wondered, why is this so hard to do? He felt butterflies in his stomach as he reached for the phone, but it had no dial tone. Neither did the next one, but the phone on the end of the row worked. He dialed zero and the number. "Collect call," he told the operator when she came on the line, "from Silvano." She placed the call. He heard the phone ring twice, heard his brother-in-law Vinnie pick up the phone, heard the operator ask her question.

"Yeah," Vinnie said. "Yeah, I'll pay for the call."

"Hey, Vinnie. What's happening?"

"Hey, Sil, how are ya? Got a good connection this time. Where you hidden away these days?"

"Brooklyn."

Stunned silence, then: "No shit!" Silvano could hear him breathing into the phone. "Jesus," he finally said. "Silvano, are you nuts? Are you out of your fucking mind?"

Silvano was mildly amused. "What would make you say that, Vinnie?"

"Don't jerk me off, Silvano. One place in the world the man wants you dead, and you gotta go visit. Little Dom finds out you're in town, he'll turn New York City upside down to get you. You know how bad he hates you, for chrissake."

"I don't care whether he hates me or not."

"You don't care about Little Dom?" Vinnie was incredulous. "You care about breathing? You care about being alive? The only reason he hasn't put out a contract on you is because he wants to do you himself. If he catches you, he'll cut your fingers off one at a time just to watch you scream, he'll cut your liver out and make you watch him do it, he'll . . ."

"Vinnie." Silvano cut him off. "Calm down."

"Calm down? Silvano, I been to enough funerals this year, I don't wanna go to another one. Assuming Dom leaves enough of you to bury. You need money, just let me know, I'll send it to you anyplace in the world but here, just go get on a plane and go somewhere else. If you're willing to forget that carpenter bullshit, go back to doing what you're good at, heh, I know a few people could really use you. I could make some calls, you could be working by the weekend, nice and safe out West, somewhere like L.A. or Vegas."

"Vinnie, be quiet and listen to me. I'm staying in an old flophouse in Brooklyn Heights, and I'm gonna be retired for a while. I'm gonna see if I run into anyone used to know Noonie. You can call Scalia yourself for all I care, tell him I'm here, I'll give you his balls for cocktail onions."

That hung there in silence between them.

"Vinnie?"

"Yeah. Jesus, Sil, listen, why you gotta do this? Why you wanna get into all that? Noonie's gone, Sil, you can't bring him back. Whyncha just let him go? Let him rest. Go find a nice Catholic church, go on in, it won't hurt ya, light a candle. Say a prayer. Your brother's with God now."

"Yeah, you think so?"

"Come on, Sil, don't start with me. I don't wanna hear any of that gook bullshit you're into. Have some respect for the dead, for chrissake, go light a candle for your brother, and then just get the hell out of town."

Why do I talk to this guy, Silvano wondered. "You know, Vinnie, you may be right. Maybe I'll do that. Ann around?"

"Yeah, course. Look, Sil, why . . . I don't understand you, you know that?"

"I don't either. Lemme talk to Ann."

"All right." Silvano could almost see him shrugging his shoulders, throwing up his hands. "Just lemme say this one thing, okay? I know Domenic, okay, and he's smarter and meaner than the old man ever thought of being. Even if you keep your head down, word's gonna get out, it has to, and he has a long memory."

"So do I."

"All right, I just want to make sure you understand I did right by you, Sil, you can't say I didn't give you fair warning. I'll go get your sister. Just watch your back, okay, Sil?"

"Don't worry about it."

A moment later she came on.

"I gotta hand it to you, Silvie, nobody can make Vin talk about going to church except you. Are you still a Buddhist?"

"Only part time. Every other Saturday." He listened to her laughing at him. She was used to it, she knew he'd spent years looking for that one real thing he could pour over his life like milk on the cereal, something that would get everything to make sense, make it all work. Once it had been the Army, but that hadn't worked in a long time. Another time it had been the Oregon woods and the marijuana maintenance program. Zen had been the last in the series, but it had come up suddenly short.

"Vin says you're back in Brooklyn, Silvie, is that right? You know you're gonna open up some old wounds. You really wanna get everything all stirred up again?"

He thought of the years that had passed since he left, the places he had lived as a stranger, always a gypsy passing through, another guy who didn't belong. "I don't care about the Scalias anymore, Ann. I'm not interested in ancient history. I'm gonna put my feet up here for a while, and while I'm here I'm gonna see if I can find out what happened to Noonie. I can't just let it go and pretend he died in his sleep. I owe it to him to at least ask a few questions."

Her voice got quiet. "You really think he's dead, then."

"I'm sorry, I didn't mean it to come out like that, but I guess I do."

She sighed. "I guess I've accepted it. It was so hard, waiting for him to call, the way he always did. For the longest time, whenever the phone would ring, I would think it was going to be him. But it's like when someone pokes you in the same spot, over and over again, it hurts so bad, but then after a while you just don't feel anything anymore. I guess I would really like to know what happened to him, you know, but I don't know if I could deal with losing you, too, Silvie. Domenic's not just a kid anymore, he's for real now. This is not like he's waiting for you at recess. I can let go of it, Silvie, I can handle not knowing about Noonie, if you would just go somewhere safe."

"Annette, I been through shit would make Domenic Scalia run screaming for his mommy. He may be a big man on Cross Bay Boulevard, to me he's just another asshole in a shiny suit. Don't worry, nothing will happen."

"You are the most stubborn person I know. I suppose I should quit wasting my breath."

"You seen the old man lately?"

"I went in to Bensonhurst last week to visit. The house is the same, I don't think they changed a thing. New TV in the living room, that was it."

"He ask about me?" It just came out.

"He don't ask about nobody, Silvie, he's like seventy something years old. Only thing he talks about, what he had for breakfast, what he's gonna eat for dinner, ooh, we got some nice Jersey tomatoes. Couple years ago me and Vin sent the two of them on a cruise, only thing he remembered was the restaurant, Monday we ate this, Tuesday we ate that, Wednesday we ate something else."

"Terrific."

"Hey, could be worse. You remember Aunt Mary?" She lowered her voice to a whisper. "Remember her stomach was all fucked up?" Silvano suppressed a laugh. More than once he'd seen his petite little sister screaming invective at someone several times her size, but in normal conversation she would lower her voice to swear. "You remember her? Last few years she was alive, all she could talk about was her bowel movements, right up until the day she died."

"Jesus, what a family. I had a nice bowl of pasta, and then I took a nice big dump. Life is good."

"Oh, come on, Silvie," she said, laughing. "It ain't just us, they're old now, that's the way old people are. Are you going to go out to see him, while you're in town?"

"Am I gonna what? Are you out of your mind?"

"Oh, come on, Sil. How can you be afraid of him if you're not scared of Domenic? It's been so many years, he's not gonna live forever. If you don't face up you're gonna feel rotten about it for as long as you live. He's not that bad."

Easy for you to say, he thought. You were always Daddy's Little Angel. Jesus Christ. And it wasn't that he was afraid of the guy, really, it was more that he didn't like how it felt to be the object of all that disappointment.

"Silvie, you still there?"

"Yeah, sorry. Some cops were going by."

"Why would you care? You carrying, you done something bad?"

"No, not yet. You remember what Noonie used to say?"

"Yeah, 'I already got all the trouble I need.' Poor guy. I'm really sorry you didn't get to see him."

"So'm I. Listen, I don't wanna run up your phone bill."

"Pfffft. Gimme a break. All right, Silvie, I'll let you go. Can I just ask you one thing?"

"What's that?"

"At least think about it, all right? Think about going down to see him. If Noonie's really gone, you're the only son he's got left now. I know he feels bad about the way things turned out."

How can you tell, he wanted to ask her, how can you tell he feels anything at all? He had never given any sign of it . . . "All right." Silvano listened to himself in disbelief. Did I actually agree to this shit? "I'll go see the old bastard before I leave."

"Oh, good." He could hear the relief in her voice. "You'll feel better when it's all over, you'll see. I'd really love to see you too, you know."

"Yeah, I know. I don't wanna put Vinnie in a bad spot, though."

"Vinnie don't owe them Brooklyn assholes nothing, there's no way they could think he's gonna give you up." The mob was a feudal arrangement, and Vinnie and Domenic were knights who owed their allegiances to different barons. The barons were called capos, and each capo would have somewhere between five and a dozen men like Silvano's cousin Domenic who answered to him, and he, in turn, would answer to one of the heads of the five families, the godfathers who ruled like kings, high above it all. They would not even know, or care, about the old hatred between Domenic Scalia and Silvano Iurata. The cement that held the arrangement together was money. As long as the money kept flowing upward, from the street level operators all the way up to the godfathers, everyone was happy. If a kink developed in that chain, though, let someone get too greedy and try to keep too much for himself, then the men at the top would begin to bury their problems in shallow graves. The money was all that mattered.

"Well," he said, "you're right about that. I tell you what, give me a few days to see what I can find out, and then I'll call you. Okay?"

"Promise me you won't go off someplace before you come out to visit. And promise me you'll be careful."

"All right," he said. He said good-bye and hung up the phone, still not quite believing he had promised her he'd go visit his father. He shook his head. Ever since enlisting, he had pretended to himself that he was alone, that there was no one who cared about him or even knew his name. Life seemed so much easier that way. They're supposed to be on your side, he thought. How is it that they can make you feel so lousy?

He looked down Montague Street. It was only a couple of blocks to the end, where the Brooklyn-Queens Expressway ran underneath the Promenade. It was just a short ride, he knew, jump on and head south, bear left at the split for the Verrazano and you're on the Belt Parkway swinging down along the southern shore of Brooklyn, where he'd grown up. It isn't home anymore, he thought, you don't belong down there. Still, he could feel it pulling at him.

• • •

"I want you to do me a favor."

It was Angelo, his uncle, and you couldn't say no to Angelo even if you wanted to. Not that Silvano wanted to say no; at seventeen, he looked up to his uncle. Angelo walked through the neighborhood like he owned it, and if you thought about things in a certain way, he did. Everyone knew who he was, they all said hello, politely. There was always a certain kind of deference in the way people looked at him. If you had a problem, say you hit the number and the guy wouldn't pay off, Angelo was the guy you wanted to talk to, because he would take care of you. The only other alternative was Angelo's father, Domenic, and the old man was so savage and unpredictable you never knew what kind of treatment you were going to get. Better you should talk to Angelo.

"Anything," Sylvano told him. "You name it."

"Come with me," Angelo told him. "We'll talk in the car."

Angelo drove an enormous Chrysler St. Regis, Silvano loved the big chrome beast. He watched Angelo drive, muscling the big steering wheel with one hand, even when the car was sitting still, when most people would have to wrestle the wheel with both hands. Angelo looked over at him. "Your aunt can never know about this. You understand me?"

"She'll never hear anything from me." It was old news, though, everybody in the neighborhood had heard the story. Angelo had a mistress, not that it was a big deal, not for a man of his stature. What had gotten everyone talking was the fact that the mistress wanted Angelo to divorce his wife and marry her, and he was actually considering it.

Things had gotten worse when Angelo's wife finally caught on. Silvano had been visiting his cousin Little Dom when Angelo came walking into the house. The next thing he knew, Angelo and his wife were having a screaming match in the kitchen. This, too, was not all that unusual, but this argument continued with an intensity and a duration that told Silvano that this time it was different. He and Dom both left the house then. "Don't say anything to anybody," Dom said to him. "Promise me."

Silvano had promised, and he had kept his mouth shut, but Angelo's wife was under no such compunction, because soon afterward, the entire neighborhood knew that Angelo was sleeping on his own couch.

Angelo looked over at Silvano. "You heard the stories?"

"I ain't said nothing to nobody."

"That's not what I asked you."

Silvano could feel his heart beating wildly in his chest. No easy way around this, he thought. You gotta tell the truth. "This has been going on for a year, Uncle Angelo. Everybody's heard the stories."

Angelo drove in silence for a few blocks. "All right," he finally said. "Fine. But now I'm gonna tell you something nobody knows, and if it gets out, I'll know it was you. You understand me?"

Silvano could feel the anxiety eating at the pit of his stomach. "Yes, Uncle Angelo."

He didn't look at Silvano when he said it. "She's been shooting dope."

"Who?"

"Who the fuck we been talking about?"

"I'm sorry—"

"Shut up and listen." But then he didn't say anything. Silvano sat in fearful silence. "I found out about this about six months ago," Angelo finally said. "I told her I was going to kill her, told her I'd throw her right out the fucking window . . . She cries, she begs, she promises me she'll never touch it again. I put her in a place where they clean you up. She gets out, I take her home, everybody's happy. Couple weeks later she's shooting up again." Sil-

vano could feel Angelo getting angrier and angrier. "Finally I said, fuck it, she loves the spike more than she loves me, let her kill herself, I'm done with her." He stopped at a red light, watched the cars go by. "How old are you?"

"Seventeen."

Angelo shook his head. "Shit. Seventeen. I'm sorry I gotta come to you with this, but I know you're tough enough to handle it. Your cousin Domenic, I ain't saying he's soft, but he's a scholar. He's gonna go to college to be something. There's too many things about the street he don't know. And I can't go to my regular people, they all owe too much loyalty to my father, and I've already taken too much shit from him over this. That leaves you."

"It's all right," Silvano said. "Tell me what to do."

The light turned green and Angelo drove off. "I quit giving her money the first time I found out. I thought, she can't pay for it, she can't get it. But I think she's whoring for it. I think whoever sells her this shit, she's fucking him." He was fuming. "Whoever this guy is, he caused me a lot of fucking trouble. Don't get me wrong, I'm walking away from her, but I want to whack the guy first. First, though, I gotta find out who he is. I rented the apartment across the hall from hers, okay, I want you inside, watching who comes and goes. You understand me?"

"Yes, Uncle Angelo."

Angelo looked over at him. "You're a smart kid. Too smart for this shit. You should go to fucking school. I was your father, I would have kicked your ass every time you brought home a lousy report card."

Silvano didn't know what to say to that.

Angelo fished a business card out of his pocket. "You call this number once a day," he said. "There's always someone there. The guy we're looking for is gonna be a guy who shows up regular, you understand? You see a guy once and he don't come back, that ain't him. You know who our guy is, you call that number, you say, 'I gotta see Angelo right away.' You understand me?"

"Yeah."

"Good boy. You do this for me, I'll take care of you. We gotta get you out of this life, it's no good for you. You should be in school, you should be learning to be something." He hesitated. "I know he's got problems, but your father shoulda seen to that. We're gonna go by your house, I want you to grab whatever you need for like three days. Three days, and this will all be over."

It hadn't worked out that way.

SHE WAS BACK in front of his door again, and she began to panic when she saw him coming.

"Claaark, Claaark . . ."

He stood there behind her, counting his inhalations, one to ten, but she didn't move. He jerked his thumb in the direction of the elevators. "He ain't here. He ain't coming back. Why don't you go downstairs and see if he's in the Dumpster." He kicked her shopping bag away from the door. "Go on, get outta here."

She scuttled hastily down the corridor to retrieve her bag, whimpering to herself as she went. He shook his head, sorry already. Proud of yourself, he asked silently.

Inside, he lay down in his bed, with an old bed you don't lay on it, you lay in it, and he stared at the green ceiling, feeling himself breathe. In the next room, some old fart was listening to a baseball game on the radio. Silvano's sense of hearing was unusually acute, but at times like this he didn't know if it was a blessing or a curse. Mets were playing Cincinnati, Mets were good that year and they were playing Cinci tough, and even though he didn't recognize the names, everything else was the same, the sound of the ball hitting the catcher's mitt, the pitcher toying with the batter, the batter working the pitcher, walk to first, get bunted over, steal third, pray for a hit, in fact it was the one thing that seemed to be exactly what he remembered it to be, and not fundamentally different in some way, challenging him to learn it all over again. Still, he told himself, gotta get earplugs tomorrow.

The pitcher struck the next two batters out, stranding the runner at third.

Freakin' Mets, he told himself. Earplugs tomorrow, definitely.

DOM HATED THIS, hated being summoned like a busboy and then forced to sit around all afternoon drinking espresso and sambuca, watching while Antonio conducted business out of a bar he owned down on Cropsey Avenue. The old man was doing it to him on purpose, of course, it was just one of his not-so-subtle ways of reminding everyone who was in charge, who held the string and who danced. It was a dangerous combination for him, caffeine, alcohol, and impatience, because Antonio was unpredictable and totally without mercy, sensitive to any slight.

"Carlo," he said to the stiff Antonio had working the bar. "Rack 'em up again." He'd been doing it for the past couple of hours, buying rounds for the house, forcing the pace, throwing twenties at Carlo. It was his own not-so-subtle way of registering his displeasure. Fuck it, he thought. Drag me all the way down here, down to the asshole end of Brooklyn, this is what you get. He watched Carlo raise an eyebrow, looking at Antonio, asking, and Antonio's quick scowling answer in return, "Yeah, why not, I'll drink him fucking blind . . ." Antonio never backed down, ever.

Domenic Scalia was his full name. Behind his back they

called him the Fish because he rarely betrayed any emotion, even under extreme stress he almost always appeared calm, cold, and logical. To his face they called him Little Dom, which he didn't mind because it reminded them all of Big Dom, his grandfather, and they would look at him with a glint of fear in their eyes because he was enough like the old man that nobody wanted to get too close.

There was a black guy and a Chinese guy in the bar, that had to be a fucking first, they were both from Jamaica, and they had started up a big bakery with Antonio's assistance and some of his money. Antonio was disabusing them of the notion that once they paid him back he was out of their hair. He put his arm around the black guy's shoulders and began walking him toward the exit, up past where Domenic sat at the bar. The Chinese guy trailed unhappily behind, followed by two of Antonio's guys, Victor and Ivan. Victor was almost as old as Antonio, he'd been Antonio's muscle for half a century. He might have lost half a step, but you wouldn't want to be the one to test the theory, the guy still got the job done. Ivan was the understudy. He had been friends with Domenic for years, Domenic knew he was the only guy in the world Ivan was afraid of.

Antonio halted the procession when they got to where Domenic sat at the bar. "My friends and I gotta take a little walk," he said. "We gotta talk a little business. You mind, hanging around a little longer? I know you don't like the old neighborhood no more." He turned to speak over his shoulder to the Greek chorus that followed him. "Greenwich Village, this *teste di gatz* lives in."

Domenic was annoyed, but he didn't let it show. It was just Antonio, breaking his balls. "Take your time," he said.

"Well, I know you got a long ride back." Antonio turned to the frightened Jamaican in his grasp. "A beautiful wife, he's got, two beautiful kids. Nice house in Howard Beach, but he has to go live in Greenwich fucking Village."

Domenic rolled his eyes. "We gotta go through all that again?"

Antonio stared at him with a sorrowful look on his face. "No," he said. "But I don't understand you."

"You didn't have to fucking live with her."

"We'll be back."

Domenic watched Antonio and his entourage go through the front door out into the bright afternoon sun. Fucking asshole, he thought, he's not gonna be happy until I'm back in with Gina.

He had given the house to her and the kids, moved to the place in the Village, that had been back before it got overrun with fags and flower children. He remembered sitting in her kitchen, considering his options coldly. What he really wanted to do was kill her, wrap his hands around her fucking neck and squeeze the life out of her, but then he'd be stuck with two kids, responsible for feeding them, taking them to school, and wiping their snotty noses, and who fucking needed that? He remembered thinking, at the time, how life is like a spider's web, you take a step without thinking and you wind up stuck. Everything you think you want, in this case Gina, later on you find out you're stuck with, and you got to fight to get loose.

Don't you call me, he'd told her, don't call me, don't write me, don't fucking sue me I swear to God I'll kill you, I'll put you down at the bottom of one of those big piles of garbage we're building out on Staten Island, that's where you belong, you piece of shit. You take the house, you take the money, it's in an annuity so I don't even have to think of your fucking name, you get a check once a month from the insurance company, and you take care of these two brats, they're the only reason I'm letting you live. You hear me? And don't you call me, don't you even fucking look at me. I don't care what you do, fuck the pool boy for all I care, but if he moves in with you I'll cut his fucking dick off, I swear to Christ . . . You hear me?

He gritted his teeth, clenched his fists until his knuckles were white, every muscle in his body tense as he felt it all over again, for the umpteenth time, every emotion he'd felt at that moment amplified by time and practice.

It ebbed out of him slowly, he could feel it seep away until he was cold and limp. That's how it is, he told himself, that's life, learn from it or do it all over again. You're better off just going to a whorehouse, you leave your money on the table, take some female into a back room, get your nut off and walk away, you don't even have to know her name, don't have to talk to her, listen to her, look at her, nothing.

Every relationship is an entanglement, every emotional attachment is a rope around your fucking neck. Look at this deal with Antonio and the others. Did he need them? No. They needed him, though, and they weren't going to let him go, either, and he had to drag his ass all the fucking way down here to try to explain Wall Street to these Cro-Magnon assholes all over again.

Antonio had to deal with some lawyer after he got done with the Jamaicans, and then somebody else when he was done with the lawyer, and someone after that. It was fully dark outside when Antonio finally got to him.

"So explain to me," Antonio said belligerently, "about this three-legged fucking horse you put my money on." It was an oil stock, Domenic had ridden it up into the thirties but not everybody had gotten out in time. The SEC had suspended trading, they'd be lucky if the thing opened at three bucks.

"Look," Domenic said. "You work the percentages. You don't

bet your house on every single roll. If you can get, say, a five percent margin on the house, you will make money in the long run, but you still gotta take a hit every now and then. You ain't gonna win every single hand."

They were sitting around a table in the back of the bar, and a lot of Antonio's cronies were there, and they broke out into a chorus of complaints. Dumb bastards, Domenic thought, you give one of them something, they pass it around like it was somebody's old girlfriend. Jesus. He listened to it for a while, and then he decided to break it down to something they could understand.

"Listen," he said, interrupting. "Let's say you own some jockeys out at Aqueduct. You don't try to fix every single goddamned race. You understand me?" He watched comprehension dawn in some of their faces. "Now you're getting it. You need to have some patience, and you can't be too greedy. Say you fix two races a week, you're gonna win, be happy. And even then, there's no guarantee, for chrissake. Say your horse is out in front by ten lengths, he could still step in a hole and break his goddamned leg, you're gonna lose once in a while. Sometimes God takes a hand, what're you gonna do?"

That got to them, that ancient superstition. Dom watched, vastly amused at the sight of Antonio making the sign of the cross and glancing heavenward. Even Ivan, that angel of fucking death, kissed the crucifix he wore around his neck. Dom gestured at the door with his head, just a slight nod. Antonio took the hint.

"Let's take a little walk, you and me," he said. He got up out of his chair, and Victor and Ivan did likewise. He turned and looked at them. "You two wait here."

"We gotta do something about security," Dom told him when they were safely out of earshot. "I know everybody likes to make money, and they wanna be nice to their brother-in-law and all that, but we can't have the whole fucking neighborhood jumping in the pool after us, we're gonna get shut down if this keeps up."

Antonio considered that for a few steps. "All right," he said. "Set up four or five dummy accounts with a broker you can trust. You come up with something, you call the broker yourself, then get word to me later. Don't call me at the bar, don't call my house either. Reach me through my daughter. You know a broker you can use, someone smart enough to keep his mouth shut?"

"Of course."

"All right." He stopped, stood looking at Dom on the sidewalk. "I'm gonna let you go now. I know you got a long ride back."

Sticking the knife in one more time, Dom thought. I'm gonna be sitting in traffic while he's swilling guinea red and eating his dinner, and I got an early morning appointment with a guy in a brokerage house. The house was working on a takeover bid, the guy needed cocaine, and Domenic needed lead time. Capitalism at work. But it was one more obligation, and he was drowning in them.

Antonio grabbed him in a bear hug. "Next time, gimme a horse with four legs."

"Come on, Antonio, add it all up and then tell me you're not happy."

Antonio released him. "Go home," he said. "Get some sleep. You look like shit."

Yeah, sure, Domenic thought, stepping off toward his car. All I have time for is work, every day, every day, every day, and I don't even know why I do it anymore.

TWO

■

HE WOKE AT FIVE-THIRTY, grouchy, back sore from the too-yielding mattress. He could hear her out in the corridor.

"Claaark, let me in, I got coffee, Clark . . ."

He wanted to lie there but he couldn't, with every passing moment it seemed his back hurt more, plus the years of conditioning itched at him, got him up and on his feet, doing his morning routine mechanically. Ain't you something, he told himself silently. You wanna be a bum but you're too lazy to break your programming. When he was dressed and ready to go, he jerked open his door, startling the woman in the hallway. She looked up at him, her face momentarily radiant, but when she saw it was him and not Clark her mouth went wide in fear.

"Aaaargh!" She struggled hastily to her feet. She did have two containers of coffee but she spilled one as she went flapping down the corridor. "Aaarh! Aaarh!"

"Ah, Jesus. You happy now? Scared the poor dimwit half to death." He watched the stairwell door slam behind her, then turned and locked his door.

He stopped at the newsstand in front of the hotel. The dark-skinned man he'd seen sleeping the night before was inside the kiosk, awake but looking hung over. Silvano picked up a copy of the *Daily News*, handed the man a dollar bill. "You know a place around here to get a good cup of coffee?"

"Dere is a deli right up the block," he said, rolling his r's, a singsong cadence in his voice. He counted Silvano's change from a pile of coins in front of him. "Or you can go farther up the hill, take a right on Court, dere is a specialist in coffee in a small shop, he has coffee beans and teas from all over the vorld. You might find it vorth your extra steps."

"You want me to bring you back a cup? You look like you could use it."

"Oh no, sahr," the man said, looking down. "Thank you so veddy much, sahr, no, I never take it, terrible stuff, terrible. Veddy bad for vun's digestion."

Silvano went on up the hill, scanning the paper as he walked. It was all about New York City's latest fiscal crisis, federal, state, and local politicians feuding about who was going to pay for what, dark clouds over Wall Street, but the Mets pulled it out late, after he'd fallen asleep they rallied to win. They were going to Pittsburgh next, they were three-run dogs for tonight's game but he didn't know a bookie, except for his old man. That would be great, call him up after all this time, say, hey Pops, put a C-note on the Mets for me tonight, willya? I'm good for it. He loitered outside the deli up the block, watched the street for a while, then went inside and got a black coffee and a buttered roll served to him by an enormous fat wheezing lady. He made a mental note to come back and try the food, must be good when the cook's that fat.

The coffee was bitter. He sipped at it anyway and munched on his roll as he wandered the neighborhood. Nunzio's last address had been the St. Felix Hotel. The city had housed him there after a lengthy stay at Bellevue. Nunzio had called Annette two years ago, after he'd gotten out, to let her know where he was, and the two of them had spoken regularly over the next nine months. Then the calls had stopped and Ann, unable to contact him, had pestered her husband into hiring some ex-cop friend of his to go look for Nunzio. When the guy had given her his report, she had called the carpenter in Oregon that Silvano had once worked for, and he had given her a phone number in Japan. When she'd finally tracked Silvano down, she read him the report over the phone. He went over it now in his mind as he walked the uneven slate sidewalks past crumbling brownstones and shuttered carriage houses. Last address, the St. Felix, room apparently unoccupied for some time. The usual personal effects left behind, electric razor, toothbrush, clothes, plus a flashlight, one hundred sixty-seven unopened bars of Neutrogena soap, twenty-one bottles of Pert shampoo, six clock-radios, one plugged in, five still in the boxes, a bunch of those strips of paper that come wrapped around stacks of bills, stamped in hundred- and thousand-dollar denominations.

There had been several cursory reports from the welfare department, but nothing in the previous three months, two reports of about the same vintage from the outpatient clinic at Bellevue with careful descriptions of the patient's condition but with the name misspelled and the age wrong by a decade. No John Does in any of the city's various loony bins matched his description, ditto the morgue and the holding pens at central booking.

He was just gone.

THE LOBBY OF the St. Felix smelled like boiled cabbage. It was a high-ceilinged room with lots of old woodwork but it had none of the ruined grandeur of the Montague, and the man behind the front desk, a young guy with a pointed goatee and a long ponytail, did not remember Nunzio.

"No, man, I only been here six months," he said. "You a cop or something?"

"Military Intelligence," Silvano told him.

"Oh, shit. I didn't even know there was such a thing," he said, suddenly nervous. "I think you'd have to come back when the general manager is here, because I don't even know where we keep records like that."

"When will he be in?"

He didn't know. Silvano shrugged, turned away, looking around the room. He recognized the woman sitting in a chair in the far corner of the lobby, she was the old lady with Errol Flynn's cane, and she'd been watching him. When she caught his eye, she winked at him.

Story of my life, he thought. The old ones and the crazy ones always love me, and this one looks to be both. He turned to go.

"Hsssst!"

It was her. He shook his head ruefully. Too proud to run away, ain'tcha, he told himself, and he walked on over, stopped just out of range of the cane. "Howdy," he said.

She leaned forward and whispered. "You don't wanna talk to him, he don't know shit."

"I think I got that part figured out."

"He's a doper," she hissed, still whispering. "You need to know something, you gotta come back when Bronson's here, ten at night to six in the morning. Give him a ten spot and he'll sell out the whole lot of us." She found that enormously funny and began to cackle loudly and wave her cane around.

Silvano took a step back. "Thanks," he said, backing away. "Thanks a lot."

"Sell us all out," she said, louder this time. "Every one."

"WHAT DID YOU SAY YOUR NAME WAS, SIR?"

"I didn't." Silvano leaned on the small counter and tried to look as unthreatening as he could. "Mr. Johansen is expecting me."

She regarded him briefly, shrugged, reached up, and slid the window shut. He stood there and watched as she picked up her telephone and had a brief conversation before hanging up. She slid the window open again. "Have a seat, sir," she said. "Mr. Johansen will be with you shortly."

"Thank you," he started to say, but she was already sliding the window shut. He sat in one of the plastic chairs in the waiting room and looked around. It was generic office space decor, fluorescent lights in a suspended ceiling made of white panels, cheap paneling on the walls, thin gray carpet. No magazines. After some time the metal door next to the sliding window opened, and a guy stuck his head out. He was tall and beefy, red face and sparse yellow hair. He didn't fit Silvano's image of a private detective. He looked more like the kind of guy would knock on your door selling pots and pans.

"Vinnie's brother-in-law?"

"Yeah."

"All right," the guy said, staring across the room at a spot three feet to Silvano's right. "C'mon in." He stood back, held the door open. Silvano followed him to an inner office. Johansen waved him to a client chair and went to sit behind the desk. He glanced at Silvano, then began riffling through a stack of manila folders. "So," he said. "You're the missing brother."

"It's a long story."

"Ain't they all," the guy said. He found the folder he was looking for, opened it up, fanned through the few pages it contained. "That Vinnie is a piece of work," he said, reading. "You in business with him?"

"No."

"Oh. Well, there's not much here." He closed the folder and handed it across the desk. "You're welcome to look it over, but we didn't have a hell of a lot to go on. The only people really knew your brother was a bunch of street rats, you don't get much out of people like that. Can't believe what you do get."

"Yeah." Silvano opened the folder. He looked briefly at the picture of his brother, turned it face down, and began to read. "You guys do much of this kind of thing?"

Johansen puffed his chest out, looked insulted. "We did a good job, we looked under every rock we could find. I always go the extra mile for Vinnie."

"I ain't saying anything, I just want to know where I stand."

Johansen subsided in his chair. "The guy I used for this is NYPD, retired. Guy is top notch, very smart. Just a little bit too Catholic school."

"What do you mean?"

"Oh, you know, by the book, by the numbers, cross every tee, alla that. You know what I'm sayin'? You gotta know when to look the other way, sometimes. Friggin' guy, would arrest his own mother, he caught her lifting a pack of gum. Smart bastard, though, like I said. There was something to find, I would bet on him finding it."

"Well, you're right, there's not much here. This guy still work for you?"

"He's doing something for me right now. I'm thinking you wanna talk to him."

"Yeah, I do."

"Well, you wanna hang around, I can get the guy back here in a hour or two. I'll pull him right off what he's doing, okay, but you gotta tell Vinnie we cooperated like a bastard."

"I'll tell Vinnie you were a peach. You mind if I take this picture, go have some copies made?"

"Go right ahead, there's a picture joint right up the block. Time you get done with that, my guy should be back here."

"Thanks." He stood up to go. "What is it you guys really do, anyway?"

The guy shrugged. "We do a lotta security, lotta divorce, you know, follow the wandering spouse, take pictures, we do insurance fraud, catch the disabled guy water skiing, and so on."

"Don't sound like a bad gig."

"There's worse. Listen, this guy I used is black, I hope you don't mind, but I'm telling ya, he's as good as they get."

WHEN SILVANO GOT BACK, Johansen ushered him into a small conference room. His guy was already in there, waiting, leaning both elbows on the table. He made no move to get up or introduce himself. Silvano pulled out a chair and sat down. "My name is . . ."

"I know who you are," the guy said. He leaned back in his chair and regarded Silvano coldly. "Silvano Iurata. Let's see. Brother of Nunzio, commonly known as Noonie. One of my failures. Father, Giovanni, bookie, numbers, loansharking, suspect in the occasional murder, lived down in Bensonhurst. Mother, Rachel, daughter of one Domenic Scalia, capo in one of the five families, I disremember which one. Bastard died in his sleep, six or eight years ago. Rachel went missing in the forties, body never found. Before my time, but I understand our side thought Giovanni did it, I couldn't find out why. Married wife number two when Rachel was declared dead seven years after her disappearance. Two more kids, Nunzio and Annette, your half-brother and -sister. Nunzio had some mental problems, in and out of institutions. Angelo Scalia, your uncle, followed his father's footsteps until sometime in the late fifties, when they found him floating in a marina down by Coney Island someplace, would have been face down in the water but wasn't, technically, because his head was missing." He shook his head. "Am I getting all of this right?"

"You must keep a lot of shit up in your head."

"You should never write anything down unless you're willing to answer questions about it in open court. Tell me if I miss anything."

"Finish your story."

"All right. So you, your brother and sister, your cousin Domenic, Angelo's son, aka Little Dom, aka the Fish, and his sister Jeannette are all growing up in Italian-American paradise. Everybody's happy, except you. You, you got all kind of behavior problems, you're always in trouble, you get tossed out of Catholic school, then public school. Your old man finally wakes up, he signs you up in some boxing gym, I guess he figures, let them straighten you out. You go twelve and two, something like that, not bad, but both losses were DQs, you can't even do that straight up. Okay, now out of nowhere Jeannette up and joins a convent, one of the medieval situations, they lock you in a closet for the rest of your life. Angelo does his headless doggie paddle routine, and in the confusion, you run off and join the circus. Little Dom goes ape shit, word is you and his sister Jeannette were doing the horizontal two-step, and that's why she's gonna spend the rest of her life wearing a black robe. He figures you popped his old man when he found out. Made your bones at seventeen, not bad."

"You believe everything you hear?"

"You saying it wasn't you? Well, we never made you for it. Never made anybody for it. Anyhow, Little Dom, he goes into the family business, no surprise there, he runs with a crew out of some social club, same neighborhood you grew up in. He worked the garment district, broke a few heads, hijacked a few trucks, four arrests, no convictions. Then, maybe eight years ago, he gets his act together, now he's some kind of investment counselor down on Wall Street. Separated from his wife, lives in the Village."

"You did a lot of digging, looking for one missing nut bag."

"Johansen offered serious money if I could turn up your brother. But the point of all this is, I am not about to help some middle-aged thug looking to settle old scores."

"Who said anything about that?"

"Stop, okay? You think I'm some kind of fucking moron? I got a look at your service records, Iurata. Whether you did what Little Dom thinks you did or not, you were no paragon of virtue when you went in, and it didn't look like the Army changed you much. You spent a fair amount of time in the stockade. And detached to the Defense Department, what the hell does that mean? My guess is, somebody figured out what you were good at, so they pointed you at people they didn't like and let you go do it."

"So what."

"I'll tell you so what." The guy was scowling, and his voice got louder as he went on. "You went from Brooklyn to Viet Nam, then Thailand, the Philippines, California, Oregon, I miss anything?"

"Nothing important."

"Fine. And what did you do, in any of those places? What did you build? Did you have any lasting relationships? Wife? Children? Employers? Friends? Anything?"

Silvano sat with that for a heartbeat. "No."

"No." His voice dripped sarcasm. "Let me guess. The Army was the only discipline you ever had in your entire life. Outside of that, you have never held a steady job, not a legal one, anyway, you have never submitted to any kind of authority, when you have money you spend it like a drunken sailor, you only tell the truth when it suits you, you have no idea where you're going with your fucking life, you're irresponsible, you're reckless, and you will fight anyone, anywhere, at the drop of a fucking hat. Am I right?"

"Not entirely."

"Bullshit. That's a typical criminal fucking profile."

"What do you want from me? You want me to show you my library card? You want to see if there's any points on my driver's license? You only work for virgins?" He paused to gather himself. "You think the whole world is just like recess at grade school, don't you. Follow the rules, play fair, be nice, listen to the teacher, and everyone lives happily ever after. Well, it don't work that way." It flashed on him then, the last time he saw his uncle, his grandfather, standing silent, smoldering. It felt so real, he could smell the old man's cigar breath, he could feel the same paralysis he'd felt then, waiting for the old man to make up his mind. He shook his head, pulled himself back to the present. "Listen," he said, "you got to play the cards you get. I could have been smarter, I admit it. But I did the best I could. You think you know everything, I'm telling you, you know dick. I wanted to whack Domenic, I don't need shit from you. I could pull the plug on him any time, be back on the beach in Malibu before you assholes even find the body, you would never make me for it. Probably wouldn't even try, wise guys killing each other, who gives a fuck. Go ahead, tell me you would stay up all night worrying." He stared at the guy. "What I want is to find out what happened to my brother, that's all."

"Suppose you do find out what happened. Then what?"

Silvano deflated, sagged in his chair. "I don't know. Visit the grave. Apologize."

"He was always telling people you were coming." The guy's voice got quieter. "Coming to visit him. Did you know that?"

Silvano stared at the guy. "No."

He hesitated, but then he seemed to decide that he was going to continue. "Your brother had a lot of friends. A few in particular, a panhandler named Special Ed, a minor league crook called the Dutchman. You need to write this down?"

"No. The government doesn't always put its instructions in writing, either."

"Fair enough. He worked off the books in three places that I know of. One, he helped out the porters at the St. Felix Hotel, I don't think they paid him anything, I guess he did it for the company. Two, he used to run errands and wash trucks at Black and White Armored Car Service. They always gave him something for his trouble. And three, he used to clean up at some supermarket, place is down at the end of Atlantic Avenue in Brooklyn. Not too far from Black and White, come to think of it. They didn't pay him anything at the market, but he was robbing them blind, anyway. He had the knack for it, they tell me. Some of the other, aah, sidewalk entrepreneurs were very impressed with his abilities."

"I'm not surprised. Tell me about Black and White. What do they do?"

The guy smirked. "I thought that would catch your interest. Black and White is a small company. Armored trucks and vans. They do cash transport, collections, and deliveries from check-cashing storefronts and small to medium stores all over Brooklyn and Queens. They also do a mobile check-cashing service. Some of their bulletproof vans are set up with windows and cash drawers in the back, and they'll go park out in front of some big place with lots of payroll, like a factory or a hospital, sit out there Thursday and Friday, cash checks all day long."

"What's in it for them?"

"They get a cut, like three percent or something."

"No kidding. They clean?"

"Squeaky."

"You sound real sure of that."

He shrugged. "Place is owned by a guy name of Joseph O'Brian. Guy's practically a hermit. No bad habits, don't drink, don't smoke, don't snort, don't gamble, don't whore around. Plus, three quarters of the guys he's got working for him are either retired or off-duty cops. It's a clean operation, no funny stuff. Nobody like you ever goes there."

Silvano decided to let that go. "What can you tell me about those two guys you said Noonie was running with?"

"The Dutchman went missing about six months before your brother did. We didn't find him, either, though I doubt anybody looked too hard. The guy had a lot of enemies, most of the other transients didn't like him. It's a hard life, living on the street. Shit happens to you, you ain't got a sister or a brother to come looking, nobody even notices you're gone. Nunzio went around looking for the guy for a while, but he, you know . . ."

"Yeah, I know. What about the other one, Special Ed?"

The guy shook his head. "Just a gimp. Just another lost soul, wandering around talking to people that ain't there. Waiting for someone to drop a net over him. Nothing there. Nothing at all." The guy stared at him for a few minutes. "That's about all I got."

"I appreciate your time."

"Thank Johansen, don't thank me."

• • •

THEY WORE BLUE work clothes, each guy's name along with the name of the hotel stitched on the shirt pockets. They were carrying black plastic garbage bags out of the dark interior of a back door of the hotel and stacking them in a big pile on the sidewalk. Silvano walked up to the biggest one, a white guy about six foot four, heavy, had Navy tattoos on his forearms. "Excuse me," he said, taking one of the pictures of his brother out of his pocket. "I wonder if you can help me. I'm looking for a guy, I was told he used to hang out with you guys."

The guy stopped what he was doing, and so did the others. They watched as he accepted the picture and looked at it. "You a cop? Ex-cop? Rent-a-cop?"

"None of the above. He was my brother."

"Yeah?" He looked at the picture a few seconds longer, handed it back. "You want Marvin," he said, pointing at the open doors. "He's carrying bags over from the elevator. This guy was Marvin's buddy."

"Thanks." He took back the picture, stepped through the doors into the darkness. The stench of rotting garbage in the enclosed space was overpowering. Silvano's sense of smell was as acute as his hearing, and he held in some special part of his memory an enormous reference library of scents, and from time to time, unbidden, it would spring into life and fill his head with the essence of some far-off experience, hammering him with the stimuli of some lost and unreachable event. In the space of a half dozen steps, he found himself transported, ripped back through time to a dark and stinking hole in the ground half a world away, bombarded by the smell of fear, shit, and the unmistakable odor of Mother Nature reclaiming what was hers from the body of some poor bastard, weeks dead. He felt his knees buckling and he struggled to remain upright. Just then a palsied hand reached out of the darkness and took him by the elbow, urging him to move, guiding him down a hallway, away from the smell.

"This way, buddy. C'mon, this way, you'll be all right."

Silvano found himself sitting on a wooden bench in a locker room that was flooded with fluorescent light. The smell was different there, it was the sharp tang of living, sweating men, and though no perfume, it was preferable to the hallway.

Sitting across from him was an emaciated shell of a man. He wore the same kind of uniform as the men outside, and his shirt pocket identified him as Marvin. He wore aviator glasses with pale green lenses, topped by a boonie hat. He pulled a jay out of his shirt pocket and lit up. "You coming back to us yet?"

Silvano rubbed his face with both hands. Second one today, he thought. "Yeah. Yeah, I'm all right. Just, for a minute there . . . That fucking hallway smelled exactly like a VC tunnel."

Smoke and words came out of Marvin's mouth. "Dead men and punji stakes."

Silvano looked at him. "How are you making it?"

He shrugged. "I have good days and bad days." He offered Silvano the joint. Silvano reached for it, took a hit, handed it back.

"So do I." He patted his shirt pocket for the picture of his brother, but he noticed Marvin holding it in his hand, looking at it.

"You must be Silvie."

"Yeah. Silvano."

"Noonie used to talk about you all the time. 'When Silvie comes to see me,' everything was 'when Silvie comes.'" He looked up. "Oh, hey, I'm sorry. You all right?"

"Yeah." He shook his head, fighting himself. "No, actually, I'm fucked up."

Marvin held out the joint. "Get more fucked up."

"No, you know, I . . ." The hell with it, he thought. "One more hit."

"Attaboy. You know, your brother was one of a kind."

"Ain't that the fucking truth." Silvano handed the joint back.

"You ever notice, it's the ones that's got the least are the most willing to share with you. Especially if I was having a bad day, you know . . ." He glanced at Silvano. "Like the one you're having. When he was around, it would just kind of dissipate. I don't know why. Maybe it was because all he ever cared about was right now, you know what I'm saying? No past, no future. Like, he would enjoy hauling trash just as much as anything else he did. He didn't carry any baggage around. No baggage at all. If I could only learn that, Jesus." He sucked a big hit from the joint, then fished an alligator clip out of a pocket, stuck the joint in it, held it out.

Silvano shook his head. "You know, I really got—"

"One more, chrissake, finish it off."

"All right." He could feel the dope pulsing throughout his body like blood through his veins. "Did you know anybody that hated him? Was he into anything heavy?"

"No, hell no." Marvin took the clip back from Silvano, pinched it out, dropped it, roach and all, into his shirt pocket. "Noonie didn't know from heavy."

"Can you tell me anything about a couple of guys he ran with? The names I got are Special Ed and the Dutchman."

Marvin laughed softly. "Christ," he said. "What a pair. Well, the Dutchman was a guy name of Lenny Deutch. Dead, they tell me, and unlamented. He was your basic scumbag, always looking to hustle you, steal your shit, or sell you a dime bag of oregano. I doubt if anyone was surprised he got popped, if that's what did happen. He was the kinda guy, you had to figure eventually he would get shot just for being annoying. Special Ed is still around, though. He shouldn't be too hard to turn up. Easy to pick him out of a crowd, that's for sure."

"Why do you say that?"

"Because he's fucked, that's why. I mean, maybe we all are, but him more than most. More than anyone I ever met. All you need to know, he's maybe three and a half feet tall, and he's fucked. Believe me, you don't recognize him from that description, you're blind."

"You know his real name?"

"No. Don't know if he does, either."

"Where do I find him?"

"He lives in the basement of a building over on Middagh. I don't know the number, but if you turn down Middagh off Henry, okay, you go down about half a block, you'll see an alley on your left, just go down in the back there. More likely you can catch him on the street. He pushes a shopping cart around, collects junk. He mostly works the neighborhoods on the far side of the Manhattan Bridge. You hang out down on that end of Henry, you'll probably see him coming back, late afternoons."

"All right. Listen, thanks for pulling me out of that hallway. Thanks for the herb tea."

"No sweat. Can I have this picture?"

"Yeah, I got more. That's the phone number of the Montague, on the back. You think of something else, you can leave a message for me there."

"Okay. One other thing. Special Ed is pretty, aah, skittish, I guess you could say. Might do well if you took along a half pint of something to calm his nerves."

"All right. Is there a different way out of here?"

Marvin got to his feet. "Yeah, sure. Come with me."

• • •

IT WAS ONLY a few blocks to Middagh Street. Silvano followed Marvin's directions and found the alley off Middagh with no problem, it was an ell-shaped alley that led to the back of a row of apartment houses and brownstones. There was no way to know which of the basement doors would lead to Special Ed. He walked back out of the alley and headed for Court Street, which would take him over to Atlantic Avenue.

He turned right when he got to Atlantic. There was a big Middle Eastern restaurant on the corner. The front door was open and Silvano caught a whiff of unfamiliar spices as he went by. The place had once been a storefront, and there were tables in the windows, white tablecloths, black chairs, plain white dishes, old silver cutlery. The next building housed a Syrian grocery, beyond that was a Lebanese bakery, and so on, all the way down the hill to the Brooklyn-Queens Expressway. There were a few more commonplace establishments mixed in, bars, antique stores, a witchcraft store with the windows painted black, a repair shop with a yellow sign that said FLAT FIX. Two guys inside were drinking beer. A tiny store next door had a sign painted on the window, GLASS CUT TO SIZE. A withered old man sat in the doorway insulting everyone who passed by.

"Where'd you get that shirt?" he asked a guy coming up the block, in a voice that sounded like Grandpa McCoy. "Find it in the back of a cab?" The guy looked at Silvano and rolled his eyes, continued on without comment. "Hey, pal," the old guy said to Silvano. "Your fly's open."

Silvano checked reflexively.

"Made ya look, ya dope," the old man cackled.

Silvano shook his head and walked on by, passing the brown brick hospital at the bottom of the hill. There was a parking garage attached to the side of the hospital, bigger than the hospital itself, butted up against an exit ramp from the BQE, which crosses over the end of Atlantic Avenue and comes to earth on the far side. Go under the overpass and you're on the waterfront. To the right is Furman Street, trucks parked in a long line on one side, the highway roaring overhead, freighters tied to the docks. No wonder they call them tramps, Silvano thought, looking at the rusted hulls that all seemed to list to one side or the other. Most of them had Greek or oriental names, the Olympic Line or something or other Maru. Not one of them looked like the sort of ship you'd trust your life to in Lower New York Bay, let alone the vast and cold Atlantic.

Straight ahead was an MTA bus garage on a concrete pier behind a chain-link fence. To the left of the MTA lot, between the BQE and the waterfront, was an industrial wasteland of empty lots and concrete buildings without windows. The closest building, next to the bus lot, also behind a fence, bore a sign that read BLACK AND WHITE ARMORED CAR SERVICE. A construction crew was busy building an addition onto Black and White's building. The addition looked like it would ultimately be bigger than the original place. The exterior was being made of concrete blocks, reinforced on the inside with sheets of steel. Silvano could hear the ripping sound of a mig welder above the more familiar racket of skillsaws and hammering. Out in front, four squat, muscular trucks sat in the parking lot. They were painted dull black with white doors, and there were stainless steel gun slots under the windows. Two black guys had the nose of the one closest to the street tilted up and they were looking at the engine. A black Cadillac sedan was parked in front of the trucks, and a heavily built young white guy with black hair and a goatee was leaning against it, just behind the open driver's door, and from time to time he berated the two black men in a loud voice. Noonie worked here, Silvano thought, in this place. He remembered the money strips the cops had found in Noonie's hotel room. Maybe that's it, he thought. Maybe he was walking out with more than just paper wrappers, maybe he was taking their money, maybe they caught on, maybe they decided to put him out of his misery.

There was an old automobile skeleton just down from the yard, half on the sidewalk and half in the street. It had been stripped and burned, but there were still some salable parts on it, because a red-faced old white guy with a long white braid was working on getting the radiator out. His tools consisted of a straight handled pry bar, a screwdriver, and a pair of slip-joint pliers. He had a shopping cart parked nearby, half full of car radiators and pieces of scrap metal.

Silvano wandered over to watch him work. "Hey, old-timer," he said. "Tough way to make a buck."

The old guy replied without looking up. "Ain't so bad," he said. "I seen worse."

Silvano thought about the price of scrap, and the labor necessary to harvest it. "Wouldn't it be easier just to get a regular job? You'd have to make more money than you're making doing this, have enough for a few amenities."

The old man straightened up. "Had my fill of regular jobs," he said. "Got all the amenities I need. Besides, you don't look all that employed yourself."

"I am currently between positions," Silvano said. "What I'm doing, I'm looking for a guy, people called him Noonie. Used to hang around down here."

"Don't know him." The old man got the last bracket loose and the radiator hung from its hoses. "Lot of people hang out down here. Freaks and stew-bums, whores, drug pushers, head cases, kids playing hooky, sailors off the boats, longshoremen, you name it. Mostly they don't stay long, they get hungry or cold and they move on." He whipped a butterfly knife open and sliced neatly through the two hoses. Just as quickly the knife disappeared and he deposited his prize in the shopping cart. "Friend of yours?"

"Something like that."

"Can't help you." He gathered up his tools and put them in the shopping cart.

A flatbed truck with a load of lumber and drywall sheets rumbled down the hill and pulled up to the gate. The kid with the goatee left off harassing the two black guys and went over to open the gate. He held up the driver while he checked his delivery ticket. "You wait here," Silvano heard him say. The driver looked heavenward in exasperation while the kid marched over to the construction site, shouting as he went. "Lee, Lee, you guys got a delivery!"

A large guy in jeans and a flannel shirt came lumbering out of the half-finished building. The kid handed him the delivery sheet and he took it in a meaty hand, but he handed it back to the kid and said something Silvano couldn't hear, turned, and went back inside.

"C'mon, Lee, I don't have time for this. Lee . . ." But Lee was gone. "Shit." He turned and made his way back over to where the two black guys were still working on the truck, and a discussion followed. The kid's voice was softer, now, pleading, but the black guys were not having any.

"Ain't no rasshole rose tree trimmer," the older of them said. "You got to take care a your own business."

Nobody wants to unload the truck, Silvano thought. The carpenters think it's beneath them, the driver just wants to dump it off, and those other two guys don't want to have to do all the shit work. Kid's going to have to do it himself. Serve him right.

A tall, thin white guy, looked to be about fifty, came out of the office and stood, blinking in the sun. He wore green work pants and a matching green workshirt with a patch on the pocket that identified him as "Joseph." He stared at the delivery truck. "Hey," he said, a trace of anger in his voice. "Sean! You plan on coming back inside to work anytime soon?"

"We got a delivery," the kid said. "We gotta get this truck unloaded."

"Well, get on with it, then. Or else, don't come crying to me when you have to work late."

"All right, all right." He walked up to the fence, right next to where Silvano and the old man were watching. "Hey, you," he said, looking at the old man. "Hey. You wanna make some money?"

The old man walked over and stood on the sidewalk, two feet away from the kid. He stood there squinting for a long count, and then wordlessly turned on his heel and walked over to his shopping cart and began to push it down the sidewalk.

"Suit yourself," the kid said. He looked at Silvano. "Hey, how 'bout you? Wanna make a few bucks?"

"What do I hafta do?"

"Nothin'. We need some help unloading this truck, is all."

Silvano shrugged. "Why not," he said, and he headed for the gate.

THE WOOD WENT FIRST.

The kid climbed up inside the building and stood in an opening about eight feet off the ground and waited there expectantly. The driver shrugged, climbed up on the back of his truck, and began to hand two-by-sixes to Silvano, who walked them over and handed them up to the kid, who took them inside. The wood was new, blond, and a little wet. Silvano hefted each piece in his hands, relishing the feel and the clean pine smell as he worked. He had worked for a carpenter once out in Oregon. The guy had liked him and had tried hard to teach him, but Silvano had been in no shape for a steady job. He'd enjoyed the work, though, especially the way you started out in the morning with what was there, and at the end of the day you saw the changes, you saw what you had done, and when the job was all finished you could look back and see something, a house or a garage or whatever it was, standing where there had been just empty space before you came.

The drywall was a little tougher to handle than the wood. The driver slid the four-by-eight sheets off the pile one at a time, and Silvano balanced them in two hands, handing them up to the kid, pressing them up over his head. The kid was sweating profusely now, breathing hard, and halfway down through the pile he had to wave Silvano off and take a break.

The driver smirked. "S'matter? Can't take it? Don't like the way a real job feels? It ain't like this at the gym, is it, Sean?"

The kid was standing in the opening of the building, leaning over, his hands on his thighs. He gave the driver the finger half-heartedly. "Fuck you," he said. "Ain't no wonder I never get anything done around here, I gotta spend all day taking shit from assholes like you, niggers that don't wanna work, and drafting bums off the goddam street just to get a truck unloaded."

The driver laughed and lit a cigarette. Lee, the carpenter the kid had argued with before, came over a minute later and looked down at the kid, then turned and walked away shaking his head. The kid's face got red.

"Awright, c'mon, let's get the rest of that shit up here. Let's go, let's go." They resumed unloading, and by the time they were finished, the kid was done for. He came down out of the building and wordlessly handed Silvano a ten, signed the driver's delivery ticket, and walked away. Silvano could hear someone approaching from behind as he watched the truck drive off.

It was Lee. "Hey, buddy," he said. "You looking for a real job?"

"Working for Prince Charming?"

The big carpenter didn't smile. "Don't mind the kid, he's nobody. You wanna work or not? You on the street? What's your problem? Your wife throw you out or what?"

"I got no problems," Silvano said. "You pay off the books?"

"Yeah, we can pay cash, no sweat." They discussed terms. "We start at seven," the guy said. "If you want to work, don't be late. No beer on the job unless I bring it. No dope on the job at any time. We quit at three. See you in the morning."

Silvano walked over to where the two black guys were finishing up what they had been doing. "One of you guys got the key to the gate? How about letting me out?"

"Why not?" said the older of the two. He had white hair cut very close to the scalp, and his belly strained against a dirty gray T-shirt. "Stop what we're doing, go let the white guy out." The other guy, younger, tall and thin, fished around in his pocket for the key.

"I should apologize for Frankie," he said, walking with Silvano over to the gate. "He's a good guy, but it's been one of those days. They throw him and me a few bucks extra to do a little bit of this and that, and he really needs the money, but he'd much rather just drive, he ain't much with a wrench."

"You guys ever think about teaching that kid to watch his mouth? Sounds to me like he could use it."

"O'Brian? Nah, Sean ain't a bad boy, just ignorant. The old man's a dick, though. Sean's uncle. I guess that's why he owns the company, we just driving the trucks."

"He the guy came out of the office, dressed like a janitor?"

"That's him. Cheap motherfucker, still got the first dollar he ever made. You a carpenter?"

"No. Not really. I got out of the Army a few years back, and I been kind of bouncing around."

"I know the feeling. I'm Roland, by the way."

"Silvano. Nice to meet you, Roland."

"You go to Uncle Sam's party, over there in Viet Nam?"

"I did."

"I lost a brother there."

It was a fresh wound, every time. Silvano clamped down hard on his emotions. "I'm sorry," he said. "I'm really sorry to hear it." He fished one of the pictures of Noonie out of his shirt pocket and handed it to Roland. "Listen, do you know this guy? I was told he used to work down here."

Roland looked at the picture. He stared at it for a minute. "Seen him around," he said, "but not lately. He was just some street kid, used to pick up a few bucks, running out to pick up lunch, shit like that." He handed the picture back to Silvano, unlocked the gate, and yanked it open. "Be seeing you," he said.

SILVANO WALKED UP Atlantic Avenue, thinking himself to be irrationally angry. I should be happy, he thought, I got my foot in the door . . . He wasn't, though, he was irritated. There had been something in Roland's face after he'd looked at the picture of Noonie. He hadn't wanted to talk about it, Silvano thought. He hadn't asked any of the normal questions, either, like, who was he to you, what do you care, he'd just given the picture back and said good-bye. That did not seem like a normal reaction. And then there was that fucking kid, Sean O'Brian. He had the trick of giving you his last shot and then turning his back so he wouldn't have to face your response. Noonie would have been impressed with you, you little turd. Let it go, he told himself. You don't know anything yet.

He stopped in front of the Long Island Medical Center, the brown building with the parking garage attached. There was a circular driveway in front of swinging glass doors where the ambulances dumped their cargoes. He turned and walked the few steps back down the hill to the corner of the building, where the driveway led into the garage, which was eleven stories high. He ambled down the alley to take a look. Sean O'Brian, he thought, I wish I had a way into your head. Little bastard can't be much more than nineteen or twenty, and advertising his insecurities at that, what with the goatee and all. See how bad I am? Bet he has a tattoo. But he wasn't little, he was actually bigger than Silvano, with a weightlifter's showy build.

There was no one in the guardhouse at the entrance to the garage. Silvano stepped around the arm that swung up to admit cars and walked inside. To his left was the doorway from the garage to the hospital. He watched the glass doors swing open and a nurse in her white uniform came striding into the garage, a slim white woman with dark hair pinned up under a cap, looked to be in her thirties. She looked around quickly, and Silvano retreated back into the shadows behind some cars. She traversed rapidly over to a stairwell and went through the gray door. Silvano waited maybe two minutes and the door banged open again and she came back out with her head held a little higher, her chest thrust out a little more, and she walked swiftly back into the hospital, wiping her nose and sniffing as she went. There must be other stairwells, Silvano thought, but this is the one I want, this corner of the building will have the best vantage point.

Leave it alone, he told himself, go find another way up, but he was still aggravated over Roland and Sean O'Brian. He felt something stirring in his blood as he walked on over to the stairwell door. You can't do it, can you, he thought, you can't step out around. He pulled the door open and went through.

The unfinished concrete of the stairwell was lit by sunlight that poured through the large windowless openings cut through the wall. In the far corner of the landing a thick man with long black hair and a black leather trench coat was sitting on an inverted five-gallon plastic bucket. He was counting some paper money when Silvano walked by. "Hey," he said. "Hey, buddy."

Silvano ignored him and walked up the stairs. He listened as he climbed, hearing the scrape of plastic on concrete as the guy got to his feet and got himself set, and then the footsteps as the guy came up after him.

"Hey, I'm talking to you!"

Silvano paused at the next landing, listening to the steps get closer, and at the last minute he gritted his teeth and stepped back around and clotheslined his pursuer just as he got to the top step. The guy's knees buckled and he lost his balance and fell backward down the steps he'd just climbed. Silvano danced down after him, but there was no need, the guy hit his head on the galvanized pipe railing and he lay on the stairwell landing, out cold.

Silvano fished the pistol out of the pocket of the guy's leather coat. Heckler & Koch, he thought, hefting it in his hand, nine millimeter, guy goes first class, fourteen in the clip and one in the pipe. He ejected the clip and put it in his own pocket, jacked the last round out of the chamber before he stuck the pistol back where he found it. An inside coat pocket held a white envelope filled with folded squares of paper. Silvano opened one up and shook it, watched the powder blow away. He put the envelope back and continued looking. There were some plastic baggies in another pocket, looked like a quarter ounce of weed in each one. Guy's a walking supermarket, Silvano thought, sticking two of the baggies in his own pocket before he put the rest back. The guy's bankroll was in one pants pocket, some keys in the other. No wallet.

He put two fingers on the guy's neck, felt the pulse, seemed strong enough, and the guy's breath was whistling through his nose. Silvano grabbed him by the arms and dragged him up to the next landing. He left him on the floor there and went over to sit on the sill of the large square hole in the wall.

He couldn't see down into O'Brian's yard, he'd have to climb up to a higher floor for that, so he relaxed and watched the traffic streaming by on the BQE, cars, trucks, and the occasional suicidal motorcyclist. He had ridden but never owned his own bike, and he sat remembering that peculiar mind-set you get when you ride at speed in serious traffic knowing that death rides inches away, when your hands and feet work the clutch, the throttle, and the brakes without conscious thought, when you're in that pure state of total concentration where all extraneous images are banished from your mind, where it's just you and the bike flowing through the crush of vehicles as you hold each vehicle and each driver in your head, individually but still all of them at once, when you're judging speeds, guessing intentions, watching for potholes and ripples in the pavement, riding the knife edge of disaster through drivers who do not see you at all.

The guy on the floor began to stir.

"Ow," he said, rolling over onto his side and holding his head. "Oh, shit." He was hoarse. Silvano walked over and squatted down next to him, waited for the guy to focus. He watched comprehension dawning in the guy's face, watched the fear and then the anger, watched him feel the outside of the pocket that held the pistol. Silvano showed him the clip.

"I coulda messed you up," he told the guy calmly. "Coulda took your piece and your money, coulda took all that other shit you're carrying, coulda dumped your ass out the window, nobody would give a fuck. Coulda cut off one a your ears, they do that in Thailand sometimes."

The guy pushed himself into a sitting position and felt around on his head. "All right," he said.

"I got business in this stairwell, higher up. Ain't none of your affair. You got business down here, I ain't interested." He stood up and looked down at the guy. "We achieve communication?"

"Yeah." The guy stopped feeling his scalp and looked at the smear of blood on his hand. "You coulda said that, first."

Silvano shrugged.

"I get my clip back?"

Silvano stepped back. "Don't push it."

"All right." The guy gathered himself and struggled to his feet. Holding on to the railing, he made his way back down the stairs.

FROM THE STAIRWELL landing one floor below the top floor of the garage, Silvano could see down into O'Brian's yard, but he was too far away to make out very much, just the four trucks parked in the yard, the Cadillac sitting in the middle of the lot with the door still open, the new building off to one side with vans parked outside, and hardhats going in and out. Have to bring glasses, he thought, can't see much from this distance. A figure came out of the building and headed for the car, he guessed it was the kid, Sean, and he wondered, again, if this kid even knew Noonie at all, let alone if he'd had anything to do with his disappearance.

What is it, he wondered. Why this unfocused hostility, why

this aggression? Is it because you think they hurt him, your brother who you didn't bother to see even one time since you walked away? Or is it just guilt? Or maybe it's just that territorial thing, he was my brother, goddammit, you messed with something that had my name on it, and now I'm gonna make you pay. No way to tell. It doesn't matter what you do about this, he thought. No way it can make you feel any better about Noonie. Regardless of what happened to your brother, and no matter what you do about it, you are still what you are. No one can go back and change the past.

He exhaled heavily and leaned on the sill, looking down into the alley. Why is it always so hard, he wondered, so hard to live with what you've become, so hard to figure what to do now, so hard not to make a bad deal worse? Just then a Harley with straight pipes ripped up the big sweeping curve onto the elevated section of the highway, breaking his reverie. Wonder what a Sportster goes for these days? he thought. Wonder what it would feel like to open one up and just ride away?

He looked back down into the yard. It had to be Sean. He squinted, trying to focus. Just then, another guy came out of the building, this one was pushing a bicycle. He couldn't tell for sure, but he thought the guy was Sean's uncle, Joseph. The guy left the bike next to the gate and went to talk to Sean. The two of them seemed to be arguing, there was a certain amount of arm waving on both sides that suggested it. After a while they stopped talking and the two of them headed for the gate. Sean opened it up and the other guy pushed his bicycle through and climbed aboard.

I can't see much from up here without glasses, Silvano thought. I might as well go see where this guy goes. If the guy really was Sean O'Brian's uncle, the bike fit the rest of the package because it was not an American Schwinn, nor was it an English racing bike, it was not even the sort of bike any self-respecting teenager would be caught dead riding. It was a heavy, ungainly, industrial sort of a bicycle, looked like the guy had stolen it from someone delivering Chinese food. When he got to the sidewalk, Silvano could see him from two blocks back, head and shoulders above the pedestrians. He settled into an easy jog, not pushing to catch up but slowly gaining ground.

The guy got to an intersection where the sign said DON'T WALK, and he didn't, he stopped and waited there like a schmuck even though there were no cars coming, people streaming past him, looking at him like he was an idiot. Another strange bird, Silvano thought, sign says wait, so he waits. It's a good thing the guy's not in a hurry, though, because he could lose me, easy.

Atlantic Avenue rises slowly uphill as you move away from the water, crests four blocks later, then slides gently back down again, flattens when you pass Brooklyn Correctional. Silvano had missed running, wondered why he hadn't kept it up. There had been a time when he would have laughed at a run like this one, but he wasn't laughing now. His lungs were burning after the first three or four minutes, protesting the abuse, the cigarettes, the last few years of relative inactivity. God, he thought, I really have to get back into serious shape. Really. The guy stopped for two more signs telling him not to walk, and Silvano silently thanked the man's obedient nature each time. The guy began to gain on him, though, at about the one-mile mark, up past the old Ex-Lax factory, no wonder the place was painted shit brown, and he turned right at Flatbush Avenue. Damn, Silvano thought, I'm gonna die of a heart attack. He slowed to a walk, sweating, shaking his head in disgust. I'll just walk up to Flatbush, he told himself, before I turn around.

He didn't make it that far. Before he got there, the guy came back around the corner, pedaling back the way he came. Silvano, shaking his head, spat nicotine slime into the gutter. After the guy passed him, going back, he kicked himself back into motion.

BACK AT HIS SPOT in the stairwell of the parking garage, he wiped his face with his shirt. It's a terrible thing, he thought, when you used to be a racehorse, discovering you can't make it to the end of your driveway and back without stopping to suck wind. He sat there watching for the remainder of the afternoon. Shortly after three the construction workers packed up and went home, and soon after that, armored trucks and vans began returning to the lot. By five-thirty it seemed they were all back, and the drivers began leaving through the gate and going home. The last three to leave were Sean, the bike rider, and another person who came out of the office after them, he couldn't tell from the distance, but from the way the person walked, he got the impression it was a woman. He headed back down the stairwell.

He got to the sidewalk in time to see Sean's Cadillac come out through the gate, followed by a crapped-out old Ford Maverick with Joseph O'Brian behind the wheel. Last through was the woman, and she closed and locked the gate before crossing the street and heading up the hill. Silvano loitered in front of the hospital, watching, and a tall, dark-haired man crossed the street a half a block up, fell into step behind her. Silvano followed them on his side of the street, not quite sure why he was doing it, happy that neither of them was riding a bike. He was berating himself for slapping around the dude in the stairwell, there had been no need for that. He could have used another stairwell to get to a higher floor and then crossed over, he could have avoided the guy altogether, but it was the same old thing, the same compulsion it seemed he'd had from the beginning of time. If there was conflict, if there was confrontation, he was like a moth to a flame, he could circle around for a while but sooner or later he'd wind up with his ass in the fire. He knew all the excuses by heart. It was his old man's fault, it was Brooklyn, it was the Army, it was the boxing ring, it was all those years he'd spent fighting Noonie's battles, keeping the neighborhood bullies off his brother's back. He'd used all of those justifications and more, and they were all bullshit. It was him, it was something that boiled up inside him, some eternally pissed off and insatiable gargoyle, and he hated it. "What I want to do, I don't do," who was it who had said that? St. Paul? "And what I don't want to do, I do." Well, sure. But it wasn't who he wanted to be.

The woman from Black and White went down a set of white stairs that went underneath a storefront bakery that made Middle Eastern pastries. Silvano stopped and leaned on a parking meter, watching. The place in the basement was a Lebanese bakery that specialized in tiny three-corner spinach pies and ground lamb pies. He had noticed it on his way down the hill, paused to catalog the ethereal smell of what they were baking. The guy who'd been following paused at the entrance, looked around, then he went in behind her. Go on, Silvano told himself, go on and look. Besides, they might have something good in there for dinner.

IF NOT FOR THAT SMELL, he couldn't imagine anyone bothering with the place, the entrance looked too much like a set of cellar stairs leading down into some dark and mousy cavity where the baker upstairs would store his raw materials. There was a small sign, white like the stairs, black letters in English and Arabic, proclaiming the name and hours of the establishment.

It was a short room. Silvano, the woman behind the counter, the old baker, and the girl from Black and White, was she a girl? It was difficult to tell her age. But all of them could stand upright. The man who had followed her had to duck his head, and he did, instinctively, as if he had knocked it before on one of the thick wooden beams holding up the floor above. Nearly everything in the room was painted white, the rock foundation walls, columns, wooden ceiling, brick floor. The tall man was having an animated conversation with the girl in a language that Silvano did not quite recognize. Not Arabic, he thought, and not Greek either, although she could have passed as a member of either ethnic group. The woman behind the counter watched impassively.

More than twenty, he thought, less than, say, thirty, an inch taller than him, she had a thoroughbred's build, with black shoulder-length hair, fierce black eyes in a hawk's face, and she was staring at the man who had followed her with a fine mixture of disdain and disapproval. The guy continued to talk at her earnestly, hands held out, palms upward in supplication. She cut him off, her voice dismissive, and she turned to the counter.

"Can I help you?" It was the woman behind the counter.

The man turned to the counter. "Excuse me," he said, "just one minute." The girl from Black and White sighed in exasperation and looked up at the ceiling. The man continued on in that strange language, his voice getting louder and more insistent. The old baker stopped what he was doing and turned to watch, his expression unreadable. Not Slavic, either, Silvano thought, her features were too fine. He would have guessed Arabic, maybe it was some dialect he hadn't heard, but he wasn't sure. She was something, though, standing there going toe to toe with the guy towering over her.

She said nothing this time, just waved the guy off like someone shooing away a fly.

The woman behind the counter was running out of patience. "Hey," she said. "Buy something or go away. You want police to come?"

The man turned in her direction again, his face a mixture of anger and anguish. He held his hand out, his meaty forearm blocking the counter. "Excuse me," he said to the woman, "please, just one more minute."

The girl got up in his face then, her own face a mask of patrician contempt. They both began talking at once, shouting and not listening. The baker hefted his shovel speculatively, and he eyed Silvano with one eyebrow raised. The message was clear: If you make me do it, I will. I may be old but I'll give him what I've got.

"Oh, fuck me," Silvano said. God, he thought, you got some sense of timing. "Hey," he yelled, louder than the two of them. "Hey, asshole." I was being good, God, he said silently, I already said I was sorry about the guy in the stairwell, I just came in here to get something to eat. This has to be your doing.

The man took a half step in Silvano's direction, his face twisted in an angry scowl. "This is not your business," the guy said, raising a clenched fist. "This is—"

Silvano cut him off. "Lady already told you to get lost. Twice, I figure. Why don't you just walk?"

The man turned completely away from her and suddenly all of his anger and frustration were focused in Silvano's direction. He faced Silvano and reached around to a back pocket.

Silvano's voice was flat and calm. "If you take that out, I'm gonna have to cut you with it. That's the rule." The other guy stood still, breathing noisily through hairy nostrils. "You understand me? Leave it where it is, you can walk up those steps and go home. Take it out, you leave on a gurney. You understand me?"

"Who the hell are you?" He was sneering, but he did it without moving anything but his face. "You big scary guy, huh, you think you're superman? Where's your cape, big man, you don't look so tough to me."

Silvano shrugged. "You can't win." He had given the speech many times, in barrooms, in dark alleys, and it was one of the rare truths that he would give up without hesitation. "I've got fourteen amateur fights and eleven years in the Army. I don't wanna go to jail, and you don't wanna go to the hospital, so do us both a favor." He stepped around to the side, giving the man a clear path to the stairs. "Walk away. Be smart. Go home."

The guy stood there, deciding, and after a minute he began to relax. He exhaled and carefully moved his hand around to the front. He looked back at her, but she said nothing, she turned her back, so he looked at Silvano one more time before he turned and went out.

She was rigid with anger, shaking just slightly. He stood watching her until she turned to look at him. "Friend of yours?" he said, with a slight smile.

She pursed her lips, shook her head in mock disgust, but then she smiled in spite of herself, and for that one split second she was beautiful, radiant, angelic in black hair and tan skin, and she had him. "No," she said, "you were right. He's an asshole."

He held out his hand. "Silvano," he said.

Her smile was gone, she regarded his hand, then shook it. He waited.

"Elia," she said, giving in. "Elia Taskent."

"Hello, Elia. You think he'll come back?"

She cocked her head, watching him. "I can take care of myself."

"I never doubted it for a minute. But could I walk you home? Just so I don't stay up all night worrying."

She looked at him, evaluating, then she smiled again, just a twitch of her mouth. "All right," she said. "Just let me buy my dinner first."

"I'M SORRY," SHE SAID, when they got back out onto the sidewalk. "What did you say your name was?"

"Silvano. What kind of a name is Elia Taskent?" They walked down Atlantic, right where he'd chased the guy on the bicycle just hours before.

"Turkish. Tell me about yourself, Silvano. What do you do?"

"I work with some carpenters at Black and White, all the way down the end of Atlantic."

"That's where I work! How come I haven't seen you there?"

"I just started. Was that guy an ex-boyfriend?"

She gave him a withering look. "Give me credit for better taste than that. I would never date a guy with that much hair in his nose. His parents were friends with mine, years ago. Some kind of distant relation. He's an old-fashioned Turk, thinks it's scandalous for a woman to be out on her own. He thinks I need some man to give me permission to walk down a sidewalk by myself."

"He offering his services?"

"No," she said. "He's a typical male. He doesn't have any solutions, only problems. Did you really have fourteen amateur fights and so many years in the Army?"

A lot of people, in his experience, did not care for ex-soldiers. Normally, he wouldn't have told her, he would have kept it to himself, but she'd heard him in the bakery, and she remembered. He prepared himself for the brushoff. "Yeah," he said. "I'm afraid I did."

She looked at him. "So you got out of the Army and came to New York City."

"Well, not exactly." Her eyes narrowed, and she waited for an explanation. "Actually, I got out a few years back. I, ah, kept working for the government for a while, out on the West Coast."

"Oh. And then you quit and came to New York City."

"Ah, well, sort of."

She shot him a look. "Complicated history."

"Yeah. I went to Japan for a while. I came East from there."

She stopped on the corner of Smith Street. "We turn here. Why Japan?"

"Well," he said. Ah, Jesus, what a long story, he thought. Why don't I just make up something simpler? Maybe she's different from all these American women, he thought, maybe she's got enough primitive tribal blood in her to understand, maybe she doesn't automatically assume every ex-soldier is a bloodthirsty murdering savage. He found to his surprise that he wanted to tell her the truth, or some part of it. "You ever know anybody who spent a long time in prison?"

She stood still, regarding him. "Yes," she said, finally. "Why do you ask?"

"Other institutions can be similar," he said. "You learn a particular set of rules, in some situations. Certain things you have to know, and do, to survive. Certain, I don't know, modes of behavior. From the outside, they are not . . ." He searched for the right word. "Comprehensible. You have to have been there, to really understand."

"Okay," she said.

"When you get out . . ." He inhaled, blew it out, started over.

"It's not so easy to keep straight, which is the real world, there or here. And those rules that you lived by for that period of time, the things you believed and what you did, they may have kept you alive, okay, but once you're out, they don't work any more, they're unacceptable. You . . . I. I was unacceptable. Even to myself. So I had to find a way to change back, and no one tells you how to do that."

"That why you went to Japan?"

"More or less. I had this friend in Nam, guy named Ramirez. I always thought he was smarter than me, quicker, mentally. Guy always seemed to know what he wanted, you know what I mean? Anyway, he gave me a call, sent me a picture of himself, he was at this Zendo in Japan, yellow robe, shaved head, and the whole bit. I couldn't believe it. So I went to see him. They wouldn't let me in, but I hung around, like, for a while. They had a guy there fixing the roof, and I sort of helped him out a little bit. So they let me stay." He walked silently for a few steps, remembering. "So they wake you up with a bell at like four-thirty in the morning, by five you're sitting on this cushion, okay, you fidget or make noise, this guy comes up behind you, he's got a stick, about the size of a Little League bat, only squared off instead of round. They call it a *kaisaku*. He bows to you, you bow to him, he whacks you with the stick."

"You're kidding."

"Nope."

"You get whacked with the stick?"

"Many times. They hit you right here, both sides." He squeezed the big muscle on the top of his shoulder. "I didn't mind it, you wanna know the truth, my back would be screaming after about twenty minutes, getting whacked makes the pain go away for a while. So anyhow, they had chants, too, you start out chanting soft, 'nah, moo, bo, sah,' like that, everybody together, and you get louder and louder, whole room full of bald-headed assholes yelling at the top of their lungs. 'Nah, moo, bo, sah!'"

She was laughing. "What's that mean?"

"Beats the shit outa me. Thousand years ago, whatever it was, Zen first came to Japan, Chinese monks were teaching it, Japanese had a hard time with the language, they had a particular way they mispronounced the words, they're still doing it. It's traditional, you know, 'we don't know why we do this, but it's the right way, so this is how you should do it.' See, I got fooled by the name. Zen. Sounds so cool, don't you think? Doesn't it? Doesn't it sound cool?"

She had a wry smile on her face. "I suppose."

"Once I thought about it, though, it didn't seem that much different from any other religion. I mean, guy comes along a couple thousand years ago, right, in most cases the guy has a relatively simple rap, 'Hey, why don't we try this another way.' Right? Maybe I'm oversimplifying. Oh, jeez, you're not religious, I'm not insulting you, am I?"

She grinned, shook her head.

"Oh, good. But anyway, the guy dies, right, now the priests are in charge, and priests are really just lawyers, okay, and pretty soon all you got left are legalities. The original point of the exercise is lost."

"This is my street," she said. "So what happened?"

"I changed the words of the chant."

"To what?"

"Moo goo gai pan."

"Oh no," she said. "You didn't."

"I figured, what the hell's the difference. Turned out, I was the only guy thought it was funny."

"We're here," she said.

"What? Oh, this is your building." It was five stories high, wide enough for two apartments, side by side plus the stairway, dirty gray brick, trash cans overflowing, ancient windows with the frames painted black, rickety iron fire escape clinging to the front of the place, made you wonder if you'd rather burn to death or be crushed when the thing fell off the building with you on it.

She stopped in front of the steps that went up to the entry. "All right, Silvano," she said, "thank you for the escort. Tell me how much of that story was bullshit."

He sighed. "Just the ending."

"Moo goo gai pan?"

"Yeah."

"I thought so. Tell me the truth. What really happened?"

"The truth is ugly."

"I can handle ugly."

"Okay." He looked down at the ground. She was up on the second step now, looking down, but he didn't look up at her. "My buddy Ramirez," he said, "my best friend Enrique, he hung himself in the Zendo. Left a note behind, said he couldn't live with it anymore."

She came back down the two steps and stood up close to him, stared at his face. "I'm sorry to hear that. How about you? Can you live with it?"

He looked at her, looked into that face, soft and yet hard. "I'm working on it."

"Good," she said, and she poked him firmly in the chest with her forefinger. "Don't bullshit me, Silvano. I don't like it."

"All right."

She turned and climbed the two steps again. "Thanks again. I'll see you around."

"Yeah," he said, suddenly feeling better. "Yeah, okay." She went the rest of the way up the stairs, winked at him from the doorway. He watched her go through, watched the door swing shut behind her. He noticed some strange feeling, he didn't know what it was, some small spark, some uncertain flutter in his chest where his heart was supposed to be. God, she's beautiful, he thought. What would she want with a lunatic like me? It was something, though, just the thought, just the possibility . . . sweet Lord. Life was never what you thought it was going to be, he thought. Just when you think you got the shit figured out, the next pitch hits you in the head. He walked back up the street, suddenly a bit unsteady.

BRONSON WAS NOT what Silvano had expected. The man looked like he was already dead. It was the skin on his face that you noticed first. It looked like onionskin paper stuck to a plate of scrambled egg whites, it seemed you could look through it to things underneath that you shouldn't be able to see. It had no texture of its own, either, no wrinkles or pores. It just lay there, pasted on.

His hands shook badly. There was an ashtray on the counter in front of him on the front desk of the St. Felix Hotel. It was surrounded by near-misses. He raised the cigarette to his lips and sucked on it until the ash was a bit more than an inch long, and then he held it in his quivering hand over the ashtray, his index finger poised over it in unsteady readiness. He seemed to gather himself, calling on all of his remaining shreds of concentration and focus. He waggled the index finger twice. False starts, Silvano thought, but then the guy did it, brought the shivering finger down on the cigarette, but not sharply enough. Instead of detaching cleanly and falling straight down, the ash split off in slow motion, spinning off to one side from the english imparted by the shaking hand and it landed among the other strays on the scarred wood of the countertop.

An aviator crouched over a bombsight could not have tried harder.

"Damn," he said. His voice gurgled deep in the mucus of his throat and lungs. "Of course I remember Nunzio. He was the nicest guy in the whole hotel. He'd stand right there, right where you are, talk to me all night sometimes."

I'm never gonna smoke another cigarette, Silvano thought, never, as long as I live. I think I'd rather get hit with a truck. "You ever hear anything about what happened to him?"

"No." Bronson pursed his lips and shook his head. "I wonder how hard anybody looked. There was that one guy your sister hired, and of course, the cops, initially, but that was it. Never heard another word."

"You know of anybody who hated him, had words with him, anything like that?"

Bronson shook his head. "No, no, no. Everybody liked Noonie. Everybody." He fell silent, looking off into the distance. "Kinda makes you wonder," he said, finally. "I mean, here's a guy, he coulda been anything. Coulda been governor, coulda been the world's best salesman, coulda been the greatest con artist in history, he had that kinda personality, but there was that one thing missing, whatever it was, that one piece left out. I mean, he was smart enough, in his own way, but that one thing was gone, and there he was. You know what I mean?"

Silvano didn't reply.

"I'm telling you, it bothered me." He took one last deep drag on the cigarette and deposited it firmly into the ashtray, leaving it there to smolder. "I even went to church once because of him. I ain't much for it, but I did go that one time. I just wanted to ask, you know. But the only question I could think of was, like, what the fuck?"

Silvano looked away. "Yeah," he said. "That about covers it."

"Yeah, really." Bronson had his hands held out to his sides, palms up in a posture of quivering supplication, a new cigarette, unlit, between two dancing fingers. "What the fuck?"

"I'll tell you a story," Silvano said. "We were kids, people had heard that there was something wrong with one of us. I remember this guy, friend of my old man, he comes to the house, I must of been twelve, he's down on his knees, he's looking at me like I'm a monkey in the zoo. Finally he stands up. 'Don't worry, Giovanni,' he says to my old man. 'I think he's gonna be all right.' Noonie's standing there, laughing his ass off."

"Hah." Bronson stuck the new cigarette between his lips and flicked an old Zippo alive. The flame was big enough to set off anything within six inches of Bronson's hand. Silvano looked at the man's sparse gray hair, but it was combed straight back, out of harm's reach. Bronson inhaled, started to cough, but he recovered and looked straight at Silvano. "For what it's worth," he said, "your brother had a good enough life, while he was here. We kept him warm, we kept him out of the rain, he had a few laughs. He had friends. Could have been a lot worse."

"Yeah, thanks."

Out on the sidewalk, Silvano stood on the corner of Henry and Clark Streets, sucking in the clean air, relishing the feel of the breeze coming up Clark Street off the bay. He gave the half-full pack of Kools in his shirt pocket to a guy panhandling on the corner. Did I tell him, he wondered, did I tell him I was Noonie's brother, or did he already know? How in the world could he have known? The two of us never looked anything alike. He went back over the conversation again in his mind, but he couldn't quite remember.

• • •

SILVANO TRUDGED DOWN Henry Street, heading for the Hotel Montague. What a day, he thought. He'd done more walking than he was used to, his feet hurt and his quads ached. He was also battling an emotional hangover. He usually got one after a fight, and his encounter in the stairwell of the parking garage had been enough to bring one on. Compounding it was Bronson's recollections of his brother. God, he thought, why didn't you just leave the women in charge? Everything would have been so much simpler. Just make man to be an ambulatory life support for balls and a dick, no brain attached. Wouldn't that have been better? Think how many more people would grow old and die in their sleep, how many more children would survive into adulthood. Why not just equip man for work and for sex and leave it at that? Be happier all around.

The stairs to the fifth floor seemed much steeper than normal. He paused when he got to the landing for his floor, leaned his head against the metal door. She was there, he could hear her.

"Clark? Let me in, Clark."

He sighed. God, he thought, I don't understand. Us on the fringe, are we all just broken pieces, are we just the by-products of your better efforts? There must have been another way. He pushed the door open, went through.

"Claark?" There was a note of panic in her voice. She watched him coming down the hallway, and he could see her fear and her need doing battle. She flinched when he got close, as if to run away, but she did not, instead she curled herself into a quaking ball at his doorstep.

He shook his head as he reached over her with the key and unlocked the door. He pushed it ajar and stepped back. "Go on," he said. "See if he's in there."

She'd been holding her breath. She looked up in surprise and inhaled convulsively, but she didn't move, didn't come out of her defensive ball. She don't wanna look, he thought, she don't wanna go in and find out he's not there, she already knows he's not there, but she'd rather sit out here and pretend. "Go on," he said in a louder voice. "He's either in there or he isn't. Go on and find out."

She unrolled herself and stood up. He was surprised to see how tall she was, she was taller than him, she might have actually been good-looking if she'd take a shower and lose the flower child clothes. There was a spark of feral intelligence in her blue eyes, though it was hard to see through the hair that hung down over her face. She glowered at him.

He leaned against the wall opposite the open door to his room. "You gonna look, or what?"

Her face twisted into an ugly mask of resentment. "He said he was coming back," she said, her voice hard and flat.

"And you believed him." This was a mistake, he thought. I shoulda left her alone. Her back was to the door, and with one unsteady hand she reached behind her and shoved the door open wide. He didn't think she'd go in, and she didn't, she didn't even turn around, she just glanced quickly over her shoulder.

"Claark?"

"Clark's a dog, he ain't coming back."

Her face crumpled but she didn't cry. She bent over and hooked her shopping bag, straightened back up, looked at him accusingly, her blond hair flowing down over her shoulders. Silvano shook his head. "I'm sorry."

She looked at the floor, turned away, and without looking back she shuffled down the corridor.

THE TELEPHONE RANG in the middle of the night, startling Domenic awake. He rolled over, sat on the edge of the bed, and looked at the clock on the nightstand. Half past one in the morning. He had to get up in four more hours. This had better be important.

He walked across the floor of the darkened room to get to the phone, bare feet on oriental carpets, then on hard wood over next to the bookcase where the phone hung on the wall. He put his hand on the receiver and watched the light on the top of the black box wired into the phone line. It was supposed to light up to alert him if the line was tapped. He didn't know if it worked or not, the light had never gone on. It didn't matter too much, he was too paranoid to do much business on his home phone anyhow.

He picked it up, the light stayed off.

"Yeah," he said.

"I know you're a busy man," the voice on the line said. "I'm sorry to bother you this late at night."

It was Ivan. Ivan wouldn't use his name, and he wouldn't use Ivan's. Gangster phone etiquette. "What's the matter," he said. "You need bail money?"

"Not just now. I got a phone call a couple of hours ago. You probably want to hear about it."

"Go on."

"It was from a mutt that works in that hotel your cousin used to live at."

Domenic came fully awake. His heart rate accelerated and he became conscious of a ringing noise in his ears, but outwardly he betrayed no sign of his heightened state of awareness. "Keep talking."

"Guy came around today asking about Noonie. From the description, it sounds like it might be him."

Silvano, Domenic thought. That fucking snake. "That's what you said the last time. Do you know where this guy is?"

"No, not yet." Ivan cleared his throat. "There's one other thing."

Domenic could feel his stomach burning. "What."

"Antonio told me I should handle this myself. He said he don't want you bothered with it. I'm taking a big chance, telling you, but I know how you feel about this."

No, you don't, Domenic thought, you don't have a fucking clue. "Antonio's just worried about his money. I want you to listen to me. I want you to find out if it's him, you hear me? And if it is, you grab him and you put him on ice, and then you call me."

"Listen, Antonio said . . ."

"Fuck Antonio!" He screamed it into the phone and his voice boomed and echoed in the empty room. He shook with rage, but he recovered quickly. He gathered himself and went on in a more normal tone. "Fuck Antonio," he said. "I want you to do what I said. Don't worry about Antonio, I'll protect you on this. Antonio ain't gonna live forever."

There was silence on the line as Ivan considered his options. "All right," he said, after a long count. "We'll do it your way."

"I won't forget it. This bastard ruined my fucking life, he ruined my sister, you hear me?"

"Don't get started up again on this."

"I never stopped," Domenic snarled into the phone, his voice low and guttural. "From the day it happened until right now, I never forgot this fuck for one minute. As soon as you have him, you call me."

"Gotcha."

Domenic hung up the phone. Fucking Antonio, he thought, you want to deny me this? When I'm done with Silvano, I'm gonna come for you. I'll make you pay for this, you old bastard.

He wasn't thinking clearly, the anger was making him reckless. Calm down, he told himself. You need to be careful, don't screw this up. You been waiting a long time. He walked over to the kitchen and took a glass and a bottle of Johnny Dark out of a cabinet. He poured the glass three-quarters full and went to sit down on the edge of the bed with it.

Even just the name was enough to do it to him, to send him into a rage like nothing else could. I had dreams, he thought, I had dreams, maybe they were small but they were mine, and I was on my way. He'd been accepted to Princeton and McGill, his head had been full of art and architecture. He could have been something real, a builder, an engineer. An artist! He'd been so close. Silvano had been a punk, a dropout, a boxer with emotional problems. You couldn't keep your hands off her, could you? Your own cousin, she loved you like a brother, and you couldn't leave her alone. And what did you do to my father? You were nothing next to Angelo, Angelo the Hammer. And he loved you, you fuck! He took care of you, he watched out for you better than your own father, you son of a bitch. Domenic would never tell me what you did, he'd never tell me how my father died, but I'm gonna make you talk, Silvano. I am gonna fucking make you talk . . .

One minute I'm on my way to school, the next minute my father is dead, my sister's locked in a cell in a fucking convent, and the old man yanks the rug out from under me. Fucking laughed at me. Next thing I know, I'm hijacking trucks in fucking Bayonne. Bootlegging cigarettes. "Higher education," he scoffed. "You want higher education? I'll teach you . . ."

The dream still tormented him, its power undiminished by the passing years. He still carried the images in his mind, buildings, houses, bridges, temples like the world had never seen. And instead, he was wasting his life. Fourteen hours a day, grubbing in the filth for money like a sow after a truffle.

Silvano, when I get my hands on you, I'll kill you for this.

I swear it.

THREE

■

IT WAS THE DREAM that woke him in the predawn darkness, the same one it seemed he'd had a hundred times, and he jerked awake, covered with sweat, grasping for the M-16 that was suddenly not there. He gasped for breath and his heart thundered in his chest while his mind changed gears frantically, no, this was just a room, just a room in a hotel, and he was back in Brooklyn, U.S.A.

He rolled over on his back and stared at the ceiling and slowly the shaking went away. He wiped the sweat from his face with the bedsheet. I'm never gonna get away, he thought. The shit just keeps following me.

He remembered then, his ongoing life. Black and White, he thought. Carpenters. He looked down, noticed how badly his hand still shook. He wasn't looking forward to it, in fact he was getting nervous thinking about it, which didn't make any sense at all. It wasn't like he cared about the job, the only reason he was bothering with it at all was there was a chance he might pick up some information about Noonie. But still, he was asking himself to function, to coexist in a normal environment with regular men, without long explanations of who he was and where he'd been. Why he was like this.

Get up, he told himself, get up, if it wasn't for Noonie you'd go find a hole, crawl inside, and pull it in after yourself. Get up and get going. He rolled out of bed and headed for the bathroom.

She was out there in the hallway. She only had one cup of coffee, though. He opened the door and stepped around her, closed and locked it behind him. He looked down at her. "Again?" he said. "Didn't we cover this last night?"

"I know, I know," she said, not looking up.

"So?"

She sighed. "Makes me feel better."

Shower might make you feel better, too, he thought. "That right?"

"Yes," she said. "I know he's gone. I know he's . . . I know. But if I sit here for a while, part of me feels better, part of me thinks he'll come back and then everything will be all right." She glanced up quickly, then looked away. "I know it sounds crazy."

"You said it, not me."

"See, this way, it's all on him, you get it? It's the lazy way out. As long as I'm waiting for Clark, it's all his fault. I don't have to do anything."

I don't know who's crazier, Silvano thought, her, or me for listening to her. "It's your life," he said. "You wanna spend it in a hallway, it's up to you."

"I know," she said. "Maybe this is just for now. Maybe I'll get tired of it after a while." She looked up at him and snickered. "Maybe I'll get better."

• • •

THE GATE AT Black and White was open. Silvano walked through it at quarter to seven and passed the row of armored trucks and headed for the construction site. Lee, the big carpenter foreman, saw him coming.

"You surprise me," he said, looking at his watch. "I didn't really think you'd show up."

"Ye of little faith," Silvano said.

"Faith without work is dead. You ever hang drywall before?"

"Yeah."

Lee raised his eyebrows. "No kidding. Can you tape?"

"I can get it screwed to the wall okay," Silvano said, "but you don't want me taping it."

"Fair enough."

LEE PUT HIM with a guy who liked to talk while he worked. The guy had long blond hair tied into a ponytail, played guitar in a band on weekends, and he told Silvano all about guitars, chord progressions, the roots of rock and roll, and why it was such a crime that no one listened to the blues anymore. He'd only worked at Black and White for a few months, though, and he couldn't have known Noonie, so Silvano listened with one ear and lost himself in the work, watching the sheets of drywall transform an open studded space into enclosed rooms with smooth paper walls and ceilings.

Lee showed up after a couple of hours and inspected their progress. "Not bad," he said. He looked at Silvano. "You got a driver's license?"

"State of Oregon."

"Is it good?"

"Yeah."

"All right. That little shit next door needs someone to help bring back a truck they got at a garage up in the Bronx. It was up there getting the air-conditioning fixed. You mind going for a ride, driving it back for them?"

"Why not."

ROLAND WAS STANDING in the yard, his face set in stone. He was wearing a blue uniform, blue hat, and he had a gun belt around his waist. Frankie, wearing the same kind of uniform, was twenty feet away, climbing into a truck, his jaw clamped shut in anger. Sean O'Brian was standing near Roland, red-faced. He fished his keys out of his pants pocket and handed them to Roland.

"I'm sick of these nigger repair jobs. You tell that guy I'm not paying for nigger work. If I have to send that truck back to him for the same thing again, I'm not paying his bill. You tell him that." He turned, saw Silvano standing there. "Go with him," he said, and he turned his back and walked away. He got six feet away and stopped. "No, wait," he said, turning around. "Come inside, I gotta get you the new insurance card for the truck, the old one expired."

Roland leaned against the car. Silvano followed the kid into the building.

They walked through the front door. Just inside the door was a small entryway. A metal door was set into the wall opposite the front door, and there was a keypad on the wall next to it. Sean O'Brian ignored the keypad and pulled the door open. "Broken," he said. "Another item on the list."

He stopped just inside the door and took a breath. "Hi, Elia," he said, obviously trying hard to be pleasant. "Did you see that latest envelope we got from the insurance company? I think it came yesterday."

It was her, it was that girl Silvano met in the bakery yesterday. "No, Sean, I haven't seen it. If it isn't on your desk, your uncle probably has it. Good morning, Silvano." She smiled at him, God, she was something, she was wearing some kind of T-shirt that showed a little cleavage. He felt like he'd been punched in the stomach. She was still smiling that smile, waiting for him to answer.

He remembered to inhale. "Hi," he said. "You look outstanding this morning."

She considered that. "Every morning," she said, "but thank you, it's nice of you to notice."

"Oh, damn." Sean was digging through the rubble on a desk over against the far wall. "Damn," he said, "it isn't here." It was obvious he wanted to avoid Joseph O'Brian.

"Gotta go in and ask him."

"Yeah, yeah," Sean muttered. "Come with me, Silvano," he said sourly. "If he starts in on me, at least you can take the insurance card and go."

The two of them walked down an interior corridor and stopped at a door near the far end. Sean hesitated, then he knocked. There was a low murmur from inside. Sean looked at Silvano, shrugged, opened the door, and stuck his head inside. "Ah, Joe," he said, his tone conciliatory, "do you have that envelope—"

"Come in, Sean," the voice said. "I want to talk to you."

"Oh, boy," Sean said, looking at the ceiling as he pushed the office door open wide.

"Don't take that tone with me." The voice belonged to an older man who looked a bit like his nephew, in his face, at least, but he was thinner, without muscle tone, and stooped over somewhat. He was the bicycle guy, Silvano was seeing him up close for the first time. His hair was gray at the temples and was cut in a conservative style. "Who is that with you?" he said.

"This is Silvano," he said. "Silvano, my uncle, Joseph O'Brian." He turned to the older man, who ignored Silvano. "He's going to go with Roland to pick up that truck in the Bronx, and I need to give him that insurance card that just came in case they get stopped. I know how much you enjoy paying tickets."

"Hmmph." The elder O'Brian glanced at Silvano. He'd been in the act of lacing up a pair of sneakers. They looked odd on him, out of place, like Larry Bird playing basketball in a pair of wing tips. He straightened up in his chair. There were papers and envelopes stacked in neat piles on his desk. Silvano looked around the room while the two O'Brians searched for the right envelope.

There were pictures on the paneled walls, lots of them, most were snapshots of Joseph O'Brian standing next to priests or brothers, arm in arm in some shots, shaking hands in others. Most of the priests were smiling into the camera, but in every shot Joseph O'Brian wore the same blank expression, lips pinched together, mouth downturned. Some of the other pictures were of pipe organs, ornate altars, stained-glass windows, church exteriors.

They found the envelope. Sean extracted the insurance card from it and handed it to Silvano. "Here," he said, and he turned back to his uncle. "You getting ready to go on your bike ride?"

"I want to talk to you first." He wore the same expression he'd had on in each of the pictures. The kid sighed.

"Okay." He turned to Silvano. "Go with Roland," he said.

Silvano closed the door behind him. The voices got louder as he walked back down the corridor. The O'Brians are taking up an old argument, he thought, one that they've had a lot, because they're both trying to talk over the other guy, not listening. They've both heard it all before.

Elia was grinning when he got to the outer office.

"What's up with those two," he asked.

"Oh, don't worry," she said. "They do that all the time."

"Why?"

She looked in the direction of Joseph O'Brian's office. "Well," she said, "Mr. O'Brian, Sr., is very spiritual. He's very involved with church and all that, and he objects to Sean's hair, his music, his friends, and so on. And Sean wants to be left alone. He wants to do his own thing. It's the same old story, right?"

"I suppose. Are you and Sean . . ."

"No," she said. "You seem very worried about my love life."

You can't have a casual conversation with this one, he thought. She bores right in on you, she actually listens to what you say. When was the last time anyone did that? "Well," he said, "you know how guys are, we get around a woman like you, we get all primitive and shit. It's not our fault. God made us this way."

She was shaking her head. "How about if the two of you just butted heads, like mountain goats?"

"Too painful. Could we just dance around and make hooting noises, the way sandhill cranes do?"

She leaned back in her chair and laughed. "Go for it," she said, "although I don't know what it would get you."

He sat down in the chair next to her desk. "You can't blame a guy for trying. Men have gone to war over a smile like yours, did you know that?"

She leaned her elbow on the desk and stared at him. "I'll have to be more careful with it in the future."

Over his shoulder Silvano could hear the O'Brians heating up. "Are they gonna get violent? Should we call the cops?"

"Nah. Sean's not a bad kid, he would never hurt anyone, he just never had anybody to teach him how to act. And his uncle has that disease old men get when they start believing so hard they think they know the answer to everything." She cocked her head, listening. "They'll be all right. They've just been reacting to each other lately. Joseph thinks Sean should be more spiritual, and Sean thinks Joseph is a religious fruitcake. I don't know which one is right. I don't think being a little bit spiritual would be a bad thing, do you?"

He shrugged. "They might both be right. The problem with spirituality is that it never looks the way you think it's going to."

"What do you mean?"

He stood up, folded the insurance card, and stuck it in his shirt pocket. "I would tell you a story about that," he said, "told to me by a wizzled up little Japanese guy. Tough old buzzard. I don't think I got time for it, though, I got to go. Next time I see you."

"All right," she said. "Catch you later." She smiled at him again, a lower-voltage version this time, but it still got to him. He went through the outer door into the sunshine and breathed the air in. It seemed to taste better than it had, just twenty minutes ago. Be careful, he told himself, just be careful. Don't go believing some strange female is going to put you right.

SILVANO GOT INTO the Cadillac on the passenger side. Roland started the engine and looked over at Silvano, his face expressionless. "Told you he was ignorant," he said.

"Yeah, you did. You ever want to take that pistol out and make him dance, like in an old Western?"

Roland sighed, dropped the gearshift down into drive. "It is a thought. Might do him some good. But you know, it ain't none of my business. The Man upstairs got His own way of teaching you. You don't pay attention, you suffer the consequences. I'm betting someone will come along, teach the boy a lesson or two," he said. He stepped on the gas and the big car started rolling. "It's His business, and I got to leave it to Him, because this is a good job, and right now I can't afford to lose it. Pays pretty nice, it's year-round, you know, no layoffs since I been here. My mother's been sick, and we got a lot of medical bills. Plus I got a niece in college, and I'm trying to help my sister keep her there." He looked at Silvano. "I ain't a free man, and neither is Frankie. Frankie's in deeper than me, he's got a wife and four kids. Works all the overtime he can get. You know, a man has to count up the cost before he opens his mouth."

"Not so easy, being a grown-up."

"No it is not."

"How long you been working here?"

"Two years."

"No kidding."

"Pretty long time for me. Before I got this job, I was a gypsy, pretty much."

"That right?"

"Oh, yeah. I been all over. Before this I worked a year in a slaughterhouse in Davenport, Iowa, and before that I was at a chicken plant in Maryland, down the eastern shore. And so on. Yeah, I been all over. I mean, hell, why not? Might as well see a little bit, before you die. But this job is nice, no blood or nothing." He settled into the driver's seat, getting comfortable, warming to his story. "You ever been in a slaughterhouse?"

Silvano sucked in a big breath and held it. "No," he finally said, exhaling. "No."

Roland laughed. "No place for a white man. You see a white

guy in there, either he's a supervisor or he's on work release." He looked over at Silvano. "Just the way it is. Not bad money, but it's a hard, hard place to make a living. Cows or hogs, they come in at the end of the building that smells like shit. They can smell it, you know, they can smell death, and they know what's gonna happen, they be oinking or mooing, shitting everywhere, trying to get away, but these places, they're death factories. They're very good at what they do, catch the animals and string them up, no cow nor no pig gonna get free. Before they know it, they be hanging by their back legs, on the conveyor. Next, there's a guy with the hammer, always a big motherfucker, arms like trees." He looked over at Silvano again. "Ain't a regular hammer, like you guys use. It's a pneumatic thing, suspended from the ceiling, looks like a jackhammer, a little bit. Dude just holds it up next to the cow's head, pulls the trigger, bang, the cow's unconscious. Not dead, mind you, but out of it. Two seconds later another guy with a pneumatic saw rips the thing from asshole to Adam's apple, guts and blood go flying everyplace, heart still beating.

"And so on.

"Pigs go the same way as the cows. Chickens, now, they're a little different. They hang from their back feet, too, well, that's the only feet they got, but they be upside down on this chain, right, they go through this pair of rails, look a little like parallel bars, traps their heads and slides them through this machine that zaps them, kills most of them, except for some of the roosters, the males. Males can be tough, but you're a rooster, all being tough buys you is you get to hold your head up, watch the next machine coming, the one that grabs you and cuts your throat. Then the next pair of parallel bars traps the head and pulls it off, drops it into this sleuceway that carries it off to get made into cat food or fertilizer, or mattress padding, for all I know. Very efficient."

"You worked there a year?"

"Little bit longer, at the chicken place. Funny thing about the chickens, a chicken is dumber than a fencepost, but it's the chickens that get away most often. I don't know if it's because they're small, or if they trust us less, or if they just want it more, but some of them do get away, at least for a little bit. But they're stupid, you know, they don't know to run and keep running, they don't know what's food and what ain't, they ain't ever been outside in their lives, so they just wander around the parking lot. Plant will have some guy looking for them, you'll see him walking around, stick looks like a golf club but with a hook on one end, he's got that in one hand, he's got a bunch of chickens in the other hand, you know, carrying them by one leg each, he be covered with shit. Taking them back inside to die.

"And I often wondered, you know, if there ain't a big cloud of bad karma hanging over these places like a bad smell. Oh, and you can believe it, brother, the smell of them places is for real, it's like nothing else you've ever smelled, and when you been in there all day long it seems like forever before you get clean of it."

"You go to the supermarket," Silvano said, "I bet the stuff looks a little different to you."

Roland laughed. "Oh, yeah," he said, "all nice and clean and wrapped up in plastic. I couldn't eat chicken for a long time after I left that place. Ain't no problem now, though, I like them precooked wings, come frozen, got spicy red sauce to dip them in. It's red but it ain't blood. You lick it off your fingers.

"I was a little boy in Atlanta, my grandmother had chickens in her backyard, run around in this little fenced-in enclosure. Yellow and fuzzy, cute when they're little. She catch one, she hold it in her hands and cut its head off with a pair of tin snips. Pull the feathers off, clean it, and cook it. It was more honest that way. Make you understand what this animal gave you, so you could eat your dinner.

"But anyway, now you know all about me, what about you? How come you're in Brooklyn? I got family obligations, right, but you look like a free man. What you doing here? Couldn't find no place better than this?"

Silvano sighed. "I grew up in Brooklyn. Joined the Army, stayed away for a long time. But Brooklyn is like an ugly girlfriend with big tits. You know you should stay away, right, but you can't get her out of your head."

Roland was laughing. "Well, I been there before, brother. I been there."

ROLAND HAD TO STAY with the car, there was no safe place to park it. "Guy's inside that garage," he told Silvano. Black guy, and I mean black. Jamaican, little bit fat, got a mustache. Tell him Sean was pissed off. That's all you gotta say."

Silvano walked through the open truck bay door into a dimly lit garage. A greasy-looking dog got to his feet and showed his teeth at Silvano, growling.

"Sit."

It was a command voice, and the dog dropped his butt to the floor abruptly, looking around behind him. A man came out of the shadows. He had the darkest skin Silvano had ever seen on a human being.

"From Black and White," Silvano told him. "Here to pick up a truck."

"Van," the guy said. "Armored van."

"Whatever. Kid was pretty pissed off," Silvano told him. "Made noises about not paying the bill."

The guy grinned broadly. "He don't got the stones for that," he said, fishing a set of keys out of his pocket and handing them to Silvano. "Him don't want I come down there to visit."

"What was wrong with it, anyway?"

"Air-condition. The gas leak out. Him use the van to cash payroll checks. Park the ting in the hospital parking lot on payday, right, everyone inside come out to cash the check. Him hire maybe four, five off-duty cops to work inside the van, hand out the money. Hot day, right, they leave the ting run all day, with the air-condition on full blast. See, you got the black van, park in the sun all day long, four, five cops inside with sweat running down the crack of the ass, well, mon, it's just too beautiful to contemplate. You know what I'm saying?"

Silvano was laughing. "All those guys driving for him off-duty cops? Anyway, I told you, right? Guy was not happy. You might lose a customer."

"Fuck him." The guy patted his stomach. "I look like I'm starving? Besides, summer's over. Don't need the air-condition no more."

THE VAN WAS loaded down with the extra weight of inch-thick bulletproof glass and steel armor plating, and it drove like a pig. It was sluggish and it wallowed through the corners. Silvano followed Roland in the Cadillac. He was happy when they got back, glad to get out of the van. He tossed the keys to Roland and went back to work.

Shortly before the afternoon coffee break Silvano noticed a guy he hadn't seen before. The guy was wandering around the construction site, young white guy with straw-colored hair chopped into random lengths, sticking straight out from his skull. He was wearing jeans, sneakers, and a blue flannel shirt. At first Silvano assumed he was working there, but there was something about the guy that caught his attention. The guy went over to where the sprinkler-fitters were installing their piping. After a short conversation he walked away with a two-foot piece of inch-and-a-half galvanized pipe. He held it in his right hand like a club, smacking it into his left. Alarm bells started ringing in Silvano's mind, and he stopped working and watched the guy.

The guy walked up to some carpenters then, and after another brief conversation one of them grabbed a piece of two-by-four and a power saw and cut a foot-long stake, broad at one end, pointed at the other. Silvano listened to the zing the saw made, reminding himself not to jump to conclusions.

"Thanks a lot," Silvano heard the guy say. "I really appreciate it."

There's a thousand things he might need that for, he thought, but the alarm bell in the back of Silvano's head kept ringing.

A few minutes later the coffee truck drove up, honking its horn, and hard hats started pouring out of the half-finished building. Silvano sat down on the steps out in front, near a group of about ten men when the guy in the blue flannel shirt, still carrying the pipe and the wooden stake, approached the driver of the coffee truck, who was busy making change, and asked him something. The man looked up in surprise, shook his head no. Silvano took note of the look of surprise on the driver's face, and he watched the guy make a slow circuit around the job site, stopping here and there, asking people his question, getting the same startled looks and negative responses in each place. He strained to hear the guy but could not. It didn't matter, eventually the guy got around to them. He stopped at the foot of the stairs and leaned in, addressing no one in particular. He kept his voice low and conspiratorial.

"Hey," he said. "You guys seen any vampires?"

Most of the men were surprised by the question and looked at each other. One or two began to smile. "What?" one man said. "What did you say?"

Silvano brightened, remembering what Roland had said about the man upstairs. Maybe this guy really is more than just a random crazy person. Maybe he was sent here for a purpose. The Lord works in mysterious ways, that's what they say, His wonders to perform.

"Vampires," the guy said, in the same low voice. "I'm hunting vampires. You seen any?"

"Oh, man," the questioner said, "you need to . . ."

"I seen one," Silvano said, interrupting. "He hangs out next door. Very young-looking, for a vampire. Black hair, got a goatee. He's a big one, though. Be careful."

The vampire hunter hefted his pipe. "Oh, boy," he said. "Thanks. Thanks a lot."

A wry smile worked its way through the group of men as they watched the guy go into the building next door. The man who had spoken up before wasn't smiling. "Oh, Lord," he said to Silvano. "I know the kid is a spoiled rich boy, but why did you do that?"

Several of the men laughed.

"No, really," the guy said. "He could get hurt bad."

Silvano shrugged. "He's got an ass-kicking coming to him."

"How do you figure that?"

"Too quick to run his mouth. That's what happens, you ain't had your ass kicked when you needed it."

They heard the sounds of breaking glass from the building next door, and then shouting, and thumping noises.

"Break's over." It was Lee, walking over to the group. "Back to work. Don't worry, I'll go check on the little shit." He was looking at Silvano, laughing, shaking his head. Silvano went back inside, and he didn't see when the cops came to take the vampire hunter away.

AT THREE O'CLOCK everybody stopped what they were doing. Lee came walking through the room where Silvano was working. Wordlessly he took a roll of bills out of his pocket and paid Silvano.

"See you tomorrow," Silvano said.

"No, you won't."

"Why not?"

"Because tomorrow's Saturday. You forget what day of the week it is?" The big man had a look of amusement on his face.

"I suppose I did."

"I'll see you Monday, then. You be here on Monday?"

"Do my best."

He walked through the gate a few minutes after three, but then he remembered the insurance card in his shirt pocket and he went back. The place was suddenly deserted, because the construction workers were gone and Black and White's regulars were still out with their armored vehicles, doing their jobs. Silvano looked around for Sean O'Brian and didn't see him, so he headed for the office. He yanked open the inner door and went in. Sean and Elia were sitting at their respective desks, doing paperwork. They both looked up in surprise.

"Forgot to give you this," Silvano said, fishing the card from his pocket.

Sean had a mouse under one eye, some scratches on his cheek, and a resentful look on his face. He stood up and walked over to get the card. "I speak to you outside?"

"Yeah, sure." Sean walked through the door, and Silvano

turned to follow him. Elia, stifling a grin, looked at him and winked. Outside, in the yard, Silvano and Sean faced each other.

"Why'd you do it? Why'd you sic that guy on me. I didn't do nothing to you."

Silvano shook his head. "There's a rat in every crowd. Who told you it was me?"

"What difference does that make? Why'd you do it?"

"I figured I'd do you a favor."

"How the hell do you figure that?"

"Remind you to get the door fixed, for one thing."

"Oh, thanks a lot."

"And the other thing was, obviously you ain't had nobody to tell you, what's okay and what's not. So I decided to help you out."

"What are you talking about?"

"See, me being a vagrant, I don't need you, and I don't need this job. You start talking shit to me, I can walk, or I can kick your ass first and then walk, if I want. But it ain't right to talk shit to guys who can't talk back. You're a man, you ain't supposed to do that, not after grammar school. You get it?"

Sean reddened. "You mean Frankie and Roland. You did it because of what I said to them."

"Not exactly. I did it because I didn't like how it felt to get into that car with Roland and feel ashamed that I'm the same color as your sorry ass. Either one of those guys is a better man than you. You had to carry what they're walking around with, you'd run to the nearest bridge to throw yourself into the fucking river to drown."

Sean was still red. "You're right," he said after a minute. "I was wrong. But next time, just tell me, okay, don't send some whacko in to get me."

"You kidding? You got off easy."

• • •

SHE LOOKED BETTER out in the daylight, even if she was still wearing the same clothes she'd had on when Silvano first saw her. She grabbed his elbow. "Wait, wait," she said. "Hold up right here."

It was Mrs. Clark, and it was the first time Silvano had seen her in the full light of day. He stopped. He couldn't look at her without wondering what had gone wrong, he had to mourn for her, Jesus, she was so close to beautiful, with the wind blowing her hair around that lost face, but there was no way to feel good, knowing she was so far gone. Why you hadda make friends with this one? he thought. The Angel of Montague Street. Teach you to talk to crazy people.

She was digging around in her shopping bag. She pulled out an old nasty brown fedora with a wide brim and jammed it down over his ears. He reached up to adjust it.

"No," she said. "Pull it down low." She took a step back to look at him. "Still need something," she said. "Got anything in that pocket?"

"No."

"Good." She reached out quicker than he'd thought possible and snatched the pocket right off the shirt. The square of material that had been underneath was a darker color than the rest of the shirt. "Better," she said, looking at him and grinned. She stuck the square piece of cloth that had been his pocket into one of her bags. "Almost there. See that patch of sand in the gutter? That dry stuff? Rub your hands around in it."

Okay, God, Silvano thought, I know you find me amusing. "Do you have some reason for this? Something that would make sense to me?"

She cackled. "You think I got a screw loose,, don't you?"

"You kidding? You got some screws missing altogether."

"Well, maybe so," she said, "but there's some men waiting in the Montague, don't look all that friendly, and I'm betting they're waiting for you."

"No shit," he said. "Why are you doing this?"

"I don't know," she said. "Maybe because you're not a complete asshole. Now go on, get some of that nice dirt on your hands."

He did as he was told.

"Good. Now rub your hands around on your face. Rub it in good. All right, all right," she said, taking his elbow again. "Now I'm gonna walk with you, and you'll be invisible. Slow down, slow down, you got nowhere to go. Limp a little bit, like you got a bad foot, and you ain't been to the doctor in about half a lifetime. No, not like that, just a little. That's better. Now you're getting it. Go check out that trash can, see if you can find us a little sumpin-sumpin." She was amused by his reaction. "Go on, don't be shy. What do you think you're gonna eat when there's too much month left over at the end of the money?"

He went over to look in the can.

"Go on," she said, enjoying it. "Dig around in there."

Go ahead, God, he thought. Rub my nose in it. Is this to pay me back for sending that guy after Sean? Don't tell me you didn't think that was funny.

He didn't find anything worthwhile in the can. Mrs. Clark looked at him sideways. "Bet you passed sumpin' up," she said. "Bet you'd find a little bit in there, you was hungry enough."

"Well, you're right about that," he said, his memory flashing him images of a rain forest on the far side of the planet. "But I ain't been that hungry in a while. What now?"

"Now we're gonna walk right on past the Montague, but we're gonna go nice and slow, take our time. Remember, your foot hurts, you're hungry, and you're just another invisible street person."

They made their slow way up the street, and as they did, all of Silvano's senses came alive. A black Cadillac with the engine running was parked on Henry Street, about twenty-five feet back from the corner of Montague, just past the rear of the hotel. The back windows were blacked out. The driver, a heavy-set dark-haired man in a pin-striped suit, sat stolidly behind the wheel.

Wonder if I'd have noticed? Silvano thought. Wonder if I'd have picked him up in time? They paused right in front of the hotel. "Go do that trash can, over there," she said. "You do it right, none of these people will ever see you at all. Don't forget, you still got a sore foot."

He limped over to the trash can and rooted around inside. Out of the corner of his eye he saw her looking casually in the direction of the hotel's entrance. "Nothing here," he said.

"All right," she said. "Come on." There was a man standing just inside the front entrance of the hotel, a somewhat younger and thinner copy of the man behind the wheel of the car around the corner. The guy ignored the two of them as they continued on their way. Silvano felt himself getting angry, but he cooled off in the few minutes it took them to get far enough up the street to be safely out of sight.

"Well," she said, straightening up and releasing her grip on his elbow, "that was that. One more in the stairwell, another one inside your room."

"I owe you one."

"I'll hit you up someday, don't worry. You got someplace to stay?"

"I could stay at the St. Felix."

"Don't be an idiot. First thing they'll do is check out the

other hotels. You can stay with my friend Henry. They'll never find you there. C'mon, I'll take you to see him."

"Time out." He stood silent, thinking. "You hungry? Someplace around here you can get lunch?"

"I guess . . ."

He handed her a twenty-dollar bill. "Go eat. I'll meet you back right here in, say, forty-five minutes. You got a watch?"

"I'll be here," she said. "You gonna go get into trouble?"

"Don't worry. Recon used to be my specialty." He set off down the sidewalk, taking the long way around the block so he'd come up Henry Street behind the Cadillac.

THE DRIVER WAS EASY. Silvano waited until there was no one else on the sidewalk, then he walked up behind the car on the driver's side and kicked in the taillight. The guy had been half asleep, and Silvano felt mildly insulted as the guy woke up with a jolt and lurched halfway out of the car. Silvano grabbed a handful of greasy black hair and whacked the guy's head twice against the roof of the car. He laid the guy out across the front seat of the car, unconscious, relieved him of the Smith & Wesson he'd been carrying in the inside pocket of his jacket. Silvano tucked the gun in his waistband, in the small of his back.

He went around behind the hotel and jumped up on the loading dock. Guy was just a driver, he told himself. Don't get cocky.

THE BACK DOOR of the hotel must have been jimmied a hundred times. He looked at the door, sprung, hanging on its hinges. Why they bother locking it? he wondered. He looked around the loading dock, noticed a wooden pallet. The pallet had been knocked together out of thin sticks of hard wood. He kicked a piece loose and jammed it in the space between the door and the frame just above the plate on the door that was supposed to protect the deadbolt. He leaned against the protruding end of the piece of wood, prying the door away from the frame until the deadbolt came out of the hole in the frame it was slotted into and the door slid open. Certain things you learn when you're twelve, he thought, you never forget.

He was in a short, dark corridor, and at the end of the corridor was the back door to the hotel lobby. The door had a small window in it, it was grimy, but he could see through. Guy was still there, but it appeared that he was getting antsy, looking around, shifting his weight from foot to foot. Silvano waited, watching him. Wouldn't do to have the guy spot you in the lobby, he thought. Eventually the guy lit up a cigarette, and that seemed to calm him down. Silvano slipped through the door and headed for the stairs.

The guy behind the front desk never looked up from his newspaper. The old guy with the potato nose, the guy Silvano had met his first night at the Montague, was sitting in a lobby chair staring out into space. His hands rested on his thighs, the left twitching rhythmically. Don't look at me, buddy, don't say anything, Silvano thought, but the guy just stared out into nothing. If not for the twitching hand he might be dead. Mrs. Clark must be right, Silvano thought. Too much month left over at the end of the money, this guy's sitting there in a state of suspended animation, waiting for the next check to come so he can afford his life's blood.

Once through the stairwell door he paused to think. One guy up over my head, one in the room. How would you do it? I was the guy in the stairwell, I'd wait one floor up, wait for the target to go into the hallway on his floor, then I'd come down, go in behind him, make some noise. Guy in the room comes out, we've got him. He took the driver's pistol out of his waistband and looked at it. Snub-nosed .38 Smith & Wesson, the kind the cops used to like back in the fifties. Lethal enough at close range, nice gun, not too big, not too heavy, does what it's made to do.

He made a little noise going up the stairs. Don't want to startle the guy, he thought. Good way to get shot. He got to the fifth-floor landing and sure enough, it was empty, but he could smell the unmistakable essence of Old Spice. He shook his head. Definitely not varsity, he told himself. They sent the water boys after me. He opened the door and went through, waited just inside the hallway.

Rapid, heavy clomping noises came from the stairwell. Big boy, he thought. He bent his knees slightly and went into a spin, and just as the door opened he jumped off his right foot, and high in the air he snapped out his left leg. It's a beautiful kick when you do it right, positively a thing of beauty, but it's kind of like an Italian sports car, you have to keep up with it, maintain it, baby it, you can't leave it in the garage for six months and then expect it to work when you need it. Six months? More like three years.

He was too high, and off balance to boot, plus the guy was shorter than he'd expected, and in a bit of a crouch. Silvano's toe caught the guy right on the chin instead of in the solar plexus. The guy's momentum carried his lower body forward even as his head and shoulders snapped back from the force of the kick, and he straightened out in midair and landed on his back. Silvano came tumbling awkwardly down on top of the guy, but the guy didn't move as Silvano rolled off him and jumped to his feet. He noticed in passing the unnatural position of the guy's head and neck. Sloppy, he thought. Should never have gone for the kick.

He grabbed the body by the shoulders and dragged it hastily through the metal stairwell door. Behind him he heard a door burst open. He left the guy on the stairwell landing and climbed up the stairs a few steps and sat down, grabbing for the .38 he'd taken from the driver. There was just one light on the landing, and the sound the gun made seemed deafening in the enclosed space. Silvano was suddenly in gloom.

The guy who burst through the stairwell door was the size of an NFL linebacker, six foot four easy, nice big target. Gym rat, Silvano thought, watching the guy vault the body on the floor and rush to look down the stairs, a big automatic in his left hand. No fat on the guy at all. Had his hair cut the way the kids were wearing it, long enough to cover his ears, and curly.

Silvano pointed the .38 at the guy's head. "I don't think your friend is gonna make it," he said. The guy froze. "You might not either, you don't do exactly what I tell you."

The guy turned his head slightly in Silvano's direction.

"No you don't," Silvano told him. "Put it down, put it down or I'll shoot you right in the fucking head. Safety on, please. Oh, nice. Now kick it down the stairs."

The guy did as he was told. This guy's so mad he can barely breathe, Silvano thought. "Okay, turn and face the wall. Verrry nice. Down on your knees, hands up behind your head. Nice, nice. Now I'm gonna come and pat you down, don't do anything to make me nervous."

The guy had a straight razor in his back pocket and an ice pick in the inside pocket of his suit jacket. Silvano screwed the muzzle of his pistol into the guy's ear while he retrieved them. "For me? Man, I love a guy believes in traditions. Do things like your grandfather did." He tossed them both down the stairs after the pistol, and he got the guy's wallet next. He stepped back with it, flipped it open, looked at the name on the credit cards inside.

"Ivan Bonifacio," he read. "Bet I know what they called you in school."

"Not more than once," Ivan said.

Guy is still steaming, Silvano could hear it in his voice, but he was under control. Unafraid. "Well, kids can be cruel. Turn around, Ivan, okay, sit down now, back against the wall, feet straight out in front. Sit on your hands, Ivan. Verry good. Now tell me who the fuck you are."

Ivan sat on his hands and stared balefully.

Silvano shrugged. "I didn't mean to do your pal over there, it was just bad luck. You know I got squeamish since the Army. I don't like to hurt anybody, not really. But since the guy's dead, already, what's one more? I mean, what the fuck? Right?"

"Little Dom sent me."

"Little Dom, that what they're calling him now? Back in school we used to call him Dumbenick. Carried books home from school every night. What are we gonna do about this, Ivan?"

"You got the gun."

"Yeah, I do. This is embarrassing, though, Ivan. I feel like I been assaulted by Huey, Dewey, and Louie. You the best he's got?"

"I might be," Ivan said softly.

Silvano shook his head. "All right. Back on your knees. Turn and face the wall again. Up close, Ivan, so you can kiss it. Good. You do me a favor, Ivan. You tell Domenic I'm in town on business. Tell him I'm gonna do what I came here to do, and then I'm gonna go away and leave him alone. Tell him I'm not worth the trouble."

"No trouble," Ivan was saying, but Silvano leaned forward and hammered him in the temple with the butt of the pistol. Ivan's head bounced off the concrete and he slumped to the floor.

• • •

THE CABDRIVER DIDN'T want to pick her up. "You got to look close," he said, "don't let that hair fool you, she be livin' on the street. You don't want her."

"Be nice," Silvano told him. "She just saved my ass."

"Your life," the guy said, but he pulled the yellow Checker cab over to the curb.

She seemed to sense the change in him, he saw her notice the slight tremble in his hands from the ebbing adrenaline, and the way his anger put a twist in his face. She handed him six dirty and wrinkled one-dollar bills. "Change," she said.

"I don't want . . ."

"Keep it!"

"All right, all right." He started to fold the bills, but then he noticed the names written on each one, up over George's head, Michelle, Tommy, and Heather, and down at one end, "Mommy loves you," and a few hearts. He wanted to ask her about it, found that he could not. Everybody got their own troubles, he thought. You don't want mine, I sure as shit don't want yours. Jesus. He folded the bills up and stuck them in his pocket.

She sat in the far corner of the backseat and directed the driver down past Black and White and then south where the waterfront curves past Buttermilk Channel, which runs between the land mass and Governors Island just offshore, and into Red Hook, a small neighborhood of high-rise projects and warehouses isolated by the BQE and by the Gowanus Canal, a stinking finger of motionless fluid distantly related to water that pokes two dozen blocks north and east up into the industrial entrails of Brooklyn. Life hangs on grimly, Silvano thought, looking out the window at the people who lived there, it sinks its claws into the most unlikely and inhospitable places, survival is its sole and intractable aim.

The cab pulled over at the corner of Van Brunt Street and Visitation Place. He looked at the street sign, looked at the grim and graffitied concrete warehouses, looked at the projects a few blocks away that went by the name of the Red Hook Houses. Not an actual fucking house anywhere in sight, he told himself. What kind of visitation could you expect around here? Jesus.

Silvano handed the cabdriver a twenty. "Don't go anywhere," he told the guy. "I'll give you another one of these to take her back."

The driver looked around. "You got ten minutes."

Mrs. Clark was looking upward, her mouth agape. "Wow," she said. "Henry's gone higher. He's moved outside."

Silvano followed her gaze with his eyes. The brick and concrete building she was looking up at was three stories high, industrial gray with blue from an earlier, more optimistic time showing through in spots. The windows were painted, too, the same gray as the rest of it, and they were covered by wrought-iron gates. There was an improbable metal and glass bubble growing up out of the roof, half dome and half sculpture, architecture in found objects, a crazy, avant-garde, postmodern Noah's Ark in mixed media, come to rest on a factory roof. Silvano shook his head. Noah on acid. "What is this," he asked her, "Mickey's castle? Mad Ludwig's revenge?"

She tilted her head down to look at him, her mouth still open. She snapped it shut, shrugged her shoulders. "Henry's an artist," she said. "He's a little bit, what you call, peculiar."

"Oh, great," Silvano said. "You think this guy's peculiar? That's a hell of a distinction."

"No need to get snippy," she said. "Truth be told, you're a little peculiar yourself. I told you, he's an artist, artists can be funny. Let's go inside." She headed for the end of the building and ducked through a hole in the chain-link fence into an empty lot overgrown with sumacs. Silvano followed her, stopped when he heard the low growl.

She ignored it. "Get over here," she commanded, and a large, fat, hairy dog the color of dirt came waddling out of the weeds, ducking his head and waving the half tail he had left. "The hell are you doing," she said to the dog, leaning over to pat his ugly head, "growling at me? You forget me already, you ungrateful mutt?" She reached into one of her pockets, pulled out a few stale french fries. She tossed them to the dog, one at a time. The dog's jaws made an audible snap as he caught each one. She turned and gave the last couple to Silvano. "Let him take them from your hand," she said. "Let him smell you."

Silvano stepped forward and did as he was told.

"Don't you bite him," she said to the dog. "He's one of us." She looked at Silvano and snickered. "You are, you know."

"Terrific."

Half hidden in the bushes was a metal door. Mrs. Clark jabbed a button set into the concrete wall next to the door, and Silvano could hear a bell ringing somewhere inside the building. Without waiting for an answer, she yanked the door open. "C'mon," she said, and she stepped into the inky blackness.

"Henry!"

A moment later, the lights came on, and Silvano saw that they were in a stairwell. Paint was peeling from the walls in dollar-bill-sized sheets. There was an empty shopping cart in one corner. A door opened up higher. "Hello?"

"Hi, Henry, it's me, Blanche."

"Blanche?" Henry and Silvano both said it at the same time.

• • •

"LAST YEAR," Henry told her. "I started building the atrium last year, because the roof was leaking." He was the red-faced old guy, looked to be maybe seventy-five, had a long white braid hanging down his back. He was the same guy Silvano had seen stealing the radiator out of the abandoned car on the sidewalk outside Black and White the day before.

Blanche (Silvano couldn't help thinking of her as Mrs. Clark) looked at him in disbelief. "Since when did you start caring about things like roof leaks?"

Silvano was sitting on an old sofa. It was in the center of what had once been an open and empty factory floor, but was now a warren of passageways, closets, storage areas filled with Henry's gleanings, cubicles that served various functions, such as a sitting room, a kitchen, library, as well as work areas and rooms whose purpose Silvano could not quite fathom. "How the hell do you find the bathroom in this place?"

Henry answered Blanche's question first.

"Well, I wouldn't care if the leak was next to the wall, because nothing serious gets wet," he said. "But it started leaking right in the middle, right on all my stuff. Right on my living arrangement, so I had to do something about it. When I went up on the roof to look, I found a real mess. It's a flat roof, wasn't nothing but layers of tarpaper and asphalt, covered all over with little rocks. When I scraped that away, I found the concrete underneath all rotted. Water must've been getting in there for years, freezing and melting, over and over. I cut a big section of it out, I was just gonna cover over the hole, make a wooden deck or something, but what happened was the weather happened to be real nice and the sun was coming in, and it gave me the idea for my solar heating system."

Silvano looked up into the floorless glass cube over his head.

From the street it had reminded him of Noah's Ark, but from underneath it looked like a junkyard in space. Rows of automobile radiators were suspended in the air in front of a wall of glass. They were interconnected with a snarl of rubber tubing that snaked around them all over to a large rectangular rust-colored tank hanging from a pair of chain hoists.

"Bathroom's easy to find," Henry said to Silvano. "Blue arrows painted on the floor. From anywhere in here, find a blue arrow and follow it to the bathroom. Blue is for the bathroom, brown is for the sitting room, green . . . I forget what green is for. But it's all very logical."

"Okay," Silvano said mildly. Another one, he told himself silently, another crazy person, this one's like a psychotic beaver, started out building a dam and wound up with his own theme park. Whackoland.

"What color arrows get me the hell out of here?" Blanche asked. "I've gotta get back, somebody's waiting for me." She winked at Silvano.

"What color for exit," Henry said, scratching his chin. "What color . . . Oh, red. Follow the red arrows. Here, I'll walk you down. Be right back," he said to Silvano.

"Okay," Silvano said. "Thank you, Blanche."

"See ya. Keep the hat."

SILVANO WAS STANDING UP, looking at the rows of radiators suspended over his head when Henry came back. Silvano glanced at him.

Henry laughed. "Don't matter if it looks crazy," he said. "Only thing that matters is, does it work."

"So? Does it work?"

"Not yet, I ain't done with it yet. No reason why it shouldn't, though. We got the sun shining in on our heat exchanger, there . . ."

"Heat exchanger?"

"Well, ain't that what a radiator is? You got cold water in that tank, see, and you got your tank hanging up higher than the heat exchanger, and cold water feeds down into your heat exchanger, where the sun warms it up."

"Okay."

"All right, now cold water is heavier than warm, so cold water from the tank displaces the warm, pushes it back up into the tank. You got natural convection to circulate it for you. Then at night, okay, you gotta do two things. You gotta close your blinds right inside the windows, they're insulated to keep down your losses, okay, and you gotta drop your tank down so it's lower than your heat exchanger. Then you turn on your ceiling fans, the moving air cools off the water in your heat exchanger, and it drops back down into your tank, and convection works for you again, the other way around."

"Sounds like a pain in the ass, you don't mind my saying. Open this, close that, raise the tank up in the air . . ."

Henry dismissed those details with a wave of his hand. "Oh," he said, "in the final version that'll all be automated. You wouldn't have to do nothing different than you do now. Set the thermostat and walk away. This'n here's just a pilot model."

"Pilot model."

"Yep."

"Suppose it works, then what?"

"Then you file for your patents. You can't patent water and old radiators, but there's a few gizmos you gotta have for this to work, water valves and sensors and so on. I patent the gizmos, then I sell the patents."

"You've done this before?"

"Of course. I'm an inventor, that's what I've always done."

"No kidding. What else have you invented?"

"Well," Henry said, "my best one was about twelve years back. It's a machine that sorts rubbish. What it does, it takes normal household rubbish and pulverizes it, okay, busts it into more or less bite-size pieces, then it feeds the pieces into a stream of air inside a tube. Different materials behave differently when they're in an air stream, so it's just a matter of mechanics after that. Paper goes one way, metal another, plastic, wood, and so on. Couldn't sort everything, only about seventy percent. Cuts way down on what you gotta dump in a landfill, though."

"No shit! Did it work?"

"Of course it worked." Henry looked insulted. "Sold it to NASA. I don't know what they're doing with it. I suppose I don't care, I got the money. Bought me this building, and I'm still paying the bills with what's left."

"I'll be damned. So how many patents have you gotten?"

"Fifty-eight. Made money on about half of them."

"You make your living this way?"

"Mostly. I got back home from the war, I had a hell of a time keeping a job, I had to find something to do. I guess that's what started it. First World War. The Great War, they called it. The war to end all wars."

"How long were you in?"

Henry looked off into space. "Four years and a bit. I was in the Canadian Army. Four years in the mud."

"At least you made it back."

"Yeah, I was one of the lucky ones, though there was times when I had my doubts. Time I got back, women had the vote and you couldn't buy a drink. And I needed one bad. Between the sweats, the shakes, the nightmares, seeing things that weren't there, I'll tell you, the last thing I needed was temperance."

"How long did it take for them to go away? The sweats and all that."

Henry looked at Silvano, squinted at his face. He took his time thinking about the question. "Viet Nam?" he said.

"Well, yeah."

"I probably shouldn't say anything. All I know is what happened to me. Common mistake, you know, making universal generalizations based on a sample of one."

"Oh, come on. Why the hell not? How long did it take for you to get, you know, back to regular again?"

Henry sighed. "Well, everyone's different. The first few years were pretty bad." He peered at Silvano, examining his face. "I'm gonna make some coffee," he said, turning his back abruptly. "You want?"

"Yeah, sure." Silvano followed him down a corridor to the kitchen area. Leave him be, he told himself. He'll tell you the story when he's ready. He watched Henry busy himself with water and a stainless coffeemaker. He had the two sections of his coffeemaker put together and he stuck the pot on the stove and lit the gas underneath with a match. "All right," he said, looking at the pot, not at Silvano. "I'll tell you a story. I was out on a patrol," he said, "toward the end of the war. It was summer, everything was wet and moldy. My boots had rotted right off my feet, you know, and you couldn't get new ones, not for love nor money. My feet weren't in great shape, either." He sighed. "Nighttime patrol. Six guys, up out of the trench, out into no man's land. It was a pointless exercise, but I was beyond asking questions by then. Anyhow, we crawl past a dead fella, he's still got on his boots, better than mine. German. I'm the last in line, and I stop for his boots, I'm talking to the guy like he can hear me, I'm whispering low, telling him I'm sorry for taking his boots, sorry he's dead and got no more use for them. I'm talking mostly to keep my mind off the smell. The five guys I'm with, they get a little ways up ahead of me, all of a sudden the mortars start coming in heavy." He stopped, leaned down and adjusted the flame under his pot. Silvano could hear how the pace of his breathing had picked up as he relived his story.

"I was startled, you know, and I flopped down quick." He stopped again, shaking his head. "My left hand went right down into the German's chest. I laid there right next to him, him dead and me wishing I was, mortars kept it up, crump, crump, crump. They left off, finally, and I got away from there. I went forward, up to where my patrol was, where I should have been. They were all dead, all five of them. I would have been, too." He looked into the top chamber of his coffeepot, awash now with water and coffee grounds.

"I went right back past the guy, on the way back. You couldn't really see his face, it was mostly teeth and skin hanging loose, like on a piece of boiled chicken. Saw the hole in him where my hand went in." He sighed again, turned off the flame under the pot. "I wondered, you know, if that's all the guy was there for, you know, just to hold me up for that few minutes. But that didn't make any sense to me. Nothing did."

"Anyhow. After the war was over, they kept me in another year, almost. I was okay, I thought, until I got home. Then I started seeing that guy's face. Every night, soon as I went to sleep, I'd hear those mortars going off, and I was right back there, right next to him, my hand in his chest, my face right up next to his, and my nose full of that smell. Jesus. I'd wake up on the floor all covered with sweat, trying to run. Scaring the hell out of my poor wife. For a long time, it got worse instead of better. It changed me, it made me ugly. Made me act mean, drink too much."

"Thought you said you couldn't get a drink."

"Not legal. Booze ain't hard to make, all's you need is sugar, water, and yeast. Mix 'em together, give her a little time. Then you just boil off your alcohol, put it through a heat exchanger."

"Another radiator, huh?"

"Nah, you can't use radiators for that, alcohol will leach the lead out of 'em. Plus, you got to be real careful when you're boiling it off. It's about like boiling gasoline on your stove. Safer to make applejack, easier, too. Take a jug of cider, let her sit until she turns, right, then just put her in the freezer. Overnight she'll turn into slush, because what's water freezes, what's alcohol don't. Just pour your slush through a strainer, and there you are. Stuff will give you a hell of a hangover, though." He separated the two halves of the coffeemaker. "You take something in yours?"

"Black is good."

Henry went looking for cups. "Took a while, but I quit making moonshine, and I made my peace with Klaus."

"Klaus?"

He smiled ruefully. "The German. I don't know why it was him I got stuck on, there was worse things than that. But one night I gave him a name, gave up trying to forget him. Thanked him for saving my ass, told him I'd remember him as long as I lived, that I'd keep him alive in my mind because he'd kept me alive. I don't know what his real name was, of course. Don't know if he had any people, or if they ever found out what happened to him. Don't know if anyone but me remembers him now at all. After I did that, though, after I talked to him a little bit, you know, the dreams weren't quite as bad, and the rest of it started to go away. Not all at once, you understand." He looked at Silvano, as if trying to gauge his strength. "Took about fifteen years," he said, finally, "after I made my peace, before I really felt right again, before the sweats and all that finally went away, but that's when it turned around. I can't tell you how to do that, you have to figure that out yourself. Meantime, try not to do any more damage than you have to." Henry looked into the depths of his coffee cup. "Blanche tell you what a windy old coot I was?"

"No," Silvano said. "Thank you for your story."

"You ever find that guy you were looking for?"

Silvano had been adrift, mentally, listening with half an ear. "Did I ever what? Oh, Noonie. Nunzio, my brother. No, I didn't find him. He worked at that place, though, Black and White, that place where you were liberating part of your heat exchanger. I got lucky and got hired on by one of the construction foremen working on their new building. I figure, I hang around there long enough, I might get a lead on what happened to him."

"You didn't tell me he was your brother. And what do you mean, 'find out what happened to him'? You think he met up with some trouble?"

"Yeah. Yeah, I do." He sighed. "I guess it's only fair that I should try to explain, so you should know what's going on, if I'm going to be camping out here for a while."

"Blanche told me what happened."

"Well, then, you got an idea who's looking for me."

Henry put a finger on the end of his nose and pushed it over sideways. "The deviated septum crowd."

"That's them. I'll leave in the morning if you think they'll cause you problems."

"We'll wait and see," Henry said. "No real reason to think they should come looking down here. Besides, this place ain't so easy to get into. Or out of."

"Door was open, downstairs."

"Yeah, but Blanche knows the dog, and the dog knows her. Otherwise, you'd have never gotten to the door."

"Suppose I shot the dog?"

Henry had a sly look on his face. "Okay, fine. But there's two of them, and you never even saw the other one, did you?"

"Oh, shit." Silvano shook his head. "No, I didn't."

"Plus, I do lock up most times. And in the morning, we'll have to go over a few procedures so you don't trip any of my security systems while you're staying here."

"Security? What security?"

Henry grinned. "I'm an inventor, remember? They might be unusual, but they are effective. Tell me about your brother."

"Yeah, okay." Silvano rubbed his face with both hands. "Noonie was like Blanche, except he was crazier than her," he said, starting in. "Cleaner, but crazier. He had a good heart, but he had too much energy, he couldn't sit still, and he didn't have any of those social filters that most people use to keep themselves out of trouble. You know what I mean? Like, he was smart enough, in some ways, but if he had a thought in his head, it came rolling right out of his mouth. No filter, nothing to make him pause and think before he said something. Same with other things. He got an itch, he hadda scratch, right then and there. If he got the urge to, I don't know, go swimming in the river, for example, he's going. He had that thought in his head, there was no room for anything else. Nothing to tell him, hey, the water's dirty, or it's cold, or it's deep, or his mother would be pissed, nothing like that."

"He must have been a joy to grow up with."

"Oh, man. I spent half my time fighting with kids wanted to kick his ass, and the other half kicking his ass myself, trying to get him off the next crazy shit he had in his head. Anyway, my old man put him in a hospital when he was twelve, because he'd gotten to be too much to handle. That's the first part of the story."

"Okay."

"Second part. My old man was a bookie. Mostly. He did a little bit of shylocking, but he didn't like it as much, in those days he did mostly the horses, college sports, some high school, even. Said it was more civilized. But he was not a good guy. Nice enough to talk to and all that, friendly, everybody liked to drink with him, but if my mother's father, Domenic, told him to put you in a oil drum fulla concrete, my old man didn't ask a lot of questions, and you got disappeared. Know what I mean?"

"I get the picture."

"Okay. So, not too long after they put my brother away, I got thrown out of high school for like the third time, and I wound up joining the Army." He looked over at Henry. "I'm skipping over a lot, here."

"All right by me. Tell the parts you want to tell."

"All right. My mother's father was the guy that was really mobbed up, my father just sort of worked through him. That's the way it worked, back in those days. My grandfather's name was Domenic Scalia, he's dead now and ain't nobody crying over it. His grandson, my cousin, same name, is the guy who's after me now. Little Dom, they call him. He and I had what you might call a falling out. Years ago, before I went in the service. Those were his guys in the hotel."

"That had to be, what, ten years ago? What'd you do to him?"

"That's another long story."

"All right. So I understand this right, you want to find out what happened to your brother before these guys find you. Again. Is that it?"

"Some plan, huh?" He shook his head again. "Maybe I

should just grab one of those two assholes down at Black and White and bounce them up and down, see what comes out."

Now Henry was shaking his head. "That won't do you any good," he said. "You have to take this in logical order. They eat a lot of rabbit, over in France. Did you know that?"

Silvano was mystified by the sudden leap. "No."

"Yeah, lotta rabbit. They got a recipe for rabbit stew, okay, line one of the recipe says, 'First, catch one rabbit.' They don't assume anything, you see what I mean?"

"Yeah. Yeah, I get it."

"You want to do this right, you got to catch the rabbit, first. You ain't got the rabbit, you're nowhere."

HE WENT TO BED thinking of the old man's story, the bad-smelling German and mortar fire, and the later part of it, too, Henry coming home, growing slowly back into a human being. It was a small comfort to know that other men and other generations had been through it, too, that he wasn't the first guy. The dream was worse, though, after he fell asleep, it was the same one, the PBR barreling up the river with him sitting alone on the stern because the guys on the boat never wanted to talk to you. He counted the islands as they roared past, gripping the M-16 with both hands. When they came to the final island, the boat dropped him off. He had barely hit the water when the boat started taking fire, and she reversed engines, clawing her way back out into the channel, opening up with everything she had, tracers arcing into the brush over his head. He came to on the floor, like always, scrambling for cover, heart pounding, ears ringing from phantom gunfire.

FOUR

■

HENRY WAS UP EARLY, impatient to be gone. Silvano listened groggily as Henry showed him his security systems. "You might feed the dogs," Henry told him. "I gotta be going. Besides, it might make them like you a little."

"Yeah, sure," Silvano told him, and Henry left him standing there with a big bag of dry dog food in his hands.

He went without shaving, and he wore Blanche's hat, a stained T-shirt, and a ratty pair of jeans. Two blocks up on Van Brunt, he happened across a car service running out of an old storefront. The guy behind the desk inside eyed him doubtfully. "I need a ride," Silvano told him. "Up to the Heights."

The man rubbed his mustache. "Eight dollar," he said, making no move to pick up his radio.

Silvano watched him, wondering what the guy was waiting for. "Yeah, so?"

The guy rubbed his thumb together with his first two fingers. "Eight dollar," he said again.

Oh, yeah, Silvano realized, I forgot, I'm a bum. "I got the money," he said, and he took a ten out of his wallet.

"Okay," the guy said, reaching for the radio. "You wait outside."

"All right. You got a card? I might need you to come get me, later."

SILVANO LIMPED DOWN Middagh Street, carrying his shopping bag. To his surprise, he found that the disguise liberated him somewhat from his eternal hypervigilance and the need to stop and scope out the street every hundred yards or so became less oppressive. He was getting into it, he imagined himself living on the street with nothing, no home, no family, no job, and no prospects, nothing beyond what to eat next, where to get enough money for the next bottle. Yeah, he thought, and die alone, no one to give a damn who you were or what you did. There was nobody in Special Ed's alley, but he ran into a prosperous-looking fat guy on his way back out. The guy gave him a look and passed him by, then apparently thought better of it.

"You looking for Ed?"

"Yeah."

The guy shook his head. "He was supposed to take out the trash for me yesterday and he didn't do it. That's not like him. I'm a little worried."

"You think something happened?"

"I don't know." The guy hesitated, then went on. "A couple of men stopped in to see him the other day. I happened to be upstairs by my back window, watching, and it looked to me like they were giving him a hard time. I didn't know if I should call the police or what, but Ed gets so upset when anyone tries to help him, he's always accusing me of meddling in his business."

The guy shook his head. "Poor bastard. I hope he's all right."

"Yeah, me too. Maybe I should go look for him."

"You know where he goes, during the day?"

"I got an idea."

"You know, that would be great if you could find him. I can't be here Monday to take out the trash, and I hate to miss it twice running." The guy fished around in his pants pocket, came out with a roll of bills, peeled off a one and handed it to Silvano. "Buy him a beer, if you see him, tell him I need him back on Monday."

"Okay," Silvano said, looking at the dollar bill. "God bless you, sir."

"Yeah, yeah," the guy said, walking away. "Don't forget to tell him about Monday."

There was a car service guy parked out in front of the Castle Arms with his motor running. Silvano walked up to the driver's window and showed him a twenty. The driver rolled down the window, looked at him suspiciously.

"What you wan'?"

"I need a half hour," Silvano told him. "I need you to drive me around, over on the other side of the Manhattan Bridge. I'm looking for a guy, and I don't think I can find him on foot."

The driver snatched the bill out of his hand. "All right, maricon," he said, growling, "but you don't gonna get sick in my car. You unnerstan'? You trow up in my backseat, I kick your fokking ess."

Silvano had to smile. "Sure you will. Let's go."

The guy gave him more than a half hour, it was closer to an hour later when they were back in front of the Castle Arms. "Sorry for your fren'," the driver said. "Maybe he sick, maybe he stay home."

"Yeah, maybe." Silvano tipped the guy a five. "Thanks."

• • •

"HEY, CUTIE! HEY!"

Elia had just come out of the grocery store. She turned, looking for the speaker, who was standing a few feet up the sidewalk. He was a vagrant, bent over, carrying a brown paper shopping bag. He was wearing a stained brown canvas jacket and shoes with no laces, toes leaking out through a split along the side. Why do they all have to do this? she wondered, shaking her head. The guy was making kissey noises now. She could hardly see his face behind the long matted yellow hair and the hat he had pulled down across his eyes. Why me? she thought. What am I, some kind of magnet for these jerks?

"Get lost, creep." She turned and walked away.

The bum convulsed with strangled laughter, wheezing and slapping the leg of his jeans with his free hand. "Wait for me, sugar," he said, limping after her.

She turned and walked backward, eyeing him. There was something familiar about the guy, but she couldn't put her finger on it. Can't blame him for trying, she thought, but she gave him the finger anyway. He broke up again, slapping his leg and croaking his strange laugh.

The city's full of them, she thought, shaking her head, turning front and walking swiftly down the sidewalk. Just a thrill a minute. Why does it have to be? she wondered; I meet a doctor or a stockbroker and he runs away like a scared rabbit, but every fucked-up guy within a hundred yards thinks I'm Miss January. She glanced back over her shoulder to see if he was still following, but he was nowhere in sight.

Men.

How is it, she asked herself silently, they can go directly from extended adolescence into old fogeydom without ever passing through adulthood? And yet, every single one of them was more than ready to tell you how to live your life, where you should go, what you should do. It was the same old story, as far back as she could remember. Her parents had not been young when they'd moved from Turkey to the United States, and her father, in particular, had never really understood that a woman could be a real person, as real and as independent as any man. Her mother had continued to live according to the patterns of the life she'd known in the old country. If she'd had any opinions, she'd kept them to herself.

Ah, so what, she thought. So you had to stand up for yourself. Who hasn't? And so your parents weren't much help, so you have to work during the day and go to school at night. They got you here, didn't they?

She turned off Smith Street onto her block, and he was waiting there, in fact he was sitting on her stoop, that wino in the brown jacket, the one from outside the store. In a fraction of a second she was pissed, balling her fists, clenching her teeth. If this guy thought for one second she wouldn't clean his clock . . .

"How'd you get here ahead of me?" she demanded angrily. "Who the hell are you?" And how did you know I live here? she added silently, with a twitch, a tiny shiver at the back of her neck.

"Don't hurt me, okay?" The guy spoke in a different voice than the one he'd used before, and she stopped, her heart racing, but then the guy reached up and grabbed his hat, wadding the crown up in his fist, and when he took it off the hair underneath came off with it.

"Silvano! You asshole! Are you trying to scare me to death?"

He held the wig in his lap, stroking it like it was his pet rat. "Sorry," he said. "I didn't mean to scare you. I just wanted to find out if this little getup here was gonna work."

"Whew," she said, still recovering. "Well, it worked on me. I was about ready to pull this pistol out of my bag and put a couple rounds into your skull."

"Damn," he said. "You really have a pistol in there?"

"Wouldn't you like to know? What the hell are you doing, anyway?"

"It's a long story," he said.

She looked at her watch. "I got time."

SHE LIVED IN A STUDIO on the top floor in the back. "This is the same color as my room at the Montague," he told her.

"They must've had a sale on it, forty, fifty years ago when they painted last," she said. "Have a seat." She went into her phone-booth-sized kitchen. "Don't go getting the wrong idea. I only asked you up so I wouldn't be seen talking to some wino. I don't want my neighbors thinking I'm that desperate." There was part of a bottle of Portuguese rosé screw-top in her fridge. She fished it out and poured two of her four glass tumblers half full.

When she turned around he was sitting cross-legged on one of the pillows she had strewn around on the oriental rug, and he was looking at the travel posters of the Mediterranean she'd tacked up on the walls. Well, it's the pillows, the floor, or the daybed, she thought, there ain't no chairs. She hadn't thought of that in a while, she couldn't remember the last time she'd had someone come up. He didn't seem to mind.

"I'm disappointed," he said, accepting the glass. "I just naturally figured it was because of my roguish charm."

"Yeah, sure." She sat on the floor across from him and leaned back against the bed. "So what's with the wig and all that?" She was eyeing the shopping bag suspiciously. He sighed. She watched him thinking it over.

"We can get to that in a minute." He pulled a picture out of his pocket and handed it to her. "You recognize this guy?"

"Noonie," she said, looking at the picture. "You a cop? You with those guys doing surveillance?"

"Surveillance? What guys?"

"No," she said, angry, shaking her head. "You first. Who the fuck are you? Is your name really Silvano? God, I hate men, you're all such liars. What about that story you told me, was that all bullshit after all? What's your real name? Let's start with an easy one."

He looked at his hands folded in his lap. "Silvano Iurata," he said. "That's my real name. I am not a policeman of any kind. Noonie was my brother."

"How could you be related to Noonie? He always told the truth."

"Yeah, he had a lot of problems like that." He looked up at her. "Elia, I think somebody killed him. Never once that I know of did he ever mean anyone harm, but he did something or he saw something or he knew something, and somebody killed him for it. I would really like to know who it was."

"Oh, God," she said, her anger bleeding away. "I'm sorry. We never found out what happened to him. I just thought . . . I figured he moved away, or something. He was your brother? I'm sorry."

He sighed. "Yeah, me too. You never heard anything about him, after he disappeared? Nobody said anything about him?"

"Well, not really. One day he just stopped coming around. For weeks after that, we all walked around with one eye open for him, but he never came back. He and Sean had been just about joined at the hip, they used to go everywhere together. Even Mr. O'Brian kind of liked him. He would take him along, sometimes, when he went off on his little projects. Everyone was so sad he was gone. I can't imagine anyone wanting to hurt him."

It was the same thing he got from everyone. "Why would cops be watching Black and White?"

She shrugged. "I doubt if it means much of anything. In that kind of business, someone's always checking up on you. It's not that unusual. They're not exactly subtle. If you hang around for about an hour after quitting time you'll see them. As a matter of fact, they're sort of hard to miss. Bunch of white guys, short short hair, suits, white shirts, ties, look like they never go out in the sun. They all pile into your basic, government-issue unmarked sedan and go home."

"Anybody else notice them?"

"Nobody said anything to me."

"How about that." He looked at her with new respect. "How come you picked up on it?"

She glared at him. "Girl's got to look out for herself. I can't see any connection between them and your brother. I can't picture either of the O'Brians doing anything to Noonie, either. Sean is too dopey to get away with much, and his uncle is too religious."

"The physical man and the spiritual man."

"You're mocking them both."

"You're right. I'm sorry."

"You told me before, spiritual didn't mean what I thought it did."

"So I did." He sighed. "Okay. Two monks. Happen to be Zen monks, but it don't matter, a monk's a monk, I figure. Anyway, one of them was very holy. Verrry holy." He shook his head. "You know the kind. Story says, guy is so spiritual, everywhere he goes, the birds stop what they're doing and start bringing him flowers. You get it?"

"Yes."

"Okay. The other monk is just a regular guy. Nothing special. So anyway, the two of them, they're on a little trip, they have to go from one monastery to another, they got to walk through the jungle to get there. Jungle's got tigers in it, okay? Sometimes a tiger will make a sort of coughing noise, like this." He demonstrated.

"You ever hear one of them do that?"

"Yeah."

"What's it mean?"

"Who knows. I figured it was the tiger's way of saying, 'I know you're there, sucka.' So anyway, they're traveling through the jungle, they hear a tiger do that, right next to the trail. The ordinary monk, he's up in front, and he flinches. He's afraid, right? And in Buddhism, you're not supposed to be worried about it. No attachments."

"Okay."

"All right, so the holy monk, Mr. Spirituality, he says to the first guy, 'Oh, I see you're still suffering.'"

"Oh," she said. "You mean, like, 'You aren't holy like me.'"

"Exactly. Story doesn't say what the first guy thinks of all this, but you can imagine. Anyhow, they keep going, after a while they stop to take a rest, they find two rocks to sit down on. After a few minutes, Mr. Spirituality has to take a leak, right, he goes off to find a tree. The other guy, he's sitting there, he takes a piece of chalk out of his pocket, right, he draws the symbol for the Buddha on the rock the other guy was sitting on. Few minutes later, the other guy comes back, goes to sit down, he's got his butt cheeks like six inches from the rock, he sees what's written there, he flinches. The first guy is watching him, right, he says to the guy, 'Oh, I see you are still suffering.' Story says, when His Holiness hears that, he becomes enlightened. Spiritual for real, not for show. And after that, the birds never bring him flowers again."

"And that means . . ."

"Story doesn't say. I figure it means that you can't see spirituality from across the room. Not when it's real. And maybe it's just me, maybe I'm reading into it, but I figure they're also saying all this other stuff, you know, buildings and statues and priests and all that, it's all format. Don't get hung up on it."

"I have to think about that one. What about the rest of that story you told me? Viet Nam, Japan, boxing, all of that? Was that real?"

"It was real, all right."

"Well, listen, I'm really sorry about Noonie. I know it's hard, not knowing. But you can't do anything for your brother now. Wouldn't you be better off just going someplace new and starting over?"

"Tried that. Kept feeling like I had unfinished business."

"This sounds very much like what happened to my father." He sat watching her, silent. "His people were farmers in eastern Turkey. He was a schoolteacher, the first educated man in the family. He had four brothers. One day when he and my mother were away, partisans massacred them all, brothers, their wives, children, his parents, all of them. He had to decide what was more important, stay and fight, or go someplace and have a life. My mother was pregnant with my older sister, maybe that made it easier for him, but he came here, to the United States, where he didn't speak the language, where his degree and his skills were no good, where he didn't know a soul, and he started all over again. I never even knew about all this until after he died, and my mother told me about it."

"I don't know if I could do that."

"Maybe he decided to be a schoolteacher, not a soldier," she said.

He shook his head. "You don't always get to choose. Some parts of the world, everyone's a soldier. Everyone has a gun, and they all know how to shoot. I bet one of the guys on the other side was a teacher himself. One of the partisans."

"It's too bad guns were ever invented."

"Doesn't matter," he said. "It's inside us. We didn't have guns, we'd kill each other with rocks. Baboons do the same thing, did you know that? They live in family groups. Tribes. Chimpanzees, too. They mark their territories, right, this is ours, stay out. If they catch another tribe trespassing, they go to war. We're no different. Take away my gun, I'll hit you with a brick."

"You know," she said, grinning, "I had you figured for that kind of guy."

He looked sheepish. "I didn't mean you, personally. I'd be afraid to hit you, you look like the type that hits back."

"Don't you forget it, either. So what happens now, Silvano? Why are you going around dressed like a wino? I'm not talking to you in public when you're dressed like that."

"That's another long story. If you wanna hear it, I'll change into my other getup so you won't be ashamed to take a walk with me. My butt's falling asleep."

"All right," she said. "I'll go wait by the door." She got to her feet, not as smoothly as she would have liked, and she noticed that he'd been sitting in half-lotus the whole time. He uncoiled and stood up, started fishing around in the bag. She walked down the hallway to wait by her front door. Elia, she asked herself, are you nuts? Don't you have enough insanity in your life yet? What do you want with some semi-suicidal ex-soldier head case? You should let him go, you should just open your hand and let him fly away. I'll do it, she told herself, even though she knew it was a lie. He was like a puppy, you know he's gonna pee on your rug but you keep him anyway, because you can't bring yourself to take him to the shelter. All right, she told herself. Just be careful. Be careful how close you let him get.

"Come on back," he said.

She walked back down the hallway. "Wow," she said. He was wearing the same jeans, but everything else was different. The ratty shoes were gone, replaced with white socks and sneakers, instead of the brown coat, he wore a gray Police Athletic League sweatshirt with the hood pulled up over a baseball cap, with oversized shades covering half his face.

"What do you think?"

"Well, I already knew it was you," she said, "but if I hadn't, I probably wouldn't have looked at you twice. You look like you're just another over-the-hill jock on his way to a basketball game."

"Oh, thanks," he said, wounded. "What do you mean, over the hill?"

"You had all this in that paper bag?"

"Yeah. Now all the other stuff is inside the gym bag. Including the paper bag. I can go from one to the other in about three minutes."

"All right," she said, "let's go. And you're gonna tell me the rest of the story, right? No bullshit this time?"

"Absolutely," he said. "I promise."

THEY GOT OFF THE TRAIN and emerged out onto the street on the southern tip of Manhattan. "Staten Island Ferry," he said, reading the sign. "That where we're going?"

"Cheapest date in New York," she said, and winked at him. "You got a dime?" He followed her through the terminal and onto the dingy orange ferryboat, then up the stairs, all the way to the other end of the boat and then downstairs again, outside on the stern, just above where the propellers were churning the dirty water, keeping the boat nose-in against the dock. "When I was a little girl," she told him, "my father used to love to bring me here." She felt herself getting a little misty and she turned away from him, faced into the breeze, felt its fingers brush softly past her face and through her hair. "He came from the mountains, there was nothing like this where he grew up. No city, no buildings, not like these, no rivers like this one. He never got tired of riding on this boat." She smiled sadly, but she was back in control. "Poor man's cruise ship. Have you been here before?"

"Nope." She watched him put a hand on the rail as the deck shuddered beneath them and the ferry began backing out of the slip. "Born and raised in Brooklyn, never rode the ferry. Never been to the statue, never went to the Empire State Building or Radio City or any of that."

"Oh," she said. "Oh, that's criminal. Why not?"

The boat nosed into the current and began picking up speed. She moved closer to him, took his elbow for support. "My father was a gangster." He took her hand in his. "Still is, I expect. My mother died when I was six. After she died it was like growing up in a morgue. Even after he got a new wife, even after Noonie and my sister came along, it always felt like my father and his whole crowd were just going through the motions. Just waiting for someone to dig the hole. Every year he pulled in a little more, a little more, like a gardener pruning back a bush until it's barely there."

"What happened to your mother?"

"I'm not entirely sure." He was silent for a minute. "I can barely remember her. She disappeared, no one ever talked about it. I know the cops thought my father killed her, but her body never turned up, and they never got enough to charge him. You know, they teach you the family rules, when you're a kid. Two of the rules in my house were, don't ask any questions, and don't tell anybody anything."

"Sounds a lot like my family. So your father remarried?"

"Yeah, he married one of the poodle women."

She blinked at him. "I'm sorry, he married one of the what?"

Silvano was nodding. "Poodle women. You know the type. Ornamental, not functional, except in one or two, ahh, limited categories. Her main jobs, besides servicing him, were getting coiffed and tanned and shined and spiffed. You know, she had to look as stylishly silly as she could manage."

"Sounds like the two of you didn't get along."

"Well, she didn't like me, because I loused up things between her and my father. I got in the way. And of course, I hated her."

"Why 'of course'?"

"I was only six. One day my mother went away, and then the poodle lady showed up. I honestly don't know if there was any time interval between the two events, I can't remember. But in my mind, over the years, I came up with the same theory I suppose the cops did, the old Henry VIII ploy, you know, I'm tired of this one, let me throw her away and get a new one."

"Do you really believe he could have done that?"

"When I was ten or twelve, I was sure of it. Now, I don't really know."

"Didn't you and your father ever talk about her?"

"We never talked about anything."

"He never told you what happened?"

"No."

"And you never asked."

He shook his head. "No."

"Jesus Christ." She was incredulous. "Well, are you gonna ask him? Don't you wanna know what happened to her?"

He thought about it for a minute. "I should have asked before now, right?"

"If he dies before you get around to it, it will be too late. Then what? So who raised you?"

He smiled broadly, she actually saw teeth. "You know, when I joined the Army, my DI used to ask me if I was raised by wild dogs."

She watched his face closely. He was showing the first signs of affection she'd seen in him yet. She shook her head. "I don't get it. You didn't like your father, you hated your stepmother, but you actually liked your drill instructor."

"I know. They're supposed to be monsters, but mine was actually a cool guy. He was always real clear on what he wanted from me. 'Private Alphabet,' he'd say, 'climb up that obstacle and knock that man off.'"

"Private Alphabet?"

"He was from down South somewhere, he had a little trouble pronouncing Iurata. But what made you acceptable to him or not was right out in plain sight. You didn't have to read his mind. 'Here's what I need you to do.' No guesswork."

"So things were ambiguous, then, in your house."

"'Ambiguous'?" He didn't smile, but she could tell he was amused. "Things were crazy in my house. Between my brother, who was out of his mind, and my psychopathic grandfather, you never knew what was coming."

"Don't use a word like that," she said. "Tell me what he was really like."

"No, psychopath is the right word," he said, shaking his head. "That's what he was. A crocodile on a riverbank was probably capable of more empathy than him. But I was young, you know, and I didn't understand. I idolized him, because it seemed to me that he knew how to live. He engaged, he stepped on the gas pedal. He used to take me to the opera, right, because nobody else would go with him. We always sat in the same place, first balcony, first row. 'You don't wanna see 'em,' he told me, 'you don't wanna know what a fat pig the soprano is, you just want to hear her, you want to believe she's a beautiful angel.' He knew the music by heart, you know, and he'd sit there fidgeting, waiting for the parts he wanted to hear. We went to see *La Boheme*, right, he's sighing, he's bored stiff, looking up at the ceiling, picking his nose, then finally the tenor starts into '*Che Gelida Manina*.'" He sung it to her, softly, just the first two lines. "All of a sudden he's transformed, his eyes are closed, his mouth is open, he's in heaven. Soon as the guy is done, my grandfather's at the rail, he's clapping, he's bellowing 'Bravo!' and all of that. Then he grabs my hand. 'We're outa here,' he says. Didn't think the rest of it was worth listening to."

"He doesn't sound like a psychopath."

"Hah." She saw him start to say something, then stop and reconsider.

"Tell," she said.

"All right." She watched him work up to it. "When I was seventeen," he said, finally, "he killed my uncle Angelo, his son, because of something he did. And he made me help him dump the body."

She held on to him, in shock. "Are you kidding?"

"No. And because of that, you know, he said I had to go away, leave the city, leave my brother. I had always taken care of Noonie up until that. It was my job to fight his battles, watch out for him, get him out of trouble. It was a little like wrestling a gorilla, because no way you're gonna win, right, and you're gonna get your ass kicked trying, but it was what I did. After what the old man did to my uncle, though, I didn't have any choice, so I left. Wound up in the Army, not too long after that.

My cousin, Angelo's son, has hated me ever since because he thought it was all my doing. Little Dom, they call him. He went into the family business. It's his guys that are trying to kill me."

"Jesus. So that's why you're going around dressed up in these outfits."

"Please. Men don't wear outfits."

"Pardon me. These getups, then. So how long do you figure you have before they get you?"

"That's not gonna happen." He dismissed the idea with a wave of his hand. "Ultimately, though, if I stay in Brooklyn, my cousin and I are going to have to settle up."

"So that's it, then?" She saw it in his face, pictured him living in a vast and sterile emotionless desert. "That's all you learned, right? You learned how to fight, and that was it. Did anyone teach you how to love someone else?"

"I did love my brother." He said it quietly.

"Did you ever tell him?"

He shook his head. She took his face in her hands and turned him to her, wrapped her arms around him. "It's not enough," she said, feeling her heart thundering in her chest. "It's not enough just to feel it. You have to tell, you have to show it." She kissed him then, crushing him against her body, and then she let him go and stepped back, seized by a sudden panic. What if he's gay, what if he's not capable, what if he's too far gone? "It's better when both people do it," she said. "Try to get into the spirit of the thing."

"Yeah," he said, reaching for her. He's more fucked up than I am, she thought, but by then he had his hand soft on her face and she felt herself drawn in, sucked under, engulfed.

They rode back home on the train, silent but side by side, maintaining contact, and they didn't talk during the short walk to her building, either. When they got to her front stoop he detached, holding her just by the hand. "Listen," he said, his voice husky. "I really . . ."

"No you don't." She felt more vulnerable than she could ever remember feeling, but some buried part of her had already decided to risk it all right then and there, even though she was sure if he turned away she would shipwreck and die on the rocks. "You're coming with me." All of a sudden they needed no more talk, their gathering momentum swept them up the stairs, it seemed to her that they barely made it inside her door.

She could hear a tiny voice in the back of her head, shouting for her attention, "What are you doing? Are you insane?" She felt a tickle of fear in her belly, because it had been so long, and the last time had been so ugly . . . She wanted him, though, that's what it came down to. He was tangling his fingers in her black hair, looking into her eyes. Already she could tell that he was different from anyone else she had known, he wasn't rushing her, he wasn't trying to tear her clothes off, and he didn't look like some guy who'd just hit the number. She closed her eyes, ran her hands up under his shirt, trying to make her hands as slow and gentle as his. She felt two small round scars low on his back, over to one side. "What are these?"

"Oh," he said, distracted, his eyes closed. "Those?" He had one hand on the bare skin of her back. "Those are . . ." She leaned into him. "Those are souvenirs, sweet lady luck put her hands on me just like you're doing, she pushed me over to one side, just not quite far enough. What's this?"

She had her cheek next to his, her chin on his shoulder. She whispered in his ear. "That's a bra, the hooks are right under your hand. Don't tell me you didn't learn how to deal with those in high school."

"I may have been out that day."

She realized then that he was waiting for her, he was letting her drive, and when she knew that the last vestiges of her fear went away. In the space of one shallow breath she gave in, she rode on a current of sudden fever. "Pay attention, then," she said, whispering in his ear. She leaned her hips away from him, just far enough to get one hand in to unbuckle his belt. "Let me show you . . ."

SHE DIDN'T GET DRESSED, after. She knew that she wasn't perfect, but she was round where she needed to be round, flat where she needed to be flat, and she had worked hard to get and stay that way. She stood up, watching him watch her. She walked into her kitchen, came back with the rest of the Portuguese rosé. She sat down beside him, rubbed her hand over a long scar on the back of his arm. "I don't think there's enough unmarked hide on you to make a good pair of shoes," she said. "Would you like to stay? There's another bed thing under here that pulls out."

"I'm a lousy sleeper," he told her, avoiding eye contact. "I have a lot of nightmares, and I'm very restless. You wouldn't get much rest."

"Maybe I don't want any rest," she said, leaning in to kiss him.

It was almost daybreak when he finally left.

"HENRY!"

The dogs knew who he was, and they let him pass, but he started calling out as soon as he reached the top of the stairwell.

"Henry, it's me. Henry, you around?"

"I'm here." The answer came from one of the back rooms. "Where you at?"

"I'm following the arrows to the kitchen."

Henry met him there. "Why all the fuss?"

Silvano was slumped in a chair. He put the sweatshirt hood back up, topped it with the hat and the sunglasses. "Didn't want to get shot for trespassing."

Henry laughed. "Nice, I like this look on you. You look beat, though."

"Yeah, I am tired. I went on a date, Henry. Now my head is all fucked up."

"Oh, my. Must've been good, then. Did you have a nice time?"

"Whoo, yeah. But she scares me, Henry. I don't know if I can take the stress."

"That's all right, it's good for you. Keep you healthy. You like her?"

"Hell, yes. But she's testing me, she's trying to find out what I'm like."

"You figure you passed muster?"

"I don't know, man. I don't know anything about women, Henry. I never been married, I never even lived with a woman. In the Army, well, I don't have to tell you."

"No, you don't."

"You were married, right? How long were you with your wife?"

"Well. I guess you can't count the war years, we got hitched just before I went off. So, middle of nineteen-twenty, say, up until she died in sixty-five." His voice softened, talking about her.

"Wow. Forty-five years. So you gotta know a lot about women."

"I don't know about that. I don't know. I would say it was myself I learned about, and the institution, maybe, not her. She kept surprising me, right up until the end."

"No kidding. So you recommend it? The institution, I mean."

Henry rubbed the stubble on his chin. "Depends," he said. "You get married so's you can get your ashes hauled nice and regular, I'd say you made a poor bargain. 'Cause it's too hard, you know, it's too hard to get it right. But I suppose it's like a lot of things, you knew what was coming, you'd never leave the house. That's why you get those hormones in your blood, so that they can override your common sense."

"Damn. That's hardly a ringing endorsement."

Henry shrugged. "I don't mean to be negative. My old lady was about the best thing that ever happened to me, but it don't always work out that way. Plus, you gotta know, going in, that you're gonna go through the fire. You'll be a better man for it, after, but that don't make it no easier. I really don't mean to make it sound bad, though. It's only the first ten years or so that suck. After that it gets better. Generally."

"Jesus, thanks, Henry, I'm more confused now than I was."

Henry was laughing again. "Well, that's okay, that's natural. Nobody can tell you what to do, anyhow, but I will say this much: You get to be friends, first, you got as good a shot as anybody."

"All right. So you can't tell me what I should do next."

"Oh, I can tell you that. Call her up and tell her that you had a good time."

"I told her that already."

Henry shook his head. "That don't count. You gotta call her and tell her again."

"Okay. Tomorrow?"

"Yeah, tomorrow. Then, in four or five days, you gotta do it again."

"What, are you kidding me? What can I say to her the third time that I didn't say the first two times?"

"Listen to what I'm telling you. You don't do what I say, here, she's gonna think you don't give a damn. That what you want?"

"No. No, it's not. Okay, I'll call her, just like you say."

"Well, all right."

FIVE

■

THE AFTERNOON SUN BLED the colors from the enormous stained-glass window and splashed them onto the white stucco interior of the church. Silvano shifted his weight on the wooden pew. Made to be uncomfortable, he thought. Elia had gotten a laugh when he'd told her, on the phone, that he had to go to church this afternoon, until he'd told her why, and where.

"Silvano, are you crazy? You're right down in your cousin's backyard. Did you already have this planned yesterday? Why didn't you tell me about it then?"

"I was gonna tell you yesterday," he told her, "but when you took off your shirt, my brain vapor-locked and I forgot. Don't sweat it, anyhow. This is all gonna work out soon enough, and anyway, I'll be out of sight the whole day. And listen, I just wanted to say, um, I had a really nice time with you yesterday . . ."

"Me, too," she said. "Please be careful. And the next time I see you, after I kill you, I want you to tell me exactly how you plan to make this all work out, and whatever other little details you might have forgotten."

"All right," he told her, penitent. "It's a deal."

He leaned back and gazed at the vaulted ceiling high overhead. He was sitting on the aisle, near the back, and he was trying to ignore the hushed mumble emanating from the confessionals on the far side of the church. He could have made out the words, if he'd really been interested, but he concentrated on ignoring the sounds instead. What a terrible job, he thought, to be a priest, to be obliged to listen to the same tired infractions, over and over, the same trespasses, repeated so many times there had to be a trail leading to them, grass beaten down and stunted from being trod by so many feet. And still worse, if you were God, imagine the constant, never-ending cacophony of all those whining voices . . . He remembered seeing a woman using a prayer wheel once. She had written her prayer on this little hoop, and she sat on the ground spinning the hoop on the end of a stick, believing her prayer to God was repeated with each spin, gimme gimme gimme gimme gimme. He'd been amused, at the time. Who would imagine a Supreme Being you could bludgeon into compliance through sheer repetition?

The mumbling ceased and the door to one of the confessionals opened. The man who came out was tall, several inches over six feet, with iron gray hair combed straight back and a pockmarked face, heavy-lidded reptilian brown eyes, a thin slash of a mouth. He was heavy but not fat. He wore a white shirt, open at the collar, and a suit that was tailored to fit him perfectly. Silvano watched him make his way slowly up the far side of the church to the front row of pews and kneel awkwardly. He didn't quite look like the force of nature Silvano remembered, but he was still big enough, still had enough of a presence to make you take notice.

The old man finished what he was doing and struggled to his

feet, leaning heavily on the railing in front of him, grunting with the effort. Silvano figured he must be having trouble with one knee, because he swung one leg stiffly forward and he walked slowly down the center aisle in Silvano's direction. He may be old, Silvano thought, but he looks like the same guy, same face, expressionless, unsmiling, same dead eyes that took you in but told you nothing. The old man stopped eight feet away, looking at him.

"Giovanni." Silvano had not called him "Dad" since he was six. The old man stood still, leaning on a pew, the other hand clenching and unclenching. Silvano gestured with his chin, up toward the front of the church where the old man had been praying. "You think it worked?"

Giovanni regarded him for a moment. "I dunno," he finally said, in his raspy voice. He had always sounded like a man with a cold, as far back as Silvano could remember. He swung back into motion, covering the distance between the two of them, his stride looking more natural. He's covering up the limp, Silvano thought. He didn't notice me before. Didn't know I was here. Giovanni sat in the adjoining pew on the other side of the aisle. It was about as close as the two of them ever got.

"You pray for forgiveness?"

"Sometimes." He cleared his throat. "You still think this is all superstitious bullshit?"

Silvano shrugged. "What's the harm," he said, "if it makes you feel better."

The old man looked up at the ceiling. "I was God," he said, "I wouldn't much like you talking that way in my own house."

"You were God, I'd have been in the ground a long time ago."

"Maybe not. You might be surprised. But it does make me feel better. Coming here, and all."

"What else you pray for? You ever say a prayer for my mother?"

"Sometimes." He stared at Silvano, not smiling. There was no apology in his face, no desire for compromise, no need for compassion or forgiveness. "Sometimes I just ask that my asshole son would come back and see me."

Silvano watched him, watched the way his eyes would look at you and then flick away, restless, not giving you much. He wondered if there had been a challenge there, in that last look. He did not take the bait. "See? You got to be careful what you ask for."

"I guess that's true."

There was no way to put it off. As far back as he could remember, he'd been trying to hang on to memories that were becoming painfully indistinct, her face, her voice, her touch. He needed to know what had happened to her, but he was afraid to find out. All these years he'd been thinking about her, and it still came down to one short and ugly sentence. "You kill my mother?"

The question hung between them in the still air of the empty church. Silvano watched the old man squirm on the wooden bench. Yeah, he thought, I got a sore ass too, but I'm not going to let you know it.

"I always wondered when you were gonna ask."

"I know the cops liked you for it."

"They liked me for a lot of things."

"I seem to remember, you were always pretty good with a baseball bat."

"I still got one, out in the trunk."

"No shit. Didn't you used to keep it under the front seat?"

"Still got one there, too," Giovanni said. "Handle sawed off, so it don't stick out." He sat quiet for a while, and Silvano began to wonder if he was done talking. He looked over, made eye contact, looked away again. "You remind me of her," he said. "Me and her went to high school together, did you know that?"

"You went to high school?"

"Smartass. Not all the way through, but I did go. Her old man ran all the numbers in Brooklyn, way back when. Back in the old days."

"I heard the stories."

"Not all of 'em, you didn't. Everybody thought I went with her because of him. Because he was a made man. Wasn't true."

"No? You fall in love with her?" He felt bad for the tone he used, but he couldn't help it, and the old man didn't notice anyway.

"Well, I fell. Who knows what it was, at first." He glanced over, then looked over at the stained-glass window. "She was smart, she was funny, and she didn't take shit from anybody. Had a short fuse." He looked pointedly back at Silvano. "She's the one you got that from, not me. Anyway, I liked her. So we started going out, you know, it got to be a thing. You know what I mean?" He looked away again. "Maybe you don't. It got to be bigger than like. I wanted her to stay with me."

"And Domenic liked you, right?"

"You kidding? No man ever likes the guy his daughter goes with. You think I like that fucking Vinnie, that bum your sister married? Your half-sister. Anyhow, old Domenic didn't much like anybody. Liked you, a little bit. That was about it."

"You were gonna tell me what happened."

"Was I?" Giovanni had always guarded his secrets. This has to bother him, Silvano thought, this has to go against what he believes in, even if part of him wants to tell. "All right," the old man said, finally. "You got a right, I guess." Somewhere in the back of the church a door closed, and the two of them sat silent, listening, but there were no other sounds beyond the faint hiss of the cars passing by outside. Giovanni shifted his weight on the pew again. "How much you remember?" he finally asked.

"Not a hell of a lot. I remember going on rides with her, until once I got lost and you took her keys away."

"You didn't get lost. She just forgot to bring you back. Anything else?"

Not much that I want to tell you, Silvano thought. "She was funny. She laughed a lot. Used to like to tell stories."

"Yeah," Giovanni said. "She sure did." He took a cigar out of his inside jacket pocket. It was long, thin, dark brown, and he held it up to his nose.

Silvano patted the shirt pocket where he used to carry his Kools. "You gonna light that up in here?"

Giovanni glanced around, looking for the priest. "Not just now," he said. "You ever hear of senile dementia?" His eyes flicked over to Silvano's face, then down at the cigar again. "They probably don't call it that anymore. Mostly old people get it. She was just twenty-six when it started. We went to doctors all over, but they didn't have nothing for it back then. I don't know, they got anything for it now, either." He sighed, shook his head. He's had a long time to get used to this, Silvano thought, but still, he could be talking about a game the Giants lost and should've won, twenty years ago. He's the same as he was, a hard old motherfucker.

"I thought I could handle her, at first. Kept her home, you know, out of trouble. But she loved people, and she loved to talk. She made the old men nervous, not just Domenic but all of them, the Mustache Petes that ran the game, back then. Old bastards off the boat from Sicily. The problem was, being Domenic's daughter, she knew too many stories, and she'd talk to anybody." Giovanni held his cigar up to the light, examining its wrinkled surface. Silvano watched his face, but he couldn't tell what the old man was feeling, couldn't tell if he saw sadness there or just anger, or maybe nothing at all.

"Domenic comes to me." He looked at Silvano, made eye contact, smiled slightly. "Her father. Tells me how sorry he is, all that shit. Tells me he'll make sure she goes easy, that she won't suffer. I told him no. Told him that I understood the necessity. Told him I'd do it myself."

Silvano leaned back and sighed, looked around at the church. This is why they do it, he thought, this is why they need the stained glass, the fancy building, the rituals, the guy in special robes. It's to con you, make you think it can still work out, that it still makes some kind of sense, somehow. He looked over at his father's face, but if there had been any compassion, any sadness there, it was gone, or else covered over so completely that no one would ever see it, because the number-one rule for tough guys, the one they all lived by was, you couldn't give a fuck. Roll the dice, walk out of the bank with a million bucks or a twenty-year hitch at Sing-Sing, you couldn't care which. You had to laugh the same laugh either way. "Okay," he said. "Go on."

"Domenic took you home with him. Kept you over the weekend. He was trying to make it easier for me, I guess. Trying to make sure I did it, too, probably. I put her in the car, we went for a long ride. She was afraid, you know, I'm not sure she always knew who I was, by that time. I drove out in the country, up into the Berkshires. In Massachusetts."

Silvano couldn't quite pull off not giving a fuck. "I know where the goddam Berkshires are at."

"S'cuse me. There was a hospital there, a sanitarium, outside of Amherst. I put her in there, under a phony name. Paid the guy a fortune to keep his mouth shut. I put a gun in his mouth, too, told him he ever opened his yap, I'd blow his fucking brains out.

"There was a kid in there, had hands about your mother's size. I cut off one a his fingers, put her wedding band on it. Walked into Domenic's house that Sunday afternoon, laid it on his kitchen counter. He's crying, it's the only time I ever seen him cry, he was probably drunk. She didn't feel a thing, I tell him, I'm trying hard not to laugh, 'cause she didn't, you know, and I took you and went home."

The two of them sat in silence. Finally Giovanni stirred again on the wooden pew. 'She didn't last long,' he said, "just over four years, I think it was. Turned out, they didn't have nothing to worry about. She wasn't in there long before she couldn't remember a thing. Didn't know who I was, didn't know who she was, most likely."

"What did you do with her, when she died? Where did you bury her?"

Giovanni stuck the cigar back in his pocket. "They cremated her for me," he said, "at the hospital. The one she was in. I took her ashes up to Oneida Lake, upstate. There's a little town there, Silvan Beach. We went up there on holiday once. You remember the place?"

"I don't think so."

"Well, you were probably only three or four. Anyhow, at the southern end of the town, there's a canal runs out of the lake, I buried her there, under an oak tree. Where her and me walked along the bank that one summer."

"What about that kid in the hospital? He mind you borrowing his finger?"

"No, he didn't care. I did him first, smothered him with a pillow."

"Jesus Christ."

"Ahh, it didn't mean nothing, he was gone already. Poor bastard, just laying there in the bed like a stick of celery. Probably did him a favor. I had a hard time knowing when he was dead, you want to know the truth."

"Nobody noticed he was missing a finger?"

"They put you in a box to bury you, for chrissake. You think somebody's gonna open the box and count all the parts up? The guy didn't have nobody, anyhow."

"No? You check first?"

"No, that's just the way it worked out." He twisted to face Silvano across the aisle. "What do you give a shit about the guy, anyhow?"

"I guess I don't, nobody else does. So my mother was still alive when you brought what's-her-name home. Your second wife."

"Her name is Elaine."

"Yeah. Her."

It was Giovanni's turn to shake his head. "Okay. Yeah, you wanna get technical, Rachael was still alive. I didn't think of her that way. You seen her in that bed, you wouldn't have, either. Elaine was just a broad, you know. I didn't mean for her to be anything more than that."

"So what happened?"

The old man shrugged. "I had needs. She moved in, and girlfriends turn into wives. That's just the way it goes. Hadda wait seven years, you know, before Rachael was declared dead. Elaine was counting the days, though I didn't know it. Time was up, Noonie and Annette were already here, it was more trouble to get rid of her than to just go along with it. So . . ."

"So that was that."

"Yeah." The two of them sat with it for a minute. "End of story," Giovanni finally said. "How'd you know I'd be here?"

"Called your wife," Silvano said. "Elaine. She told me you do this, most Sundays."

"She never mentioned that you called. You ask her not to?"

"No. She probably forgot."

"Could be. You wanna come to the house? We got some nice veal for supper."

Hell, no, Silvano thought. "Can't," he said. "I gotta wait here until it's dark, and then I got business, over in Howard Beach."

"He don't live there no more."

"Who's that?"

"Don't play stupid. He moved to Manhattan, a couple years back."

"Yeah, I heard."

"You're gonna have to whack him, you know. Either that or you gotta run. Is that why you came back?"

"No. I came to look for Noonie. See if I could find out what happened. I figure, Dom lets me be, I let it go."

"He ain't going for that."

"Yeah, I know. His mutts already tried for me once."

"I heard." The old man's face broke into a wolfish grin. "They gonna bury Massimo in a coupla days. He's the one, you broke his neck."

"Short fat guy?"

"Yeah."

"Wasn't my fault. They should be glad the other three walked. The driver's half asleep, for chrissake, the one guy's standing out front like he's the freaking doorman. I shoulda walked away, when I seen 'em there. I had the choice. I shoulda just went on by."

"Don't matter. You can't leave things the way they are."

"What's the difference? I hit Domenic, you guys be looking for me forever."

"They're looking for you now, for Massimo, but I don't think it matters all that much. You lay low for a while, everybody will forget about him. It's Little Dom you gotta worry about. Why don't you get him when he's alone? Who could tell what happened? That way, coulda been anybody."

I'm like a horse, Silvano thought, I'm going off at ten to one and he's got fifty bucks on me. He wants to win his bet, beyond that he don't give a shit. "I didn't come here for that," he said. "I came for Noonie. I ain't going looking for Little Dom, but if he comes after me, I'll finish it."

"Oh, he'll come, don't you worry. He says it's all your fault. Angelo dead, Jeannette turning into Sister Mara, him being what he is instead of Frank fucking Lloyd Wright, Jr., all of it would have been different, wasn't for you. Everything would have been strawberries and fucking cream."

"He can think what he wants." He wants to hear the story, Silvano thought, but he's too proud to ask. "You ever hear anything about Noonie? Any of your South Brooklyn buddies ever say anything?"

Giovanni leaned forward, resting his elbows on the back of the pew in front of him. "Nobody ever said a thing," he said. He stared up past the altar where the light from a rack of small candles flickered up against the wall. "I thought at first, it might have had something to do with this business between you and Domenic, but everybody said no."

"You believe that?"

"Yeah, I do. Otherwise, after some time went by, a little birdie would have whispered in my ear. You know how that goes. Funny thing was, last year he was alive, I kept trying to decide if I should have him put away, you know, find someplace nice where he'd be happy, keep him out of trouble. I went to talk to one of his doctors, this guy over at Bellevue was seeing him, guy told me Noonie would be better off learning how to function in normal society. So I left it alone."

"Yeah? So what'd you do to the guy told you to leave him on the outside?"

"The doctor? Why you always gotta think the worst about me?"

"Come on. What'd you do?"

"I didn't have to do nothing. Guy's car caught on fire, with him inside. Terrible thing." Giovanni gripped the back of the pew in front of him and pulled himself erect. He stepped out into the aisle, stiff from sitting so long. "You ready, for when Little Dom comes for you?"

Silvano reached down and pulled the black Beretta out of the ankle holster under his pantleg. "Yeah."

"Okay. Anything you need, call me."

"All right. Sure."

"I gotta go home. To Elaine." A hint of a smile lurked near his mouth.

"Yeah? You still got needs?"

"On occasion," Giovanni said, grinning. "On occasion I get one, but at my age, you gotta use it right away or it folds up on you."

HOWARD BEACH IS A SMALL, hermetic square of neighborhood, an enclave of quiet streets, small houses, postage-stamp-sized green lawns. It is bordered by the Belt Parkway on the north, by JFK Airport on the east, and by the Atlantic Ocean on the other two sides. It was, in the seventies, overwhelmingly Italian, fiercely defended by some of its inhabitants.

"Damn." The car service driver was black, and he looked around suspiciously at the streets they were driving past. "You sure know how to pick 'em, buddy. First Bensonhurst, now Howard fucking Beach. You trying to get me killed?"

"Not me. You driving a cab. You really think anyone would mess with you?"

The driver swiveled in his seat to glare at Silvano, sitting in the back. "That a trick question?"

"All right. Tell you what, I need to talk to someone, shouldn't take no more than an hour. Place is halfway up this block. You drop me here, you can shoot up to the stop sign, grab a left, and run straight up Cross Bay Boulevard, go have a short one up near Aqueduct someplace. Come back down this block in, say, an hour and fifteen minutes, go slow, leave your right-hand turn signal on so I know it's you, we'll both be out of here before anything bad can happen. You okay with that?"

"Sounds like a lot of hanging around to me. I got expenses, man."

"Don't worry, I'll take care of you." The big Lincoln glided silently over to the curb. They discussed terms, and then Silvano got out, slammed the door shut, and watched the car pull slowly away.

THE HOUSE DIDN'T LOOK like anything special, it was a Cape, same as all the other houses on the block, short driveway, one-car garage. A '68 Mercury Cougar was parked in front of the garage door. Silvano ran his hand over it as he walked up the driveway and stood in the pool of darkness between the garage and the house. Over the rumble of traffic in the background, he could hear the noise of a television from the house next door, voices from a loud argument over on the next block, a jet on its final approach to JFK, but nothing from the house he was interested in. There was light coming from what he assumed was a kitchen window, but the glass was opaque and he couldn't see through it. Be best if she wasn't home, he thought, but there was no way to hang around and wait for her to go out. Not on this block.

What if Little Dom's in there? he thought. He pulled the Beretta out of the ankle holster and stuck it under his belt. If he is, it'll all come down right here and right now . . . He walked up and tapped on the glass of the window in the back door, then stepped back into the shadows.

He heard someone stirring, heard the creak of a floorboard, but no footsteps. The door opened and she leaned out, shaking long hair out of her eyes. She looked around, saying nothing, until she spotted him standing in the darkness. "Yeah," she said, combative, no fear in her voice. "What?"

He stepped forward into the light so she could see who he was. He kept his voice low. "Can you talk?"

She worked at a smile, couldn't get it more than halfway on. "I'll be damned," she said. "If it ain't the Antichrist himself. How the hell are you, Silvie?"

"Okay so far," he said. "He around?"

"You kidding? I haven't seen Domenic in months." She looked at the pistol and rolled her eyes. "You guys," she said. "Put the cannon away and come inside."

He stuck the Beretta back in the holster and stepped up to the doorway. She stood there, blocking his path, long straight blond hair, dark brown eyebrows, brown eyes. Standing barefoot on the first step, she was almost at eye level with him. She let go of the door and inclined her face to be kissed. She embraced him when he did it, crushing him to her chest with surprising strength for such a small person. He stood there with his hands on her back and his face buried in her hair until she was ready to let him go. "Come in," she said finally, pulling away. "Come on inside."

"The Antichrist," he muttered, half to himself. "Gimme a break."

"Hey, listen," she said. "In this house, you are the big, bad bogeyman." She preceded him into the dimly lit kitchen. It had a yellow tile floor, yellow cabinets, yellow refrigerator with children's artwork taped to the door. "Have a seat," she said, gesturing to the table. "You want something to drink? I don't even know what I got, maybe some wine . . ."

"No thanks, Gina," he said. "I'm okay, I don't need anything, really."

She was looking in the refrigerator. "Man, Silvie, I really got nothing to offer you. I'm sorry." She closed the refrigerator door. "I'm not much used to entertaining, these days."

"That's okay," he said. "I'm fine. Last time I saw you, you had brown hair, and you were wearing it all piled up on top of your head."

"Beehive," she said, grimacing. "Don't remind me. Well, Domenic still wears his hair like Frankie Avalon, but I see you finally quit getting yours cut like Sergeant Rock. How about I make us some coffee. You want a nice cup?"

"Gina, stop, I'm fine."

"Silvie, listen to me. Domenic left six years ago, I been stuck here in this jail cell with two kids ever since. Everybody in the neighborhood knows him and me are separated, and every guy I know is scared shit to even say hello. All I get to talk to is girlfriends, wives, and old ladies, and even that's only on the phone, most of the time. I haven't had a man in my kitchen, not one I like, anyhow, for so long I can't even remember. Let me make you some fucking coffee already."

"Coffee would be nice." He watched her busy herself at the counter. Damn, he thought, she looks better than I remember her. She was wearing white shorts and a blue denim work shirt with the sleeves rolled up. "Why don't you leave, things are that bad?"

"He's got me sewed up here, Silvie. Bought and paid for." She was pouring water into the pot, and she didn't turn to look at him. "The house ain't mine, it's in the name of some lawyer friend of his. He sends me enough money to feed the kids, pay the bills, and that's about it. I've never had a job, Silvie, I leave here, I leave with nothing, I gotta support two kids, I wouldn't know where to start. You take milk and sugar?"

"Black is good. You really wanted to go, you could find a way."

"Maybe I could. Maybe I will, when the kids get old enough. Unless someone puts a bullet in Domenic's head first, then I won't have to wait. That what you came here to do?"

"No," he said. "I didn't come here to get this thing with Dom started up again. I just want to find out what happened to my brother Nunzio, that's all. You remember him?"

"Course I remember Noonie." She turned around and leaned back against the counter. Behind her, the coffeemaker coughed into life. "I was real sorry to hear about him."

"What did you hear?"

"Somebody seen him, down at some check-cashing place they were sniffing around at. I heard that, and then I heard he come up missing."

"You sure it was a check-cashing joint?"

"Something like that."

"No kidding. Who was it, had his fingers in?"

"Guy named Ivan. I don't know his last name."

"Big guy, right, couple years younger than us?"

"That's him."

"Ivan tied in with Domenic?"

"They both run with old Antonio's crew. Ivan was Domenic's

boy, probably still is. They were like Heckle and Jeckle for a few years."

"Okay. You ever see Domenic?"

"It's like I told you, Silvie. On very rare occasions, maybe once or twice a year, he comes over the house, drunk out of his mind. Terrorizes the kids, slaps me around, brags what he's gonna do to me, passes out on the floor before he gets around to doing it." She crossed the floor and sat down across the table from him. She had this look on her face, he couldn't tell if it was resignation, sorrow, or just fear gone stale from the passing of time. "He's an empty hole, Sil. He don't care about anything or anybody. Since you left, he just kept getting meaner and meaner. The only thing he got excited about, the last year we were together, was getting back at you. He had some guy from the feebies calling him every time you got a new posting. He knew where you were the whole time, from when you went in all the way up through Viet Nam. Then, when you got sent over to the Defense Department, the guy couldn't trace you anymore, Dom went wild. It was like he lost his mind. That was about the time he moved out. He blames you for everything, Sil, everything that's wrong in his life is because of you."

"That's funny. I used to think all my problems were because of him." He looked into her face. "What went wrong with you and him?"

She shook her head. "It was like a gradual thing. When we first got married, he was just like, you know, normally unhappy. You know what I mean? He didn't like his job, he didn't like this house, he was like everybody else. But then he started getting weirder. Like, he couldn't stand it if I made any noise, he had some guy putting soundproofing in the walls, he had to have it like a freaking monastery in here. He even started talking quiet himself, you had to strain to hear him. I was all the time, 'What,

what?' and that pissed him off no end. And you couldn't argue with the guy no more, I couldn't fight with him the way regular people fight about things, he would sit there, and then he would just blow up. It was all life or death. Then, when the kids came, sheesh. I mean, kids make noise, that's what they do. They cry and shit. He couldn't take it. I had started to worry, you know, he was gonna do something permanent to me or to the kids, but what happened, it all came to a head when his grandfather died. 'You're free now,' I told him. 'Why don't we just sell everything and just leave? You could go to school, like you always wanted.' We had enough money for that, we could have just went. I guess I pushed him too hard. I mean, all those years I hadda listen to him complain, now he's got the perfect chance to go do what he wants and he won't take it. We had terrible rows over it, Silvie, terrible. Then they made Antonio Malatesta the new capo, to replace old Domenic, that was it, he beat the shit out of me and moved out." She laughed, but it wasn't much of a laugh, just one short, humorless exhalation. "You know, I think he was actually jealous of you. You know, you being in a war, going all over everywhere, and all. Old Dom never even had to get him a deferment when he got out of high school, did you know that? When he went before the draft board, they gave him a 4-F."

"How come?"

"Mentally unfit."

"Wow."

"Yeah, coo-coo. Listen, nobody knows that, you say anything about it and he'll kill me."

"Him and me, we're always having these long conversations."

"Hey," she said. "I had to mention it. What did you do, anyhow, for Defense? Dom was convinced they turned you into James Bond, it really ate him up, you know, him still stuck here in Brooklyn."

He shook his head. "James Bond." The coffeemaker stopped gurgling and she got up to get cups.

"Go ahead," she said. "I'm listening."

"Yeah," he said, thinking about it. The muscles in the backs of her legs flexed as she stood on tiptoe to reach the cups. He figured, then, that she became conscious of him watching her, because it seemed to him that she began to pose, just a bit, as she stood pouring the coffee. When she came back over with the coffee she leaned over in front of him to put his cup down. The top three buttons of her shirt were undone, how had he missed that before? Her shirt hung open and he caught a glimpse of creamy white skin where her tan ended, and then her hair cascaded down and spoiled the view.

"Go on," she said, watching his face as she straightened back up. She sat down across from him again and wrapped her hand around her cup. "Tell me what you did."

"Tell you one story," he said. "The Army had a big drug problem, because Charlie made sure that the south was flooded with great dope, selling for next to nothing. A guy that's wrecked all the time is gonna have trouble keeping his mind on his business, you know what I mean? Someone decided that the heroin, in particular, was coming from Laos, up in the hill country. Very remote, up in there, rough country. The villages were very isolated, basically they were on their own. Each village would have a headman, kind of like a warlord, and it was his job to make sure they got a fair price for their shit, that they didn't get ripped off, because that's how they fed their kids, that's how they lived. So, anyway, we started flying up in there, we were like a civilian air taxi, you know, trying to work with the headmen, help them out if we could, give them arms and equipment, freight their product out in choppers. The idea was to get them to go back to normal channels, so that the dope would wind up on the street in Paris, or Detroit, or here, where it belonged, and not in Saigon."

"Funny. You go halfway around the world, you wind up working for Antonio after all."

"In a manner of speaking."

"Did it work?"

"Depends on how you look at it. Most of the time they'd work with us. Why not take the money? But we couldn't stay and protect them, and sometimes you'd get a guy that was too afraid of the North Vietnamese, or you'd get one that was just too stubborn, and he wouldn't go along."

"What happened then?"

"Well," he said, and he stopped for a heartbeat. "I heard stories about napalm and gunships."

"Jesus. That what you did? Fly a gunship?"

"No," he said quickly. "I was in logistics."

Gina was used to men lying to her. "Sure you were. Do you think all of that did any good?"

He sighed. "Stand in the river," he said. "Try to hold back the water with your hands." He studied her face, trying to understand what he saw there.

"You aren't drinking your coffee."

"Sorry." He tasted it. "Not bad," he said, "not bad at all."

"Nothin' but the best. What are you gonna do now, Sil? Suppose you find out about Noonie. Suppose you get past that. Then what?"

He hadn't thought about it. He shook his head. "No idea."

"Domenic is sick," she said. "You could have said what you wanted about his dreams, maybe they were silly, maybe he could have never done it, but when you quit on what you love, Silvano, it don't leave you nothing but what you hate. He's sick, he's not gonna get any better, and he's coming after you." She stared at him. "And if he gets you, Sil, it won't even matter, he's too far gone. He'll just have to go on to the next guy, whoever else's fault the whole world is. You get me? There's nothing else left of him anymore."

He shrugged. "Maybe," he said.

"There's no maybe," she said. She looked at him oddly. "You don't even care, do you? Him wanting you dead, and all. Am I right?"

"No," he said. "Maybe a week ago I would have agreed with you, but not now."

"Must've been a hell of a week." She stood up again. "You really don't want that coffee, do you?"

"Not really. But thank you for—"

"Please," she said. "Stop." She took both cups over and dumped them into the sink. "I just miss having somebody to do for once in a while," she said. "That's all." She stood there at the sink, her back to him. He got up out of the chair and went over to stand behind her. He started to say something, but she cut him off.

"Be quiet, Sil. I know, you don't wanna ask me out, 'cause you know I'm going steady with Domenic, right?" She turned to face him, put her hands on his waist. "You think I want to use you to get back at him? Is that what you think?" She put one hand up on his cheek. "This ain't the fifties anymore, Sil, you gotta come out of hibernation. It is 1973, and this don't mean a thing. It's just what it is. It don't mean anything at all." She pulled his head down to kiss her, and the last thing he saw on her face was that look, and he still didn't know quite what it was, until it flashed on him how he'd felt, in Viet Nam, when he finally reached the point where he'd been afraid for so long that he didn't much care what happened, anymore. He put his hands on her shoulders, held her out away from him.

"Gina, I can't."

"Oh, God . . ." She shook her head, stood up straight. "Why not? Did something happen to you?"

Yeah, he thought, Elia Taskent happened to me. He didn't want to talk about it. "You could say that."

"Well, I'm sorry." She turned away.

"So am I." He could feel the sweat breaking out on his forehead. "I guess I better go."

"Silvie," she said, not turning around. "Be careful, okay?"

HE STEPPED OUT of the bushes when he saw the turn signal, the driver slowed for him, and he was in the backseat before the car came to a stop. The driver looked back at him. "You get what you came for?"

Silvano shook his head. "I don't know," he said.

"Where we headed now?"

"You know where the St. Felix is at?"

"Yeah." The driver glanced over his shoulder at Silvano. "Someplace more normal, thank God." At the end of the block, they turned left on Cross Bay Boulevard, the main artery into and out of Howard Beach, passing by Fortunato's, a large and garish Italian restaurant, bright lights, dark windows, a valet out front waiting to park your car.

THERE WASN'T ENOUGH of them to occupy all the seats around the long table, so they filled the ones nearest the end where Antonio sat. It was the only table in the long, narrow room, a private room in Fortunato's, Antonio's favorite restaurant. They were not there to eat, though some of them might, after they were done with their business. For now, though, no waiters would disturb their privacy. The lights were down, and Domenic squinted at the other faces in the gloom. No candles on the table, he thought derisively. We should have candles, and a secret handshake, we should have a dagger, we should all have to cut a finger with it and mix our blood. Ignorant people, he thought. They love ritual, mystery, and bullshit.

Careful, he told himself. Things go bad enough tonight, there could be blood on the floor before they were done, it had happened before. This time it might be his. He went over the speech again in his mind while he listened to them debating over the fate of Ivan Bonifacio. Hell of a chance you're taking, he thought, but if you never risk, you never win. He looked at his friend Ivan, who sat alone at the far end of the table, staring at nothing. The abrasion on his forehead stood out dark against his skin.

It seemed to take forever for them to sort themselves out, and he didn't listen to any of it. It was all bullshit, anyhow, macho posturing about honor, respect, and responsibility from men who had, at best, only a passing acquaintance with such things. It didn't matter what any of them said, in the end, nothing mattered except what Antonio said, and he was sitting silent at the head of the table, his face an unreadable mask of stone. Domenic waited patiently for silence, and when he finally got it, he calmed himself, took his life in his hands, and stood up.

All the eyes in the room turned in his direction, all except Ivan's. Ivan continued to sit and stare into space. Domenic called each man by name, starting with the man next to him, and ending with the only name that mattered.

"Antonio Malatesta," he said. "I must begin by saying these empty words to you, by telling you how deeply grieved I am by the death of your nephew Massimo, who I know was like a son to you. Although these words are true, they are truly empty because nothing I can say can bring him back. And the next thing I must tell you is that the blood of your nephew Massimo is not on the hands of Ivan Bonifacio.

"It is on mine." He felt like he was imitating James Caan playing a character.

The old man scowled, and Domenic could swear that the temperature in the room went down several degrees. Even Ivan was staring at him now. Be careful, Domenic told himself silently. Stick to the script. You screw up and smile at the inanity of this act you're putting on, even just a tiny bit, Antonio will have you strangled with your own guts.

"Please do not think I say this out of loyalty to my friend Ivan," he said, "because I do not. The truth is, Ivan Bonifacio could not have known what he was dealing with when he made his move on Silvano Iurata." He felt his own hatred then, and he allowed some of it to show, in case Antonio had forgotten. He calmed himself and swallowed before he continued.

"I could have warned him, but I did not, and now Massimo is dead. And worse than that, worse than that, it was my . . ." He paused, letting the tension build. Let Antonio think I don't know he sent Ivan after Iurata, he thought. "It was me. I was the one who set Ivan watching for the return of my childhood enemy. I should have taken care of this business myself. I never should have involved Ivan, or anyone else. It was personal business. I should have kept it that way." He turned in Ivan's direction, making his voice louder, angrier. "Why didn't you come to me?"

Ivan looked down at the table as Domenic's voice echoed in the room. He can't look at me, Domenic thought, he's probably afraid of laughing, if he laughs Antonio will feed both of us to the crows. He also understands that I'm telling Antonio that it's his own fucking fault that this happened. He never should have tried to keep me out of it.

Domenic looked back at Antonio.

"What's done is done," he said coldly. "But allow me, please, to atone in some small measure by telling all of you, here and now, what sort of animal we now have on our hands." He turned from Antonio and stared at the other men around the table, and he allowed his voice to rise as he continued. "And every one of you, if you take nothing else from this room today, remember this one thing: be careful what you ask for. For years I have prayed for this, I have begged for Silvano Iurata to return to Brooklyn so that I could wrap my hands around his throat, so that I could avenge the loss of my father and my sister . . . or die in the attempt. Now he's here and I wish he had never come." He turned back to Malatesta. "I was wrong, Antonio. I'm so sorry. I don't know how you can ever forgive me."

The old man, uncharacteristically silent, stared at him for a long count, and for one heart-stopping moment Domenic thought he might have misjudged him, might have overestimated his own salesmanship. This is it, he thought, this is where I find out if this works. You think the tigers at the zoo look tame, but you go inside the cage, you find out different.

Antonio inhaled, held it, and sighed. The spell was broken. He cleared his throat, hacked, and spat on the floor. "Well," he said, "what's done is done, Domenic, you're right about that. Go on and tell us all, now, what you should have told Ivan, before."

The danger is past, Domenic thought. Antonio doesn't give two shits about Massimo. He just needs to save face, get through this without too much disruption. I've been making too much money for him, that's his real problem. He doesn't want to jeopardize that. He sat back down in his chair, spread his hands, palms down on the table in front of himself. "It's a long story," he said. "I'll try to be brief. Some of you in this room are too young to remember much about my grandfather Domenic, the man for whom I was named." He glanced over at Antonio, who did remember. "You may have heard the stories. You probably wondered if they were true, how they could be true. I'm here to tell you that they are true. My grandfather was all that you have heard, and worse."

He looked at his audience, warming to his story. "Don't get me wrong, there are no priests here tonight." That got a laugh. "I apologize to no man for what I am. But like every one of you, I am a human being. I care about my family." *You are such a hypocrite*, he told himself silently. *I can't believe they're buying this bullshit. Can't believe I'm selling it. Never mind that*, he told himself harshly. *Focus.*

"I bleed for my friends. I wish evil upon no man. I walk with my head up. But there are some men who are not like us. Honor means nothing to them, they do not understand respect. To them, you and I are only prey animals, put here to satisfy their needs. They will sit at your table and eat your food, they will slap you on the back and call you 'brother,' and then if it pleases them, they will kill your sons, rape your daughters, cut your throat just to see if your blood is the same color as all the rest. God forgive me," he said, glancing up at the ceiling, where these superstitious dolts thought that some cosmic male parent named God lived, "God forgive me, my grandfather was such a man.

"He was a bloody-minded man. Violent by reflex. Look at us, sitting here at this table, talking to one another. If blood must be spilled, so be it, but we do it reluctantly, with regret. We do it only after we have tried, and failed, to find another way." He shook his head. "My grandfather did it because it amused him. It satisfied his appetite.

"My father, God rest his soul, he was not like his own father, he was a good man, he was a man of honor. I bear my grandfather's name, but I struggle, every day, to live up to my father's legacy, to be the man he taught me to be. But the evil that lived in my grandfather's heart did not die with him, he passed it on, through his daughter Rachel, to her son, my cousin Silvano Iurata.

"We were children together, we even slept in the same bed sometimes, under my father's roof. My grandfather loved Silvano, loved him as he had loved nothing else in his life, because he must have recognized what I was too young to know." Domenic was not playing a part anymore. His face was red and his hands were balled into fists. "I did not know what he would do to my family, to me." He pushed his chair back from the table and made an effort to relax. He heard himself breathing, felt his heart beating, felt the tension in his muscles. "I thought the Army would kill him for me," he said, "but they used him, instead. They found out what he was, and they sharpened him into something even worse than what he had been before. Now he's back, and one of us is already dead. Antonio, give me permission. Let me do what must be done."

Antonio was looking down at Ivan, still at the other end of the table. "Ivan Bonifacio," he said, and the blood drained from Ivan's face. "I do not hold you responsible for Massimo's death. I have listened, and I hope you have, too, to Domenic tell his painful story, and I thank him for laying himself bare. But I must say no, Domenic, and for this reason: Unless Ivan avenges Massimo's death, he could never be sure, he could never know that I have truly forgiven him."

Ivan stood up, but he still looked down at the table in front of him. "Thank you, Antonio," he said. "Leave him to me."

He doesn't get it, Domenic thought, fucking old bastard doesn't understand. He thinks he's got me in a box, and he doesn't want me getting out. "Be careful, Ivan," he said. "Iurata will not make the same mistake again. He won't let you walk away the next time."

OUTSIDE, IVAN PUT a hand on Domenic's arm. "Thank you," he said. "I'm impressed. That was quite a performance."

Domenic glared at him. "I don't know who's the bigger asshole," he said, "you or him. I'm telling you, you can't handle this on your own. You need me."

"Is this guy as bad as you say? I thought most of that was for Antonio's benefit."

"I tell you what," Domenic said, "I still can't believe he didn't wax all four of you assholes. I don't care what Antonio said, we have to work together on this."

Ivan looked at him. "I know I owe you for bailing me out in there. Antonio told me to take care of this, and he told me to keep it quiet. I fucked up on both counts. But you heard what he said." He stopped, and the two of them stood in silence as one of the restaurant's regular patrons came out of the building. They all waited without a word while the valet brought the guy's car around. "All right," Ivan said, as the guy drove off. "I'll call you in a few days. We'll set this up between the two of us. You can be in it, all the way up to when we take him down. But that you gotta stay out of. Okay?"

We'll see, Domenic thought, we'll see who fucking stays home. "All right," he said. He looked over his shoulder to see that they were still alone. "Is this gonna fuck up the timing on Black and White? What's the holdup with that?"

Ivan shook his head. "Cops are still all over the place. They won't sit there and watch forever, eventually they'll pack up and go home. Then we can do it." He looked at Domenic's face. "If you still want to."

"You bet your fucking life I still want to do it. You stay in touch."

SILVANO WALKED INTO the lobby of the St. Felix, and Bronson, standing behind the front desk looking like an extra from *The Night of the Living Dead,* froze when he saw him. As Silvano got closer he could make out the beads of sweat on the man's forehead. Bronson looked at his cigarette, smoldering in an ashtray, and made a try for it with a quivering hand and missed, knocking it out of the ashtray and onto the counter. It rolled to the edge and fell off. "Shit," Bronson said. "Dammit." He steadied himself on the edge of the counter with his left hand and went for the butt with his right, came up with it cleanly, but then he dropped it again as he stood up. "Oh, shit," he said, gave up, stomped it out. Silvano leaned on the other side of the counter, watching him.

"Hey," Bronson said, shaking a new cigarette out of the pack and sticking it in his mouth. "Hey, it's you. You find out anything?" He flicked his Zippo lighter twice, three times, but it refused to light. There was a small glass jar on the counter, filled with books of matches bearing the hotel's name. Silvano took one out and lit a match, held it out steady, and let Bronson navigate the dancing end of the butt into the flame. "Thanks," he said, sucking hungrily.

"Yeah," Silvano said, flicking the match at him. "Found out you ratted on me."

"Wha . . ." Bronson took a step back, but there was nowhere for him to go. "Who said . . . I never—"

"Shut up. Don't make it worse, okay? I know you did it. It's okay, I can understand it, it was just business. You didn't know me, right? But now you do, and I know you. From now on, you don't see nothin', you don't know nothin', you can't remember what I look like. You got that?"

Bronson blew out a big cloud of smoke. "All right," he said. Even his voice was shaking. "All right, listen, I . . ."

Silvano shook his head. "I don't wanna hear it. I told you I understand the first one. Do it again, though, and I'll break one of your knees. Maybe both. Guy as fucked up as you, you'll never heal right. You won't be able to work anymore, you're lucky, you'll wind up in a wheelchair in some stinking roach palace like this, hanging out in the lobby, wondering what happened."

Bronson held up both shaking hands like he was being robbed. "Hey," he said. "I don't see nothing. I just went blind."

Silvano shot him in the chest with his finger, turned, and left.

THE DOG CAME NOISELESSLY out of the bushes and stuck his nose into Silvano's hand. "I'm sorry, I forgot about you," Silvano whispered to the dog. "Next time I'll bring you something. I promise." The dog licked his palm. He forgives you, he thought. How about that.

He pushed Henry's door open. It's so late, he thought, that it's early. He decided that there was no point in going to bed just to sleep for two hours and then have to get up and go to work down at Black and White. He let himself in as quietly as he could and felt his way into Henry's kitchen. He sat at the table there in the darkness, listening as the old building seemed to talk to him, creaking and groaning in the night. His imagination peopled the empty kitchen with ghosts out of his past, and risen to haunt him, they complained to him of the unfairness of it all. He shook his head, trying to wake himself up, drive them all away. Keep your head where your ass is, he told himself. The past is the worst neighborhood around.

Where does Henry keep his coffee? he wondered, and he got up and went looking. The old coffeemaker was there on the stove. In the dark, it was hard to tell if it was clean or not. He decided it didn't much matter, the thing was empty, at least. He tried to remember how Henry had made coffee with it. Oh, forget it, he told himself. How hard could this be? Water in the bottom, coffee in the top. He found the coffee can on the counter, loaded the thing, set it on the stove and lit a fire under it. A few minutes later it began to boil, filling the kitchen with its comforting smell. He got up and went to look at it. It seemed dangerously close to boiling over, so he turned the heat down partway. He waited a minute longer and then shut the burner off, went back to sit down while the thing resolved itself into separate chambers of coffee and spent grounds.

Despite his intention to remain where he was, his mind went back, back to the house in Bensonhurst where he'd grown up, empty rooms, black-and-white television sitting on a wooden box, mattresses on the floor. He didn't know how the old man had gotten the place, had to have been a score of some kind. It was inconceivable that the old bastard would have purchased it, sat down and applied for a mortgage, filling out paperwork like a regular person. Had to have been a scam. They had lived in it without furniture for what had seemed like an eternity, because nobody hijacked furniture trucks except by mistake, there was no money in it, and the stuff was hard to move, in more ways than one. Too much like work.

Henry must have smelled the coffee too, Silvano heard him rustling around somewhere in the dark recesses of the building, and a few minutes later he came wandering into the kitchen in his boxer shorts, thin white bony sticks holding him up, long white hair still unbraided, hanging down all crazy in the back.

"Damn," Silvano said. "You look like who did it and ran."

Henry drew himself up, insulted. "Least I come home last night, went to bed when it got dark, like a human being. Didn't stay out half the night howling at the moon with the werewolves."

Silvano wrapped his hand around his cup, relishing the warmth. "Wasn't howling," he said. "I had business."

"Yeah?" Henry fished his cup out of the sink and poured coffee into it. "You find out anything?"

"Hard to say. I went looking for this guy, supposed to be a friend of my brother, but I didn't find him."

"Son, you make a rugged cup of coffee. What was his name?"

"Special Ed. There was one other guy, they called him the Dutchman. He's supposed to be dead."

"Hmmmph." Henry sounded disgusted. "I don't know no Special Ed, but the Dutchman was a guy name of Lenny Deutch. He was the kinda person would steal your wallet and then help you look for it. Every time you run into him, the sonuvabitch is looking you over, trying to see what you got, wants to know where you got it. Dirt bag. Always claimed to be connected, but I never believed him."

"Terrific. And you never heard of anybody named Special Ed? Guy's a dwarf. Lives up off Middagh Street. Pushes a shopping cart around. Might be your competition."

"I got no competition." Henry scratched his chin. "Walks all crooked, hangs on to the cart to keep from falling over?"

"Sounds like him."

"I seen him around, but I don't know the guy. I hope he ain't like Lenny Deutch. I think I did hear that Deutch was dead. Last time I saw him, he was blowing smoke out of his ass about some big score he had lined up." Henry shook his head. "I don't mean to talk vulgar, but I never liked the guy. He was too stupid to pull off anything big, anyhow. He was the kinda guy, he'd break into your place to rob you, right, but he'd be so drunk he'd fall asleep on your living room sofa with your television in his lap. I figure, whatever he thought he had lined up, it blew up in his face."

"World is full of 'em, isn't it."

"Yeah," Henry said sourly. "And more coming, every day."

"I MIGHT HAVE A LINE ON YOUR GUY."

Domenic stared at Ivan. "What the fuck does that mean? Might? You might have a line? Exactly what is it you think you got?"

Ivan lit up a cigarette, rolled the driver's side window of his car halfway down. "The other night," he said, "after you left, Antonio grilled me pretty good. I think he's starting to wonder about you. I don't like that." He looked pointedly at Domenic. "When he wonders about you, he starts wondering about me."

"Oh, for Christ's sake . . ."

"He thinks you're losing it."

Domenic stared up at the ceiling of the car. "You know, I worry about the same thing myself." It was true, of late, he often wondered if he wasn't slipping, if some misplaced or malformed protein in his brain might not be altering his consciousness, or if some essential but as yet undiscovered or misunderstood nutrient might not be absent from his diet, thus causing him gradually to lose his mind. Or maybe it was some flaw in the basic design, maybe the old superstitions were right after all, maybe God was amused by insanity, maybe He dreamed up the whole mess just to alleviate His own boredom. Or maybe it was just Time, lapping on the rocks of his being, eroding the civilized superfluities, leaving behind only the primitive skeleton of fear, rage, and the will to survive. "You fucking guys are driving me crazy. You're not gonna be happy until you see me chained to the fucking wall someplace, talking to myself. Forget Antonio, how many times do I have to tell you that? He's a hundred years old, for Christ's sake. Tell me what you got on Iurata."

Ivan took a deep drag on the cigarette. "It's easy for you to tell me to forget Antonio, you hardly ever see him. I got him up my ass all day long, and I'm telling you, he's starting to suspect something. I think he might have heard something."

Domenic's arm flashed out, and he whacked Ivan on the back of the skull with his open hand. "Yeah, from who? If I keep my mouth shut, and you keep your mouth shut, who the fuck else is there? Nobody, that's who. Nobody but you and me knows shit about this. To Antonio and the rest of them, Black and White ain't nothing but some ten-cent armored car company across the street from one of his grocery stores. Antonio's probably picked up on you and your case of the fucking shakes. All you gotta do is keep your trap shut, you hear me? Quit worrying. Tell me what you got on Iurata."

"Yeah, you wanna hear what I got? I got a fucking speech from the old man, that's one thing I fucking got. He told me to make sure you stayed out of this. I think he wants to use this thing to find out if I'm in your back pocket. If he even knew that I was sitting here having this conversation with you . . ." He looked around, checked his rearview mirror reflexively. "It wouldn't even matter what we said, all right, we could be talking about pussy, okay, but you and me, in this fucking car, that would be enough for him. He would put me in the fucking ground, you understand? You know what he told those Jamaicans the other night? He told them he don't always learn from his mistakes, but he does always bury them."

"So what are you telling me? You're telling me you're gonna

do Silvano without me, and then we're both gonna walk away from Black and White and leave all that money sitting there, after all the time we put in setting this thing up. Is that what you're telling me? Because of Antonio? You're telling me your balls have shriveled up to the size of fucking raisins, is that what you're fucking telling me?"

"Dom, this is not what I wanted."

Domenic was laughing in disgust. "Not what you wanted? Not what you wanted?" He slid over next to Ivan on the seat. "You listen to me," he said, lowering his voice. "The day you brought Black and White to me, you sold out. You understand? You sold Antonio down the fucking river. Now, there is no fucking way to back out of this without taking a bullet in the fucking head. Do you hear what I'm telling you? We do this right, we both walk away from Brooklyn with everything. Do you even know what that means? That's what it comes down to. Those are your only two choices, you can take two rounds in the skull or you can have the whole fucking world. There's no third option. Now, we both know you're smart enough, and we both know you've got the fucking opportunity. Here's what I want to know: Do you have the fucking balls?"

Ivan stared straight ahead, out through his windshield. "You don't need to worry about me. I just want to keep him off my back until the time comes."

Domenic slid back over to his side again. "Fine," he said. "You grab Iurata, make Antonio happy. Just don't kill him. I'll stay away until you've got him. Now tell me what you got."

Ivan looked at him for a long count. "All right," he said, finally.

• • •

DOMENIC STOOD ON the sidewalk and watched the car pull away and turn the corner. Ivan would not be human if he didn't have second thoughts, he told himself. It's always easier to get into shit than it is to get out of it. Hell, if he had only known how things would work out, he'd have walked away when his grandfather died, shit, man, he would have run. Gina was right, he hated to admit it, but she'd been right on the money. He just wished she hadn't shoved it down his throat, but that's when you sold out, he told himself, back when you took the easy way out, when you took the money, when you turned your back on what you really wanted. Now your obligations keep pushing all the good things in life back just out of reach. Give yourself the same speech, he thought, the one you just gave Ivan. You can pull this off, you can get Iurata, and you can suck the money out of Black and White. If you have the balls, you can walk away from here with enough money to do whatever you want. He turned and walked down the sidewalk. Better days coming, he told himself. Iurata first, then Black and White.

SIX

■

"WE OUGHTA HAVE A GUN."

I got one, Silvano thought, feeling lucky that no one had made him for it. Thank God for bell bottoms, this would never fly with those peg leg jeans he'd grown up wearing, and still, the gun made a bigger bulge under his pant leg than he wanted it to. It was not the kind of gun the carpenter was talking about.

"A nailer," the guy continued. "You know, pneumatic. We'd be done in no time." They were installing subflooring made of four-by-eight sheets of compressed wood shavings and glue. They'd spent the first two hours laying it out, cutting and fitting pieces to fit the odd shapes of the room, securing each one with two or three nails, and now it was time to finish the job. "You want the nails on a six-inch square." The guy was on his knees with a nail bag around his waist and a heavy framer's hammer in his hand, and he kept up a steady rhythm with the hammer while he talked. He hit each nail three times, no more, no less, one whack to set the nail in place, one to drive it most of the way in, one to send it home. Silvano watched his hands, particularly the left one. The guy had a handful of flooring nails in it, and he would finger out the nails one at a time, spin the pointed end down, and position the nail on the wood, all without looking, without varying the steady pace of the hammer unless he had to shift to a new spot or grab another handful of nails.

"Damn," Silvano said. "I feel like I oughta just stay the hell out of your way."

"Ain't nothing to it. Why don't you start over there in the closet. You gotta go slower in the closet, anyhow. On six-inch squares. Get it?"

"Yeah," Silvano said. "I get it." His mind had been occupied with fruitless speculations about Noonie, Special Ed, and the Dutchman. He found now, however, that he needed to concentrate, because whenever his mind wandered, he would hit his left hand with the hammer.

"Ow! Shit!"

The carpenter got up and came over to watch. "Don't choke up on the hammer," he said, looking over Silvano's shoulder. "Hold it down at the end. Yeah, like that. Okay, now just tap the nail in so that it's set in place. Now move your hand out the way. Okay, now hit the fucking thing, no, don't look at the hammer, keep your eye on the head of the nail, and just whack it. There you go, that's better. Don't try to kill it, just let the hammer drive the nail. Yeah, there. That's more like it."

He improved, somewhat, with practice. After a couple more whacks on his left hand, he managed to put all thoughts about Noonie, Special Ed, and the rest of it out of his mind and did what the guy told him, set the nail, feel for the next one as you watch the nail head, swing the hammer three or four more times, put the next one into position, and after a while he found his head as empty as the room, nothing in it but the nailing.

Some time later Silvano noticed Lee standing in the doorway

of the room they were working in, watching the two of them. Lee took up most of the space in the doorway. Silvano, figuring his attention was now compromised, did not want to hit his hand in front of the foreman, so he stopped what he was doing and turned to look. "Hey," he said.

"You know," Lee said, "we could avoid all these interruptions from next door, we might actually be able to make a carpenter out of you."

Silvano shrugged. "Tell them I don't want to do it."

Lee shook his head. "Black and White is a nice account," he said, with a hint of a smile. "Nice, nice. We get time and materials for every man-hour on this job, including whatever time you spend helping Sean. I want the O'Brians to have a warm fuzzy feeling whenever they think of us. The little turd's got some errand to run, says he needs a hand." He looked at Silvano. "You don't mind, being a gofer?"

Silvano laid his hammer on the floor and stood up. "Pay's the same," he said. "Why would I care?"

SEAN O'BRIAN STOOD in the middle of the floor, distracted. "Thanks, Lee," he said, his mind obviously elsewhere. "Uhh . . ."

"Silvano."

"Yeah, sorry. Silvano. Why don't you have a seat somewhere, I got to get a check for my uncle." He turned, headed for his uncle's office, stopped by Elia's desk. "God, I hate this."

She did not look up from what she was doing. "Well, he's only your uncle, Sean, he doesn't own you. You can leave if you want to."

"Easy for you to say," he said, walking away. "It isn't that simple."

When the door to Joseph O'Brian's office closed, she looked up at Silvano and smiled. "Hey," she said. She pointed at the chair next to her desk. "Come, sit. You miss me?"

He complied. "Oh, man, you better believe it. I been thinking about you all day."

"Good," she said. "When am I going to see you again?"

"Watch for me," he said. "I'll catch up with you."

She reached out, brushed his hand with her fingertips. "Little Domenic didn't find you yet."

"No," he said. "Everything okay in here?"

"Well . . ." She shrugged. "Mr. O'Brian has been helping the Brothers of the Immaculate Reception." She smiled again. "It's some old empty seminary, way down the other end of Brooklyn. The fathers there have some sort of reconstruction going on, and Mr. O'Brian is working with them."

"O'Brian know anything about construction?"

"What he knows about is money. How to get it, how to keep it, how to squeeze it out of your suppliers, how to spend it. He says people don't know how to spend money. They do it, but they don't do it right. That's what he says."

"He might be right about that. Is that what he's doing? Helping the fathers spend their money?"

"He does a lot of that for the Church. He says they are too trusting. He says every organization needs an asshole, and they don't keep anyone around who's mean enough. So when they need an asshole, they call him."

Silvano regarded the back of his hand. "Couple of nuns I can think of," he said, "plenty mean enough, they're still alive."

She laughed. "No doubt, but most men are too proud to listen to a woman. Anyway, Sean thinks his uncle spends so much time on his church activities that he isn't taking care of business here, and it means more work for everyone else. He and

Sean had another screaming match here this morning. I'm surprised you didn't hear it next door. I think you probably could have heard it from New Jersey."

SEAN TOOK THE on-ramp to the Brooklyn-Queens Expressway and got in line for the exit to the Brooklyn Bridge. He shook his head, looking around at the traffic. "Shoulda took the local streets."

Silvano relaxed, savoring the comfort of the soft leather passenger seat. "Where we going?"

"There's a place on the Lower East Side, sells gold leaf and shit. I got to pick up an order that my uncle made and run it down to this chapel he's working on, St. Whoever-the-Fuck, I forget the name, way down on Rockaway someplace. He don't like me going to this gold leaf joint by myself, he says the locals keep watch, see if they can rob somebody coming out." He made a face.

"See, that's nice," Silvano said. "He's worried about you."

"It ain't that," Sean said. "He just don't wanna have to pay for his shit twice."

"Oh. You carrying?"

"No, I ain't got a permit. It ain't like that, anyhow, gold leaf ain't really worth that much. It's like this thin foil, so thin you can't believe it, comes on these little sheets of tissue paper. The way they use it, they paint this glue on whatever it is they wanna cover, right, and then the gold foil sticks to the glue. Sorta like painting, except you gotta polish it up, after. So anyhow, the gold leaf isn't worth the bother, if you're like a professional crook, but if you're a bum on the street and you don't know any better you might be tempted. So what I'm saying is, you got nothing to worry about, just, like, hang out next to the car, keep me from getting a parking ticket."

"All right."

The stop in the city went quickly. Silvano got out of the car and sat on the trunk while Sean made his pickup, and a minute later they were on their way again.

"See, that was easy," Sean said. "Now we gotta fight our way all the way down the Belt Parkway to get to this fucking place. You know, I wouldn't mind doing this kinda shit, but I got things I hafta do, you know, back at the ranch, and wasting all this time means I won't get out of that place until who knows what time tonight. And my uncle don't care about that, he don't think anybody's got anything else to do, because he's got no kinda life, don't understand why I want one. He don't care what time he gets home."

"Maybe he doesn't want to go home to his wife."

"Wife? He ain't got no wife, he had one once but she left his ass, he ain't social enough to handle a pet fucking parakeet, forget about a wife. I'm telling you, he ain't got no life at all. Guy's got more money than God, right, lives all by himself in this apartment house he owns out in Douglaston. I don't even know for sure he's got a television. He drives a Ford Maverick, for chrissake. You ever see the guy go out for lunch? Brown-bags it every stinkin' day, don't see the point of going out. Don't take vacations, don't do shit. Wasn't for this church obsession, he wouldn't come out of his hole at all." The kid was mad now, gritting his teeth. "I don't understand him. He started this construction project at work, got all you guys putting up a new building, and then he just seemed to lose interest. It's like he doesn't pay attention at all."

"Maybe he's just comfortable. Maybe he's made enough money already, don't care anymore. Nice problem to have."

"Oh, bullshit." The kid was still steaming. "I would never want to trade places with him, no matter how much money he's got, and neither would you. He's all worried all the time about what's a venal sin and what's the other kind, the worse one, I forget what they call it . . ." He looked over at Silvano.

Silvano shrugged. "Whatever."

"A mortal sin, that's what it is. Don't do this, don't do that, don't touch your thing unless you hafta take a whiz. What the hell kind of way is that to live? You really think God is that much of a cock teaser, fill up the world with all of this good shit and then tell you that you can't have any of it?"

Silvano had to laugh, and Sean looked over at him, and then he laughed too, his mood broken. "Sorry," he said. "I didn't mean to go off on you. But lately, I've really begun to think my uncle is losing his mind."

"This is all your fault, you know."

"How the hell do you figure that?"

"Look at you. Guy says jump, what do you do? You jump. Sure, you might bitch about it, but he's used to that. What if you put the shoe on the other foot? Suppose you went off and pissed the day away instead of the other way around, left him there by himself. Maybe then he'd have a better understanding of how it feels."

"Oh, man." Sean looked mortified.

"I bet you weren't even going to stop for lunch. I bet you were gonna go running right out there, deliver your package, and come running straight back."

Sean looked at his watch. "Well," he said, "I got so much work to do . . . You hungry? You wanna stop someplace to grab a bite?"

"I ain't grabbing nothing. I eat my lunch like a man, I sit down at a table and eat with a knife and fork. You know, Sean, I'm going to give you another piece of free advice. Okay? Very important for a man to learn when to say 'Fuck it.'"

Sean looked over at him, stared for a few seconds. "You know a place?"

Silvano permitted himself a half a smile. "Used to be a nice place down on Baxter Street, in Little Italy. Let's go see if it's still there."

It was. Silvano palmed the waiter a ten to let them use the room in the back of the restaurant. The room was painted white, had Astroturf on the floor, vines stenciled on the wall, plastic grapes hung from a trellis surrounding a huge skylight, which was open, admitting the air and the sounds of Manhattan. Silvano ordered in Italian, starting them off with a big antipasto and two bottles of Orvieto, followed by the main course and another bottle, Chianti this time. By the time the waiter cleared the table, Sean was plotzed.

"I think I'm fucked up," he said.

"Not yet, you're not," Silvano said, winking at the waiter, giving him two hundreds. The guy left, came back promptly with two glasses and a bottle of brandy and then left them alone. Silvano still had the two plastic baggies he'd taken from the guy in the garage stairwell in an inside pocket. He took one of them out, tore a piece of paper off one of the placemats and rolled a huge joint.

"Oh, geez," Sean said, stumbling over the end of his tongue. "Whass that shit?"

"This," Silvano said, holding up the finished product, "is proof that there really is a God. You ever do this before?"

"High schoo'," Sean said. "Once or twice." He looked doubtful.

Silvano fired it up but didn't hit on it. "All right," he said, handing it over. "This shit is pretty lame, okay, so you gotta take a nice big hit. Inhale, inhale, that's good. Now hold it, hold it in . . ."

Sean coughed out a big cloud of smoke, giggling when he saw it. He handed the joint back to Silvano, who just held on to it for a minute before passing it back. "Here you go," he said. "Nice big hit."

"I am really ffffff, oh, shit. I am fffff . . ." Sean had an idiotic grin on his face.

"Yeah, you are. Now you are fucked up." Silvano moved his chair around next to Sean, took a picture of Noonie out of his pocket. "I want you to do me a favor," he said. "I want you to see if you recognize this guy. Look at the picture. You know him?"

Sean tried hard to focus. "Nnnnoomie," he said after a minute. "Nnnoomie, my pal. Poor fffuck." His face wrinkled up and he started to cry. "My besss fren," he said, reaching for the picture. "Besss fren I had."

"What happened to him? Do you know what happened to him?"

Sean shook his head. "Sick inna head," he slurred. "Happiess mothafucker I ever met." The tears were rolling down his face. "Never wan nothin', never got nothin'. You give him somethin', he juss give it away to the nex guy."

"Do you know where he went? Where is he now?"

Sean was shaking his head. "Livin' onna street," he said. "Dinn have nobody taken care of em. Prolly dead, someone prolly kill em, take his money." He lowered his head and sobbed.

The joint was probably overkill, Silvano thought. "But they never found his body," he said. "Right? Nobody ever saw him again."

"Maybe he wen away," Sean said, wiping his face. "Maybe he got losss . . ." He looked over at Silvano, and a light went on somewhere in his sodden brain. "Silvie?" he said. "You Silvie? He loved you, man . . ."

"Yeah, I'm Silvie."

"You come too late, Silvie. Noomie's gone." He shook his head, collapsed onto the table. "Nnnoomie's gone."

SEAN O'BRIAN LIVED in a basement apartment in a brownstone in Sunset Park. Silvano found his address on his driver's license and left him there passed out on his couch. He stood there, looking down at the kid, wondering how much he'd remember when he came to. Not that it mattered. It had happened before, his gut feelings could be wrong, but that didn't make it any easier to take. He'd been so sure that Sean knew something, but there was no way the kid could be that messed up and not give himself away. It didn't seem that he knew much, though, other than the fact that he hated his job, and that his uncle had his head up his ass. Silvano turned and walked out.

He walked for a while, giving the air and the sun and the exertion time to burn off whatever alcohol was left in his system. He had been careful, feeding most of it to the kid. He felt lousy about it now, but it wasn't the first rotten thing he'd done in his life, probably wouldn't be the last. He caught a cab when he got to Fourth Avenue.

JOSEPH O'BRIAN WAS BACK, because the Maverick was parked in the lot.

Silvano was better prepared this time. His shopping bag with wino clothes in it was on the floor beside him. He sat in the garage stairwell and sipped at his coffee while he watched the comings and goings at Black and White through his binoculars. If anyone missed him and Sean, you couldn't tell from this distance, the business of the day went on as it had before, with the exception that Joseph O'Brian had to find someone else to let him out of the gate when he went on his bike ride. Silvano stashed his glasses high up on a ledge and headed down the stairs while the elder O'Brian stood inside the gate waiting. He crossed the street and headed up Atlantic, glancing back over his shoulder. O'Brian started out on the other side, stopping for the lights as he had before. Silvano didn't stop when O'Brian did, this time he kept up a nice steady jog, and O'Brian didn't pass him until they were nearly to Flatbush. He stopped on the far side of the street, watched O'Brian chain his bicycle to a parking meter. There was a bar on the corner of Atlantic and Flatbush, place looked like a real bucket of blood, exterior painted flat black, door, windows, and all. Silvano, wiping the sweat from his face, watched in disbelief as Joseph O'Brian went inside.

Can't be, he thought, there's no way this guy rides his bike all the way down Atlantic Avenue just to go have a beer in that dump. He stayed where he was, watching the street, waiting to see if anyone else had been trailing O'Brian, and then he walked across the street and headed for the bar.

There was a small vestibule, also painted flat black, with a pay phone on one side, set of stairs heading down into the basement on the other, and a set of swinging doors in the center. The windows on the swinging doors had been pasted over with posters advertising a free concert in the park. Silvano didn't recognize the names of any of the bands, and the date of the concert was a little better than a year past. He pushed the door open and went in.

The place was dark inside and it smelled bad, the essence of beer, urine, and vomit mixed in the undercurrent of decay. The only light came from a couple of frosted globes and some neon beer signs. There was a group of guys collapsed around a table in one corner, but none of them was Joseph O'Brian. None of them looked conscious. Silvano walked over to the bartender, a heavily muscled white guy who had both arms covered with tattoos, one running up the side of his neck.

"Looking for someone," he said. "Weaselly-looking guy, wearing green work clothes."

The bartender crossed his arms and looked at Silvano coldly. "Can't help you."

"Yeah, all right." He walked away, looked over at the guys in the corner, but they weren't going to be any help. He went past them into a little corridor in the back where the bathrooms were, both of them smelled even worse than the rest of the bar, but O'Brian was not in either one. There was a small door at the end of the corridor, probably led out into the back alley, but it was chained shut. He turned and went back out into the main room. The bartender, looking irritated, came out from behind the bar holding a baseball bat in his hands.

"Hey, asshole," the guy said. "You got a problem?"

Silvano was not in the mood. "No, but you do," he said, grim-faced. He peered behind the guy to see if there was anyone hiding down behind the bar, but there wasn't. "You shoulda sawed the knob off the handle of that bat."

"Yeah? Why?"

"That way it won't hurt as much when I shove it up your ass." He could feel it building up, waiting to go off. The bartender saw something in him, looked at the end of the bat, decided not to chance it.

"You done in here?"

Silvano looked around the dingy room one more time. "Yeah," he said.

"Good-bye."

He walked on over to the swinging doors but stopped when

he heard footsteps clomping up the cellar stairs into the vestibule. He waited, but whoever it was did not come into the bar. He cracked one of the swinging doors open and peered out in time to see Joseph O'Brian bent over, unchaining his bicycle.

GOING DOWN INTO HOLES in the ground was not one of Silvano's favorite activities. There was no light switch that he could find, and he didn't even have a match or a cigarette lighter with him. Breathing heavily, he went through the door at the foot of the cellar stairs, let it swing shut behind him. He waited for his eyes to adjust. The darkness smelled like mice and damp cardboard. It seemed that no light leaked in from anywhere, though, and he began to make his way by feel, an inch at a time. He made them out with his hands, random stacks of cases of beer. Off somewhere in the darkness a refrigeration compressor clicked into life, hummed for a few minutes, shut down again. Got to be a light over there, he thought. Guy had to run power to the compressor, stands to reason he'd put in a light, too. Counting his steps, he made his slow and silent way around the piles of boxes into the corner where he'd heard the compressor. The thing kicked on again when he'd gotten close and the noise guided him the rest of the way. A string brushed against his cheek, it was attached to a bare bulb hanging from the ceiling. Turning his face away, he pulled the string.

It was a vast relief to see with his eyes what he'd seen with his hands and nothing more, none of the images from his raging imagination, just a cellar, just cases of beer, compressors for the coolers upstairs, dirt, dust, shadows, rat turds. What would O'Brian want down in this hole, he wondered, but there was nothing. Fuck it, he told himself, maybe the guy sneaked down here to take a leak, there's nothing down here, get out. He plotted his course back to the door, hit the light, made his way gratefully back out onto the street.

Silvano headed back. He shook his head. The guy has a heart condition, he's trying to get in a little exercise. Just trying to stay alive. That's why the feebs don't follow him. There's nothing here.

Back in his stairwell, he watched through the glasses as quitting time came for the construction crew and they all packed up and trooped through the gate. Not long after that, the trucks began showing up in ones and twos, parking in the lot in front of Black and White's building, and the drivers went inside to do whatever they had to do to settle up. He changed into his wino clothes and headed off.

SPECIAL ED HAD BEEN half out of the mold when the die came down; he was badly stamped, misshapen, twisted, gnarled, poorly served by fate, and anyone who made eye contact with him could tell it was eating at him from the inside. Walking behind his shopping cart, he barely came up to the handle, and from the rear he appeared to have been knocked into a half-moon crescent, in the shape of a backward C from his ankles to his shoulders. He had thick, black, furry eyebrows that seemed to have lives of their own. They were always in motion, squirming across his forehead as he squinted first one eye shut, then the other, depending on which way he was looking. He never had both eyes open at the same time, even staring straight ahead he would peer through one eye and squinch the other one shut, and he would twist his mouth as far as he could in the direction of whichever eye was closed. The effect was that he did not so much look at you as chew at your consciousness, furiously demanding your attention, although he did not seem to enjoy it. "The fuck you looking at," he would yell angrily at anyone who stared too long. "The fuck you looking at?" Spraying spit, showing a lot of small teeth in his lower jaw.

He hung on to the back of the cart, holding himself semi-erect with thick stubby fingers and corded forearms. He kept some cinderblocks in the front of the cart, underneath whatever swag he'd happened to have scored that day, so that when he sold his load to the junkman he didn't lose all of his ballast. He was going bald on top, and what was left writhed from the fringes of his skull like Van Gogh's trees.

He saw Silvano coming in his direction, wearing his wino clothes and carrying his shopping bag. He yanked an aluminum baseball bat out of the cart, and he hung on to the cart handle with one hand and he smacked the side of the cart with the bat with the other. "Lemme alone," he growled, trying to sound tough, but he had a thin, reedy voice. "Lemme alone. The fuck do you want?" He looked at Silvano out of one eye and then the other, his face doing its scowling dance as he did. "I don't got nothing, I don't know you. Lemme alone!"

"Ain't gonna hurt you," Silvano told him. "I just want to talk."

"I don't know nothin'! Why you wanna bother me?" He screwed his face into an ugly mask of fear and resentment, and for a few seconds it appeared that he was going to burst into tears, but instead he smacked the shopping cart with renewed vigor. "Lemme alone!" he shouted. "Get the fuck away from me!"

"My brother was a friend of yours. I want to talk to you about him."

Special Ed hefted the bat in his hand, glaring at Silvano through one eye and then the other. "I don't got no friends."

"His name was Noonie."

"Ah, shit." The tension drained out of Special Ed's body. "Noonie," he said, his voice softer. He crammed the bat back into his shopping cart. "Noonie. The poor fuck." He looked at Silvano, and a grin spread across his unlovely face. "You must be the guy," he said. "You must be the one them was lookin' for."

"I might be. Who's them?"

Special Ed shook his head violently. "I dunno! I didn't ask! I tol you, I don't know nothin'!" He grabbed for his bat and missed, leaned too hard on the shopping cart handle, and the cart lurched forward a few feet. He almost fell, but he grabbed the handle with both hands and hauled himself back into his semi-erect position. Silvano caught the front of the cart and steadied it.

"Easy," he said. "Easy does it. You all right?"

Special Ed seemed to calm down a bit. "I'm okay," he said. "But I don't know nothin'. I don't. Awright?"

"These guys, looking for me," Silvano said. "They give you anything? They take care of you?"

"No," Special Ed said sourly. "They knocked me down and they dumped my cart out. Said they'd pay, though. Said they'd gimme a C if I turned you up." He glared at Silvano, his face a closed fist, impossible to read.

"Well, that's fair enough," Silvano said. "I can match that, and I won't knock you down for it." He reached into his pocket. "Matter of fact, I'll do you better than that. I'll tell you how you can collect from both ends. How's that?"

Special Ed squinted at him. He watched Silvano count off twenties. "All right," he said. "We gotta get off the street, first. I ain't takin' nothin' from you out on the street. I'm gonna start yellin', okay, and I'm gonna grab my bat. You run away, okay, and I'll meet you in the alley down behind my building. You know where I live at?"

• • •

IT WAS A LOUSY SITUATION, tactically. Silvano walked halfway down Special Ed's alley, stopped where it made a ninety-degree turn to the right before dead-ending behind a row of four- and five-story brownstones. There was only the one way in and out, except for a couple of locked doors and one fire escape. Silvano surveyed it from the corner of the L. You were here before, he told himself, what are you worried about now? But the layout didn't feel good, so he headed back out onto the sidewalk. There was a storefront liquor store down the block, it occupied the first floor of an apartment building. He went inside and found himself in a vestibule made of bulletproof glass. The merchant and her wares were on the other side, and business was conducted through a drawer. Silvano stood close enough to speak to the clerk and still keep an eye on the street.

"Kinda blackberry brandy you got?" He couldn't help it, when he was wearing his wino clothes, he wanted the cheapest high he could get.

"Huh?" Behind her partition, she hadn't heard him. He repeated his question, louder this time.

"Old Mr. Boston," she said, and she went and got the pint and half-pint sizes, and they discussed prices.

"That's a little steep," he said, still talking louder than normal so she could hear him. "What you got that's a little more cost-effective?"

Fortified wines were the best value, in the clerk's opinion, and Silvano continued to divide his attention between their conversation and the street, outside, while they debated the merits of the various brands the clerk had in stock. "I hate sherry," he told her. "And that Mad Dog gives me a bitch of a headache. Make it Richard's Wild Irish Rose. I always like a square bottle." He dug in his pocket and put a five-dollar bill in the tray. Special Ed was making his painfully slow way up the sidewalk. She passed his change through with the bottle. "Mad Dog," he said, shaking his head. "Stuff tastes like they cut it with formaldehyde." Through the glass door he watched Special Ed make his way down into the alley. He waited another minute, but there were no other pedestrians, no cars coming down the street.

He'd been worried for nothing, Special Ed was on his own. Silvano helped him hump his cart down the two steps and through the door to where he kept it chained to the wall outside his basement room. "Fuckers!" Ed shouted, red-faced. "They steal my cart, steal my shit, they even take my cement blocks! What kind of asshole would steal a man's cement blocks, ain't even good for nothin', ain't worth shit! Can you answer me that?"

"It's a hard world."

"Nobody knows that better than me. Nobody!"

Silvano didn't argue with him. He sat down on an inverted milk crate and slid his bottle out of its brown paper bag. "You got any cups, Ed?"

"Hey. Hey, now." He held up a stubby finger, and then made his way over to the wall and leaned on it for support and went off to rummage in some cardboard boxes in the corner. He came back dragging a wooden chair, carrying two Styrofoam coffee cups. He spun the chair around sideways so that he could perch on the edge of the seat and lean on the back, in as close to a sitting position as his unusual shape would allow. He noticed Silvano looking at a stack of siding in one corner.

"Lumium," he said. "They ain't payin' shit for it right now, and I'm waitin' for prices to go up."

"Sounds smart."

"Well, they're always tryin' to fuck ya," he said in a wounded voice. "Every which way you turn, there's always somebody there waitin' and watchin'." He handed Silvano a cup. "Brand new," he said, peering into his. "Nice and clean. I just took 'em out of the package." He turned his cup upside down and tapped it on the bottom, just in case. "The cops threw out a whole box of 'em, I found 'em in the Dumpster behind the precinct house."

Silvano looked into his cup, and finding nothing there, he poured it a quarter full, trusting that the Richard's would kill anything he couldn't see. Special Ed held his cup out in Silvano's direction.

"You said you'd pay," he said. "Said you'd pay me a hundred."

"So I did." Silvano poured Ed's cup full and then sat the bottle on the floor and fished out a twenty. "Let's start with that. Who are these guys looking for me?"

"Two guys in a Caddy."

"Caddy have a busted taillight?"

Special Ed twisted his face up, concentrating. "Yeah," he said. "Driver's side. Two guys, one of 'em was a big son of a bitch. Bigger'n you. Him and the driver, I didn't see the driver very good."

"This guy have a name?"

Ed grinned. "Driver called him Ivan, that's what pissed him off . . ." Suddenly he scowled. "That's when he kicked over my cart. Bastard. Asshole." He screwed his face into a knot, grinding his teeth, holding his breath, and then he recovered, inhaled, opened one eye and glared at Silvano. He took a swig from his cup and swallowed convulsively. "Some day," he said, "I'd love to push the button. The one the President carries around with him everywhere. I'd like to sneak into the White House while he's asleep and push that button. See who laughs, then."

Silvano took out another twenty and handed it over, poured Ed a refill. "You'd have to move to D.C., you wanted to do that. Next question. Who or what is the Dutchman? And where can I find him?"

"Who." Special Ed wrinkled his face into an expression of contempt. "Lenny Deutch, is who. Another asshole. Another mean fuck, thought I was funny. Noonie liked him, though." He squinted at Silvano. "Noonie was your brother? You don't look nothin' like him."

"We had different mothers."

"Oh. I'm sorry he's gone." Special Ed tucked his chin into his chest, both eyes closed, and then he started to cry, his body shaking with the effort. Second time today someone's crying for my brother, Silvano thought. Special Ed fought with it for a minute, shrugging a shoulder up to wipe his nose and his cheeks on his sleeve. He started in talking again, his eyes squeezed shut. "He always treated me nice. It wasn't pity, neither, he didn't feel sorry for me or nothin', he didn't know nothin' about that. He would come here early in the morning sometimes, an' he would knock on the door. 'You goin' to Lantic, Ed?' he would say, 'cause he knew that was where I would sell my scrap metal, and then he'd load up the cart, right, an' he'd push it, he'd let me ride, all the way down to Lantic. Do the same thing, comin' back, if he seen me." He wiped his nose on his sleeve again and peered at Silvano. "You ain't like him, are you?"

"No."

"No. Nobody is." Special Ed drained off what was left in his cup, held it out for another refill. "I tol him to stay away from that Lenny Deutch. I tol him and tol him."

"Where is the Dutchman now?"

"Dead. Dead and in hell, I hope, with his balls on fire."

"Metaphysically speaking," Silvano said, "maybe he is. But there's got to be something left of him up here somewhere, right?" He peeled off a couple more twenties. "Do you know where those parts of him might be?"

Special Ed squeezed his eyes closed tightly and shook his head violently. "No," he said, fear heavy in his voice. "I don't know nothin' about that."

Silvano sighed. He looked at what was left in the bottle. "Drink up, Ed."

"All right." Special Ed drained what was left in his cup, not savoring it anymore, just gulping it down and then holding out his empty cup. His hand was shaking. Silvano poured him full again.

"Okay. Let's try this another way. You're a survivor, Ed. You must be a pretty smart guy, making it on your own, like you do. There's nobody giving you a free ride, am I right, Ed?"

"All by myself," Ed mumbled, peering down into his cup.

"So I figure, sharp guy like you, you gotta know what the Dutchman was doing wrong. You gotta know why he got whacked. Am I right?"

Special Ed peered at him through one eye and said nothing.

"C'mon, Ed. Tell me where he made his mistake."

Special Ed looked at the floor. "He din't know who he was," he said after a minute. He stopped, thinking it over, and Silvano sat silent, waiting him out. "See, I know who I am," he said, after a minute. "An' I know what I hafta do. If I don't go actin' like somebody I ain't, I'll prolly be safe. Safe enough." He took another swig from his cup. "Lenny Deutch din't wanna be what he was. I mean, I wanna be something else too, everybody does. I wanna be you. You prolly wanna be some other guy." He said it without looking up. "But you ain't. An' I ain't, neither. Different, I mean. Lenny Deutch was a nothin' but a drunk, but he wanted to be a tough guy. He wanted it so bad, he started believin' it. When he started out, he'd drink his wine, stay out of everybody's way, din't get into no trouble. After he decided he was a gangster, he started workin' for these guys, they was from down in Bay Ridge or somethin'. They used to use him to run errands an' shit, an' he started thinkin' he was better than us." He looked up, finally. "Better than me, anyhow. But they was just usin' him, like he was tryin' to use Noonie. They sent him inta places he din't belong, got him doing things he shouldn't have did. That's why he's dead. That's all I know."

"All right," Silvano said. "Bottle's almost gone, let's finish it." He poured the last of it into Special Ed's cup. "How come I heard that Noonie found the Dutchman?"

Special Ed's hand was shaking again. "They'll kill me," he said. "If they think I know somethin', they'll kill me."

"They're not going to find out anything from me."

Special Ed sat and stared at the floor for a while. "We was junkin'," he said, finally. "You know, collectin' stuff. Me an' Noonie. We was way down Lantic, by Flatbush. I lost track of him somewhere, he went in, someplace. I couldn't go look for him, I don't do stairs very good. I started gettin' scared, 'cause we was so far from here, you know, an' I needed him to push me back, on the cart. I woulda had a hard time by myself. An' he coulda forgot about me, you know how he was, be just like him to forget me and go off someplace, an' I din't know what to do. So I jus waited. After a long time, he come back, all excited. Said he found the Dutchman. He wanted to show me. An' I din't wanna know nothin' about the Dutchman, an' I wouldn't go. There's a bar on the corner, Flatbush and Lantic. Basement stairs ain't locked. That's where he found him."

"I was down there, I didn't see anything."

Special Ed was still staring at the floor. "Front corner of the building," he said, his voice almost inaudible. "'Nother set of stairs down to the subbasement. Noonie said he found the tunnel, found the Dutchman down inside the tunnel."

"A tunnel? Shit. God, I hate tunnels. What kind of tunnel?"

Special Ed sighed. "There's a abandoned railroad tunnel under Lantic. I been hearin' 'bout it for years, but nobody knew where it was. Noonie said he got in, down through the subbasement."

"So the Dutchman was dead, I take it. What else did he find?"

"I din't wanna know, I tol ya. I got him to push me back home, I got him talkin' about somethin' else." Special Ed was looking down again, and his voice got quiet. "I don't wanna know things I ain't sposed to know. I don't wanna go places I don't belong." He glanced over at Silvano, looked back down at the floor. "Maybe you ain't exactly what you look like. Maybe you ain't afraid of those guys." He looked around, reassuring himself that the two of them were still alone. "I can't be a tough guy," he said. "I can't. I got all I can manage, jus collectin'. Pushin' my cart."

Silvano counted off another hundred. "Ed," he said, "I want you to do me a favor. I want you to stay off the street for a few days. Take it easy for a while. Okay? If that guy comes around again, you tell him I came around to talk to you. Tell him I was asking about Noonie, tell him you said you didn't know anything. Okay? And tell him I told you I was at the Montague, that you could find me there if you remembered anything. Okay? Think you can remember all that?"

"Yeah, sure." Special Ed sounded despondent. "You're lookin' for Noonie, an' you're at the Montague. Maybe if I jus stay home they won't bother me."

"Maybe not. But if they do, you just tell them what I said. Okay?"

"Yeah. Yeah, sure." He squinted at Silvano. "They killed the Dutchman," he said. "They prolly killed Noonie, 'cause he found where the Dutchman was at. You go messin' around, they're gonna kill you, too."

Silvano stood to go. "Maybe," he said, "maybe not."

"Be careful," Ed mumbled. "Don't forget your shoppin' bag." He didn't look up when Silvano let himself out.

SILVANO WENT FOR THE MAD DOG AFTER ALL.

He figured he needed it to complete the look, and he went on down past the car service office where he'd seen Bonifacio and his crew, found a liquor store up closer to Henry's building, bought the bottle, and headed back. The bastards must have found out I used this car service, he thought, someone must have seen me getting out of the car. Sons of bitches, you think you've found a safe place, and they show up on your doorstep. He'd been immediately angry when he saw them. Try to do this the easy way, he thought, so nobody else gets hurt, and they don't cooperate. He cracked the bottle of Mad Dog and tossed the cap into the gutter. For a drunk, open is empty, you ain't gonna need the cap again. He took a swig, just a small one, wrinkling his face up in distaste. Jesus, he thought. You really have to be willing to suffer, you wanna get a buzz from this shit. He poured some more of it out before he got there, and then he limped right past them, pausing not fifty feet from where they were to rummage through a trash can. Stupid bastards, he thought. When are they gonna get that taillight fixed? He'd made them from two blocks away.

His heart rate was up and there was a tingling sensation in the pit of his stomach, but mostly what he felt was anxiety. God, don't let them get Henry . . . He straightened up, finding nothing edible or salable in the trash can. Neighborhood like this, a gentleman of the streets would starve to fucking death.

There was no one sitting behind the wheel of the car, but the back windows were darkened and he couldn't tell if there was anyone inside or not. He limped his way over to a recessed doorway in the brick wall of the factory building on his side of the street. He leaned on the brick wall next to the doorway, doubled over, pretending to be sick to his stomach, careful not to spill his wine. There was a security gate on one side of the doorway, the expandable kind that you could open and padlock to a hasp on the other side. This one was rusted in place, though, and he guessed that whoever occupied this building didn't use this doorway, probably sealed it from the inside. Someone used the outside, though, there were some sheets of cardboard stacked up in the recessed space behind the gate, and a hairy green blanket hung from a nail driven into the mortar between the bricks, shoulder-high. Silvano straightened up a little, looked into the space, and then he limped on past.

Where were they?

When he got to Henry's building he paused next to the fence, looking into the jungle. The dogs were used to him now, and the one with half a tail came out of the undergrowth and looked at him expectantly. He felt a wave of relief wash over him. Maybe Henry's all right, he told himself. These two mutts would both be dead, they would have never gotten past the dogs. He turned and headed back.

The car was still sitting there when he got back to the doorway. He set his bottle off to one side and got the green blanket down off the nail. Sitting down in the doorway, he wrapped the blanket around himself, ignoring the smell. There was very little of him to see, that way, just his head sticking out of the top, and that was covered by his wig and Mrs. Clark's hat. Beneath the blanket he eased his pistol out of the ankle holster, clicked the safety off, and settled in to wait.

There were four of them, Ivan Bonifacio and three other guys, and they were all in the storefront office of the car service he'd been using. They spilled out onto the sidewalk, the four of them plus the guy who ran the car service. Ivan was the only one he recognized, two of the other guys were in suits, and the fourth guy looked like California, muscular and tanned, jeans, T-shirt, sneakers, long blond hair, shades. Hired help.

The car service guy was shrugging his shoulders and shaking his head, speaking Spanish, telling them he didn't know anything. One of the suits grabbed him by the elbows from behind, held him steady while Ivan backhanded him, stepping into it, putting some steam behind the blow. A cut opened up on the guy's cheekbone and blood began to run down his face. He looked over Ivan's shoulder and made eye contact with Silvano for just the briefest of moments, then looked back at Ivan, shaking his head violently, his voice going higher and quicker, still denying. Ivan drew his hand back again, big muscles flexing across his shoulders, loading up. The suit holding the car service guy was laughing, and the car service guy braced himself, but just before he did his eyes flicked Silvano's way again, just before he squeezed them shut. Ivan stopped, half-turned, looking over his shoulder, just a guy in a hat, rolled up in a blanket, but then his eyes went wide and he spun, reaching inside his coat, coming out with a big Colt Python, bringing it down, victory shining in his eyes. Car service guy took a punch for you, didn't rat you out, Silvano thought, you gotta give him a chance to get away. He flipped the blanket aside and put two rounds into the face of the suit holding the car service guy's elbows. The two of them went down, tangled up in Ivan's legs, and he went down with them. The other suit was reaching for something in his armpit and Silvano hit him next, two rounds in the center of the chest. The guy in the jeans had a Ruger .22 automatic in his hand, and he had Silvano all lined up, and Silvano's heart seemed to stop, but then the Python boomed, throwing the guy off. Ivan had fired from a prone position and his shot went high, recoil pushing the Python's barrel skyward. Silvano used the eye-blink of time to fire twice more, and California went spinning down in the middle of the street.

The car service guy leaped to his feet and vanished inside his office. Ivan rolled over behind the car. Silvano looked down under, watching Ivan's feet, and sent a couple of rounds punching through the sheet metal, but it was too late, Ivan had gotten in on the passenger side and slid over behind the wheel. The car engine roared, the back wheels smoked, the car fishtailed wildly, and then it was gone. The suits were both motionless, dead or dying where they'd landed. California still lay on his back in the center of the street, arching his back, kicking his feet, the Ruger still in his hand. Struggling for his next breath.

He'd never get it.

Silvano stuck the pistol back in his ankle holster, turned and looked around. No one had come out to look yet but they would soon, stupidly curious. The car service guy lurched out and slammed his front door, hastily locking it with an unsteady hand, shaking his head, looking down, avoiding eye contact. He yanked his keys out of the door and took off. He don't know nothing, Silvano thought, ain't seen nothing. Tough guy, but careful. He'll probably go back wherever he came from, visit his family for six months or so.

The street was still empty, and quiet. Silvano retrieved his shopping bag and his bottle of Mad Dog, wrapped the green blanket around himself, and walked away. In the distance, faint, he could hear sirens.

• • •

THEY WERE GHETTO OREOS, some other brand he was not familiar with, but they looked the same, black cookies with white stuff between. The dogs liked them fine, though. Silvano sat in the weeds in Henry's vacant lot, it was a pretty good spot because he was out of sight but he could still see what was going on down the street. The dog with half a tail came over and flopped down beside him in the bushes, resting his head on Silvano's thigh. He held out a cookie in his shaking hand, and the dog took it carefully, licking his palm afterward. "You love me, don'cha," he said to the dog. "You don't care whether I got something for you or not. You're still happy to see me, either way . . . I'm happy to see you, too." He patted the dog on the head. The other one sat under a bush about eight feet away, watching him. That didn't bother him. He had two more in his locker at the St. Felix.

The cops had half the street closed in front of the car service joint. The guy who ran the place had not returned, and neither had any of the drivers. They would all see the yellow crime scene tape and decide that it wasn't worth the risk, take the prudent course, go cruise for fares somewhere else. The three bodies were still where they had fallen. The cops were in no hurry, they went around taking measurements and locating spent brass. Won't do them any good, Silvano thought. His Beretta was already sinking into the mud at the bottom of Buttermilk Channel.

He'd gone over the thing a hundred times in his head, trying to think it out of having happened, but no matter how many times he turned it over in his mind, those three guys in the street stayed where they were. He couldn't see their faces from where he sat, but his memory provided him with the images whether he wanted them or not.

He ate one of the cookies himself and then fed a couple

more to the dogs. The clear plastic wrapper made a hell of a racket, he'd had a bitch of a time getting the thing open to begin with, his hands had been shaking so badly. He was much calmer now, but he was beginning to get that familiar feeling, and that internal chorus was starting up. You were lucky, he told himself, all the breaks went your way this time. One of these days the ball is going to bounce into the other guy's hand, and what are you gonna do then?

He got to his feet and went inside, looking for Henry, who was not home. He changed out of his wino clothes and left by the side door, the one that opened out onto Visitation Place.

THE STORE WAS A RIOT of exotic sights and smells. Most of the grocer's wares lay in open boxes, on countertops or in burlap bags on the floor, and they all competed for Silvano's attention. There were two aisles in the store, and he made his slow way down the one, up the other, admiring a knee-high sack of red lentils, a row of small wooden kegs full of dried beans, red ones, black ones, green, beige, spotted, striped. A cardboard box with a plastic liner was filled with wrinkled little green and red peppercorns. There were bags and bags of rice, and not the Americanized kind, either, not the homogenized, bleached, presorted, cleaned, processed kind that comes in a cardboard box with instructions printed on the side, petrified little maggots of starch with all nutritional value removed, boil for three minutes and you're done. The rice that leaked out of these bags onto the wooden floor came in various shades of brown, the color of tree bark, the color of old leaves, the color of coffee with cream in it. From the back of the store he watched a woman arguing with the grocer over every purchase she made. She was buying a paper bag of dried chickpeas, some spices Silvano didn't recognize, and a tin of olive oil. Before his eyes she was transformed, changing from a plump middle-aged woman with dark skin and a faint mustache into a round and sensuous alchemist who could change such unlikely makings into a delicacy whose dusky aroma could pull men in off the streets. An alchemist, he thought. Lead into gold, boys into men.

He compared her favorably, and, he knew, unfairly, to his second mother, the woman his father brought home when Silvano was six years old. She had been tall and thin, with phony blond hair and big tits with impossibly large, saucer-shaped nipples. (He'd seen them twice by accident and was still repulsed by the memory.) No alchemist, she, her efforts at cooking had been limited to removing from the package and boiling, opening the can and heating on the stove, defrosting in the sink and sticking in the oven, dumping into a bowl and pouring milk on.

After the woman left he looked at his watch and made his way to the front of the store. He looked out through the big plate-glass window, watching the sidewalk outside. He glanced at the grocer, then at his watch again. Any minute now, he thought. The grocer watched him from behind his cash register.

"You had to buy something from this store to give a woman," Silvano asked him, still watching through the glass, "some little present, what would you buy?"

"Ah," the grocer said. "You sound like a wise man. Something sweet, candied almonds, perhaps, or some dried flowers . . ."

"Yeah," Silvano said, interrupting him. "Dried flowers, gimme what you got, quick, here she comes."

The grocer leaned forward to see, and seconds later he was chuckling, shaking his head, wrapping the flowers in white paper. He wouldn't take any money. "Go, and good luck."

He caught up to her on the corner where Court crosses Atlantic. He was wearing his Police Athletic League sweatshirt and all the other stuff that went with it, shades, hat, sneakers, and all that. His face lit up when he saw her, and he handed her the flowers, checked the street while she opened the parcel.

"Hey," she said. "I know you?"

He raised his eyebrows behind the shades, cocked his head. "You forget me already?"

She grinned at him, just a little bit, offered him her arm. "You wanna walk me home?"

"That would be nice," he said gravely, checking the street one more time before he moved.

"What's the matter? You looking for somebody?"

"I usually watch the street. It's just an old habit."

"Yeah, I noticed that, but this is twice in like thirty seconds." He turned to go, and she fell in step beside him. She squeezed his arm. "So?" she asked, after a few steps. "Who are you looking for?"

"Other than you?" he said. She doesn't miss a damn thing, he thought. Might as well just tell her. "I need to be sure nobody is looking for me. They tried for me again, about an hour ago."

"What? Are you hurt? Are you all right?"

His steady pressure on her arm kept them walking. "I'm fine," he said. "Keep walking, pretend to be normal. I'm fine."

"Ooh," she said, "that was a shot." She punched him in the ribs with her right hand. "Where did this happen?"

"Down by Henry's."

"They were waiting for you at Henry's?"

"Just up the street. Couple of blocks."

"Is Henry okay? Do you think they knew you were staying there?"

"I didn't see Henry, but I think he's probably out doing his thing. Making his rounds." He walked on in silence for a few paces. "I think they picked me up at a car service joint I was using. It's my fault, I used the same guy too many times. Fall into a pattern, you become predictable."

"I see." Now it was her turn to think it over. "Am I part of the pattern, too?"

"I'd like you to be," he said, not looking at her. "But maybe not just yet. Not until this is all over with."

"Why?" she said, and left it there, waiting to see which part of it he would answer.

He inhaled, held it for a couple of steps, blew it out.

She shook her head. "This can't be that hard to do."

He looked at her. "Maybe not for you," he said.

"Gimme what you got."

"All right." He stared down at the sidewalk as they went on, working at it. "I never met anybody like you before." He took another breath, blew it out. "Whew. I never, ever, felt before, what I feel when I'm with you."

"That's a good start."

"Yeah, but I don't know what to do about you. And I'm afraid."

"Of me?"

"Ahh . . ."

"Tell it," she demanded. "Just tell it, and tell the truth, goddammit, don't tell me half now and save half for some other time. Just spit it out."

He stopped and looked at her. "I'm afraid if you find out who I really am you'll run away. You'll hate me."

She was mystified. "Why? Are you such a horrible person? I think I would know, if you were. I'm good at this, Silvano, I can always tell who the creeps are from a mile off. I don't think you're a creep."

He took a few steps in silence. "Guy told me, earlier today, nobody wants to be what they are. Everybody wants to be something different. I never thought I had a problem with that, until I met you."

She stopped, and he looked up. "We're here."

"Yeah," she said. "You wanna come up?"

"I would," he said. She was already climbing the stairs, her key in her hand, and he went on up behind her. He was focused on Elia, watching her go through the door, and he failed to notice the red Alfa Romeo that came down the street, or the grim-faced man behind the wheel who peered at the building on his way by, leaning over to catch the number.

INSIDE, HE SAT ON the same pillow on the floor as last time. He took off the hat and the sunglasses, and she could see more of his face. He sat there looking out of the window. He doesn't know how to pick it up again, she thought. He's probably never in his life spoken to another human being like this before. She sat down across from him. "Scare me, Silvano. Get it over with."

"You don't fool around, do you?"

"I'll make you a deal. You tell me what you're afraid I'm gonna find out, okay, and I'll tell you what I'm afraid you're gonna find out. How about that?" She waited. "I'll even go first if you want."

"No," he said.

"I'll even do better than that," she said, her voice rising. "What if I told you I already know what you're so afraid of telling me? What would you think of that?" He watched her, silent. "You're no fucking carpenter," she said.

"I never said I was. I said I was working with . . ."

"Don't start that shit, not with me. I am not a goddam

lawyer, and I'll be damned if I'm going to start thinking like one." She let him think that over for a heartbeat. "That guy in the bakery was twice your size. Easily. You didn't know who he was, he could have been anybody. Or anything. What if he'd had a gun?"

"He didn't. I'd have seen it."

"What about the ones that tried for you today? What happened to them?"

"One got away. Three of them didn't." He looked up at her. "I'm sorry. I really wanted to be a carpenter. Once I spent—"

"That's not the issue, Silvano."

He felt like he was in the ring with Ali, and he just couldn't react fast enough to cover up. "What—"

"This is what your father did, all his life. Am I right? He hurt people, and he didn't feel it. So you ran away. But all these years later, you're afraid you're just like him. Right?"

Even the thought of that pissed him off. "I am nothing like . . ."

"It's Viet Nam, isn't it?" She sighed, turned away as though she didn't want to hear his answer. "Is that why you think I'll hate you? Why don't you just tell me? Why do I have to drag it out of you? Start with why you joined. What made you want to be in the Army?"

This is it, he knew it, this was that inevitable crossroad, this was why Nam became such a dirty secret when you got back, some dark thing you carried around in your heart and never talked about, not to anyone. She already knew, though, she knew he'd been there and she was going to have to decide how she felt about it. Was he really a murderer, rapist, baby-killer? That was the popular opinion. He remembered the flight back to L.A. You had to fly in uniform to get the military rate, and he was returning the same way he'd left, alone, his haircut and his clothes branding him, setting him apart. It felt like the whole world was wearing love beads and long hair, and there you sat with blood dripping off your fingers. The first thing you did when you got back, you got out of those fatigues as fast as you could. There was no pride in having gone, no pride in survival.

She glanced at him. "Listen," she said. "If you're not ready for this—"

"No," he said, "it's all right. I just got lost there for a minute." He inhaled, seeing her walk away, in his mind's eye, leaving him by himself again. Fuck it, he thought, fuck trying to justify yourself, it's too hard. Just tell it, let her do what she wants.

"I was so young," he said, and he shook his head. "All of my life, up until then, I had been . . ." He wondered how to say it. "On the inside. In the middle. I was another Italian from Brooklyn, I lived most of my life surrounded by people who looked the way I looked, talked the way I talked, all of it. They knew what I was just by looking, and I understood them. I belonged to the tribe. I knew what to do and what not to do. Then, the next day, I'm in Chicago. I don't know anybody, everybody there talks funny, I'm always getting lost." He shrugged. "I took it for a while, but it was no good. I guess I was just too young, you know? Too young to handle being on the outside. There was a recruiting office not far from the boardinghouse where I was staying. One day I went in and talked to the guy. Next thing I knew, I was in boot camp." He knew she was watching him but he was afraid to look at her. He was jonesing for a cigarette, but he didn't have any. He looked at the two fingers where he would have held it.

"That's how I got in. It was a few years before Nam got going big. I guess I didn't think about it all that much. In sixty-eight, I volunteered to go. The strange thing about Nam, one of them, anyway, they didn't ship you over in your unit. You went by yourself. So I finally get over there, I'm in a tent with five other guys. They'd all been there different lengths of time, one guy had eight days to go, another guy had two months, and so on, down to me, I was the FNG."

"What's that?"

"Fuckin' new guy. But every one of them came to Nam by himself, he fought his own war, and he went home alone. Far as the Army was concerned, we were six potatoes in an olive green sack. After I got back to the world, I never saw any of those guys again. Well, two of them are dead, but you get the idea.

"So anyway, for the first eight months, I'm in a rifle company. You go out on patrol, a sniper shoots at you, you gotta find him and shoot him. You schlep to this village, you schlep to that one, you set up an ambush, you go back to base. Once in a while a mine blows somebody up. I was bored shitless most of the time, scared shitless here and there, you know . . .

"So after about eight months, I'm on R and R, I run into this guy in Saigon. Enrique Ramirez. He works for the Company, the CIA. We go drinking together, right, I find out he grew up in East Harlem. We met one another here, okay, we wouldn't even look at each other, but in Saigon we're asshole buddies, because I know him, and he knows me. He tells me he can get me out of the mud, you know, get me reassigned. 'Yeah, sure,' I tell him, I'm thinking, the guy's drunk, he ain't gonna do dick. Guy surprised me, though. For the next four months, I'm like his pet snake. On paper, I was assigned to a motor pool, but the deal was, up until then I'm shooting at some guy up in a tree, now I get a picture first, and an address. Besides me and Ramirez, there were four of us that I knew about. Probably weren't the only ones. Sometimes we worked together, sometimes we went solo."

"Did you like it better than what you were doing at first?"

He shrugged. "Slept in a better bed." He looked over at her.

"Sorry. I'll give you a real answer. Picture you and me, we're out for a walk in the woods. Or it could be you and anybody, right, just some person that you know. Okay? But your friend steps on a mine and it blows his foot off. Or maybe his leg. So they show me a picture of some guy, he's with the ones that put the mine there. When I connected it up that way, I didn't have much trouble pulling the trigger.

"So, anyhow, when I got back the first time, I had two years to go on my enlistment. I hit California again, I'm on leave, right, but I can't go home. I didn't know what to do with myself. I'm telling you, I didn't think I was gonna survive that first month. All kinds of crazy shit went through my head. Anyhow, I finally get orders for Germany, okay, I'm all ready to go, I get a visit from these three guys. One of them is Ramirez, but he doesn't say anything. They're all dressed in civvies. 'We're with the Defense Department,' the guy says, 'and we're interested in you.'"

"Did they send you back to Viet Nam?"

"Twice, but not as a soldier. I was now a civilian contract employee." He sighed. "Fly over, do the hit, fly home."

"Is that what you did?"

"Shoot people? Occasionally, but not always. But see, Uncle Sam wanted to conduct his business the way my grandfather did, but these guys were from, like, Harvard and Princeton and they didn't have the moves."

"Why didn't they just go to your grandfather? Or someone like him?"

"They could never trust a guy like him. He wouldn't tell them shit, he'd just take their money, use them for his own purposes, and that would be the end of it. So they used guys like Ramirez and me."

"So what other things did you do for them?"

"Well, for example, guy gets elected to something in the Philippines, I don't remember if he was a senator or what. Anyhow, he's yelling about closing Subic Bay, the big base over there. Wants to throw us out. Now that's never gonna happen, okay, but who needs this nutbag running around agitating? The question is, how do you shut him up? What does he want?"

"So they send you over to find out."

"Yeah, basically."

"Then what? Do you just do it or do you write a report?"

"I was never any good at reports, they gave me a special dispensation on that. No, I would meet someone, usually Ramirez but not always, and I would tell them what I found."

"What happened to the guy?"

"Ramirez? I told you what happened to him, he hung himself."

"No, the guy in the Philippines."

"Oh. He had a cousin, guy was a doctor, wanted to practice in this country."

"That was it?"

"That and some money."

"What if he didn't go for it? What if he really believed in his heart that Subic Bay should be shut down? What if he really wanted to fight for that?"

"Then I would have to find some way to squeeze his nuts, but that almost never happened. The world is hell on true believers, that's why there's so few of them around."

"So now you're out. Ramirez is gone, and you don't work for Defense anymore. Right? So now what?"

"Now I work at finding what happened to my brother. And I need to find a way to do something different with myself. All I've come up with so far is this carpenter thing . . ."

"I'm glad you want to be something else, Silvano." Her voice was softer. "I want to be something else too. That's why I go to school at night." She glanced at her watch. "The real issue here, is this. It's very very hard for a woman to find one of you assholes that's all grown up. A real man, not just a guy. Do you get what I'm saying? Not a cowboy, not an astronaut, not a race car driver. A carpenter would be fine, if that's what you want, just as long as you could manage to be a grownup. Someone who can tell the truth, and not run away. That's the issue."

He looked up at her, and the corner of his mouth twitched. "You're asking a lot."

"I know I am."

"You got school tonight?"

"I didn't mean you had to run."

"I ain't running. Are you?"

"Not yet," she said.

He unfolded himself and stood up, and so did she. He was looking into her face. "What are you going to school for?"

"I'm going to be a nurse."

"Ah," he said, and he looked away. "Listen," he said, not looking at her. "I know I'm behind the curve on a lot of this. But I'm working on it."

"I know that, Silvano."

He shook his head. "I can't stay where I'm at," he said. "I've gotta climb out, or I'm gonna fall back in."

"All right," she said, and she stepped up to him, put her arms on his shoulders. She squeezed, feeling the muscles in his upper arms. "Are you good enough, they won't get you next time?"

He shook his head. "I was lucky today," he said. "I've got to go talk to someone, see if there's a way to settle this."

She put her arms around him, pulled him in, filled herself with his animal smell, and then she kissed him, hard, hard enough to show him she meant it. She let him go and stood back. "You staying with Henry?"

"Tonight," he said. "After that, I don't know. I might be out of touch for a few days."

"Be careful," she said. "Don't keep me in the dark."

"All right," he said. "I won't."

You must be nuts, she thought, after he was gone. Son of a South Brooklyn mobster, boxing, jail, Viet Nam, Japan, and that's just what he'll admit to. Jesus. You must be losing your mind.

"LET ME MAKE THE COFFEE. Your technique needs a little work."

"Okay." Silvano sat down and Henry went over to the sink.

"I was wondering about you," Henry said, his back to Silvano. "I seen the cops outside, seen those dead fellas in the street. I wasn't sure what to think. Figured they got you, or the cops did." He glanced over his shoulder. "Glad to see you still walking around loose, got all your parts and so on."

"I'm pretty happy about that myself."

"Were they waiting for you here?"

"No. Car service joint down the street, I used them a few times. They were having a conversation with the guy that runs it, and he was not enjoying the experience, when I came walking up the sidewalk. They didn't recognize me, but he did. Didn't mean to give me up, I don't think, but he kept looking over at me, and you can guess the rest."

"Yeah. Well, at least they don't know you're staying here."

"No, but it's not that much of a stretch. They know I'm holed up down here somewhere, and they're gonna be looking. I can't stay here anymore. Matter of fact, I should leave tonight."

"No hurry." Henry dismissed that thought with a wave of his hand. "Besides, where would you go?"

"I don't know. Staying in Brooklyn is turning into a high-maintenance situation, but I'm not ready to leave just yet. Besides, I don't like the idea that I'm letting some guy run me off."

"No place like home, huh?"

"That's not it. It's this woman, Henry. Her name is Elia." He shook his head. "She makes me feel like I'm back in high school, tripping over my own tongue. She really shook me up. I never met anyone like her before."

"Sounds promising."

"Yeah, you ain't kidding. But the deal is, I can't hang around here if these guys are gonna be taking potshots at me every five minutes."

"I can see how that would get on your nerves. How did all of this get started?"

"It wasn't my fault," Silvano said, and he told him the story. "I was seventeen . . ."

HENRY GOT UP and refilled his coffee cup. He came back to the table, sat down, looked at Silvano. "It's a private vendetta, then."

"Yeah. It's between me and my cousin."

"There's the obvious solution. Kill him before he kills you."

Silvano looked down at the table. "Everybody's got the right to self-defense, I suppose. I could justify it if I tried hard enough, but it don't feel right, Henry. It ain't who I'm trying to be."

Henry looked relieved. "Well. Some other way, then. What have you got to work with?"

"I don't know that I got anything to work with."

"Not true. You got to think logically, here. First of all, the guy's a criminal, right?"

"Yeah."

"So find out what he's doing. You must know a lot of his associates from back when you were a kid, there's bound to be a few that don't like him. If you can turn up enough on him to get the authorities interested, maybe he'll be too busy to worry about you, even if he doesn't go to jail. It isn't a long-term solution, but it might buy you some time."

"I suppose."

"Another thing you might try is going over his head."

"What do you mean?"

"Well, the mob does have a hierarchy. Doesn't he have someone he answers to?"

"Yeah. He works for a guy named Antonio Malatesta."

"You know him?"

"Yeah, him and my old man were friends when I was a kid."

"You could try talking to him. Maybe there's something he could do for you."

Silvano was shaking his head. "Even if we were old buddies, Henry, Little Dom is Antonio's guy. Little Dom puts money in Antonio's pocket. Guy like Antonio is always gonna do what's best for his own wallet. Unless I found some kind of leverage to use on him, or something to make him think Little Dom is getting ready to roll over on him, he would give me up in a second."

"Hmmm. I know a guy, writes for the *Post*. Maybe we could get him to do a story, you know, 'War hero haunted by the guys who didn't go,' something like that. If we could generate enough bad publicity, maybe they'd leave you alone."

Silvano shrugged. "You could ask the guy, but I personally don't see it. There weren't any war heroes in Viet Nam. With what most people think about the war these days, they'd probably have a hard time deciding who was the villain of the piece, me or Little Dom. Probably figure we deserved each other."

"Well. That just leaves you with the first option, then. Dig up something on Little Dom and give it to the cops. Turn up the heat on him. Or . . ."

"Or what?"

"Pack it in. Whisper sweet nothings in your lady's ear, take her away with you. Gotta be some other place where the two of you could live."

"I thought of that. Maybe I'm being stubborn, but I don't like the way that feels either."

"Feel better than getting shot."

"You got that right. But I still didn't find anything about my brother, Henry. I don't know much about him that I didn't know to begin with."

Henry scratched his chin. "Don't know that I agree with that. You know where he lived, you know the places he worked, you know some of the people he was running with."

"I suppose, but what's that worth? All I have is this gut feeling that the O'Brians, down at Black and White, got some kind of a game running, but I can't believe either one of them would kill anyone. And if that's true, whatever it is they're doing is none of my business."

"Didn't Noonie work at a bunch of other places?"

"Yeah. He helped out the hotel porters, and he did something for the grocery store up the street from Black and White. I checked out both places, and I don't know what the hell they could have to do with anything. Black and White was more likely, I thought, because they're all about money, and money makes the world go round. I thought Nunzio might have seen something or someone that he wasn't supposed to see, maybe one of the guys from the old neighborhood. He never could keep his mouth shut. It's the only reason I could think of for someone to kill him, but it's beginning to feel like a dead end."

"Maybe you're giving up on it too soon. I would think a place like Black and White would be a magnet for a guy like Little Dom."

Silvano was shaking his head. "For Domenic, the problem with a place like Black and White is that there's too many eyes watching. You've got to worry about the Banking Commission, the FBI, and even the stinking IRS. When a place like that gets robbed, ninety-nine times out of a hundred it's an inside job."

"What if they didn't want to rob the place? What if they wanted to use it to launder money?"

"Same problem, too many eyes watching. You had a hundred grand you needed to wash, why would you bother with a place where everybody's going to be looking up your ass with a microscope? Much easier to buy a grocery store. You do that, right, nobody cares how many felony convictions you got, no one cares where you got the money to invest in the place, hell, you could put it in your dead grandmother's name for all anybody cares."

"How does that wash your hundred grand?"

"Lots of ways. If your suppliers are crooked enough, you can pay them with cash, off the books, and when you sell the merchandise, it shows up as a profit. You give Uncle Sam his cut, everybody's happy. Or you can cash checks from the people in the neighborhood. Give them your dollars, you wind up with nice clean paper."

"I thought they went to one of those check-cashing storefronts."

"Sometimes they do, but those guys get a percentage to cash your check. Lots of poor people don't have a bank account, they live from week to week. You was that broke, would you walk a few extra blocks to cash your check with some guy who'd give you face value, save you a few bucks?"

"Yeah, I guess I would." Henry scratched his head. "You know, I'm not saying you're wrong, but I would bet that whatever happened to your brother started out at Black and White. Those goobers from the FBI still camped out, down across the street from there?"

"You hear about them?"

"The whole neighborhood was talking about them. The thing is, they might all look like they're from Kansas or someplace, but they're not stupid. Something had to catch their eye. I say, where there's smoke there's fire. I don't know that I'd give up on the place yet."

"Maybe you're right. Listen, I should get outa here while it's still dark, Henry, I gotta find another place to crash for the next few days."

"Relax. I own a building over on Clinton, there's a garage attached, got a couple of rooms over top of it. Nobody's been in there for a long time. We'll get you over there tomorrow morning."

"Henry, I don't know what I'd do without you. I didn't know you owned another building."

"Some things it don't pay to advertise."

Silvano was silent for a minute. "Henry," he said, after a minute, "you suppose there's a rabbit here, in all this?"

Henry didn't turn around. "Could be," he said. "Rabbit sign all over it."

Silvano remembered, then, something else he had to do. "You got a flashlight I can borrow?"

HE TRIED TO THINK of a good reason not to do it. He'd already done his time going down into holes in the ground. In his experience, going into dark tunnels was a bad deal for everyone concerned. Yeah, he thought, but you gotta go look. He clicked the flashlight, just to check it, for what must have been the fiftieth time.

It was the same bar, the stinking hole where he'd seen Joseph O'Brian visit the basement. The place was actually pretty busy at night. Not much light escaped through the painted windows, but plenty of noise did, and there was a fair amount of traffic in and out. He waited for a lull, crossed over, and flowed down the cellar stairs.

He waited inside the cellar door, as before. The noise from upstairs drowned out the compressors, and he was not sure he'd be able to hear if someone were to come down the stairs. Move your ass, he told himself. The quicker you get down there, the quicker you can get back out.

The stairway to the subbasement was right where Special Ed had told him it would be, and it was no wonder he'd missed it the first time, a dark hole in a dark corner of a dark hole. Jesus. He looked once more at the door to the outside, then made his way down the stairs. The walls of the basement had been made out of concrete cinderblock, but as he went down the second set of stairs he felt like he was going back in time. The walls and the steps were made out of roughly squared blocks of stone. How much of this city lies buried, he wondered, how many old secrets are layered over by our more recent efforts. At the foot of the stairs he shone his light down at the stone floor. The room was partitioned off into what appeared to be labyrinthine passageways, but whoever used this space walked the same way every time, and it was easy enough to follow the pathway worn through the dust.

The sounds of the bar up over his head receded as he went along, and he found himself facing an ancient iron door, dimpled by time and rust. It was in what had to be the exterior foundation wall of the building above him. Just like old times, he thought, and he pulled his pistol out and clicked the safety off. Come on, he told himself. That fucking O'Brian does this, get on with it. You didn't see him peeing his pants, did you? He checked the perimeter of the door with his flashlight carefully, then slowly pushed the door open. Behind it was a brick-lined passageway just wide enough for a man to walk through. Should've brought bread crumbs, he thought, just to keep from getting lost . . . The passageway was only about thirty feet long, and he made his way to the other end, flashlight in one hand, gun in the other. He was sweating profusely, finding it hard to breathe, but then at last he stepped through the far end into what was, by comparison, a vast chasm.

It appeared to be what Ed had told him it would be, an abandoned railroad tunnel. The round ceiling soared far over his head, and a single set of railroad tracks ran down the center of the tunnel, receding in the darkness in each direction. He pointed his light at the ground, thinking that he would continue to follow the trail through the dust, but it was not necessary. Out of the corner of his eye he saw the chair.

It was on the far side of the tracks, up near the wall. There wasn't much left of the guy who'd been sitting there. The bones were still there, though a few had been scattered or dragged away, but most of the clothing and some of the skin was intact, dried a hard and dusty black. The chair itself was stained black, as well as a dark circle of ground underneath the chair, and a forest of rodent footprints ran through the dust.

He shone his light on the guy, mouth sagging open but empty of all but a few teeth, strands of hair stuck to the top of the skull, copper wire ligatures still knotted around what had been wrists and ankles. It was the Dutchman, Silvano didn't know why but he was sure of it. "Lenny Deutch," he said softly,

"I don't know what you did, but it's hard to believe you deserved this." He shut the light off then, letting the darkness wash over him as he listened, wary for the sounds of humans still alive, but there were none.

He clicked the light back on and turned to go. Over against the far wall, right next to the opening he'd come through, he saw a metal footlocker. He went over and opened it up.

Yeah. Well, he thought, it always comes down to money. He shone his light up and down the tunnel, every nerve ending in his body screaming at him to leave, but he knew he had one more thing he had to do before he could go.

SEVEN

HENRY'S APARTMENT BUILDING was a six-story brick walkup that fronted on Clinton, with an alley going down one side where the garage was. It was a three-car garage, and all the garage doors were chained and locked. There was a personnel door at the end of the garage closest to the building. Henry fished around in his pocket for a key ring and unlocked the door. "You don't have to come and go this way, if you don't want," he said. "There's another door inside that unlocks with the same key, that way you can just go down the hallway on the first floor next door, and use the main entrance on Clinton, or you can go out the side door on the other side."

"Okay." Silvano had been watching his back, peering down the alley through the predawn darkness, watching the taxi pull away. Henry had called the guy, and he had met them outside the back door at Henry's factory building. Silvano had watched out the back window during the ride over, and if someone had been following them he had not seen them, but that did not mean they were not there. And the alley could be a bad spot, too easy to cut you off once you entered it. Henry must have been reading his mind.

There were three cars in the garage, all of them covered with canvas tarps topped with a coating of dust. A set of stairs went up the back wall behind the first car. "You gotta lock this door behind you," Henry said, clicking the deadbolt closed. "I should fix that, so she locks when she closes." The apartment went the full width of the garage, and it was mostly one big room, with a small bedroom at one end and a tiny kitchenette at the other. There were bars outside all the windows, and ratty green shades were pulled halfway down.

"Damn." Silvano was looking in the kitchenette. There were two cockroaches in the sink, an inch and a half long apiece. "Damn, Henry. Those things roaches or are they Dobermans?"

"Water bugs," Henry said, flicking the light on. As soon as he did, the bugs jumped out of the sink and scrambled down behind the stove. "Those ones eat the regular kind," he said. "I'm surprised to see 'em, tell you the truth. Ain't nobody lived in here for ages. I wonder what they been living on."

"You could put saddles on 'em and give pony rides."

"I got stuff to kill 'em," Henry said in a mildly wounded voice. He turned and looked at Silvano. "I'll drop something off this afternoon." He watched Silvano a minute. "First time I seen you smile," he said. "I was beginning to think your face was broke."

"I'm fine, Henry," Silvano said, wondering at himself, trying to understand this strange mood he was in. "Don't worry about the bugs. I'll take care of 'em."

"All right." Henry clicked the light off. "I used to rent this out as a furnished apartment," he said, "but over the years, I guess the furnishings left with the outgoing tenants. I don't know if there's even a bed in here anymore."

"I've slept on the floor before." He walked over and looked out the window, listened to the sounds of his footsteps on the wooden floor echoing in the empty room. What is it about this place? he thought. Maybe it's just that it's not a barracks or a hotel room. Or a tent.

"Listen," Henry said. "There ain't a lot of people know that I own this place, or the other place, neither. Most of the folks living here think I'm sort of a handyman, or maybe just a harmless old fart losing his marbles. I'd kind of like to keep it that way."

Silvano looked over at him, shaking his head. Crazy old white dude, long white braid, wearing jeans as old as he is, ratty old sweatshirt, sneakers that look like they already walked around the world. "No danger there, Henry. Way you dress, nobody would believe me if I told 'em. What you get for rent for this place?" He was shocked when he heard the question coming out of his mouth.

"Well, I get extra from folks that insult my sartorial situation."

"That right?" He had already decided to stay. All the reasoning and logic come after the fact, he thought, you just want to justify something you already decided to do. The hell with it, anyway. No more running.

"Don't you want to see it in the daylight, at least? Wait until the sun comes up? Besides, you can stay here as long as you want."

"I appreciate that, Henry, but I don't want to stay here. I want to move in. Is that all right with you? You weren't keeping this place empty on purpose, were you?"

"No. Not really. I'll rent to you, if you're sure. You made up your mind on this kind of sudden. I figured you were gonna take the smart way out, take your lady out to see the world, get you both out of harm's way."

"I never claimed to be smart."

"Well, all right, then." Henry shrugged, started taking keys off his key ring. "Glad to have you," he said. "You still got a tough row to hoe, here. You gonna keep me posted on current events? Hate to get a new tenant all broke in, then have somebody shoot him."

Silvano was looking around, feeling his way. "Things look better in the daytime," he said. "I got a feeling the next couple days ought to tell the story. I'll do a wire transfer tomorrow. You want cash or a check?"

Henry was laughing, shaking his head. "Wire transfer," he said. "And here I was, thinking you was a poor homeless grunt."

"Homeless, maybe."

"I'll leave you the address for the real estate company. Send 'em a check, the end of the month."

AT FIRST LIGHT the traffic moved freely on the BQE overpass and only a few pedestrians dotted the sidewalk, early birds beating the rush. An ambulance rolled up to the hospital emergency room entrance, but the attendants took their time unloading their cargo. The sheet on the gurney was pulled over the occupant's face. The city was grinding into gear, powering up for another day.

Joseph O'Brian was already in, Silvano could see the beat-up Maverick parked in its usual spot in Black and White's parking lot. The sun rose, burning in behind his shoulder and reflecting off the buildings in Lower Manhattan. The Statue of Liberty looked lost and lonely, small and green out on her island with New Jersey in the distance behind her, but Silvano's glasses were not strong enough to show him anything that far away. Four suits in an unmarked sedan pulled up on the other side of Atlantic Avenue, all of them with hair cut so short that he could see the whitewalls with his naked eye from 10 floors up, but at least they had the sense to park the car somewhere out of sight. Soon after that, the traffic began to slow and thicken, more and more people making their way to work. The hardhats showed up at Black and White, seemingly all at once, and then after them came the regular drivers, off-duty or retired cops, mostly. The only ones he recognized were Frankie and Roland. The morning rush was in full swing by then, and Sean arrived last, parking his Caddy out in the middle of the lot with the door open while he went to have an argument with Lee, the carpenter foreman. Silvano watched through his glasses as Sean shouted and waved his arms around, then stopped abruptly, turned on his heel, and walked away holding his head. I wonder how much he remembers from yesterday? Silvano thought.

Two delivery trucks pulled up in front of the grocery store, momentarily blocking his view of that section of the storefront and the sidewalk, but then one of them pulled out and double-parked on the avenue to leave the fire hydrant clear. The drivers both rolled up their rear doors and began unloading cardboard boxes and stacking them on hand trucks, wheeling them into the store. A guy from the store came out and stood on the sidewalk, ticking items off on a clipboard. Ordinary guys, Silvano thought. Ordinary life. He allowed himself to envy them, just for a moment.

By this time the BQE overpass was clogged with cars, everybody in the world, it seemed, headed for Manhattan, and he wondered how there could be space for all of them on that small island, and why there wasn't a better way to transport them all there and back, and why the hell would they do it, anyhow, sit in traffic like that every morning and every night, wouldn't it turn you into a raving lunatic, after a while?

His coffee had grown cold. He sipped at it anyway, and watched, trying to empty his mind. The armored vehicles did not leave Black and White's yard until rush hour had begun to ebb. The drivers had to go through their morning routines, getting their assignments and loading their vehicles. Most of that took place out of sight, inside the big room where Elia sat behind her desk. Something about her, he thought, something that made you feel better. You weren't so bad, how could you be, when she smiled at you that way that she did? Funny how some women can do that to you, he thought, just give you a look, make you think that maybe you're not such an asshole after all, maybe you're a real human being, underneath all of your bullshit. It seemed he always walked out of Elia's presence looking at the world through slightly different eyes. I bet she doesn't even know she does it, he thought. Bet she doesn't even think about it.

One of the trucks outside the grocery store finished up and left, but an ice cream delivery truck took its place a few minutes later, double-parking in the same spot. Silvano watched through his glasses, trying to keep his mind from speculating, trying to simply gather information, noting where the trucks were from, what the drivers looked like, but then a Lincoln Town Car double-parked in front of the ice cream truck. What a stupid car for the city, he thought, too long to park very well, too wide for clogged streets. Who would buy such a thing? The driver of the car got out and went to stand on the sidewalk in front of the store, looking in both directions. It was the same guy who'd been the lookout in front of the Hotel Montague. Probably had to promote the guy, Silvano thought. The guy stopped looking around and made a motion with one hand, and Ivan Bonifacio got out of the backseat of the Lincoln, unconsciously patted his coat pocket, and went into the store.

Information, Silvano thought. Don't jump to conclusions, gather information. He swung his glasses to the building where the FBI was set up, wondering if they were looking at the same thing he was, but of course, there was no way to tell. The angle didn't seem right, though. You would have to lean out of a window in the front of that building to get a really good look at the sidewalk in front of the grocery store. He looked back, the driver was still standing there, and Ivan was still inside.

Joseph O'Brian came out of the yard over at Black and White, pushing his bicycle, looking faintly ridiculous in his green work clothes and white running shoes. He pushed his bicycle out of the front gate, waiting until Sean came out to lock the gate behind him. The two of them stood there jawing at one another for a few minutes, and then the older man pushed his bicycle across the avenue, mounted up, and began pedaling up the hill. Ivan Bonifacio came back out of the store, walked over to the rear door on the driver's side of the car and stood there with his hand on the door handle, waiting. O'Brian pedaled past, watching the cars coming down the hill at him, and he nodded slightly at Ivan on his way past, and Bonifacio returned the nod, just a tiny bob of his head.

Son of a bitch, Silvano thought, those two bastards know each other. Don't jump to conclusions, he heard Henry's voice saying. Could have been saying, thanks for waiting, for not forcing me out into traffic to get around you . . .

Yeah, sure. He swung the glasses back to the building where the feebies were, waiting to see if any of them came out to chase O'Brian on his bike, but none did. They're probably sick of following the guy around, he thought, same routine every day. Guy's got a heart condition, that's what I assumed, does this twice a day, most days, trying to exercise, trying to stay alive.

Sure he is. They're waiting for someone connected to show up, and meanwhile the guy is stealing his own money, walking out with it right under their noses. And he and Bonifacio know each other.

Silvano stuck his glasses up on the ledge in the stairwell and ran down the stairs.

IT WAS A LONGER RUN this time because he was winded from his trip down the stairwell and O'Brian had a head start on him, but he felt a little better than he had the first two times, his breath came a little easier, and besides, he hadn't had a cigarette since that first time he'd met Bronson in the St. Felix. When he crossed Court Street four blocks up, he could see O'Brian waiting at the next light, and he eased up the pace, coasted down the hill. Slow down, he told himself. Let the guy go on ahead. Give him room.

Joseph O'Brian's bike was chained up to a parking meter when Silvano got to Flatbush Avenue. He leaned on a mailbox and waited. Joseph O'Brian came up the steps and out of the bar entryway, blinking in the sun, looking like he'd seen a ghost and not just a dead guy.

Silvano stayed where he was. "O'Brian!"

Joseph O'Brian stopped, looked over his shoulder at Silvano. His face was white, and he looked away, distracted. Silvano walked on over to him. O'Brian was staring at his shoes. Guy looks like one of the nuns just caught him jerking off, Silvano thought. He reached into his shirt pocket and pulled out the picture of his brother.

"You seen this guy before?"

"Huh? Yeah. No, I mean. Don't know him." His hands fluttered, and he looked around, looked out at the cop directing traffic in the middle of the intersection of Flatbush and Atlantic.

Guy looks like he's having a stroke, Silvano thought. "You want it back?"

O'Brian swung back, his mouth wide. "What? What? You . . ."

"Got time for me now, don't you, motherfucker?"

"You took my money?" He looked over his shoulder, out at the cop again.

"Look at the picture," Silvano told him. "You wanna talk to me or you wanna tell the cops?"

He swallowed convulsively. "Not out here, not out on the street." His eyes darted around, nervous. "It's not mine, not all of it. They'll kill me . . ."

"I don't give a fuck whose money it is," Silvano told him, "or whether they kill you or not."

THEY SAT AT A TABLE in the back of a coffee shop on Atlantic, a block up from the bar. Silvano watched O'Brian wordlessly, let him tell it his own way.

"You get used to it, I guess. After a while, you could just as well be counting books, or record albums, or cabbages, for that matter. Even after my divorce, after my ex got done raking me over the coals, I never really gave it much thought. And I was in a real pinch, there, for a while, but the only thing that bothered me about it was that I had to scale back what I was doing with the Church." He was looking down, avoiding eye contact.

"I didn't mind losing the house. I actually prefer my apartment, at least it's quiet in there. I don't mind driving the Maverick, not even when I park it next to Sean's Cadillac. Taking the money never really crossed my mind, until Noonie." He looked up, his face haggard, and quickly looked back down at the table. "Your brother. I don't mean to suggest that it was his fault. Your brother was a good person, and I'm not saying that now to try to get out of trouble. He was pure, there wasn't a hypocritical bone in his body. He was one of a kind.

"Where I made my mistake was, the first mistake, he was hanging around in the office one day when we had the safe open. We had gotten a big delivery the day before, for the vans that go around doing payrolls. I was showing off, I guess, and I showed him a stack, it was about half an inch thick. 'Ten thousand bucks,' I told him. 'Every one of these little bundles is ten thousand bucks.' I don't even know why I bothered, because I'm not sure Noonie really appreciated the difference between five hundred and five hundred grand. Hell, he used to like Sean to pay him in ones. Made him feel like a rich man, he would be so happy, he made the rest of us feel rich, too. Anyway, he says to me, 'I bet one of these would hardly make a lump in your pocket.' And he winked. I couldn't stop thinking about it, after that. I started playing games, take ten grand, put it in my pocket, carry it around for a couple days, put it back. I was taking something of a chance, you know, because every so often we get an audit, the FBI or the IRS will come in and look at the books, count up all the money, and it had better come out right. It always had, before that.

"I don't know if I would have ever gone past that, I don't know if I would have taken the next step, but I had Noonie with me in the car one afternoon, I forget where we were going, but on the way up Atlantic, Noonie sees this guy he knows out in front of that grocery store up the block. He's waving to the guy, wants me to honk the horn. 'Who's that,' I ask him, 'That's the Dutchman,' he tells me. 'Who's the Dutchman?' I ask him, and he starts telling me how the Dutchman is the bagman for whoever owns that store, they got some way to cycle their money through the store so that it comes out looking legitimate. 'See,' I tell him, 'everybody's stealing but me.' 'Oh, you could do it,' he tells me. 'Just walk out the door with it.' 'I can't,' I tell him. 'The FBI would put me in jail the next time they counted it.' He shrugs. 'I bet Ivan could tell you when they're coming,' he says. 'Besides, if you take what you want, first, then you could tell Ivan to come steal the rest, and then there wouldn't be anything left to count.' I should have just left it alone, but I didn't. 'Who's Ivan?' I ask him. 'Oh,' he says, 'Ivan is my friend from the old neighborhood, where I grew up. Ivan is the guy the Dutchman works for.'" He glanced up at Silvano again. "I guess you're starting to see the shape of this."

"Yeah. Noonie put you together with Ivan?"

O'Brian sat at the table, breathing heavily. "Yes," he said, after a minute. "I thought about it for a couple of months, feeling resentful about how the courts and my ex had treated me, and then one day I just decided. I told your brother that I'd like to meet Ivan. He knew what I was up to right away, your brother, got all excited. I had to yell at him to quiet him down, get him to keep his mouth shut. Anyhow, he passed word along to the Dutchman, and word came back, and we did have a meeting. I met Bonifacio out at the monastery, out in Rockaway. I was amazed to find him a religious man."

"I'll bet. How soon after you two set this deal up did it start going bad?"

O'Brian was shaking his head. "Almost right away. First thing that happened, Ivan killed the Dutchman. He said he had to do it, claimed the guy knew too much about what we were going to do. I'm not sure I believed him, maybe the guy just put two and two together and invited himself in, I don't know."

"That's him, down in the tunnel."

"Yeah. It was horrible, at first, going back down in there, that poor man falling apart, the rats chewing on him and all. You never get used to that smell."

"No kidding. Why'd you leave the money there?"

"That was my agreement with Ivan. His people own that bar. They used to use that tunnel during Prohibition. We're supposed to split the money up, later. He keeps whatever he gets out of the robbery, and we go fifty-fifty on what I manage to get out ahead of time."

Silvano shook his head. What an idiot. "Why didn't you just take the money and run? Head for the Cayman Islands or something?"

"I was daydreaming of Costa Rica." O'Brian ventured a rueful smile. "Funny," he said. "If I had really wanted to, I probably could have done it. You know, before all this. Before I started up with the financial masturbation. I could have sold out, dropped out, gone and lived the rest of my life on a quiet beach somewhere. Stiff my ex out of her alimony, she'd have to go get a job. What could be closer to paradise?" He shook his head. "Looks so attractive now, I don't know why I didn't do it then."

"Go now. What's keeping you?"

O'Brian shook his head. "I'm caught between Bonifacio and the government. Your brother was right, Bonifacio got to someone in the FBI district office, but something must have leaked. They audited us twice, Bonifacio got word to me both times, I was able to juggle the books and paper over the shortfall, but I don't think it was good enough. They're watching my bank accounts, they're tracking my credit cards, they've been through my apartment a couple times when I was out. I suspect my phones are tapped, home and work, both. Ivan says he's waiting for them to back off enough for us to pull the trigger. If I run now, I'll have the whole bunch of them chasing me, Bonifacio and Uncle Sam, both. I'm stuck."

"Sounds like it." The son of a bitch, Silvano thought, all he's thinking about is his own trouble, not the two lives that ended because of his greed.

"I've really done it to myself. I even thought about turning myself in, you know, just going to the feds and telling them what I'm telling you." He shook his head again. "You believe in God, Iurata?"

"That depends on how much trouble I'm in."

O'Brian laughed, but there was no humor in it. His face was pale and waxy, he looked like he was ready to throw up. "You know," he said, "there's a scripture that says, in so many words, you got business at the temple, get it done and then get out. Don't hang around. 'It's a fearful thing, falling into the hands of the living God.' Bonifacio made me watch, back when he killed the Dutchman, down there in that hole." He shuddered. "He told me he wanted me to be an accessory, that way we were both committed. He didn't make it easy on the poor bugger, either. Kept sticking him with that ice pick, listening to him scream. I suppose it was for my benefit, but the man really enjoys his work. He wanted me to understand who I was dealing with, what he was capable of." He looked up, stared at Silvano. "I have to answer for that, Mr. Iurata. Not only the man's life, but the manner of his death, as well."

"What about Nunzio?"

"That's on me, too. Noonie spent a lot of time looking for the Dutchman. I thought he'd forget about it after a week or so, but he didn't. What happened, finally, I think he followed me out here one day, went down there after I left. Found the Dutchman, found the money, too. Started telling people he'd found the Dutchman. I didn't hear about it right off, by then he wasn't hanging around with us as much. Plus, I was preoccupied with my work down in Rockaway. By the time it got to me, it was too late. Bonifacio had already killed your brother." He looked at Silvano, his fear showing in his face. "I know it sounds pathetic, but I'm sorry. It's all I can say."

"Yeah." Silvano was surprised that he felt nothing like what he'd expected, no rage, no grief, just something cold and implacable. "You weren't there, you didn't see it."

"No."

"He down in the tunnel, too?"

"No. I don't know where he is, Bonifacio didn't tell me."

"Fuck." Silvano stared into O'Brian's watery blue eyes until the man looked down at the table again.

"What now? Are you going to go to the police?"

"No." Silvano stood up to go.

"What do I do now?" There was a note of panic in O'Brian's voice.

"I don't give a fuck what you do now."

"You asked me if I wanted it back, that's why I talked to you. Are you going to tell me what you did with it? If Bonifacio goes down in there and it's gone . . . I've gotta have that money back."

"Behind the Dutchman's chair. Go look over next to the wall, you'll find a spot where the concrete is all broken up. I buried it under there."

"Oh God," he said, relieved. "What if I hear from Bonifacio? What if he wants to pull the trigger?"

Silvano ground his teeth. "You won't hear from him," he said. "He only has a couple of days left." He looked down at O'Brian. "He'd have never let you keep it, you know. You would have died in the robbery, and he'd have taken your share, too."

O'Brian shook his head. "I guess it's true, then, what they say. You don't get punished for your sins, but by them."

"Listen to me. Sit tight for the next two days. No more bike rides, and stay out of that cellar. After that, you can do whatever you want. Take your money and run." Or choke on it, he added silently. "Meantime, if I find out you lied to me, you won't have to worry about Bonifacio getting you. Understand?"

"Yes." It was that Catholic schoolboy voice, subdued, ashamed, penitent. Silvano turned and walked out into the bright sunshine on Atlantic.

"GOOD AFTERNOON, SAHR." The Indian guy in the newsstand made change for Silvano's paper from the pile of coins on his counter. He leaned in close, lowering his voice. "Dere vere some men here de udder day. Looking for you, perhaps."

Silvano looked around. "When was this?"

"Day before yesterday. Dey vent into de bar for a time, den dey came back out and vent avay. Dat is all dat I know."

"You seen them since?"

"No, sahr, but vun cannot be sure. Dey looked like disagreeable men, sahr."

"Thanks." He stuck the *News* under his arm and went into the lobby of the Hotel Montague and looked around. The usual cast lent their earthy ambience to the soiled elegance of the place, but none of them seemed to be looking for him. He walked through the thick glass doors of the hotel bar. Might not be a thing of beauty, he thought, but it beats the hell out of the last one. The potato-nosed old guy, sitting at a table in the far corner, recognized him right away.

"Hey," the guy said. "You decided to visit us after all."

Silvano went over and sat down. "Nice joint," he said.

"Ain't so bad," the guy said, looking around. He looked at Silvano. "Guy in your business, though, you gotta watch where you walk. Gotta watch for land mines. This is a good table for it, you can see out the windows to the street and through the glass doors, into the lobby."

"What are you drinking?"

"Dewar's," he said happily, "with a beer chaser." He raised his hand to the bartender. "Thomas!" he said. "The gentleman is buying." He lowered his voice, kept his eyes on the bartender. "Several lifetimes ago, I was a combat photographer in the Pacific Theater. Pretty cherry assignment, all things considered, for an ignorant young fool such as myself. The Japanese didn't have any good land mines, nothing with remote detonators or anything like that, so their solution was the soul of simplicity. They would dig a big pit in the road, and they'd put a bomb in the pit, the kind they normally used for air drops, and they'd put a soldier down in the pit with a ball-peen hammer. Cover over the pit with boards and dirt. What the poor boy was supposed to do, of course, was wait until he heard a truck over his head, and then whack the primer with his hammer. Sometimes he didn't even have a hammer, just a rock. Why, thank you, Thomas, you're a scholar and a gentleman."

Thomas, who had heard it all before, accepted a twenty from Silvano, nodded at Silvano's hand signal to keep them coming. "Club soda for me."

"Sometimes they would actually do it." The old guy watched Thomas go back behind the bar. He sipped at the Dewar's. "Sometimes they'd bang on the boards instead, and we would have to dig the poor bastard out. Self-preservation triumphing over ideology. Better that way, I suppose, ideology is a bitch."

"I've heard that. Any land mines in this hotel?"

"Well, sir, three Mediterranean gents went in, but only two came out. That was Sunday, two days ago. Course, I can't watch the back door, the guy might have gotten bored and gone home, but I wouldn't count on it."

"I should just watch out for a guy with a ball-peen hammer?"

The guy downed the rest of his scotch with a gulp, looked at his watch. "Might be more useful," he said, "to wait here for another forty-five minutes or so. I would bet you a delivery boy from the deli up the street will show up with lunch for one in a brown paper bag. Man's gotta eat."

"You are an observant son of a bitch, aren't you."

"A useful trait, and strictly in my own self-interest. You can sit here and buy me drinks while we wait. We'll tell each other sad stories."

Silvano sat back and watched the old boy put away double shots and beers at an alarming rate. No wonder he was broke the other day, he thought. Guy can't drink enough to get drunk.

"Here he comes," the guy said, interrupting a long story about Leyte, a touch of sadness in his voice. "You got just enough time to buy me one more before you catch him in the lobby. Black kid, white apron, just coming up the block. Yeah, that's him, he's turning in."

SILVANO TRADED TWENTY BUCKS to the kid for the paper bag. "Okay," the kid said, pocketing the bill. "Fifth floor, number's on the bag. Guy don't tip for shit."

"That's all right," Silvano said. "I owe him one."

Sure enough, the number on the bag matched the room across the hall from Silvano's, the one where Mrs. Clark had camped on the floor. He didn't see her anywhere, she hadn't been in the lobby, either. He stood off to one side of the door and knocked. Hope she's all right, he thought. Hope she had enough sense not to mess with these guys. He heard creaking noises coming from inside the room. Lazy bastard, he thought. Guy was probably asleep. "Deli," he called out, trying to sound like a kid. He heard the lock on the door snap back, and he flattened himself against the wall, gritting his teeth.

The door swung open and the guy inside stuck his head out. It was the guy who had been driving the car the first time. "Took you long enough," the guy said. "I musta called—" He stopped when he saw the bag on the floor. "Fuck!" he yelled, going for the gun he was carrying in a new shoulder rig, but it was too late. Silvano swarmed him, knocking him back into the room. It didn't take much, somebody had already worked him over pretty well, when his sunglasses went flying Silvano could see the swelling in the guy's face, and there were stitches in his upper and lower lips.

Silvano took the guy's gun away and held it on him while he retrieved the lunch bag and kicked the door closed. The guy struggled to his feet, stood there uncertainly. "You look like shit," he told the guy. "Boner face do this to you?"

"What do you think?" The guy was trying to sound tough but he couldn't manage it. Plus, he could smell his lunch in the bag and it was compromising his attention. Silvano handed it to him.

"Sit down," he said. "Eat."

"My last meal?"

"Doesn't have to be."

ANTONIO HAD NEVER BEEN the kind of a guy who liked to travel like a head of state, bodyguards and all that. Sometimes he had a driver, sometimes he didn't. Sometimes he drove and made his driver ride in the backseat. He might be a little nervous lately, though, Silvano thought, and it might not be the smartest thing to pull up to his front door in a car service limo or a cab.

Improvisation is the soul of all good plans, he thought. He tossed the gun he'd taken away from the meatball in his room into the Dumpster behind the hotel; then he stopped and bought a screwdriver at the hardware store on Montague Street, used it to boost a delivery truck. It was an International, had small vent windows you could open in two seconds, open the door, pop the thing in neutral, open the hood about six inches and short out the starter solenoid with the same screwdriver and you're in business. He'd watched the driver and his helper go into a bar for a belated liquid lunch. With luck, they'd be in there at least an hour, plenty of time.

The truck was gutless, the diesel choked and gagged, and the suspension was shot, the thing crashed over every bump in the road, but it was fun to drive anyhow, the cars on the BQE yielded to superior bulk, if not speed. He caught the off-ramp to the Long Island Expressway, took it out to one of the last exits in Queens and turned into the tree-shaded streets of Jamaica Estates, a neighborhood of oversized brick Tudor-style homes behind tall fences, long driveways, and green lawns. He found the right street, parked the truck. He broke the cheap padlock on the rear door with his screwdriver and looked in the back. Frozen beef, he thought, reading the boxes. I'm in luck. He grabbed the deliveryman's hand truck and loaded it up. Antonio might be rich enough to buy half the cows in the country, but everybody likes getting over. Free always tastes better.

He pushed the hand truck down the block to the house he remembered from his childhood. His father and Antonio had played cards here when he was much younger, and Antonio had always seemed happy to see him coming with his old man. There was no lock on the gate at the end of the driveway, nobody outside watching the house, no dog, even. Things must have been quiet for a long time.

He went up the driveway, left the hand truck and its load of boxes just around the rear corner of the house, out of sight from the street. He crouched under a window. There were voices in the house, and he stood quiet, listening. Maid, Spanish accent, moving around on the first floor. Male voice, crude, coming from the front of the house, probably a guard, it wasn't going to be the guy's best day. One more voice, female, older, upstairs, had to be Antonio's wife. Antonio's study had been on the first floor in the back when Silvano had last been in the house. He heard a vacuum start up, and he crouched low and ran across the back until he was under what had been the study window. Just an ordinary catch on the window, no locks. There was an alarm, but he was betting that it would be turned off during the day, with people in the house. He pried the window up with the screwdriver, breaking the latch, and eased inside. The vacuum continued, covering the noise.

It was still a study, and he went through the darkened room quickly, trying not to disturb anything. There was a pistol in the middle drawer of Antonio's desk, a big Colt .45. He left it where it was and went and sat down in a chair in the darkest corner of the room. He didn't look at his watch again, instead he settled in to wait, resigning himself that this would take whatever time was necessary. If he made some noise he would no doubt get Antonio home quicker, but the old man would be agitated, then, which would not be a good thing.

The maid finished her vacuuming, the guard and Antonio's wife watched the "Phil Donahue Show" on the television in the front room, the maid went about the business of preparing dinner, beginning a process that would be finished by Antonio's wife. Silvano sat motionless in his chair, emptying his mind, eyes half closed, the rise and fall of his chest the only outward sign that he was alive. It was something he was very good at, this quiet, empty watchfulness, and it went on undisturbed into the deepening afternoon. When the maid finished her work for the day and went out the back door to go home she found the hand truck and sparked a flurry of activity. Antonio and his driver arrived home forty-five minutes later.

There was a short conversation just outside the back door. Antonio had a thin, hoarse voice that tended to go higher and crack when he was excited, which was fairly often, and it did so now while he yelled at the guard in a mixture of English and Italian that was punctuated by loud slaps. A few minutes later Antonio and his driver came inside and made their way through the house methodically, leaving the library for last. The old buzzard knows there's someone in here, Silvano thought, and he's letting me know it.

He heard the driver's muffled voice just outside the study door, heard him being overruled, shoved aside. "Get the fuck out of the way," Antonio said, shoved the door open, and walked into the room. Silvano stood up, held his hands out to the side, empty. "Forgive the dramatics," he said. "I hated to do this this way . . ."

Antonio was about Silvano's height but he was much heavier. He was a muscular, barrel-chested man with long arms and bricklayer's hands, wiry gray hair, and a rubber face that betrayed everything he was feeling. He came striding across the room and grabbed Silvano in a bear hug. "Silvano!" he yelled. "Silvano! You're back! God, it's been a long time, Jesus, it's good to see you." He released Silvano and stood back. "Why are we losing, Silvano," he asked in an aggrieved tone. "How can those riceball motherfuckers beat us? Look at this country, look at them! How the fuck did this happen?" He didn't wait for an answer. "And how come you hadda go, you stupid fuck? What's wrong with you, you lose your fucking mind?" He grabbed Silvano by the shoulders. "I understand why you went," he said. "You were all alone, you didn't have nobody to counsel you, but I woulda never let you go. Never!" He let go with one hand and began poking Silvano in the chest with his finger. "I blame the old man for this mess. I blame Domenic! Look at what he did, all of these years later and we're still trying to finish burying him." He turned to his driver, who was standing in the doorway. "Hey, Rocco, go get that asshole . . ." The guard, though, was standing uncertainly, just behind Rocco, and Antonio bull-rushed him. Rocco stepped back out of the way just in time. Silvano winked at him, and Rocco rolled his eyes. Silvano could hear Antonio going at the guard in the next room, sounded like Dick Butkus head-slapping some poor offensive lineman.

"*Gagootz!* You stupid bastard! Go out in the kitchen and make some coffee, that's all you're good for, you stupid fuck, I should give you a dress and make you clean the fucking house, I should make you wash the fucking toilets with your fucking tongue, is what I should fucking do." He came striding back into the room, his face locked in dismay, and grabbed Silvano by the shoulders again. "What went wrong in Viet Nam? Why can't we win?" he demanded, his voice rising. "Why can't we beat those fucks?"

Some inside part of Silvano curled back away from the question, but he knew this was the price he was going to have to pay for his conversation with the old man, and you couldn't finesse him either, he wanted his answer. At least, Silvano thought, he's not asking me how many people I killed. "Antonio," he said, and he stopped. The old man let go of him and stepped back, waiting.

"It's like any fight," Silvano said. "Can you hurt them bad enough to make them stop before they hurt you bad enough to make you stop? What's your capacity for violence, what's your tolerance for pain?" He stopped, looking at the old man's face.

"You remember what my grandfather Domenic was like? He was never the toughest guy around, or the smartest, either. It was just that he was always willing to get after it, he never had to stop and think. While you were working yourself up for it, he already had his knife in your guts. You know what I mean?"

"You're telling me we don't have the stomach for it. Is that what you're fucking telling me?"

"You live the good life, Antonio. You have a family that loves you. You have success, you have the respect of your friends, you have this house . . . you have everything. If you get in a fight with a man who has nothing, can you take as much pain as he can, or has the good life taken away some of your taste for it?"

Antonio sneered. "I fight with a man, it's not over until one of us dies."

"No matter what you stand to lose."

"No fucking matter what! I let you beat me, I lose everything anyway! I'm gonna let you walk over me? I'm gonna let you take my house, I'm gonna let you fuck my daughter? Fuck, no. You go to war with me, you better not stop until I am fucking dead, because I'm not stopping until you are fucking dead."

"You'd never get elected president, Antonio, but you would have made a hell of a general."

Antonio straightened up to his full height and thrust his chin out. "One Sicilian general. You're telling me that's what we need."

It was as good an answer as any. "We at war, Antonio? You and me?"

"You already put four good men into the ground." He walked over behind his desk and sat down, and Silvano watched him carefully, but the old man made no move for his drawer. "Well, three," he said, leaning on the desk. "Massimo was fucking useless, you told him he had two heads, he'd go buy two hats. I never woulda let them use him, I knew what they were gonna do." He sat there and stared at his desktop. He's counting it up, Silvano thought, he's balancing his interests, trying to figure which way he comes out ahead.

"You were never at war with me," the old man said, finally. "I don't want to lose any more guys trying to settle this madness between you and Little Domenic. It has nothing to do with me or the family, it's that sick old man, reaching out from his fucking grave, that's what it is."

"Little Dom ain't so healthy himself."

"Ohh!" Antonio looked up at Silvano, his face the picture of wounded disbelief. "Ohh! Are you kidding me? Are you kidding me? Little Domenic has a beautiful wife and two beautiful children. Beautiful! And do you know what he fucking does?" Antonio was affronted, horrified. Silvano clamped down hard on his amusement. He knew that family was sacred to Antonio. You could have all the girlfriends you wanted, but you always went home for dinner. "He moves to Greenwich Village, he leaves his wife and his son and his daughter all alone in Howard Beach and he moves out! What the fuck is he thinking, will you tell me? What is he looking for?" Antonio was bellowing his questions.

Silvano could swear he saw tears in the old bastard's eyes. "You know anything about an armored car heist? Supposed to be all set up and ready to go, just waiting for the feds to back off."

The old man turned deadly serious. "Where did you hear this?"

"The horse's mouth," Silvano told him. "Guy's been clipping his own money, figures he'll have somebody take the place down, cover his tracks."

It was not what Antonio wanted to hear. "Who?" he said, veins standing out in his neck. "You tell me who."

I've got him now, Silvano thought. They didn't clear it with him, big hit like that going down in his own backyard, and the heat that goes with it, and they never cleared it with him. They were going to stiff him out of his cut. "Word I got," Silvano said, "Little Dom has one of his boys on it. Guy named Bonifacio. I was told Little Dom is too big for anybody to touch. I was told the guy turned out to be a genius, you guys need him too badly, so now he does what he wants."

Antonio leaned slowly all the way back in his chair, leather and wood creaking as he put a foot up on his desk. He was calm now, his face went back to its usual color. He watched Silvano for a minute. Silvano sat in his chair without moving, without a twitch, but he was completely prepared if the old man made a move for the desk drawer or a coat pocket, or even if he shouted for Rocco. He didn't, though.

"There's a fine line between a genius and a idiot," the old man said. He's decided, Silvano thought. He's made up his mind. Silvano fought to remain calm. "Domenic turned out to be a very smart boy," he continued. "He has taken us in some new directions. Very smart boy. But that does not mean the rest of us are stupid."

"You've got someone ready to step into his shoes."

"We have been paying close attention. Learning. Branching out. Silvano, Silvano. Do you need to teach a fox to steal chickens? No. You just whisper in his ear. 'Mr. Fox,' you say. 'There's a nice henhouse, just across the river.' He'll do the rest."

He's gonna do it, Silvano thought, he's gonna sacrifice Little Dom. He relaxed, just a little, you could never totally relax around a predator like Antonio, even if he liked you. Who's to say the cat feels no sorrow for the mouse?

Antonio put his foot down and stood up. "Hey!" he bellowed. "*Gagootz!*"

His chastened guard rushed into the room, bearing coffee on a tray. Antonio looked at the ceiling in disgust. "*Mange di gatz,*" he said, "I don't want any fucking coffee, you fucking idiot. Go get rid of that goddam truck." The guard turned and fled. "Find someplace to empty it out, first!" he bellowed at the doorway. Silvano couldn't help chuckling.

Antonio turned to him. "Civilization," he said, "is going down the fucking toilet. You hear me? Right down the fucking toilet. You should never listen to anybody under thirty, they're all brain dead." He walked over to Silvano and embraced him again. "It's good to have you back," he said. He grabbed Silvano by the shoulders and held him out at arm's length. "The old man thought you were the crazy one and Domenic was the smart one. Turned out to be the other way around. You're staying for supper," he said. "I insist." He stepped back, held his arm out for Silvano to precede him out of the room. "The fuck were you talking about? I woulda made a great president."

ROCCO DROPPED HIM OFF on the corner of Atlantic and Court. He stood in the closest doorway and watched the receding taillights, not even wanting to give them the general direction of where he was going. Who are you kidding? he thought. If Antonio had decided the other way, they'd be mixing the concrete for your new overcoat right now. He turned, finally, and walked down Atlantic, past the bakery where he'd talked to her that first time. God, he thought, what are you doing to me? I've never felt like this before . . . There had been that one girl, in Yelapa, down on the coast of Mexico, but that wasn't really about her, that was just about the way she stood in that doorway with her hair hanging down in her face . . . Her mournful expression had haunted him ever since. But this one is different. Isn't she, God? Is it her or is it me?

• • •

DOMENIC GOT OUT of the cab on Eleventh Avenue and Twenty-eighth Street, stood on the sidewalk watching the departing car vanish in the gloom. He turned on his heel and walked east under the last remaining section of the elevated highway that once ran down the west side of Manhattan. After the road began to fall down in the late sixties the city barely had enough money to tear it down, and this was the last piece, it no longer connected to anything. That's New York City, he thought. Falling down around your fucking ears. Just a few pieces left, here and there, to tell you what it used to be like.

There was a gray Lincoln Town Car parked in the middle of the block. Dom walked up to the passenger side and got in. Ivan Bonifacio was sitting behind the driver's seat. Domenic looked at him. "What happened to your Cadillac?"

"In the shop."

"Oh, yeah?" He decided to have some fun with it. "Having problems? What is it, engine trouble?"

Ivan stared at him. "It's got some fucking holes in it, okay? All right? Does that make you happy? It's got fucking bullet holes in it."

Domenic stared back. "You know what your problem is? You got no vision."

"What the fuck does that mean?"

Domenic shook his head. "Vision. Initiative. Now Iurata, you have to give it to the son of a bitch, he has vision. He has initiative. He's had you dancing to his tune right from the beginning. He knew you were coming, he's one step ahead of you already, what does he do? He leaves a trail of footsteps, then he circles back around and hides in the bushes to see who comes looking. That, asshole, is vision."

"Hey, the guy got lucky, all right?"

"Lucky? Is that what you think? This is twice now he let you walk away. I think he's fucking with you." Domenic suppressed a grin. "I think he just wants to see if you have any vision."

Ivan stared out the windshield. "Hey," he said, "if vision is what got me into this bucket of shit I'm in, maybe I don't want vision. Maybe my life was a hell of a lot easier before I got vision."

"You're still worried about Antonio, aren't you?"

Ivan continued staring out the windshield.

"You know, I'm really sad to see this. Really, I am. You're sitting around waiting, you have to get permission from Antonio to go to the bathroom, and meanwhile Iurata is kicking your ass." He watched Ivan, but Ivan sat without moving, without saying anything. Domenic sighed. "If you don't have the intestinal fortitude to take what's yours, then you don't deserve to have it. Certain things in life, Ivan, don't get given to anyone, they have to be taken. You have to take them by blood and by will. That's how Antonio got where he is, he didn't sit around waiting for permission to take a shit."

"You're out of your fucking mind, you know that? Antonio is right. You are out of your motherfucking skull."

"Antonio only says that because he can't understand the way I think. He doesn't read, Ivan, he doesn't know anything except what he learned hijacking trucks and twisting arms. I bet you don't read, either. Do you know what the basic principle of life is? Do you have any idea?"

"I got no clue what you are talking about."

"Yeah, no shit. Natural selection is what I'm talking about. Survival of the fucking fittest. That's why the Russians are winning and we are losing. They understand how it works. The fucking Russians survive through strength. Through power. And what are we doing, over in this country? We're all getting stoned and marching for peace. You believe that? Marching for peace. Fuck peace. Do you hear me? Fuck peace. You want to win, you want something more than what you got? Then you have to fucking take it away from the guy who already has it."

"Give me a fucking break," Ivan said. "You think Antonio is just going to stand there and watch you take your dick out and wave it around? You think him and Victor are just gonna retire, because you're ready to step up? What's he gonna do, move to Boca, walk up and down the beach every day with a metal detector looking for nickels? You're all ready to go to war, but you got no soldiers, motherfucker, you got nothing."

"I got vision. Look, Ivan, Antonio's a hundred years old, for chrissake. Victor's been following him around for so long, living off the leavings, he don't know how to do anything else. You got nothing to worry about."

Ivan turned to look at him, leaned back in the corner of his seat. "Maybe you're right," he said, after a minute. "Maybe I got no vision. I was ready to come in with you on this thing down at Black and White because I thought there was a nice score there, I thought there was a good chance the two of us could walk away from it with some nice scratch, but you know what? All I heard outa you so far is talk. You got vision? Hey, great. Terrific. You wanna take on Antonio, be my fucking guest. You come out on top, I'll be your fucking butt boy. Okay? But until then, I have stuck my head in the lion's mouth for the last time."

"I don't believe this. We're this close, you're losing your fucking nerve."

"I told you before, it's easy for you to say it, you don't have to . . ." He saw the gun in Domenic's hand. "Hey! Hey, wait . . ."

Domenic shot him twice in the chest. The car was suddenly filled with noise, smoke, and blood. Domenic opened the door and got out, looked inside, shot him once more in the face, just for the hell of it, and then he slammed the door and walked away.

EIGHT

■

SILVANO HAD THE DREAM again that night, he got further into it this time, made it up onto the island in the river. He was carrying an automatic shotgun, a ten-gauge alley sweeper, but the damned thing was empty, and the ammo he carried was all .22 longs, useless unless you were going to throw the shells at someone. He worked his way past a village, keeping just inside the jungle, but the place was deserted, not even any dogs around, the villagers must have eaten them before they died, or ran. There was a school at the far end of the village, wooden building raised a few feet off the ground, about fifteen feet square. He eased up the steps to look inside, saw two dozen kids inside sitting on the floor. They all sat there silent, looking at him. The teacher was a woman, skinny, long dark hair, impossible to tell how old she was but she had a round face, God, she looked like the Madonna, except she stood there in the corner watching him through the saddest eyes he had ever seen.

He backed away, holding the empty shotgun across his chest, retreated back into the jungle. There didn't appear to be any other buildings on the island and he found no sign of people, so he made his way back to the village and went through the empty habitations one at a time and found nothing. It was as though the place had been deserted for years, or like it had been kept that way as a museum, this is how we used to live, before you came. He went back to the schoolhouse, back up the steps, but when he got to the doorway he stopped in his tracks. They were all dead, butchered, hacked, the floor was awash in blood. The teacher was in her corner, she was dying, her throat slashed, she looked at him with accusing eyes. He could read her thoughts, we all died because of you, because you had to come here . . .

He woke up on the floor in his apartment over Henry's garage, doubled over, retching, covered with sweat. It took a long minute for him to remember where he was. He rolled over on his back, looking at the ceiling, and he became conscious of faint scratching noises coming from the kitchen. Mouse, probably, getting an early breakfast. Bastard, he thought. Why couldn't you wake me up five minutes ago?

THERE WERE COP CARS parked on the sidewalk in front of Special Ed's alley, and an ambulance was double-parked in the street nearby, back doors open, lights flashing. Silvano walked on by and went over to the St. Felix, stashed his pistol and ankle holster in the locker he kept there, and then he went back. By the time he got to the alley, someone had shut off the ambulance and killed the lights. A uniform stopped him halfway down the alley.

"Where you think you're going?"

"Looking for a guy I know, lives in a room down in here."

The cop regarded him coldly. "Your friend got a name?"

"Everybody calls him Special Ed."

"Cute. Was he a gimp?"

Was? "Yeah." Silvano got a cold feeling at the pit of his stomach.

"Let me see some ID." The cop took his driver's license, walked him back out of the alley and deposited him in the backseat of a cruiser. No door handles on the inside, windows don't roll down, nothing to do but wait. He leaned back, tried to relax, despite the circumstances. They didn't leave him there long, though, not more than a half an hour. A cop wearing a brown suit and a green tie opened the door and let him out.

"Sorry to make you wait, Mr. Iurata," he said. "This your current address?"

"Yeah, but I'm staying at the Montague for a couple weeks."

"What's your business in Brooklyn, Mr. Iurata?"

"I got family here. Haven't seen them in a while."

"I see. The patrolman said you were looking for Special Ed?"

"Yeah. He was a friend of my brother's. My brother died last year."

"Sorry to hear it. You may as well come with me, see if you recognize the guy. You ain't got a queasy stomach, do you?"

SPECIAL ED WAS EVEN UGLIER in death than he had been in life. Both of his eyes were open, and he lay in a pool of blood on the concrete floor of his room, his baseball bat on the floor beside him. He had a dinner fork gripped in one hand. He'd been worked over with the bat, whoever had done it had finished him off with a blow to the head, there was a groove in his skull matching the shape of the bat. Ed's face was frozen in two of his favorite expressions, resentment and outrage.

"Aaah, Jesus Christ." Silvano flashed on the dream, the

butchered children, the teacher with her throat cut. *We died because you had to come here.*

"Hey." The cop was tapping him on the shoulder. "Hey! This your guy?"

"Yeah, sorry. Yeah, this is him. I don't know his real name. Special Ed, that's what they called him."

"All right. Come back outside."

They had a short conversation back out in the alley. The detective took a few notes, but the answers Silvano gave him were probably not much help. "No," Silvano was saying, "he wasn't into dope, not that I knew of. He'd take a drink. You see what the guy was. All he wanted to do was stay out of trouble."

"A worthwhile goal," the detective said.

This doesn't look like Antonio's doing, Silvano thought. Even if the old buzzard had some reason for it, Silvano couldn't picture him working on Special Ed with a bat. He'd put a bullet in the man's skull, if he needed to, but he wouldn't make a mess like that out of someone already as fucked up as Ed had been. It would have offended his sense of fairness. "Far as I know, he just wanted to be left alone."

"Didn't work out that way. You said you got relatives here local?"

"Yeah. My sister."

"Gimme the number." The cop put him back into the cruiser while he made the call, came back and let him out ten minutes later. "You're free to go, Mr. Iurata," he said, his face a total blank.

SILVANO DECIDED TO LEAVE the gun in the locker; New York City cops had definite attitude problems when it came to unlicensed firearms. Made him uncomfortable, though, given the events of the last few days. Special Ed had not died easy.

He walked past the St. Felix. A dark blue Plymouth Fury that had been parked in the no-standing zone in front of the hotel followed him up the street. He began to feel naked, thinking about the Beretta sitting in the locker back in the St. Felix, not a hundred and fifty feet away. He didn't turn to look at the car, but whoever was driving it was not being careful. The hell with this, he thought, and he stopped on the next corner and turned to look. It was Roland behind the wheel, the driver from Black and White, and he was dressed in street clothes. The car drifted up to him and pulled in at the curb. Roland leaned over and unlocked the door. It was the car that bothered Silvano, though, and it took him another minute to figure out why: it was the same car the feebies had arrived in yesterday morning. He sighed, not sure whether to be irritated or relieved, opened the passenger door, and got in.

"You know, I had a feeling, when I met you."

"Do I still call you Roland?"

"Why not. I gotta tell you, man, you got a gift for stirring up shit. I worked on this case for a year and a half, this was the one was gonna make my career, and you had to come along and fuck it up."

"What are you talking about?"

"Goddammit, you know what I'm talking about. I had a major organized crime bust about to go down, and now all I got is two dead guys and one old guinea cocksucker, maybe, if we can find him, for attempted extortion."

"You with the feebs?"

"What did you do, eat stupid flakes for breakfast? What were you doing down at Black and White?"

"Damn, I thought all the brothers on J. Edgar's payroll worked in the dining room. Who are the dead guys?"

"Most of them do. One guy is a soldier named Ivan Bonifacio."

"Fuck!" Silvano gritted his teeth. "What happened to him?"

Roland shrugged. "Pissed off the wrong man. They found him behind the wheel of his car, early this morning, couple bullets in him. It's usually a message, you know, when they do that."

"Damn." Could it have been Antonio? But the old man did work fast.

"You sound disappointed."

"Maybe I am. Who's the other guy?"

"You ain't heard?"

Silvano shook his head. "Heard what?"

Roland eyed him speculatively. "Guess it don't much matter now, I can't see what difference telling you makes. Joseph O'Brian fell asleep behind the wheel of his car last night. Trouble was, the engine was running and the garage door was closed."

Silvano shook his head. "He leave a note?"

Roland thought about it. "Yeah. But first I gotta know what you were after. I know you ain't no motherfucking carpenter, so if you don't want me holding your ass as a material witness for the next six months, baby, you better start talking."

Silvano still had Noonie's picture in his shirt pocket. He pulled it out, handed it to Roland. "You were lying, when I asked you about him. Right?"

Roland's shoulders sagged when he looked at the picture. He shook his head. "Shit. Who was he to you?"

"My brother."

Roland slumped behind the wheel, looking out the window, not at the picture in his hand. "Sorry," he said, handing the picture back.

"Sorry don't cut it."

"I know. We had that guy Bonifacio dead to rights for doing your brother. Powers that be figured there was no hurry on it, we could pick him up for that any time. See, this thing running at Black and White is conspiracy, and we wanted to go further up the ladder than Bonifacio. There had to be some heavier players than him in on this."

"Just one. That's why they whacked him, him and his buddy were doing this on their own."

Roland regarded him with suspicion. "Who was the other guy?"

"What was in the note? And what do you know about my brother?"

Roland scowled at him, dropped the gearshift lever into drive and jerked the car away from the curb. "This is the kind of shit keeps knocking me back down the ladder," he said.

"You're in the wrong agency," Silvano told him. "You wanna play with the big dogs, I can give you a name. Guy I know in Defense. You're never gonna look enough like a Boy Scout to make it with the feebs, anyhow. What was in the note?"

"Note was to his priest," Roland said, a sour expression on his face. "Asking for absolution. Apparently, O'Brian thought he was gonna get off the hook, but last night some guy named Victor paid him a visit. Told him the original deal was still on, except the names had been changed. O'Brian said it was more than he could take."

"That's too bad."

Roland blipped the siren a few times and swung out around the cars waiting for the light on the corner of Atlantic, swung left and headed east.

"You have any idea who Victor is?"

"Muscle. Works for Antonio Malatesta, same guy Bonifacio used to work for. You might be able to put him away for a while, but you won't get anything out of him. Victor is old school. Anything else in the note?"

Roland glanced over at him. "As in, where's the money? No, but don't worry, we'll find it. So they whacked Bonifacio for freelancing, who was his buddy? Who was he working with?"

Fair enough, Silvano thought, and maybe a bargain at that . . . They turned south on Flatbush. "Domenic Scalia, alias Little Dom. Where we going?"

"Heard the name," Roland said. "We're going to the beach. I hear white boys love the beach." He looked over at Silvano. "You know how to keep your mouth shut, I'll show you what I know about your brother."

Silvano sat with that for a couple of minutes. "You want Scalia," he said finally, "you're going to have to move your ass. I would guess, same guys did Bonifacio are looking for him right now."

Roland picked up the radio mike from its hook on the dashboard, reconsidered, put it back. "Fuck it," he said. "Let them have him."

"You wouldn't prosecute anyhow," Silvano told him. "You guys would kiss his ass to get at the stuff he knows."

Roland perked up. "That right? You telling me this isn't a total loss after all?"

"Maybe not."

Brooklyn stretches a long way from what most people think about as "the city," by which they mean the southern half of Manhattan. The subway ride from "the city" to the neighborhoods along Brooklyn's southern shore can be murderous. During rush hour you are crushed among the herd for a trip that seems interminable, and at other times, trains that go to Starrett City or Sheepshead Bay come along about as often as an ice age. And yet, there is little empty space in those places, they are filled to bursting. Silvano looked out the passenger side window as Roland blipped the siren and bulled his way through traffic. What do they think when they get here, he wondered, those lucky souls who survive the trip from China or Haiti or Eastern Europe, do they think it's worth their sacrifice? Every block, every square yard is filled with people fighting to hang on to their piece of the dream, fighting to keep their places in line. And still, the rest of the world overflows with malcontents who want to come and live here, in every foreign port he had seen he'd met them, dreamers blind to the costs of Paradise. If Brooklyn pushed another ten miles out into the Atlantic Ocean tonight, we would fill it up tomorrow.

He looked over at Roland. "Gimme a clue."

Roland glanced at him. "Rockaway."

"Brooklyn-by-the-Sea."

That got a short laugh. "God's country."

Silvano looked back out his window. Why isn't it? he wondered.

There is a green ribbon of grass and trees near the Belt Parkway, the highway that runs along Brooklyn's southern shore. They emerged from the traffic and rode across the overpass, and then, south of the highway, they came to the overgrown runways and boarded-up buildings of Floyd Bennett Field.

"You serious, you really know a guy in DIA?"

"Always looking for talent, and they love poaching on J. Edgar."

Roland pulled into a marina parking lot across the street from the southern extremity of Floyd Bennett Field. He got out of the car, waited for Silvano to do likewise.

"Over there," he said, pointing at the chain-link fence that surrounded the unused airfield. "Follow the fence line down to the water. You'll come to an old wooden lobster boat beached on the inlet. Bonifacio buried your brother right next to the boat."

"You bastards knew all about this?"

Roland grimaced. "We were gonna get to it, I told you." He looked at his watch. "Get going," he said. "I'll give you half an hour."

"You gonna wait here?"

"I'm gonna go over to that pay phone over there and have a private conversation about a certain Domenic Scalia, who I heard about from an unnamed source."

HE FELT THE WEIGHT of every incident he'd survived, every year he'd lived. He crossed the road and followed the path along the fence. The path stuck to the high ground, up near the fence, out of the mud. About a hundred and fifty yards in, the fence turned left, away from the water, toward the city. He stood there at the corner and looked at it, two widely separated clumps of tall buildings looking small and insignificant on the far side of the low rubble of Queens. The southern group of buildings was dominated by the twin towers of the World Trade Center. The northern group was midtown, more uniform, but he could pick out the pointed spires of the Empire State and Chrysler Buildings. In the near distance a jet roared down the runway at Kennedy and clawed its way through the brownish haze at ground level up into the dirty blue. This city needs wind, he thought. No wind and she'd choke.

He turned his back on the city and looked at the narrow trail leading down through tall reeds and clumps of spartina grass. Leave it alone, he thought, God, why do I have to go look at this? What the hell difference does it make? But after a minute, he went off down the trail to where the vegetation petered out.

He stood on the muddy bank of Rockaway Inlet. On the far side of the inlet stood the narrow sand bar known as Far Rockaway. The neighborhoods there still look like Brooklyn, for the most part, but blue water calls to you from between the buildings, and you can catch the faint smell of the ocean, just a hint of clean salt air over the stale, twice-breathed smell of the city.

To his left, a hundred feet away, the rotting wooden hull of a fishing boat was mired in the marsh. The sun's fractured reflection winked off the incoming tide moving sluggishly up the inlet into the vast uninhabited marsh. A pair of snowy egrets worked the margins of the shore, stepping delicately through the shallows on spindly legs, long beaks and sharp eyes, white feathers, instinct and reflexes. A blue heron, taller, darker, uglier, stood motionless on the far side watching him through an eye that comprehended neither love nor mercy. Why would you guys come here, he wondered, thinking of the birds, wishing he could ask and they answer, why come here, why not fly down to the Chesapeake, or stay up in Labrador, where men never go? Then again, maybe the city had cast her spell on them, too. Maybe they liked the view.

It was just avoidance, he knew it, just a way to keep from thinking about Noonie sleeping out in the lee of that wooden boat, with no one to visit him but fiddler crabs. I'm sorry, Noonie, he wanted to say it but the words caught in his throat, I'm sorry, not just for this but for the whole stinking trip, sorry for whatever happened to you being born, sorry for the fights, sorry for the doctors, the institutions, sorry for the Thorazine, sorry I had to go, run away, and leave you to fend for yourself.

Not that Noonie would give a shit. He'd never had much capacity for sorrow and none for introspection, if he were standing, alive, next to Silvano he would have taken a pure, unalloyed joy in the moment, he would have reveled in the sight, the water, the wading birds, the jets, the mud, the laughing gulls wheeling overhead, fighting over some scrap of food one of them had found. The Buddhists had a saying, Silvano had heard it years before and it stuck in his mind. The words came to him now: joyful participation in the sorrows of life. He himself had never managed it, he had participated, all right, he'd waded in up to his ears, but he'd done it in anger or in fear or in lust, never in joy. He would never have known such a thing to be possible, would have dismissed the whole idea as another example of soft-brained uncritical religious thinking, had he not grown up watching Noonie do it. He might never have been able to explain it to you, but, baby, he had lived it.

Whassamatter, Sil, that's what Noonie would say if he were standing here, whassamatter, Sil, why ya cryin'? He would tug on your arm, you okay? Can we go swimmin'? Is that water too cold for swimmin'? He'd feel sorry for me and I'd feel sorry for him, both of us would stand here thinking the other guy had gotten a raw deal.

The blue heron spread his wings and leaped into the air, transformed by the act of flight into a creature of grace and beauty, a being of wonder and light. He soared farther up the marsh, seeking, perhaps, some more inaccessible shoreline unspoiled by ruined wooden boats or grieving men. You sorry motherfucker, he thought, you couldn't do anything for him when he was alive and you can't do anything for him now, he's gone on ahead, and who knows if you'll ever see him again. I can't even get the guy for you, Noonie, he thought, some other son of a bitch beat me to it. Noonie wouldn't care about that, either, he'd never liked fighting, never liked being mad. He had always been ready to forgive you, forget what you'd done to him.

I miss you, Noonie, God, I miss you. I always had to reel you back in when we were kids, I always had to track you down and bring you home, but I'm not gonna do it this time, this time I'm gonna let you go, you can stay out here with the birds. Go swimming whenever you feel like it.

He felt the breeze pick up as he made his way back up the path, and wind-borne grains of sand pecked at his eyes. He stopped when he got to the road, at the end of the fence, tried to pull himself together. A tall, thin black girl wearing a blue denim miniskirt and a halter top walked by him, giving him a look on her way past, taking him for one more whacko standing by the side of the road. On the far side of the street a fat guy carrying a fishing rod, a white bucket, and a small beer cooler trudged in the opposite direction. Silvano crossed over and went to sit on the car and wait for Roland, who was still on the telephone.

ROLAND DROPPED HIM in front of the St. Felix. It had been a quiet trip back, Silvano sitting in the passenger seat second-guessing himself, Roland driving, silent, probably doing the same thing. He pulled the car up into the no-standing zone in front of the hotel. "Listen," he said, "I don't think anyone will ask, but if they do, this little excursion didn't happen."

"All right. Thanks."

"You really know someone in Defense, or were you yanking my chain?"

"I know a lot of people. You're interested in talking, I need to know your real name."

"Winston. Winston Taylor."

"All right, I'll pass it on. Someone might get in touch with you, but you never know. They'll come sniffing around, send someone to have a look at you. You decide to make the jump, don't go on anyone's verbal offer. You understand what I'm telling you?"

"Cut the cards, is what you're saying."

"Yeah."

"All right. Listen, I'm sorry about your brother. He seemed like an okay guy."

Silvano didn't know what to say to that, so he opened the door and stepped out. He leaned down and looked in. "See you," he said. He shut the door and walked away.

THE NEIGHBORHOOD SEEMED DIFFERENT, somehow, like he'd been gone a couple years instead of a couple hours. Before, he'd seen character and history, now he saw dirt. Someone had puked on the base of a small tree outside a bar on Clark Street. Half a block down, a lady stood at one end of a leash looking idly off into the distance while her little white dog stood at the other end and took a shit on the sidewalk. The woman who looked like Tip O'Neill's sister stood in her usual spot outside the Margaret, silent this time, glaring belligerently at people going past. Silvano looked at her.

"Fuck you," he said.

"Assholes!" she exploded, her face red and her eyes clamped shut. "Whole damn city is assholes and eyeballs! Eyeballs and assholes!" She kept it up as he crossed the street and went down onto the Promenade. My good deed for the day, he thought.

The buildings on the Brooklyn side of the Hudson all looked older than they had the last time he'd seen them, crumbling, decrepit, falling down. He hadn't noticed, before, how the refuse containers in between the park benches were overflowing, how the flower beds behind the wrought-iron fences were littered with empty bottles and beer cans. He sat down on a bench and stared out across the harbor, looking past the Statue of Liberty, past New Jersey, even, out into nothing, listening to the whispered promises of some distant highway telling him those same old seductive lies, the ones he'd always been willing to believe before, stories about what he might find if only he'd take the trouble to go and look. A part of him still wanted to listen, but he knew he wasn't going to be able to talk himself into buying it this time around.

I have to tell somebody, he thought, I have to talk to someone. Who the hell knows where Henry would be, this time of day? Elia's probably still at work. He decided to go find a pay phone, see if he could get her on the phone.

An unfamiliar voice answered the phone at Black and White.

"Can I speak to Elia Taskent?"

"Hold on." It was a male voice. He heard the guy ask who Elia Taskent was, heard another voice, muffled, sounded like Sean O'Brian. A second later the guy came back on. "She didn't come in today."

"No? She call in sick?"

"Buddy, she ain't here. Beyond that I can't help you." The guy hung up.

Silvano stood there looking at the receiver in his hand. He could feel worms crawling in his stomach. Go look, he told himself. Go see if she's at home.

The lock on Elia's door refused to surrender to his ministrations. After ten frustrating minutes he gave up and stood back in the hallway, tempted to just kick the door in, but then he reconsidered and headed for the roof instead.

God, he thought, looking down at the fire escape from above, God, don't let this thing fall off the building, not today, and he dropped down onto it and made his way down to her floor. The windows in Elia's apartment that fronted onto the fire escape were pinned closed from the inside, because what was a way out was also a way in. He peered into the darkened room in frustration, his anxiety building. He was tempted, once again, to simply smash his way inside. Great idea, he told himself. You'll do a lot of good locked away for breaking and entering, and you can't sit out on this rickety iron trellis much longer, either.

There was a narrow ledge in the brick face of the building that ran horizontally under the row of windows on each floor, it was barely two inches wide. Her bathroom window was ten feet from the end of the fire escape, and it had been open when he'd visited her last. He went over the railing and put his toes on the ledge, holding on to the rail for support. Don't lean in, he told himself, don't freeze up, just get over there. This is idiotic, some small inner voice in his head was saying, this is the stupidest thing you've done in a while . . . Get on with it, he thought, his desperation overruling his common sense. He inched along the ledge, holding on to individual bricks with his fingertips, narrowing his focus until all he was conscious of was the feeling of weight on his toes and the gaps between the bricks he could feel with his fingers as he felt for the next hold. He reached the window and pushed it open, began breathing again, slid into the room.

She wasn't home.

He had been worrying that he'd find her inside, beaten to death like Special Ed, lost to him forever, but she wasn't. He could smell her in the room, though, the scent of the perfume she wore, traces of the soap she used. Droplets of water clung to the shower stall, and her towel was still damp. She got up and got ready, he thought, she went out of here this morning. Probably headed for work, he thought, although there was no way to know for sure. She might have had a test, or a doctor's appointment.

Black thoughts came into his mind but he pushed them away. God, You gotta help me, here . . . If someone has her, there's nothing you can do, he told himself. Just go where they can find you, and wait. Is it self-centered, he wondered, to automatically assume her disappearance is related to you? Maybe she went off on business of her own. She does have a life, you know, had one long before you came along.

You can hope, he thought, you can hope for that, but in the meantime you have to go someplace they would look for you, and you have to wait. He closed the window he'd entered through, let himself out of her apartment, listened to the lock snap shut behind him.

NINE

■

THE CRAZY ONE WAS NOT BAD-LOOKING, but she was too vacant, and besides, she hadn't bathed in some time. The other one was not to Little Dom's taste, either, too muscular, for one thing, too dark and too pissed off. He toyed with the idea of doing her, just to get at Silvano, cause him as much pain as he could, but he didn't want to push her over the line into incoherence, because then she would be impossible to handle. He had them both stashed in the same hotel room, Iurata's girlfriend lashed securely, facedown on the bed, gagged to keep her quiet. The crazy one was tied to a chair, she wasn't gagged because she didn't seem to have anything to say. She just sat there looking at him, she didn't rage and scream and curse the way the other one had. God, what a waste. Too many trips without luggage, he guessed. She seemed compliant, though, and maybe it was just his general good mood, but he was actually beginning to like her. In the meantime, though, he needed her calm, she had to be sane enough to function, to talk, she had to be able to deliver her message. Why are you bothering with this shit? he asked himself. If you want to take Iurata down, you have to keep your mind on business. I can still fuck with Iurata's head, he thought. As soon as you're dead, he would tell him, I'm gonna do your girlfriend. Yeah, that was it. He felt better, warming to the idea. Every time she thinks of you, as long as she lives she'll feel me inside of her, with every tear she cries for you, motherfucker, she'll remember what I do to her. And you know what? No matter what she thinks of you now, she'll come to hate you, eventually, you asshole, because all this is gonna happen to her because of you.

He turned away from the window and walked around the bed, feeling the bitch's ass on his way by. She recoiled from his touch as much as her bonds would allow, making angry noises in the back of her throat.

He looked at his watch. Another hour and it would be fully dark. He looked at the crazy one. "You think you can find Silvano Iurata?"

"Probably."

He picked his bag up and plopped it on the bed between the bitch's legs, unzipped it, took out his sawed-off shotgun. Most of the stock and all but a few inches of the barrel had been removed. What was left was barely eighteen inches long, easily hidden, incredibly lethal at close range. It was already loaded. He moved the bag and nestled the business end of the gun right up into the bitch's crotch so she could feel it, but gently, gently. He went to whisper in her ear. "You better lie still," he told her. "It's not time for you to die yet."

He reached into the bag and pulled out a roll of duct tape. He stripped tape off the roll, wrapped it twice around the end of the shotgun barrels, then he grabbed a handful of the bitch's hair, jerked her head back, ran the tape twice around her neck. Now the shotgun was a part of her, it would go everywhere she went, when she stood it would hang, suspended from the back of her head. He had a shawl in the bag, he would wrap it around her shoulders, walk next to her with his hand beneath the shawl, on the gun, nobody would even look twice. Just two good friends out for an evening stroll. He snickered, looked over at the crazy one.

"You see that?"

She didn't say anything, she just nodded.

"No way for her to get loose," he said, "not alive, not unless I decide to let her go. I want you to remember that."

She said nothing, just continued to stare at him. He yanked at the ropes that bound her to the chair. When her hands were free, she rubbed her wrists, flexed her fingers, watched him as he finished untying her, freeing her legs, too. She shook her head, flinging that long hair back over her shoulders.

He watched her for a minute. "Pay attention to me now. I want you to go find Silvano Iurata. I want you to tell him everything you've seen here tonight. Tell him about the gun, the duct tape, all of it. Can you do that?"

She nodded wordlessly.

"I want you to tell him he has to meet me, right now, tonight, at the southern tip of the Promenade, all the way at the end, past the entrance from Montague Street. I'll be there waiting, and I'll have his woman with me." He looked at his watch. "I'll give you two hours to find him. If you don't find him, I'll kill her. If you find him too late, I'll kill her. If he doesn't show up, I'll kill her. Her life is your responsibility. Do you hear me?"

"I hear you. You want him tonight, you gotta give me carfare. I might have to check a few different places."

"Jesus Christ," he said. "You want money from me?"

She actually sneered at him. "I look like I'm rolling in it?"

Shaking his head, he reached into his pocket and peeled a

couple of twenties off his roll. He handed her the bills, then stepped back away from her, went over and opened the door. "Go now," he said, watching her. "Hurry." She stood up and walked out.

He went over and lay on the bed next to the other one and began caressing her. She didn't recoil this time, she just lay there. "Don't worry, I'll let you go," he told her. "If you're a good little girl, if you be quiet and cooperate, you'll live through this. But I want you to understand, I don't actually need you anymore. If you died right now, it wouldn't matter. Do you hear me?"

"Mmm-hmm." She nodded her head slightly.

"Good," he said. "We're almost ready. You better hope she finds him."

The hotel had had a dumbwaiter once, the small square door was still there, painted shut. He walked over and kicked it. It buckled with the first kick but it didn't give way. He put all of his anger into the second kick and the door shattered. He went over and looked inside, stuck his hand into the opening and felt the warm air moving up the shaft.

In his bag there was a plastic jug full of gasoline. It had a timer and a blasting cap taped to it. He set the timer, wrapped duct tape around the jug, and suspended it in the dumbwaiter shaft, running the end of the tape out through the opening and down the wall.

"Time to go," he said, and he went over to the bed. "Now, if you want to survive, you're gonna have to listen very carefully . . ."

SILVANO HEARD THE SIRENS IN THE DISTANCE, not cop sirens, going swiftly, chasing someone, but slower moving, more insistent.

He stood watching the usual evening parade on the Promenade, gay guys out shopping, walkers, joggers, a guy moving through the crowd selling nickel bags and loosies from a leather bag hanging from one shoulder. Word moved through the crowd, then, like a wave rolling up the beach, Margaret's on fire, hey, the Margaret Hotel is burning, she's going up like a torch, man, you knew this was going to happen, what a firetrap, someone probably fell asleep with a lit cigarette . . . They all hurried away to watch, and a few minutes later he was alone, leaning on the corner of the railing down at the end, northbound traffic rushing by not twenty feet below. It was a good move, he thought, torching the Margaret, he never would have thought of it.

It unnerved him, though. Margaret was where he'd been keeping them, that's what Mrs. Clark had told him. She hadn't seen it, going in, he had carried her in there unconscious, but she knew it as soon as she came to, the place had a distinctive smell, and then, of course, she had walked out under her own power, and there was no mistaking it. He had to believe what she said, had to trust this wasn't some delirium, some walking nightmare of her own imagining, had to hope she hadn't left out anything important. He had to depend on her, is what it boiled down to, and he was uncomfortable depending on anyone, let alone her. She might have the best of intentions, but that didn't mean she was in more than incidental contact with reality.

"How did he know," Silvano had asked her, "how did he know that you knew me?" She had the impression that Little Dom had been watching, she'd seen him in the Montague, hanging around, spreading a few bucks, asking some questions. He had jogged off, then, not stopping at the St. Felix for a weapon.

The fire made him nervous, they always did, you could never be sure what would happen in a fire, and maybe Domenic had fucked up, maybe the building had gone up so fast that he hadn't gotten her out, maybe Elia was trapped in there with him right now, and how many others were going to die in that stinking dump this night, people who didn't get the word in time, or were too old to move fast enough, or maybe just drunk and passed out, waiting for the flames? The thought agitated him, and though he knew he had to stand and wait, his feet itched to run, to charge in, the way he usually did, go for it, go find her, drag her out. He couldn't see the Margaret or the fire from where he stood, but he could see an orange glow haloing the buildings between the two of them, more sirens from fire companies farther away, coming hard. Smart, he had to admit it. Nobody would remember anything about this night except the hotel going up, it was a primal thing, big bonfire in the dark, everybody wants to go dance around it.

He saw them then. It looked like they were arm in arm, taking their time, working their way toward him, past the empty park benches. When they got closer he could see the silver tape around Elia's neck, some of her hair was caught up under it on one side. She had some kind of gray thing around her shoulders, reminded Silvano of the serape men wore down in Colombia. She wasn't looking at him. She walked with her head down, listening to Domenic, who was leaning down, whispering in her ear. He glanced in Silvano's direction, a smile spreading across his face, but he kept his head down, his voice in her ear, one arm hidden behind her, up under that gray thing, where the shotgun had to be. God, Silvano thought, I'm just gonna bother You about this one time . . .

He hadn't seen Little Dom since they were both seventeen. Dom had kept on growing after he left. He was about Bonifacio's size now, still had all his hair. He looked like he'd spent some time in the gym, he was a little paunchy but not bad, he carried it okay. He was jittery, though, kept talking to Elia, kept looking around, laughing nervously. Silvano wiped his palms on his jeans and calmed himself, controlling his breathing, pushing his heart rate down, clearing his head. He focused on the two of them, tuning out the fire engines, the traffic noises below, putting his anxiety high up on a shelf. He turned his back and leaned on the railing, looking at the lights of Manhattan winking off the surface of the East River, over where one of the Staten Island Ferries vectored into the current, lining up for the slip.

"Silvano Iurata."

He could hear triumph in the guy's voice. They came up and stood next to him at the railing, Little Dom right at his elbow, Elia on the far side. He wants me to try for him, Silvano thought. He wants an excuse to blow her head off, right here. "Hello, Domenic."

"I want you to know I didn't fuck your girlfriend. I might, though, later on." He chuckled.

Silvano leaned forward, looking past Domenic. Elia's face was white, and her jaw was clamped in anger. "You all right?" he asked her. She closed her eyes, nodded twice. Good thing she ain't the one with the gun, he thought. She looks like she wants to kill both of us.

"You taking in the sights?" Domenic said. He was enjoying himself.

"Yeah," Silvano said. He noticed some small puncture marks in Dominic's forearm, three rows of four holes. Special Ed must have gotten a couple of licks in with his dinner fork. "Nice night. You ever wonder what this place must have looked like when Henry Hudson sailed in here for the first time? Just trees, just water, animals? It must have been beautiful." He turned to face them, one elbow on the railing. "Sometimes I wonder," he said, "if the human race is just some kind of skin disease that the Earth caught, you know, like a planetary psoriasis. She'll feel better after she's gotten cured of us, go back to the way she was."

"Oh, that's deep," Domenic said, mocking him. "That's heavy, man, I can dig it. You tune in and turn on after you dropped out? You need to see the shotgun?"

"Probably should, just to make it official."

"Step out around us. Way out around, then come up on the other side. Okay, stop there. Reach out, take one hand, just pull back the shawl and look under. That's it, that's enough, now drop it and step away. Step away."

It was an old double barrel, the kind you had to break open to reload. Looked like a Mossberg. Domenic didn't have his hand anywhere near the triggers, though, he was cradling the thing in his hand, had his trigger finger indexed up on the stock, like they teach you in shooting school. It wasn't much, but it was something. It might buy him a half second. "I wanna go back over in the corner where I was," he said.

"Fine," Domenic said. "Turn your back to us, go way out around."

"Don't get nervous," Silvano told him. He put his back to them and did his slow half circle. There was a tall, long-haired woman straggling down the walkway from Montague Street in the shadows. Doesn't matter, he told himself. Pay attention.

"You see enough? You satisfied?" Domenic couldn't keep the stupid grin off his face.

"Yeah." He leaned both elbows on the railing and sighed.

"There is no way out of this for you. You do exactly what I tell you, I might let your girlfriend go. This whole thing is all your fault, you know."

"Yeah, you're probably right." He turned to face the two of them again. He thought he saw movement out of the corner of his eye, but he focused completely on Domenic. "I keep promising myself," he said. "I keep promising the Great Beyond that things are gonna be different, I'm gonna change, I'm gonna be a guy that builds things instead of a guy that blows them up. It never seems to work out, though, no matter what I do, I'm always back in the same old shit."

Domenic's voice was low and vicious. "How does it feel? You're finally gonna get to pay up for what you did to my father and my sister. Too bad for your woman, but she's gonna pay, too."

Silvano shrugged. "You might get away with it," he said. "Your grandfather ever tell you why he killed your old man?"

"What!?" Domenic turned toward him, his hand drifting a few inches down from where it had been. Not far enough, Silvano thought. "What did you say?"

"Yeah," Silvano said, not moving. "He made me drive the car that night. Big old tank, I don't remember what kind it was, but it didn't have power steering, had a steering wheel the size of a manhole cover just to give you enough leverage to turn the thing. Your father was up front, he was gone already, the old man was in the backseat behind him, holding a .357 in his lap." He glanced over at Domenic, trying to gauge the position of his arm just using his peripheral vision, but he couldn't tell for sure if he had enough space.

"You are making this shit up." Domenic spat the words.

"Angelo was already dead. Old Dom made me help him, the two of us carried your father down onto this boat some friend of his kept at a marina down in Sheepshead Bay. The guy had a machete on the boat, when the old man found it he lost his mind all over again, he hacked your father's head off, then he dumped both pieces in the water." He looked at Domenic again. "He's standing there on the boat, right, he's got this big fucking knife in his hand, his whole body is shaking . . . I thought he was gonna kill me, too."

Domenic was transfixed, his face a mask of horror and fascination. He came out of it momentarily, long enough to slide his hand back up on the shotgun. Silvano cursed inwardly, turned away. God, he thought, the guy's hand has got to be getting tired. He looked over the railing at the traffic just below him.

"He didn't, though. Kill me, I mean. I guess that much is obvious. He thought about it, though, for a good two minutes it could have gone either way. Finally he washes the knife off in the bay, puts it back." Silvano shook his head. "'You shoulda come to me first,' he tells me. 'You see what you made me do? You came to me first, none of this woulda happened.' He put me on a bus that night, gave me a couple grand. 'You can call me if you need money,' he tells me, 'but you can't come back. And you gotta swear to me, swear on your father's life, you never say a word about what you seen tonight. You ever talk, I'll kill your father first, then I come for you. You understand?' That was the last time I saw him." He could see the vein throbbing in Domenic's neck.

"Why?"

Silvano turned to face him again. He sighed, weary of the story. "Your father had this female he was seeing . . ."

"You are a fucking liar. I will kill this bitch . . ."

"Don't be hasty." Silvano shook his head. "Look, let me tell Elia the story, you just listen in. Okay? Otherwise we'll never get through it. Elia, you with me?"

She nodded her head, just barely.

"Domenic's father, Angelo, he had this chippy he saw on the

side. Maybe it's an old country thing, I don't know, but nobody bothered to hide it, nobody made an issue out of it. She was no spring chicken, either, she had to be in her thirties, but she was beautiful, man, she was a knockout. Anyway, Angelo has it bad for this woman. Him and his father, old Domenic, they used to fight about it a lot. I mean, they fought about everything, they were all the time screaming at each other. What they called each other, you wouldn't believe. You went over their house, it was a three-ring circus. It was never calm there, always emotional, emotional. You walk in, it's never 'hello,' you're always coming in at the middle of some big thing.

"So anyhow, Angelo's girlfriend is pushing him, she wants him to get a divorce and marry her. This is the fifties, remember, we're Italians, we don't do that. You kidding? Old Dom is having a fit, which he was good at, he's making all kind of threats. Angelo's wife finally catches on, now she's mad, she stops putting out, she won't talk to him except to yell 'Fuck you!' and lock herself in her bedroom.

"So Angelo's not getting any at home, meanwhile things go south with the girlfriend. Somewhere along the line, she gets into horse." He pantomimed shooting up. "It takes Angelo a while to find out, he's got his mind on his own problems, but when he sees the tracks, he pops a gasket, he threatens to kill her, he's gonna have her locked up, she's crying, she promises to quit, she'll never do it again, she's gonna go to the doctor, please give her one more chance, you know, all the usual shit. But you know how it goes, right, she goes away, gets cleaned up, she comes back, she does okay for a while, then she starts getting high again. He finds out, they replay the scene all over. I don't know how many times they go through this.

"Finally, what happens, Angelo figures out she's whoring for it, right, she's putting out to her connection to get her shit. So he figures, he's over it, but he decides to get the guy first, all the trouble the guy caused, he's going to find out who the guy is and whack him, then maybe she can get her act together. Call it a going-away present. So he rents the apartment across the hall from hers, he puts a guy in there to watch, see who shows up. Long story short, it's old Dom, right, he's ruining her so that his son Angelo will wake up and do what the fuck he's supposed to do." Silvano could hear strangled noises coming from deep in Domenic's throat, but he ignored them, kept his attention on Elia.

"One little detail I left out. The whole neighborhood has been following this story, right, it's like *Days of Our Fucking Lives* or something. So Angelo can't put one of his regular crew up in the building to watch for whoever's been selling smack to his girl, he's already taken enough heat for this, but he needs someone who can keep his mouth shut. So who can he use? He uses me." He looked into Domenic's eyes. "I was seventeen years old. I promised your father I would do what he told me to do, I promised him I would keep watch. I was just a kid, I thought a promise meant something. My instructions were, you know who it is, you call this number. So I call the number, some Guido answers the phone, I tell him I have to see Angelo. 'Sit tight,' he tells me. Couple hours later, Angelo shows up." He looked back at Elia. "Now Angelo might have been my uncle, but he was a scary motherfucker, and he was madder than a wet cat. I was in too far to get out, I didn't know what else to do, so I sat him down and I told him my story. When I finish, he sits there, he's looking at me, I ain't saying another word. After a while he picks up the phone, he dials, someone answers. 'Put him on,' he says. He waits. A minute later Angelo starts screaming into the phone. I mean, screaming, just calling names. Then he slams the phone down. He looks at me. 'This has been coming for a long time,' he tells me. 'Let's go, you're coming with me.' He grabs me by the arm, and we take off.

"Old Domenic was in the basement of his house when we found him. He has a bar down there, he's sitting by himself, drinking. Angelo starts in on him, just like a thousand times before, except when the old man gets up to say something, Angelo pops him, slaps him in the face, I mean, he really let the old man have it. Domenic goes down, right, he can't believe it, Angelo goes off on him, this time the old man keeps his mouth shut and listens. Angelo says his piece, finally he's done, he sits down at the bar, but his mistake was, he still trusts his father. He sits with his back to him. Domenic picks a bottle of scotch off the bar, he swings it as hard as he can, he catches Angelo just above the ear with it. I don't know if he meant to do it or not, I guess it doesn't matter, but he caved Angelo's skull in." He shook his head. "After he hit the floor, he never made another sound. Domenic goes down on his knees next to Angelo, he grabs him by the hair, he's still screaming at him, he's punching him in the face. I always knew he was nuts, but that night I thought he'd lost it, I thought he'd gone all the way around the bend, I was trying to think of a way to get out of there, but the old man came out of it. He stood up, he's got blood all over his hands, he looks at me. 'This is all your fault,' he says." He looked out into the night, there were a million lights piercing the darkness. New York City, he thought, how much shit have you seen? He turned back to Little Dom. "You know the rest of it," he said. "Maybe you think like the old man, maybe you think it was my fault. Hell, maybe it was, I don't know." He watched Domenic carefully, never letting his eyes leave Dom's face, because Mrs. Clark was creeping up the rail behind him. He could see her clearly, it took everything he had to keep his eyes focused on Domenic, but he did, even when she leaned over and pulled the knife out of her shopping bag. She held it out, the blade gleaming in the glow of the streetlight. She grinned then, showing those rotten teeth of hers. He couldn't breathe, he couldn't move, he couldn't think of any way to come out of it with Elia alive.

"I don't believe a fucking thing you say." Domenic's face twisted into a sneer. "Domenic told me you were fucking Jeannette, she joined the order to get away from you. He said my father found out, you knew what he was gonna do to you so you killed him. He said you were family, Jeannette made him promise not to hurt you, that's why he let you run."

Silvano shook his head. "Dom, you gotta know I'm telling the truth. Jeannette was all ready to go in, you know she was, it's all she ever talked about. The old man just used her, like he used everyone else. You don't believe me, you can go ask her, she's cloistered but they'll let her talk to you. Let it go, Dom. Don't make the same mistakes the old man made. Be different, make a new one. At least let Elia go, she's got no part in this." Despite his best efforts, Silvano's attention wandered, because Mrs. Clark was right up behind Domenic, crouched down low. Domenic sensed her, then, and he turned to look. "Crazy bitch!" he yelled, and he turned a little farther, and for a fraction of a second he only had the shotgun with the tips of his fingers. Silvano drove his shoulder into the tiny space between Domenic and Elia, separating the two of them, he had her by the shoulders and began twisting her away, but his back was to Domenic and he could feel Domenic grappling with something at his belt. There's no way, Silvano thought, there's no way Elia can get far enough away in time, that has to be a pistol he's reaching for, and if he's any kind of a shot at all he'll get all three of us. He tried to shove Elia away from him but he was afraid to push her too hard with that gun hanging there, he just wanted to get her going, and he turned in Dominic's direction, Domenic had Mrs. Clark by the shirtfront but he had to let her go when she hacked at him with her knife. Elia wasn't running and it was too late, Domenic had the gun out . . .

Domenic leaned back away from the knife, his gun in the hand that flailed for balance. Silvano let go of Elia and grabbed Little Dom by the shoulders, bending him backward, over the railing. A half second later he was hanging there, dangling over the roadway. Silvano had him by one hand, the one without the gun in it.

"Let it go!" Silvano shouted at him. Domenic turned his head away slowly, looking at the gun in his other hand, pointed at the roadway below. "Domenic, let it go!" Silvano could almost sense Domenic making up his mind, he felt Domenic squeezing his hand harder, saw him turning back, his face a mask of hate. The gun hand came around, it seemed to move as slowly and evenly as the second hand on a clock, Silvano waited as long as he could, but Domenic was not going to let anything go, he wanted to kill them both. With a convulsive twist Silvano shook his hand free and spun away. He could feel the shot before he heard it, it went past his ear and up into the night sky. He reached for Elia, who was still standing right there, a stick woman. He gathered her up into his arms, looked over her shoulder, down at the BQE where Domenic had landed not fifty feet in front of an oncoming semi, he was on his knees right in the truck's path. The driver tried to stop, smoking black tire tracks streamed out behind the tractor while the brakes shrieked. The trailer jackknifed, it came out around into the center lane like God's own flyswatter, Domenic was on his feet then, crazy as old John Brown himself, he had his head back, you could see him howling but you couldn't hear him over the terrible sound of the truck coming apart . . .

Silvano had to look away because he felt Mrs. Clark's hands

reaching for the shotgun, he got loose from Elia's grip and broke it open, pulled the shells out with a shaking hand.

"Hold still, doll," she was saying. "Hold very still while we cut this thing off you." With a surgeon's precision she sliced through the duct tape with her knife, peeled the tape away from the skin, trimming Elia's hair on the side where it had gotten stuck. Silvano wound up standing there with the shotgun in his hand, tape hanging off the end. Mrs. Clark looked over the railing, down at the carnage unfolding on the roadway below. She shook her head. "Seen it before," she said. "Devil always claims what's his. Wrap that thing up in the cape. Cops be here soon, we got to go."

TEN

■

"BLANCHE SAYS YOU'RE NOT A BAD PERSON. JUST MISGUIDED."

"Blanche?" Who would listen to her?

She looked at him with distaste. "Mrs. Clark."

"I knew who you meant." They were walking slowly, making their way through the crowd of people on the Promenade, next to one another but not touching, a clear space between them. He'd been conscious of it, but every time he tried to close the gap she would move away, just slightly. It was causing him more hurt than he thought he could feel. "Sounds like the two of you have become good friends."

She looked into his face then, searching. "I hate it when you do this."

"Do what?" He was mystified.

"You put up this wall, and you don't let me in. It's like one of those metal grates they close down over the storefronts in bad neighborhoods, you shut me out and I can't even see inside."

He'd heard the argument before, and a million just like it. It had been one of his stepmother's favorite complaints, and it never failed to irk his father. "I'm not closing you out," he said. "Really, I'm not. What you see is what I've got. There's no 'in.'"

"Yes, there is." She looked over at him, and then away, out over the bay. "Anyway, that's not why I wanted to see you. I need to apologize."

"Elia, you don't have to—"

"Yes I do, be quiet." She stopped then and went to lean against the rail. He followed her, respecting her distance, keeping that painful little space between them. "I'm sorry," she said. "I'm sorry for staying away from you. Sorry for not explaining. I just needed to hole up for a while."

"I didn't blame you. I know I been a lot of trouble. Cost you your job . . ." He trailed off, looking at her.

She was having trouble with it. "What have you been doing with yourself."

"Carpentering," he said, looking at the swollen back of his left hand. "I caught on with those guys who were putting up the building, down at Black and White."

She glanced up, smiled just slightly, just a twitch. "They weren't mad at you, because of what you did?"

"I didn't tell them what I did."

She thought about that for a minute. "Is that what you're going to be? A carpenter?"

He shrugged. "For now."

She turned and faced him then. "Do you remember, back when you were afraid I was going to run away?"

"I do."

"Do you remember, I said I'd tell you the thing I was afraid you were going to find out about me?"

"Yeah. Listen, I'm not—"

"Be quiet." She looked down at the ground. He noticed her

hands trembling, and it was killing him to just stand there, but he did it.

"I was coming home from school one night, about a year and a half ago. I must have fallen asleep on the subway because I came to and I had missed my stop and gone by. I got off at the next station to turn around and come back, there was nobody there but me and this guy. He dragged me into a bathroom and raped me."

He could feel his heart thumping right underneath his chin.

"For a long time after that I hated men. All of you. I didn't think I could ever feel any desire, or, or . . . or anything for a man, ever again. Until you. Until that one night we had . . ." She laid her hand on his arm, then, cold and unsteady, and he could feel how afraid she really was.

"But then," she said, letting go of him and looking away, "then Domenic, when he got me, he kept talking about it, he kept telling me he was going to do it, after he killed you. But you got him first."

"Yeah. I'm sorry all of this had to happen, Domenic and all that. I'm sorry about the first guy, too."

"Well, they got the first guy," she said. "At least he's in jail."

"No shit! How'd they catch him?"

She looked up at him, and a little bit of that fire came back into her eyes. "I bit off his thumb," she said. "He had to go to the hospital, and they matched him up."

"You what?! Bit off—"

"His thumb." She grinned, then, side to side and full on, the one he thought he'd never see again. "Just the bottom half of it, like from the first joint."

"Jesus Christ." He thought back, remembering those arguments, the fear his stepmother had that she'd be left outside in the cold. Maybe I'm more like my old man than I thought, maybe she thinks I don't feel anything, maybe she thinks I don't care. It dawned on him then, this stuff was not from Viet Nam, it was not from the violence in his childhood, it wasn't karma or anything else. It was just normal shit. They could handle this . . .

"Elia Taskent," he said, taking her up in his arms, "I really think I love you."

"Oh, God," she said, "Oh, Christ. Is it all right if I'm still a little shaky?"

"Baby," he said, holding on, "we're all a little shaky."

■

TIME, A GUY ONCE told me, ain't nothing but one goddam thing after another. I met the guy in Ossining, New York, last time I was up there. I was a guest of the state, and so was he. He was like me, I suppose, a little too smart for his own good. Not smart enough to figure a way out of the life, not stupid enough to enjoy it. I heard he got shanked after I got out. I never found out why. I suppose it doesn't really matter. These things happen. Right?

The reason I remembered the guy, I was trying to figure out what got this whole thing started. You never know, when it happens, what's going to change your life, what's going to bounce you out of the rut you been in, send you flying off in some new direction. It might have been that guy and his theory of time, it might have been that I was worried about Nicky growing up to be like his old man, it might have been that I didn't want to have to kill Rosey, because we'd sorta been friends for too long, but I really think it was Leonid.

I don't know who he was, the paper didn't say. They named a

meteor shower after him, though, I read about it in the *Post*. I know, another bad habit. The *Post* said it was the last time any of us would see it, because it wasn't coming around again until 2099, by which time I will be dead, and so will you, along with everybody you ever knew. I don't know why it bothered me. I mean, shooting stars, who gives a shit. Right? But I couldn't get it out of my head, this idea that tonight, this thing is coming by, doesn't matter if it's a big deal or not, you, my friend, and I are both gonna be worm food before it happens again. Little Nicky might make it, if he lives to be a hundred and five, but growing up in foster homes in Bushwick, you gotta figure his chances are not good.

Rosario is this guy that I work with from time to time. I was just a burglar before I met Rosey, not a great one, but pretty good. I did all right. Rosey was more of an armed-robbery guy. First thing we did together, it was a card game down in Canarsie, it was just him and me. They ran the game on Friday nights, we watched the game four Fridays running, make sure nobody too heavy was there, then on the fifth Friday, we hit them. We wore ski masks so none of them would know who we were, and it went down easy even though it was just the two of us, mostly because Rosey's a scary guy whether he's got a mask on or not. He's slightly taller than I am, maybe six foot two or three, and he's a few pounds heavier, he probably goes around two-thirty-five or two-forty. He got his physique for nothing—as far as I know, Rosey has never had to lift a weight or run a mile. Everything I have to work hard for, he gets for free. The thing that sticks in your mind, though, is not his build. I guess you would have to call it his aura. They say God gives you the face you're born with, but you earn the one you die with. Rosey had eyes that looked like they had seen a lot of pain, though how much of it he bought and how much he sold is anybody's guess.

It's not just in his eyes, either, it's in the way he holds himself, it's on his face, it's in his bones. You meet the guy, you know instinctively you gotta watch him. People shake hands with Rosario carefully, and I've known him long enough to know that he's worse than he looks. Rosey's one of those people who believes that you were put here on this planet to be miserable, to suffer, and to die. It's almost as though he knows he's predestined for trouble, so he's never surprised to see it coming, and he never runs away from it. Rosey looks like he's right on the edge, all the time. You just know, he thinks he needs to pop you, he's gonna do it. He won't have to think about it much, not until it's over with.

So anyhow, when you hit guys that know how to hit back, you have to be careful, you have to be absolutely certain you can't be recognized, you have to plan thoroughly so nothing goes wrong, and you can't go stupid afterward, either, buying jewelry for your favorite hooker. Most guys in the game find those rules too restrictive, believe it or not.

The last job I did with Rosey, there was this brokerage house run by a couple of Russians. They had a stock scam running; it was your basic Ponzi scheme, and they were getting ready to pull the plug. The trickiest part of a scam like that is cashing out, okay, because everybody is worried about getting screwed or going to jail. Most of the money we couldn't touch because it's already in some bank in the Cayman Islands or someplace, but there are certain elements involved that don't trust banks of any kind, they got to be paid off in cash. Now the brokerage house is in Manhattan, but the Russians are running it out of an apartment house in Vinegar Hill, which is this neighborhood down on the Brooklyn waterfront, used to be mostly factories but half of them got people living in them now. The place is too big for me and Rosey to take down by ourselves, so Rosey picks up three other guys, one guy to drive and two to handle the exits while Rosey and I go in. I'm only twenty-eight, right, already I'm getting gray hairs from this shit.

So we go in, and right away two things go wrong. One, there turns out to be way more money there than we thought there was gonna be. I mean, way more, the kind that comes with serious heat. We weren't even out of the place and I'm hearing the wheels turning in everybody's head. And two, the doorman must've called the cops, because we were just a couple of blocks away when the sirens started up. We got away clean, but now you got the cops looking at the Russians and the Russians looking at the cops and all of them looking for us. One whisper of this gets out, one little peep, and it's all over. We dumped the car we used over in Fort Greene, down by the projects. We transferred the money into a van we had parked there ahead of time. The three guys Rosey picked up to help out, their eyeballs are spinning, they're all excited, they never seen so much money. They had agreed beforehand to a flat fee of ten grand apiece, but now that's out the window. They're looking at each other, then at Rosey and me—man, I can practically smell it coming.

The thing is, a job where the payoff is too small is actually better than a job where it's too big. Five guys and a bunch of cardboard boxes full of money in one van, we had achieved critical mass. That's when you get too much fissionable material in one spot, right, once the chain reaction starts, it's not gonna stop until it runs out of fuel. Rosey climbs into the back of the van. "Mohammed," he says to me. "You drive."

What can I tell you, street names tend to be dramatic.

I'm driving down Flatbush Avenue, I hear him bust open one of the boxes. The shit's in all denominations, but they got it banded into ten-grand bundles. I watch him in the mirror, he's got this box cradled in his arms, he looks like a proud papa, he's in love. He hands each one of those characters one banded stack of hundreds. Half-inch thick, ten grand, that's what they agreed to, but now they're all disappointed, we're screwing them. He should have given them one of the fatter bundles, made up of tens and twenties instead of hundreds, it would have made them happier. As it was, it started to look like the whole thing might blow right then and there. I still had the piece I used in the stickup. I started looking for a place to ditch the van in case one of these guys decides to renegotiate. Rosey got them calmed down, though. "Look," he said, "me and Mo, we got to stash this money in a safe place until the heat is off. What I'm giving you is just for now, it's just to tide you guys over, you hear me? Then, when it's safe, we gonna make a good split. Don't worry, I gonna take care of you all." We were supposed to ride them down to Red Hook, this neighborhood where one of them lives with his mother, but I pulled over on the corner of Flatbush and Fulton Street.

"Okay," I told them. "Out."

"Why you leavin' us way over here?" It was one of the two that had gone up with us. "You 'posed to drive us home."

"You're a rich man now. Take a fucking cab." I'm half turned in the driver's seat, I've got the pistol in my hand but I'm not showing it.

"Hey, bro," Rosey says to the guy. "Gimme a break, okay? We din know there was gonna be this kinda money in there. We gotta get it under cover before the heat comes down. Every cowboy in Brooklyn gonna be all over this, it ain't smart to be drivin' aroun' with this shit. We don' got a lotta time. You unnerstan'?"

"Yeah, yeah." They weren't happy about it, but they got out, slammed the side door to the van closed behind them. Rosey climbed back into the front passenger seat. He rolled the window down and stuck his head out.

"Listen," he said, "you muthafuckas keep your mouths shut, you hear me? Don't say nothing to nobody, not your momma, not your baby's momma, nobody. I gonna call you in the morning." I pulled away, looked back at them standing there on the corner, watching us.

THE STORAGE PLACE WAS this old warehouse way the fuck down near Coney Island. We had already rented a stall there. The building was an old printing plant, fourteen stories high, poured concrete, bars on the windows, metal doors. It was on a block where the other buildings had all been torn down, the neighborhood was all chain-link fences and weeds, just this one big art deco–looking warehouse, nothing around it. Our stall was on the twelfth floor. Rosey grabs a few more stacks of money out of the box he had broken open, he hands me a couple, sticks the rest in his pocket. "We did it, Mo." He's grinning ear to ear, first time I ever saw him do that. "We did it, muthafucka. We rich now."

"We ain't in the clear yet."

"Don' worry," Rosey said. "Everything gonna be fine."

Rosey showed his ID to a security guy behind a bulletproof glass window. The guy checked it against a paper list, opened the door and let us in. We piled the boxes on a wooden pallet. I was trying to do the math in my head as we went. I figured there was about four hundred pounds there, give or take. I tried to guess how much in each box, and how much altogether, but without sitting down and counting it, there was no way to tell. The guy fired up a forklift, picked up the pallet, we all rode up the freight elevator. We got it all put away, right, locked up, the place looked pretty secure. I guess that's why Rosey picked it. We got back in the van, Rosey held up the key to the storeroom. "Look," he said. "I got an idea. Just so nobody gets any bad things in his head, okay. Let's leave this key in a hotel safe somewhere. We'll tell the guy we need two claim tickets, he has to get them both back before he gives up the key. Time comes, we both gotta go back together for it. That way, we can both feel comfortable. You okay with that?"

"Yeah, sure." I felt like a guy buying a new car, he knows he's getting fucked, he just doesn't know how. That's the way we played it, though, we dumped the van, and we left the key in the hotel safe at the Omni on Fifty-third Street in Manhattan, just the way Rosey said. We separated on the sidewalk outside. Rosey gave me that shit-eating grin again, walked away looking like a winner. I put the claim ticket in my pocket, went home to catch some sleep. I had a feeling I was gonna need it. I had the thought then, I should have settled for one box. I should have taken one box from the van, let Rosey drive away with the rest, but I hadn't thought of it in time.

I SLEPT MOST OF that next day away, woke up in the early afternoon. I took the twenty grand Rosey had given me out of my pocket and laid it out on the kitchen counter, and I put that claim ticket on the counter next to the money. I didn't want to think about it, I didn't want to have to go where thinking was going to take me. I wanted to trust Rosey. I wanted to believe that the two of us would meet in a week or so, split the money, and go our separate ways. I couldn't, though. What's that old rule? Do unto others? I remembered a big hit some guys pulled off back in the seventies. People still talked about it, it was like Captain Kidd's treasure was buried in Brooklyn someplace.

What happened, a bunch of guys, maybe ten or twelve, took down a cash shipment out at JFK. The take was just short of six million. Talk about critical mass—over the next year, all of those guys came up dead except for one, and he died in prison, of cancer, couple years later. If anybody knows what happened to the money, they ain't talking. Six million, whatever it was, it was too much to handle. I don't know if it says anything about the guys involved. Maybe not. Maybe there was just no safe way to cut it up and walk away. Bad things had to happen, and they did. It was inevitable.

The claim ticket lying on my kitchen counter was never going to buy me anything, I knew that. I remembered it as I sat there, it's an old scam, they used to call it the pigeon drop. It was Rosey's idea of getting fancy, switch the real claim ticket for another one he had in his pocket already, he winds up with the two tickets the attendant would need to give up the key, and the one I had gives you the booby prize. That was why he picked the Omni, he must have gone there ahead of time to get a third claim ticket, which was the one he'd given to me. It was touching, in a way. Rosey was giving me an out. As long as I had that ticket, he didn't have to kill me. I could walk around with it in my pocket, all happy and shit, and he could take care of business. That way, he gets away with the money, and I live to talk about it.

Ah, but there it is, there's the rat turd in the oatmeal. I'm still alive, right, I can still talk. When they come looking—and brother, they will—I can say, guy you're looking for goes by the name of Rosario Colón, about so tall, all of that. My guess was that Rosey hadn't followed the logic that far yet, and I was safe until he did. But Rosey was no dope. It wouldn't be long. I went into the bathroom of the place where I was living and looked at my face in the mirror. You talk yourself into it yet? That's what I wanted to know. You all right with it yet? It would really be self-defense anyhow. Right? But I couldn't tell, from that face looking out at me, much of anything at all.

It isn't just your face that forgets how to smile. For a long time, growing up, I hadn't found a hell of a lot to laugh at. And that expression you wear on your puss all the time, sour or hostile or resentful or whatever it is, it sinks in, it seeps into you, it prints itself on what you are inside, and then it's not a mask anymore, because you can't take it off. It's you, you're it. I got all the excuses you want, but they don't mean shit.

IT WAS IN THE *Post* the next morning, same day as the meteor shower, right, cops found three dead guys in a Dumpster out in Queens. Rosey was as good as his word, he had taken care of them.